Praise for
COLD BLOOD

"Forget Florida. Lose L.A. It's Minnesota that's heating up contemporary mysteries. Monsour's *Cold Blood* is almost excessively creepy crawly. This novel's strength is suspense—the 'Oh God, no!' kind. Cuticle-destroying." —*Booklist*

"Efficient plotting and crisp dialogue mark Monsour's second Paris Murphy thriller . . . [a] disturbing novel . . . harrowing . . . satisfying." —*Publishers Weekly*

"With cliff-hanger suspense, Monsour takes the reader . . . into the mind of the killer." —*BookPage*

"With her complex characterizations and tight and complex storylines, it is easy to see that [Monsour] is going to be one of the new stars in the crime thriller galaxy. *Cold Blood* is a powerful tour de force, a police procedural that takes the reader into the investigation from start to finish." —*Midwest Book Review*

Praise for
CLEAN CUT

"Paris Murphy, the heroine of this superb new novel, is a force to be reckoned with. So is Theresa Monsour. Suspenseful and relentlessly paced, *Clean Cut* will leave readers breathless for an encore." —Daniel Silva, *New York Times* bestselling author of *The English Assassin*

"The novel works because of the precision and tough-mindedness of [Monsour's] writing." —*The Washington Post Book World*

continued . . .

"Featuring a compelling protagonist and a cast of complex, fleshed-out characters, the thriller speeds us from start to finish under the guidance of a master storyteller. Hope we see more Paris Murphy in the future."

—Jeffery Deaver, *New York Times* bestselling author of *The Stone Monkey*

"Theresa Monsour takes the reader on a terror-coaster ride. A sparkling debut, written with panache."

—John Case, *New York Times* bestselling author of *The Genesis Code*

"Intuitive, gritty, and completely entertaining, Paris Murphy stakes a claim to the front rank of crime fiction heroines." —Chuck Logan, author of *Absolute Zero*

"*Clean Cut* will leave you hoping Monsour and Paris Murphy come back soon." —*Fort Worth Star-Telegram*

"About two chapters into this most effective page-turner, you'll forget this is a debut novel." —*The Philadelphia Inquirer*

"This perfectly paced search for a serial killer concludes with an at-all-costs ending that homicide investigators secretly dream of." —Paul Lindsay, author of *Traps*

"A female cop heroine who breaks the mold of recent women cop sleuths . . . the way Monsour paces this cat-and-mouse game is truly chilling. Monsour's journalistic background shows in her realistic depictions of cops, the press, and prostitutes. She also takes full advantage of the quick changes, from high-end to down-and-out, within the Twin Cities. Stunning." —*Booklist* (starred review)

"Monsour launches her mystery-writing career with a winner and one that bodes well for a long series." —*BookPage*

"This is Theresa Monsour's debut novel but nobody reading this exciting police procedural would ever believe it . . . fast-paced . . . believable . . . the heroine is the star of this work." —*Midwest Book Review*

DARK HOUSE

THERESA MONSOUR

BERKLEY BOOKS, NEW YORK

THE BERKLEY PUBLISHING GROUP
Published by the Penguin Group
Penguin Group (USA) Inc.
375 Hudson Street, New York, New York 10014, USA
Penguin Group (Canada), 90 Eglinton Avenue East, Suite 700, Toronto, Ontario M4P 2Y3, Canada
(a division of Pearson Penguin Canada Inc.)
Penguin Books Ltd., 80 Strand, London WC2R 0RL, England
Penguin Group Ireland, 25 St. Stephen's Green, Dublin 2, Ireland (a division of Penguin Books Ltd.)
Penguin Group (Australia), 250 Camberwell Road, Camberwell, Victoria 3124, Australia
(a division of Pearson Australia Group Pty. Ltd.)
Penguin Books India Pvt. Ltd., 11 Community Centre, Panchsheel Park, New Delhi—110 017, India
Penguin Group (NZ), Cnr. Airborne and Rosedale Roads, Albany, Auckland 1310, New Zealand
(a division of Pearson New Zealand Ltd.)
Penguin Books (South Africa) (Pty.) Ltd., 24 Sturdee Avenue, Rosebank, Johannesburg 2196,
South Africa

Penguin Books Ltd., Registered Offices: 80 Strand, London WC2R 0RL, England

This is a work of fiction. Names, characters, places, and incidents either are the product of the author's imagination or are used fictitiously, and any resemblance to actual persons, living or dead, business establishments, events, or locales is entirely coincidental.

DARK HOUSE

A Berkley Book / published by arrangement with Dark House, Inc.

PRINTING HISTORY
G. P. Putnam's Sons hardcover edition / May 2005
Berkley mass-market edition / December 2005

ISBN: 0-425-20427-8

BERKLEY®
Berkley Books are published by The Berkley Publishing Group,
a division of Penguin Group (USA) Inc.,
375 Hudson Street, New York, New York 10014.
BERKLEY is a registered trademark of Penguin Group (USA) Inc.
The "B" design is a trademark belonging to Penguin Group (USA) Inc.

PRINTED IN THE UNITED STATES OF AMERICA

10 9 8 7 6 5 4 3 2 1

For my parents,
Esther and Gabriel,
with all my love,
respect and gratitude

ACKNOWLEDGMENTS

I'd like to thank my family and friends for their continuing support; David for his hunting and shotgun wisdom; Rita Monsour, Marilee Votel-Kvaal and Daniel Hafner for their knowledge of medicine and health; Bernadette Monsour for tips on cats; John Lewis for his ice-fishing advice; Officer Randy Barnett for answering my law-enforcement and firearms questions; Kent Bales and Laurie Burnham of the University of Minnesota English Department for the tour of Lind Hall and background on their profession; Patricia Freeman for help with natural-resources issues; Jamie Jurkovich for information on the Iron Range; and my agent, Esther Newberg, and editor, Leona Nevler, for their good work.

WARNING SIGNS

JANUARY WASN'T HALF *finished and five snowmobiles already gone through the ice. Five separate lake accidents under identical conditions. Men drinking too much and going too fast and overdriving their headlights on unseasonably warm evenings. By the time they saw the open water ahead of them, it was too late to stop. Too late to do anything except curse. All of the riders drowned. Two took passengers down with them. One had his wife onboard. The other, his daughter. Three all-terrain vehicles went through. Separate nighttime accidents again. All men again. One made it out. Two didn't. On a Saturday afternoon, under clear skies, a lake swallowed a minivan with a family of four inside. Late for a wedding, they were taking a shortcut and tipped into a hole. Divers found the youngest first; the flower girl was still strapped in her booster seat. Two teenage boys spinning a car, doing donuts on a frozen lake, crashed through on a Sunday morning. The driver made it out his window, crawled through the crack in the ice and collapsed on a snowbank. He lived. His buddy didn't. The body was hauled out with the car. An old woman out walking her dog at night was presumed drowned. The next morning, sheriff's deputies found a plastic bag with dog feces frozen to the ice. Two yards away, a patch of open water. Divers found the dog's corpse, but not the woman's. The lake was big, and the dead stay down longer in cold water.*

The winter of 1982–83 set the bar in the state with twenty-two ice fatalities. Decades later, a winter of cold snaps followed by warm spells threatened to match that record before January's end. The roller-coaster temperatures had covered Minnesota's lakes with bad ice. The snowfall didn't help; it disguised the corrupt surfaces. Insulated them.

In the Twin Cities, deputies posted warning signs on Forest Lake around a rectangle of open water the size of a football field. They took an airboat because it was too dangerous to walk. Bald Eagle Lake was closed to cars and trucks after three fish houses plunged into open water. The Ramsey County Sheriff's Water Patrol banned traffic from White Bear Lake after a car broke through. Cops got on the television news and told people to keep their trucks off the ice. Newspapers ran stories with ice safety tips. Commonsense stuff anglers knew but often ignored: Check for the lake's known thin-ice areas with a local bait shop. Test the thickness using a chisel or auger. Wear a life jacket under winter gear. In a car, keep the windows down and seat belts unbuckled. Heed the minimum ice thickness needed to be safe. Twelve to fifteen inches to support a truck. Eight to twelve to hold a car. Five for a snowmobile. Four to keep a person from crashing through. From drowning. From dying in dark, cold water. Water so cold it paralyzes the limbs and steals the breath and numbs the mind. So cold it convinces you to stop struggling. To rest.

Television weathermen stood in front of maps and pointed to the only slice of the state with thick ice. The northern quarter, where the lakes are frigid in July.

ONE

SHE PICKED UP her drink and took another sip. Terrible. Tasted like rubbing alcohol. Too much sweet vermouth. She could have ordered something easy, but she wanted to see him work for her. She'd watched him rummaging around under the bar after he took her order. It amused her that he had to serve it in a makeshift martini glass. He seemed embarrassed by it. Humbled. Humble was good. He could have refused to make it. Could have offered her beer or wine instead. He didn't. He mixed her a Brandy Manhattan. Even came up with a maraschino cherry. Good boy. Was he too big, though? Could she handle him? He was twenty-two. Possibly twenty-three. Older than her habit. Still, small-town boys were easier than city kids. More pliable. Clumsy in bed at first, but eager to please. This one was tall. Broad shouldered. India-ink hair framed his face. High, surprised brows arched over dark eyes. Delicate nose for a man. Smooth instead of chiseled. Full mouth. A poet's mouth. He had the face of Percy Shelley and the body of a

Greek god or some other mythological hunk. Which one? Prometheus. The Titan fire stealer. She sipped again and thought she noticed him limping. It fascinated her. She kept watching to make sure she wasn't imagining things. She knew she had a habit of romanticizing. Bad habit. Got her into so much trouble. No. She wasn't fooling herself. A slight limp. Prometheus after he was taken captive and bound. Pecked by Zeus's eagle. Tortured. She set down her drink. Picked up her smoke. Took a long pull. Exhaled. Set the cigarette back in the ashtray. Picked up her pen. Sifted through her memory for the right piece of literature. Scribbled. She set the pen down. Picked up her glass and emptied it. Rattled the ice around and looked at the clock. She'd have to make her move soon. She picked the cherry out from among the ice cubes, vacuumed the fruit off the stem.

WIND rattled the storefront windows. Phantoms banging to get in. He glanced outside. Floodlights mounted over the bar entrance illuminated the falling snow. So white, someone could have taped tissue paper over the glass. A bad night to stand outside scraping ice off a windshield. A good night to nurse a drink in a bar the size of a garden shed. The wood floors were creaky and uneven and so worn and dirty they were black. Smelled musty and damp. Wet dirt in a garden shed. Underneath that, locker room odors: Sweat. Damp socks. Wet hair. The last layer of stink: beer. He pulled a rag from under the counter and walked to the end of the bar, a slab of wood the size of an ironing board. He grimaced and limped as he went. His ankles were giving him trouble. Must be the change in weather, he thought. He wiped the bar down, moving his right arm in ovals. His biceps bulged out of the sleeves of his tee shirt. He tossed the rag under the counter. Turned around and shut off the television hanging from the ceiling. He didn't like having it behind the bar. Always bumping into it with his head. Maggie didn't want to pay for a satellite. The set got two stations, and they both came in gray and crackly. He appreciated the background noise—it drowned out the memory of another noise—but he wanted something better than static. Someday he'd get his own place. No television. A jukebox. He'd do a better decorating job, too. Maggie was so cheap with her beer posters stapled to the walls. Checked tablecloths made of vinyl. Only thing she painted on a regular basis was the front door. Barn red.

He surveyed the place. The four tables were empty. Someone had spilled a Coke on one of the tables; he could see a puddle. Beer glasses in a circle on another table, all licked clean. No matter how hammered they got, people in this town didn't spill their beer. Drinking money was too hard to come by, especially with the mines letting workers go. Three of the four booths that lined one wall were occupied. The booth closest to the door had two of his regulars, miners lucky enough to still labor in the taconite pits. Harlan Siguard and Tommy Gille. Full beards, barrel chests and arms as hard as rocks. He wished they didn't wear their hunting jackets in here. Deer season was long over. He could handle seeing the blaze orange out on the street. He could look the other way. No place for his eyes to go when the jackets were inside. He reminded himself the miners were nice guys. They knew his dad. They lived and worked around Hibbing but had a spear-fishing shack on Whitewater Lake, outside of Hoyt Lakes. He had a dark house on Whitewater, too. In the booth next to the miners was another regular. Floyd Petersen. He lived on the outskirts of town. Came in a lot since his wife died and his kids moved down to Minneapolis. He didn't drive anymore, but managed to mooch rides. Tonight would be the miners' turn to give Petersen a lift. He'd chase the miners and their jackets and the old man out and lock up.

The booth at the far end. He wasn't sure he wanted her out fast. Eyes the color of blue Popsicles. Lips that looked swollen and chewed on. Vanilla-ice-cream skin. Since breasts were always a couple of shades lighter than the face, he figured her breasts must be whiter than the snow falling outside. Hair long and straight and shiny. Yellow as butter. Did she have a good body? He couldn't tell. His back was turned when she'd walked in a couple of hours earlier. Since then, she'd sat with her legs tucked under her butt and her ski jacket wrapped around her like a blanket. Wrote in a book. When he went to her table, she'd said two words: "Brandy Manhattan." Her voice didn't match her face. A little girl's voice. He'd turned around and gotten her drink without telling her how ridiculous it was to order a drink like that in a bar like this in a town this size. You'd have to drive an hour in any direction to find a martini glass. He'd served it in a wineglass. Finding the sweet vermouth was a miracle. No bitters, though. At least he had the cherry. He found a dusty jar of them under the counter. He'd throw them out after tonight. No one up here ever ordered drinks with fruit in them.

When he brought her the drink, she'd closed her book and looked up at him with those Popsicle eyes. Rubbed her arms over her jacket. Asked in that little girl voice: "Why do you keep it so cold in here?"

"So the snowmobilers don't overheat."

She'd reached out and brushed his bare arm with her fingers as he was setting her drink down. "Aren't you freezing?"

He'd liked her touch, but it had made him nervous. He'd quickly pulled his arm away. "I'm used to it."

Then she'd picked up her cigarette—one of those long, skinny smokes—and taken a drag. Exhaled and asked through the cloud: "Where am I?"

He'd wondered if she was lost. Lost little girl. "Northeastern Minnesota," he'd said. "Iron Range."

She'd smiled. "I mean the name of this place."

"Maggie's Red Door." He'd nodded toward the front door. "The town."

He'd blurted out, "Hoyt Lakes" and walked away. She probably thought he was an idiot. When he went back to see if she wanted another drink, she gave him a check. "You can run up a tab," he'd said.

"All I need is one." She'd pushed the check toward him. "There's a tip for you in there."

"Thanks." He'd taken it without looking at it. Popped open the register. Lifted up the cash box and slipped it underneath. He'd look at it later—he'd like to know her name for the hell of it—and then rip it up. Maggie didn't take checks.

She wrote in the book and played with that one drink the whole time. What was a babe doing in a dinky bar in a dinky town by herself, and so late at night? The ski jacket. She was at Giants Ridge for the weekend. They had bars in the lodge and the ski chalet. Why wasn't she at one of those bars?

He pulled a fresh rag from under the counter and limped out from behind the bar. Headed for the miners' booth. "Time to pull the plug."

"You betcha," said Gille. He drained his beer glass and set it down and slid out of the booth. He dug in his jacket as he stood up. Fished a stocking cap out of his right pocket. "Come on then, Siggy. Get your ass up so we can get outta here. Let Catch clean up and go to bed."

The bartender came up to the table. Tossed the bar rag over his left shoulder and leaned down to pick up Gille's glass. Siguard didn't move. He sat with his empty beer glass between his hands. "What's the rush?"

"Don't be a butt hole," Gille said. He pulled his stocking cap over his head.

Siguard: "Go drain the lizard and let me talk to the kid."

"Okay then," said Gille. He walked to the back of the room, giving a sideways glance to the woman as he went.

Siguard waited until he heard the toilet door close. He looked up at the bartender. "Sit down."

The bartender hesitated, the dirty glass still in his hand. He looked over at Petersen. His head was down, his chin touching his chest. The woman was curled up in the back booth and writing in her book again. He set the glass down and slid into the booth to face the older man. "What?"

Siguard spoke in a low but intense voice. The words came out quickly. He'd been saving them for a long time. Now he had to dump them. "*What*? I'll tell you what. What kind of shit life is this? Living above a bar. Working your ass off day and night in a lousy beer joint. What's Maggie paying you? Minimum wage? Why ain't you with your mom and your sisters in Duluth? You got that one brother. Where's he? St. Paul, right? Go down to St. Paul. Go to school. Get a real job." He paused, then said in a louder voice: "What the hell are you doing hanging around here? Get a life. Get laid."

"Been laid plenty."

The older man growled his next question: "Maggie paying you in pussy or what?"

The bartender's face reddened and his eyes fell. "No."

"She's too old for you."

"Ain't humping Maggie."

Siguard didn't believe him, but he softened his tone. Leaned across the table. "What's wrong with you? Had any fun lately? When's the last time you picked up a hockey stick?"

Eyes still down, he said in a voice that was almost a whisper: "You know I can't. Haven't been able to for a long time. You see how I am. Some days, I can hardly walk."

Siguard pulled on his beard and looked out at the snow. "Sorry. I don't know why I asked." He sighed and looked across the table at the bartender. Saw only a black head of curls bent down. "Hunting. Did you get out at all?"

"No."

"Why not? Stop being afraid. Stop being so down. You gotta pick up a gun again. It's been way too long."

"Not long enough to bring him back," said the younger man. He slid out of the booth and stood up. As he headed back to the bar, he tried hard to keep from limping. He failed. He kept his back turned to Siguard. Pulled the rag off his shoulder and started wiping the bar again.

The sound of a toilet flushing. The bathroom door creaked open and Gille walked out, buckling his belt as he went. He stepped up to Siguard, who was sitting in the booth, staring straight ahead with a frown. Gille looked at the bartender's back and back at his friend. Decided to save his questions for the ride home. He zipped up his jacket. "Let's hit the bricks."

Siguard slid out of the booth and stood up. Pulled a stocking cap from his right jacket pocket and yanked it on. Took some gloves out of his left pocket and slipped them on. He headed for the door. Put his hand on the knob. Turned and looked at Gille behind him. "Grab Floyd."

Gille stepped over to Petersen and touched his shoulder. "Floyd. Wake up." Petersen lifted his head. His bifocals were crooked and resting on the tip of his nose. Gille reached over with both hands and adjusted the glasses back over the old man's ears. "Time to go home." Petersen slid out of the booth, stood up, swayed a bit. He shoved his hands in his jacket pockets and followed Gille toward the door.

Siguard looked at the bartender one last time. Now he was behind the counter drying glasses. Siguard pulled the door open a crack. A blast of wind rolled inside along with puffs of snow. "Call me, Catch," he said to the bartender's back. The three men stepped outside, slamming the door behind them.

*   *   *

THE woman clicked her pen and set it between the pages of her journal. She closed her book. She'd strained to listen and caught bits of the drama: *What the hell are you doing hanging around here? Get a life. Get laid.* Heated words over hunting: *You gotta pick up a gun again. It's been way too long.* Then the sentence that made her pen move faster: *Not long enough to bring him back.* What was the eagle pecking at on this young man? Something over a gun. Too tragic. So ready for her. He'd get laid, and then some. She dug around in her purse until she found her makeup case. Pulled it out. Flipped open the top. Looked in the mirror while patting her nose with powder. She put the pad back and snapped the lid shut. Dropped the case in her purse. She slid out of the booth and stood up. She slipped her jacket off and draped it over her left arm. Picked up her journal and tucked it under her left arm. Her shirt was long-sleeved, but made of thin cotton. She'd take advantage of the cold air. She walked toward the bar. On her way there, she stroked her breasts with the fingers of her right hand.

His back was turned. She stepped in front of the bar, set her book on the counter and threw her jacket on top of a stool. "Need a shoulder?"

He froze, glass and towel in hand. "Got two of my own," he said to the row of liquor bottles in front of him.

"I'd like to help."

He set the glass down and swung around to face her. Noticed she was slender and tall. Not as tall as he, but close. Her middle seemed to go on forever. He'd never seen a woman with a waist that long. What was it like, wrapping your arms around all that? He liked that long look. Didn't like her snooping, though. Wondered how much she'd taken in. "You got big ears."

"I'm observant."

He threw the dish towel under the counter. "Nosey is a better word."

"Small bar. I couldn't help overhearing." She smiled. "I work with young people. Young men. I enjoy mentoring them."

"Is that so?" He could see her nipples under her shirt. Silly shirt for a grown-up woman. Pink with pink lace around the neckline. Her jacket was pink, too. Pink little-girl clothes to go with that little-girl voice. No little-girl breasts. She had big breasts for a skinny woman. Didn't look like they were sagging yet, and she was older than he was. By at least ten years, he figured. That wasn't what bothered him. She wanted more than a screw. The way she looked at him made him feel like a bug in a jar. "You some kind of shrink?"

"I've lived a lot. Had my share of problems."

"You don't know problems."

She hopped up on a stool. "Trade stories over a drink?"

He thumbed toward the clock behind him. "Closing time."

She rested her arms on the counter. "Sure you don't want to talk?"

He rested his arms on the counter across from her and leaned close. He could see powder on the tip of her nose. She lays the makeup on too thick, he thought. "I'm sure," he said. He noticed that book on the counter between them. Covered in leather with gold trim. "What is this, anyways?" He pulled it toward him and said in a high-pitched voice, *"Dear Diary."*

"Don't," she said. She lurched forward and tried to snatch it away but he turned his back to her.

He opened it to the pages where the pen was tucked and scanned the words. "You been copying down private conversation. What's all this crap about an eagle and pain? Writer's bullshit. Don't tell me you're another one of those bloodsucking reporters." He swung around to face her.

She snatched the journal out of his hands and snapped the book shut. She opened her mouth to say something. The front door pushed open, sending another wave of cold air into the bar.

A man dressed in a snowmobile suit shuffled inside and pushed the door shut behind him. He stomped his feet in front of the door, leaving a pile of snow from his boots. He pulled off his helmet and balaclava. His hair hung down to his shoulders and was wet with sweat. Pimples peeked through a scraggly beard. His jacket was black with flames on the shoulders and matched the fiery helmet. He tucked the helmet under his left arm. He stuffed his balaclava inside one jacket pocket. Pulled off his gloves and stuffed them inside another pocket. He unzipped his jacket, revealing black snowmobile bibs underneath. Under the bibs, a black turtleneck. From under the collar of the turtleneck, the tattoo of a cobra coiled up the right side of his neck, slithered across the front of his throat and continued up the left side of his face. The head, with its forked tongue, rested above the man's left brow.

The bartender wondered why he didn't hear the sled pull up outside. Too distracted talking to the pink lady. He didn't even know her, and she was starting to piss him off. "Don't get too comfortable, mister. We're closed."

"The hell you say." He walked toward the bar, weaving as he went. He reeked of engine exhaust and whiskey. He was as tall as the bartender and as big, but looked twenty-five years older. Gray streaked his beard. Deep lines cut under his eyes and around his mouth. A jagged scar on his forehead gave the appearance of a lightning bolt striking the cobra's head. He eased himself onto a bar stool and set his helmet on top of the counter. "A quick one. How about it?" He drummed his palms on the counter. Crude hand-drawn tattoos on his fingers. He eyed the bottles of liquor. "Shot of J.D. should do it. Make it a double." He looked at the woman. "Hey, mama."

She glanced at him and quickly looked away. Her jacket

was on the stool between them. She picked it up and set it on her lap and stuffed her journal into one of the pockets.

The bartender grabbed a rag, limped out from behind the counter. Locked the front door, closed the shades and flicked off the outside lights. He headed for the tables. He addressed the snowmobiler as he wiped. "Seriously, mister. I can't serve you. It's closing time. I'll let you sit and warm up. Then I gotta chase you outta here."

"Got a phone then? Lost my party out on the trail. Dropped my cell."

"Sorry. No public phone. They got a pay phone across the street. Spike's Saloon."

"Tried there," said the rider. "All locked up. Lights out. Nothing else open. Street's dark."

He didn't want to bend over backward to help this guy. He didn't look like the usual snowmobiler. "Gas station's open. A few blocks down. Same side of the street. Won't take you any time on your sled." The bartender tucked the bar rag in the waist of his jeans and started stacking the empty beer glasses on top of each other. He heard the sound of heavy footsteps. Looked up. Saw the guy behind the counter. "Hey!"

The guy grabbed the Jack Daniel's from the row of liquor, yanked off the top, took a swig. He turned and set the bottle on the counter. His eyes fell on the cash register, and then under the counter to the right of the register. "What have we got here?" He looked over at the bartender and smiled. A top front tooth flashed gold.

"Son of a bitch!" The bartender dropped the empty glasses on the table and hobbled as quickly as he could to the bar. Too late. He heard the clap of the pump shoving a shell into the chamber. The bartender froze in front of the register and raised his arms. He was staring into the barrel of the sawed-off 12-gauge Maggie kept behind the bar. He heard a sharp intake of air. The pink lady. He quickly turned his head and looked at her. Motionless on the bar stool, eyes wide, clutching her jacket in front of her as if it were a bulletproof shield. He looked back at the robber. "Ain't worth it."

"We'll see about that, gimp." The guy rested the gun barrel on the counter to the right of the register, but kept his right index finger on the trigger. With the fingers of his left hand, he punched buttons on the register until the drawer popped out. The robber kept his eyes and the barrel trained on the bartender while grabbing bills with his left hand.

"Ain't shit in the till," said the bartender.

The guy's eyes darted down to the bills in his left fist. Mostly ones and fives. "Fucking right about that." He crammed the money in his jacket pocket. Lifted up the cash box and looked underneath. One check. He didn't want to hassle with it. He dropped the box back in the drawer. Slammed the drawer shut, grabbed the shotgun with both hands and stepped out from behind the register. He shoved the tip of the barrel into the younger man's side. "What's in back?".

"Nothing. Nobody. The can."

"Anybody in it?"

"No."

"The back door?"

"Locked."

"What's that other door?"

The bartender turned and looked in back. "Janitor shit."

"Good. Stay where you're at."

"Yeah. Okay." The bartender felt the gun in his back. Felt the yearning in the pit of his stomach. A desire that he beat down every day. This was his chance to surrender to it. It could end here. It wouldn't be by his own hand. There'd be no shame. In fact, he could go out a hero. He closed his eyes for a moment and tried to muster the courage to do something that would make the guy pull the trigger. A sudden move. An insult. Then the urge dissipated. Evaporated as it had so many other times, in the heat of his will to live. He opened his eyes again and took in his surroundings as if he'd never set foot in the bar before. The register was on his right and the booths were on his left. He watched the woman. Still frozen on the stool, facing the bar.

The robber looked past him and eyed her. "Where's your purse, bitch?"

She swiveled around on the stool and nodded toward her booth. "On the bench."

"Get it, bitch. No funny shit or I'll pop your boyfriend." She slid off the stool, dropping her jacket. Her journal fell out of the pocket. The robber glanced down. "What's that?"

"Nothing," she said in a small voice. She picked it up and held it to her chest.

"You're awfully attached to *nothing*. Bring it here."

"It's nothing valuable. My personal thoughts."

He stepped from behind the bartender's back and pointed the gun at the younger man's left side. He ran the tip of his tongue over his top lip. "Sounds hot. Bring your personal thoughts over here." She didn't move. He swung the barrel of the gun toward her and stretched out his left arm. Opened his hand. "Give it." She walked toward the robber, her eyes down. "Stop," he said, when she was an arm's length away. She looked up and handed it to him. He grabbed it and stuffed it inside his jacket. "Closer, bitch." She took two steps. He reached out with his left hand and grabbed her right breast. Squeezed hard. "Those tatas real?"

She pushed his hand off. "Stop it!"

"Leave her alone," said the bartender.

"Shut the fuck up!" The robber swung the gun back around and slammed the barrel against the bartender's head. He fell against the register and went down on the floor. The robber pointed the gun at the bartender's shoulder. "Back on your feet, gimp."

The bartender slowly rose, resting his right hand on the register and his left against his head. "Jesus," he muttered.

"Arms back up." The bartender raised his arms. The robber jammed the gun into his left side. "You're not giving the orders. Got that?" The robber looked at the woman. She was frozen in front of him, her arms crossed protectively over her chest. "Don't worry about those titties." He motioned toward the booth with the gun barrel.

She turned and walked to the booth. She unfolded her arms from her chest and saw a smudge on her shirt. His greasy print over her right breast. Like a brand. She could feel her face growing hot with rage and shame. Her breast throbbed with pain. She'd done nothing to help the bartender. Hadn't uttered a word, and he'd been hurt trying to stand up for her. Worst of all, the bully had taken it from her. *Sounds hot.* An image popped into her mind. His big, dirty hand wrapped around his cock. Semen all over the book's pages. She leaned over the bench and grabbed the strap of her shoulder bag. Pulled it across the bench toward her. Picked it up. Thought about how she regretted coming into the bar. Regretted the entire vacation. Should have gone somewhere warm, she thought. Arizona or Florida.

"Hurry up!" yelled the robber. He watched the woman, but swung the gun barrel back to the bartender. Again jammed it hard in the younger man's waist. "Keep them arms up. What's wrong with them legs anyways?"

"Busted ankles," he said in a low voice. "Long time ago."

She was glad her back was to the men. She thrust her hand into the purse. Tried to remember what was in her wallet. Not enough cash to make this guy happy. Her cell phone was . . . in her car. Damn. She did have something else, and she was furious enough to use it. She pulled it out. Dropped the purse on the bench. Turned around and extended her arms out in front of her.

"Shit," breathed the bartender. The pink lady had a pistol.

The robber laughed. Another flash of gold. He withdrew the gun barrel from the bartender's body and swung it toward the woman. "Better hope your aim is good, bitch."

"What about you?" Her voice was quavering. So were her hands. "How's your aim?"

"Dumb cunt," said the robber. "This is a shotgun. Just got to wave it in your general direction."

The bartender figured he had nothing to lose. One or the other was going to nail him. The pink lady by accident or the robber by design. Either way, he was gone. He found that idea comfortable. Relaxing. The calm lubricated his movements. His eyes darted from the armed man on his left to the Jack Daniel's on his right. He stretched out his right arm and snatched it off the counter. He wrapped his fist around the neck and swung the bottle around. He slammed it into the guy's face. The robber dropped the shotgun on the floor, grabbed his nose with both hands and fell to his knees. The woman's book slipped out of his jacket and skid across the floor. The robber let go of his nose and reached for the gun. The bartender dropped the bottle and dove for the 12-gauge. Both men were next to each other on the floor, on their bellies. The robber had his right hand on the stock and the bartender had his left. The younger man brought his right arm over, locked both hands on the stock and yanked it out of the robber's grasp. He rolled over and crawled to his feet with a grimace. Took a couple of steps back and aimed the gun at the man on the floor.

The robber stood up and raised his hands over his head. His face was smeared with blood. He stumbled backward until he felt one of the bar stools against his legs. He touched his nose again and examined his fingers. Red. He snatched his helmet off the counter. Turned and ran for the door.

The pink voice. Little-girl voice. High-pitched and angry: "Shoot him! Don't let him go! Shoot the bastard!"

The bartender looked at the gun in his hands. It felt

good. Solid. Right. Siggy's lecture ricocheted inside his aching head, mixed up with his own spoken words and the robber's insults and the writing he'd read in the woman's book: *Tortured by the eagle. Stop being afraid. Gimp. You gotta pick up a gun again. You know I can't. He's in such pain. Bound by his ankles. Gimp. Not long enough to bring him back. Tortured by the eagle. You gotta pick up a gun again. The eagle. Pick up a gun. Gimp.* Drowning out the chorus, the pink voice. Calling him by name.

"Catch! Shoot him, Catch!" He took two steps forward. Fired into the robber's back as the man fumbled with the lock. The impact hurled the robber against the door. The bartender pulled back on the fore end, ejecting the spent shell. The man was still alive. He'd dropped his helmet. Was leaning against the door with both hands. A second blast into his back. Not from the shotgun. The pink voice again. "Finish him, Catch!" He pumped forward, chambering a new shell. He pulled the trigger again. The man jerked and slipped down to the floor.

Maggie's red door was covered with more red.

TWO

TWO MEN AND a woman hiked on the floor of the Sonoran Desert northeast of Phoenix. One of the men—a skinny guy in his twenties with blond hair and freckles—was dressed like a cowboy. Straw Stetson. Red bandana. Jean shirt. Wranglers stiff as a board. Boots with fat heels and pointed toes. Holstered revolvers hanging from his hips. The other man and the woman were in shorts, tee shirts, sneakers and Minnesota Wild baseball caps. Talking as he walked, the cowboy was leading the couple to a cactus as tall as a house. "The saguaro. Signature plant of the Sonoran Desert. When lightning strikes, these old boys take the hit because they're the tallest thing for miles. They can reach a height of fifty feet and live up to two hundred years or more. Up ahead is the granddaddy of them all."

The couple fell back a few yards. The woman hooked her right arm with her partner's left and leaned into his ear. Said in a low voice as they walked: "You told me I could shoot at stuff. When do I get to shoot at stuff?"

"The concierge at the hotel said since nine-eleven, they don't let people do that anymore," he whispered back.

She let go of his arm. "That sucks."

"You're a piece of work, babe. How many other women get pissed because they can't blast away with a pistol?"

Sergeant Paris Murphy wasn't like many other women. At five feet ten inches, she was a few inches shorter than her companion, husband Jack Ramier. The desert hike didn't tire her; she had the hard calves and thighs of a runner. She had a small waist and trim hips, but large breasts. Her olive skin, high cheekbones, violet eyes and long lashes were an exotic combination that came from having a Lebanese mother and an Irish father. Her hair was thick and black and fell past her shoulders.

The cowboy stopped and waited for the couple to catch up. When they were beside him, he pointed to a knee-high barrel-shaped cactus. "Nicknamed the compass cactus because it grows to the south. After a heavy rain, it can lean too far and fall over. That's why it's also called the suicide cactus." The cowboy paused. "We've never known one to leave a note. It just clocks out."

Jack laughed. He pulled a digital camera out of the front pocket of his shorts. Aimed the lens at the cactus and looked at the tiny television-like screen in back of the camera. He pressed a button and widened the angle. When the cactus was framed the way he wanted, he snapped a picture. He took two more.

"You are such a nerd," she said. "Three shots of a cactus. Not even a big one. A chubby little one."

Jack turned the camera on her. Snapped a photo while she stuck out her tongue. "Lovely," he said. At forty-two, he was six years older than his wife. He had curly brown hair and brown eyes. His athletic build came from rowing; he hated running. He wasn't much interested in pistols, either. The biggest difference between the two of them involved her job as a homicide detective in St. Paul. She loved it, and he hated it. He was a doctor at Regions Hospital, a level-one trauma center in St. Paul, and he was sure one day she would end up in his emergency room. On a stretcher.

Jack lowered the camera, and the cowboy continued leading the couple. Murphy inhaled and savored the desert air as she hiked. She was surprised at how cool it was. The guide said there was a lot of moisture on the ground because January was the rainy season. Her previous visits to Arizona had been over the summer, when temperatures topped one hundred degrees and the air felt as intense as the heat from a blow-dryer.

Jack watched her taking in the landscape. "Not the Death Valley scene you expected?"

"Not at all," she said.

"So snowbirds aren't so bad?"

"I wouldn't go that far." Murphy told Jack snowbirds were really snow chickens. She loved Minnesota winters. Still, he'd talked her into this vacation. Their marriage needed it.

He took her left hand in his right while they walked. "Think you could live here someday?"

Whenever they visited the state, he asked her that question. He was the only offspring of two university professors. They had a house in Minnesota, but spent as much time as they could in Arizona. His parents were always lobbying to get their son to relocate because they were planning on moving to warmer climes permanently. She figured they didn't care if she joined him or not. "I don't know," she said. "What's the homicide rate in Phoenix?"

He let go of her hand and asked dryly: "Higher is better, right?"

"I'd need a job," she said.

The cowboy stopped again and pointed to a cactus with short, lime-colored fingers jutting out. The plant appeared furry. "Teddy-bear cholla. Surgically sharp needles." He pulled a jackknife and pliers out of his front pants pockets. He gripped the tip of one of the fingers with the pliers and cut it off with the knife. He held the stub up in front of the couple. "Apaches used it for weapons. Would throw it on soldiers." He closed his knife, shoved it back in his pocket and pulled out a cigarette lighter. He flicked it on and held the flame under the piece of cactus. "They're edible and if you burn them, the smoke has a light hallucinogenic effect."

While Jack snapped three photos of the guide burning the hunk of cactus, Murphy flipped a rock with the toe of her shoe. A scorpion scurried from underneath and headed for another rock. The cowboy turned off the lighter and dropped the burned cactus on the ground. "Ma'am. Please. I told you. Don't be poking around like that. Nasty things hide under them rocks." He slipped the pliers and lighter back in his pockets, turned and continued walking and talking. "No guide or guest of Wild West Jeep Tours has ever been bit, and I don't plan on messing up that record today."

The couple let the guide get several feet ahead. Jack jabbed his wife in the ribs with his elbow. "Would you behave?"

Murphy didn't like getting lectured by a skinny kid in cowboy boots. She thought he looked like Dennis the Menace. She yelled ahead to him: "What about snakes? Got any snakes? They climb around in the wash?" She wanted to hear him say *wash* again. He pronounced it *warsh*.

"Rattlers. They don't necessarily hang out in the *warsh*." He wondered where she got that goofy idea. "You kind of have to keep snakes in perspective here. Be alert but not paranoid."

"See, Jack," she whispered. "Stop being paranoid."

"As long as we're on the subject of wildlife, I'll tell you what else you can find in these parts," said the cowboy, while still keeping a brisk pace. "Black bears. Mountain lions. Bobcats. Mule deer. Bighorn sheep. Coyote." He stopped and waited for the pair to catch up with him. "Ring-tailed lemur here, too. Looks like a house cat on drugs."

This time Murphy laughed. Her husband looked at her while they walked beside the cowboy. "You *would* find a stoned cat funny."

The cowboy pointed to a squat cactus with spindly arms growing amid some brush. "Strawberry hedgehog. Also called the horse crippler. You can figure out why." Jack took two photos. The three continued walking.

"Do you ride horses?" asked Murphy. "Are you a real cowboy?"

"Depends on how you define 'real cowboy.'"

"Where you from?" she asked.

"Indiana," said the guide.

"Why do you call yourself Montana Jones?" she asked.

"Last name is Jones. Most of the fellas take the name of their home state as their first name when they're working on the trail. Montana Jones sounded more original than Indiana Jones."

The trio stopped at the foot of the giant cactus. "Where you folks from?" asked the guide.

"Minnesota," said Jack, pointing to the "Wild" hat on his head.

"Cold there," he said.

"That's why we're here and not there," said Jack.

"January's bad?"

Murphy: "Depends on how you define *bad.* I don't mind a little snow and cold."

"I do," said Jack. "Enough weather talk. What's the story on this big fella?" He bent his head back to take in the entire cactus.

"Like I said, it can live for a couple of hundred years. It doesn't even start growing those arms until it reaches sixty or so."

Jack stepped back and aimed his camera. "Paris. Get in

front of it." The cowboy stepped off to the side. Murphy turned to face the camera. "Babe. Lose the hat. I can't see your face." She took off the cap and used her fingers to brush her bangs. They did more than fringe her face. They served to cover the crescent scar on her forehead—a souvenir from a case she'd worked the previous summer. She was still self-conscious about the mark, and Jack knew it. He worried that the case had scarred her on the inside as well, but he didn't know how to talk to her about it. "You look fine, babe. My desert flower in the desert."

She loved it when he called her that, even in jest. She grinned while he snapped five photos of her in front of the saguaro.

Jack lowered the camera. Looked at the cowboy. "How about taking one of us together?"

"Sure thing." The guide stepped over to Jack, took the camera out of his hands and stepped back.

Jack stood next to his wife and threw his right arm around her. "I love you," he said into her ear.

She twined her arms around his waist. "I love you, too," she said in a low voice. She squeezed him close. She couldn't believe after everything they'd been through, they were here. Together.

The cowboy took a photo, lowered the camera and looked at all the buttons. "Let me work this telly photo thing. Zoom in for a tight shot." He held the camera up again and pressed the telephoto button until it framed their faces. He took two close-ups. Lowered the camera. Saw Jack plant a kiss on Murphy's lips. "You two on your honeymoon?"

"Not exactly," said Jack. "We've been together awhile." He paused. "Off and on." Murphy untangled her arms from his waist and put the cap back on her head. He stepped away from her and took the camera back from the cowboy. Turned around and eyed the saguaro. "Stand over here, babe. I want to get some shots of the big guy alone."

She stood next to Jack. Watched him framing the cactus in the tiny screen. "That looks good," she said. Jack snapped three photos, one after the other.

"Got any kids yet?" asked the cowboy.

"No kids," Jack said shortly.

"We got our third on the way."

"You don't look old enough," said Jack.

"Gotta start while you're young," said the cowboy. "While you got the energy to chase after them."

Murphy wanted to get off the kid subject. "How about a picture of our guide?"

Jack turned the camera on the cowboy. "Smile, Indiana Jones."

"Montana Jones," said the cowboy, tipping his hat back from his head with his right index finger and resting his left hand on his pistol.

"Sorry," said Jack. "Montana Jones." He took two pictures. Lowered the camera, turned it off and slipped it back in his pocket. He checked his watch. Already two in the afternoon, and they'd missed lunch. "Let's head back to the hotel," he said to his wife. "Get some eats and a brew. Hit the pool."

The three of them headed back to the Jeep. "I don't know," the cowboy said as they walked. "Maybe I should go with Indiana Jones."

SHE smoothed suntan oil on her arms and watched the other people catching rays by the pool. A couple of older women in lounge chairs. They'd already spent too much time in the Arizona sun; their skin looked leathery and dry. A middle-aged man sitting by himself at a table, typing madly on a laptop. A waiter brought him a beer and a burger. He hardly looked up. A knot of preteen girls sat together on a towel, taking turns braiding each other's hair. She flipped

over on her stomach and felt the heat on her back. Even
though it was cool out, the Arizona sun felt hot. She stayed
still for ten minutes and got bored. Even as a teenage girl, she
ignored the usual female concerns like suntans and makeup.
She didn't have the patience and was too much of a
tomboy. Her mother fought with her to get her into dresses.

She flipped again and sat up on the chair. She surveyed
the pool, a man-made lagoon divided into two sections. The
sections were separated by an artificial mountain. Water-
falls cascaded down its sides and emptied into the million-
gallon body of water. A channel connecting the two pool
areas ran under the hill. Tucked inside the mountain on one
side, and overlooking the channel, was a bar that served
sandwiches, beer, wine and smoothies. Tucked into the other
side was an exercise room. The resort also had tennis courts,
gift shops and restaurants. La Posada's pool was the big draw,
however, second only to its location. The foothills of the
Camelback Mountain.

Because it was barely in the seventies, the lagoon was all
but empty. A pair of boys wrestled in the channel. She stood
up and walked over to the pool. Sat down on the edge. Kicked
her feet in the water. She lowered herself in, walked out a
few feet and then went on her back. She looked up at the
cloudless sky as she floated. A different shade of blue than
the Minnesota sky, she thought. Almost turquoise, like the
Indian jewelry they saw in the tourist shops. She rolled over
onto her stomach and did the breaststroke across the pool.

Jack had wanted to stay in Phoenix at his folks' condo,
but she'd talked him into Scottsdale. Now that they were
here, he said he was glad. She wished he didn't have to keep
leaving her alone at the hotel to run errands. Even today. On
a Saturday. This time he took off right after grabbing a bite
and changing. Said he had to meet with his parents' lawyer,
talk about their finances and set them up for their impend-
ing retirement. She and Jack were supposed to have a late

dinner with his folks that night. She wasn't looking forward
to it. Murphy was never comfortable around his mother and
father. Their St. Paul house in the upscale St. Anthony Park
neighborhood was so quiet, she felt as if she was expected
to whisper. They kept it as orderly and undisturbed and for-
mal as a museum. Even the kitchen. She'd never once wit-
nessed them use the copper pots hanging from the ceiling.
Their Phoenix condo wasn't any different. Clay cookware
on display instead of copper. She couldn't complain about
them too much, however. Her family had caused more friction in their marriage than his.

She reached the channel and decided not to swim
through it. The wrestling boys were still going at it. She
flipped and swam back to where she'd started. She climbed
out. Tugged at the sides of the one-piece Speedo; the high-
cut leg openings were crawling up. She headed for the hot
tub. She stepped into the steaming water and closed her
eyes. She thought about what had brought them to Arizona
in the first place: their floundering marriage of eight years.
Her work had always been a major source of friction. The
previous fall, however, an even bigger problem was thrown
into the mix. Jack discovered that while they were separated
and working on getting back together, she'd slept with another man. Erik Mason. An investigator with the Ramsey
County Medical Examiner's Office. Jack confronted her at
her houseboat. Told her they were through. Walked out in a
fury. To make matters worse, Jack returned to her houseboat one night and found Erik there, going over a case file
with Murphy. The two men got into a fistfight. After the
dust settled, she'd told Erik it was over. She didn't even
want to work with him professionally. She'd called Jack.
Begged for forgiveness. They'd talked about counseling and
instead decided to get away. Take a vacation. She thought it
was working. They were loosening up. Talking more. Making
love as though they meant it.

She climbed out of the hot tub and slipped back in the pool. She heard yells and saw that the wrestling boys had migrated to her half of the pool. The bigger one would lock his arm around the smaller one's head and fall backward into the water. They'd separate and come up for air. Then the smaller one would put the bigger one in a headlock. Try to drag him under. They reminded her of her nephews. She'd love to have her own wild boys. That damn Dennis the Menace cowboy and his talk about kids. Another touchy subject in her marriage. She and Jack could never agree on when the time was right, especially with a relationship that was hot one minute and cold the next. They weren't even living under the same roof. He kept the house they'd bought together, and she lived full-time on her houseboat on the Mississippi River. She wondered if that would change after this vacation. Maybe it was time to sell the boat. Go back to his house. Their old home. Start that family. She had nine brothers, and they all had kids. Her folks wanted their only daughter to start producing. Their meddling was another ir-ritant to Jack. Another reason for him to be annoyed by her large, loud clan. If she could keep her family out of it, keep them from getting involved, maybe her reconciliation with Jack would stick this time.

She bent in half and dove under the surface. Swam under-water as long as she could. Enjoyed the repetitive, mindless work of kicking her legs. Of bringing her arms straight in front of her and pushing them to her sides. Pushing against the water. She came up for air. Went back down. She came up again, in the channel. She climbed out and hopped onto a stool. The bartender handed Murphy a towel. She rubbed her head with it and wrapped it around her waist. "What have you got on tap?" She felt something hit her back. She turned around. Now the two boys were going at it with a beach ball. One had apparently missed his target and nailed her by mistake. The ball was on the ground behind her stool.

"Sorry," said the bigger one, treading water in the channel.

"Sorry," repeated the smaller one, swimming up behind his buddy.

They were flaming redheads. Brothers or cousins, she thought. Junior-high age. "Yeah, yeah. I suppose you bums want me to toss it back."

"Yes, please," the pair said in unison.

She slid off the bar stool, turned around and crouched down to pick up the ball. While she was bent over, she looked into the water. They were at the edge of the pool, hanging on to the side and staring at her cleavage. "You turds." She stood up and tossed the ball to the other side of the channel. "Hit me again and I'll pop it." They laughed and swam after it.

SHE was peeling off her wet swimsuit when Jack walked into their room. Her back was turned to him. "That's a view that never disappoints," he said. She stepped out of the suit and picked it up. Turned around to face him. "That's an even better angle."

She walked into the bathroom and draped the suit over the shower rod to dry. She looked in the mirror. Her face looked a little browner, and she could see tan lines on her shoulders from her suit. She raised her hand to her forehead and stopped before her fingers reached the bangs. Forget about the damn scar, she told herself. "How'd it go with the lawyer? Get it all taken care of so we can enjoy the rest of the trip?"

"Pretty much." He set a manila file on the nightstand. He sat down on the edge of the bed and pulled off his shoes. Pulled off his socks and tucked them inside his shoes. Their room phone rang. "I'll get it. Probably my folks." He picked it up. "Dr. Jack Ramier."

She wondered why he answered the phone so formally.

He never threw around his doctor title. She turned on the cold tap, bent down and splashed some water in her face. She listened to bits of his end of the conversation.

"Yes . . . Yes . . . Wonderful. Thank you . . . Certainly . . . I'm excited as well . . . Looking forward to it."

She stood up, turned off the faucet and reached for a towel. Only one left. She smiled. They'd left the DO NOT DISTURB sign on the door so they could make love late into the morning. Forgot to take the sign down so the maid could come in. She patted her face dry with the towel and hung it back up.

He hung up as she walked out of the bathroom. She eyed the phone suspiciously and then noticed the folder. Fat with papers. "Don't tell me you've got paperwork to do. It's Saturday, for God's sake."

"Don't worry about it." He stood up and walked over to her. Wrapped his arms around her. She smelled like the poolside. Chlorine and coconut oil. He liked the combination. He kissed her, his tongue darting past her teeth. His hands moved down her back to her bottom. He withdrew his tongue and then his mouth. "Your ass is cold."

"Warm it up, then."

"I know how to do that." He turned her around and pushed her onto the tangled linen of their unmade bed. Unbuckled his pants and dropped them. Dropped his boxers. Tore off his polo shirt. He fell on top of her and buried his face in her neck. Moved his mouth down to her nipples. Chewed on her left nipple until she squirmed. He peeled his mouth off of her skin. "Too rough?"

"Never too rough," she said hoarsely. He went to her right nipple. Bit down and pulled. She moaned. He pushed her knees apart with his and entered her. She wrapped her legs around him.

Sex was never one of their marital problems.

THREE

HE PULLED BACK on the fore end, ejecting a second spent shell. He lowered the 12-gauge and took in the mess in front of him. Blood dripping down the door. Man with a crater in his back crumpled on the floor. Crazy lady with a handgun standing next to him. Crazy Pink Lady. He set the shotgun on the floor and sat down cross-legged next to it. Put his face in his hands. "Fuck no," he said into his hands. "Fuck no! No!"

The woman took her finger off the trigger and lowered her arms. Tried not to look at the body and the red puddle under it. Turned her attention to the gun instead. Still holding it in her right hand, she turned it sideways and studied it. Ran her left index finger over the words engraved on the slide. SMITH & WESSON SPRINGFIELD, MA USA. More words on the grip and frame. SMITH & WESSON. MODEL 3913. Words. All her life, words had comforted her. Given her something to hang on to, something with meaning and beauty. That comfort eluded her now. The words on the gun meant nothing to her, except that she'd just shot a man.

He asked through his fingers: "Is the safety on?" She didn't answer. He asked again. Louder and slower, as if speaking to a child or an old person. "Is the safety on?"

She could see the red dot. *Red means fire.* She answered him without looking up. "No." The steadiness of her own voice surprised her.

"The safety. Please."

With her left index finger, she pushed the safety lever on the left side of the gun. It pivoted down, covering the red dot. "Safety's on."

"Set it on the table before you shoot one of us," he said.

She hesitated. Walked over and set it down on the table with the empty glasses and pitcher. She walked toward the bar. Bent down and picked up her journal. Brushed off the cover and the back. Briefly wondered if it was worth the price of a man's life, then set the thought aside. She laid it on the counter. Noticed her jacket on the floor, at the foot of a stool. She picked it up. Shook it off. She felt cold.

He looked at his own gun on the floor next to him, and over his shoulder, at her. She was busy slipping on her jacket. He pulled the bar rag from the waist of his jeans, picked up the 12-gauge and wiped it down. Set it back down. He noted where the spent shells were on the floor. He rose to his feet, the bar rag in his hand, and went over to the pistol. Her back was still turned. She was fumbling with the zipper of her jacket. Using the rag, he picked up her gun by the grip. Examined the pistol. "Ladysmith," he said in a low voice, more to himself than to her. "Good gun for a woman."

"The name," she said.

"What?"

"I like the name. Ladysmith." She zipped up the jacket.

He shoved her pistol in the front pocket of his jeans and tossed the bar rag on the table. "Why do you carry?"

She was starting to come out of her daze. She turned around to face him. "Personal protection. I live alone. Travel alone." She combed her hair with the fingers of both hands. Wondered if she looked as bad as she felt. "Are you okay?"

"What do you care?" He hobbled over to the bar, rested both hands on the counter. She forced herself to look at the dark heap. "Should we check for a pulse?"

"Take my word for it, lady. That fucker is dead."

She stared at the red splattered all over the red door. Still had to ask: "You sure?"

"I know what dead looks like. Believe me, I do." He lowered his head. His shoulders started shaking. He was crying.

She stood watching him for a couple of minutes. She felt bad for him. At the same time, her eyes were pulled toward her journal sitting on the counter. She fought the urge to pick it up and start writing again. Such lavish drama, and all of it real. When his shoulders seemed still, she said: "It wasn't your fault. It was self-defense."

He grabbed the hem of his tee shirt to wipe his face and saw there was blood on the front from wrestling on the floor with the man. He noticed he stank like whiskey. The Jack Daniel's bottle. He wiped his eyes with his hands. Leaned against the bar again. Inhaled deeply and exhaled slowly.

The little-girl voice behind him: "What should we do?"

"Get the twelve-gauge. Don't pump it or anything stupid like that. Bring it over. The empty shells, too."

She ran her eyes around the room. Saw the sawed-off on the floor in front of the door, not far from the body. Next to the gun, a couple of shells. She went over to the gun, crouched down and picked it up by the stock. Stood up and carried it with both hands over to the bar. Set it on the counter next to where he was resting his hands. She went back for the shells. Picked them up one at a time. Red plastic tubes only a little larger than a lipstick case. She glanced over at the body and back at the shells cupped in her hand.

Wondered how something so small could do so much damage. Empty of the shot, they were so light. What was written on the side? WINCHESTER SUPER X. GAME LOAD. 2¾ IN — 1-7½. A foreign language to her; she hardly knew how to operate her own firearm. She cupped them in her left palm. She saw something even smaller on the floor, near where she'd been standing when she'd fired. Shiny and metallic. She walked over, crouched down, picked it up with her fingertips and dropped it into her left palm. Stood up. She tried not to look at it. Unlike the plastic shells, she didn't want to examine it any closer. She knew it had come from her gun, not his. She carried the works over to the bar. Dropped them on the counter next to the gun. "What else?" she asked. She wanted to help him. Wanted a role in the drama. Most of all, she wanted him to owe her.

"The bottle," he said.

She looked around again. Saw it on the floor. She was amazed it wasn't broken. She picked it up by the neck and set it next to the 12-gauge. "The police," she said. "Where's a phone. We have to call."

He pulled his hands off the counter and straightened his back. Rubbed the back of his neck with his hand. "The fuck we do."

"What do you mean?"

He wiped his nose with his shirtsleeve. "We ain't calling."

"They'll believe us."

He turned around. Pointed to the front door. "We got a guy—an older guy—with his face smashed in and holes in his back. Holes from a fucking illegal firearm. A sawed-off shotgun. And that handgun of yours. Don't suppose you have a permit for that piece?" She shook her head. He laughed dryly. "Holes from *two* fucking illegal firearms."

"He was going to kill us. It's our word."

He folded his arms over his chest. "I don't know about

your word, lady. Mine ain't worth jack shit around here, especially when it comes to guns."

"What are you talking about? What's your story? I've got a right to know."

"My story. Thought you had it all figured out in that book of yours. I'm a tortured eagle or some shit."

"No. Tortured *by* the eagle. Who is your eagle? What is it about the guns?"

The muscles in his neck and jaw tightened and flexed. "None of your business." He unfolded his arms and went to the back of the room. Pulled open the door to the janitor's closet and walked inside. She heard banging and water running. He came out pushing a wheeled bucket with a mop. She could smell ammonia. He limped toward her. "Take off your jacket, lady. You ain't going anywhere. You got work to do."

She was horrified. "I am not going to clean this bloody mess!"

"You'll take care of this while I dump the body."

"There's no time. Morning will be here. People will be knocking to get in."

"Plenty of time. Bar doesn't open until noon on Sunday."

"No!"

He ran the head through the wringer. Tossed the mop toward her. It clattered at her feet. "You'll do what I say."

"Why should I?"

"Your prints are on both guns."

The shotgun. Is that why he had her pick it up? Her prints were on the shells and the bottle, too. Was he that devious? This could be an interesting dance. She'd never had a young one that matched her wits. He wasn't well educated, but he was sly. She saw her gun was in his pocket. She pointed to it. "Yours are on both, too."

"So we're in this together."

"In *what* together? We aren't killers. Criminals. It was self-defense. We've got physical proof." She put her hand over her right breast. "I'm sure I've got a bruise where he grabbed me. I'll bet you've got a goose egg on the side of your head. His pockets are filled with cash from the till."

"A bruise and a bump and a handful of ones. Will the cops believe that's worth three shots? In the back? Or will the cops think something else happened?"

"Something else? What else?"

"They'll cook up some bullshit."

She repeated her mantra: "Self-defense." He stared at her. Expressionless. She yelled without realizing it: "Self-defense!"

"They won't believe me," he said evenly. "So they won't believe you."

Her shoulders sagged. She brought her hand to her forehead. "I'm so tired I can hardly think. I came here to get away from the families and the couples at the lodge. Have a quiet drink. This can't be happening. I'm on vacation. Vacation." She lowered her hand and looked at him. Decided to try using his name again. "Catch. We can't do this. Normal people don't mop up blood and hide bodies. Then what do we do? Go about our business? Someone is going to notice this guy is missing. We can't do this."

He went over to her. Unzipped her jacket. Gently turned her around. Peeled her jacket off her body and dropped it on the floor. He brought his hands to her shoulders and massaged them. Spoke into her ear while he stood behind her. "We have to do this. You have to help me. Please. We can do this together."

"It's wrong," she said weakly.

"The guy was scum. Deserved to die."

"He did," she said. His voice was soothing. Convincing. His hands felt like fire on her shoulders. "But why can't we call the police? Tell them?"

He kept massaging. He felt her softening. He whispered: "You want my story?" She nodded. "I shot my father. Deer hunting. An accident. The sheriff believed me, but barely."

"Why barely?" she asked.

"I don't think they'll believe this was another accident, or self-defense." He stopped rubbing and rested his hands on her shoulders. "They'll put me away."

His voice was starting to break, and it moved her. At the same time she wondered: Is it an act? He moved his hands from her shoulders to her waist. He wrapped his big arms around her midriff. He molded his front into her back. Buried his face in her hair. His breath. So hot. He smelled like whiskey and sweat. She liked those smells together; they were one step away from a sex smell. She could feel his erection pressing against her. The only sounds were their breathing and the wind buffeting the windows. She untangled his arms and took his hands in hers. Large, hot hands. Rough hands. She moved them up to her breasts. He didn't pull away. He didn't have to be told what to do. He cupped them and squeezed. Gently. She moaned. A perfect pupil, she thought. Perhaps her first advanced student. He squeezed again. Harder. It hurt her sore breast, but she didn't care.

"That turn you on, Pink Lady?" he said into her ear.

"Yes." She liked that name. Pink Lady. His right hand moved from her right breast and slipped down into the front of her jeans. She wondered how such a large hand could slide so easily. She felt him against her skin. Cupping her crotch with that hot, rough hand. "Why barely?" she asked again. He didn't answer.

FOUR

A PICKUP TRUCK barreled down the dark county highway, fishtailed and turned south on the road leading to Fisherman's Point Campground. The road was narrow and ran the length of a peninsula that jutted into Whitewater Lake. Hardwoods and evergreens crowded the road on both sides. A few utility poles spiked the finger of land, but their lamps were out. The light poles stopped at the edge of the lake. Nailed to the last pole was a sign: NO SWIMMING OR DIVING FROM DOCK. The dock—half buried in snow—had been pulled up onto shore and was parked to the right of the pole. In the summer, the peninsula was dotted with tents and campers. In the winter, all the action was on the frozen water, where dozens of shacks sheltered ice fishermen. The truck sailed past the last light pole, rolled down an incline of packed snow and glided onto the ice. He didn't see other trucks on the lake—anyone would have to be crazy to be out in this—but he didn't want to risk being spotted. He punched off his headlights. The blizzard and the nighttime blackness on the lake didn't bother him. He knew White water from memory. Less than two miles outside of town. He'd walked to it when he was a kid. Fished it thousands of times in all seasons. He drove into the middle and took a sharp left. Headed for a bay where his shack was the only one. Bouncing around on the truck bed behind him was a snowmobile and helmet. Next to them, the body of a man encased in vinyl tablecloths and wrapped in rope. A red-and-white-checked mummy in bondage. Wrapped with him were his balaclava, gloves and an empty bottle of Jack Daniel's. The bottle was smeared with blood.

While he navigated across the ice, he thought about the Pink Lady. He'd taken a big chance leaving her back at the bar to clean up the mess. She could take off. Go back down to the Twin Cities. He guessed that's where she lived. In addition to the Giants Ridge lift tickets on her jacket, he'd noticed a bunch from Afton Alps in the metro area. Worse than fleeing, she could call the cops. If she squealed on him, he had something he could use against her. On the seat next to him were the shotgun, her handgun, the spent shells and brass casing. He'd pulled on his gloves before handling them to make sure all stayed free of his prints. The shells would have Maggie's prints on them as well. She'd loaded the sawed-off. He'd never touched it before this night. He could concoct a story that would make him look good and the Pink Lady look guilty. He could say she went nuts because the guy grabbed her tits and her book. He'd tell the cops she took the gun from behind the counter and shot the guy. Then she nailed the poor bastard again with her own piece, an illegal handgun. He knew gunpowder tests could determine who'd fired what, but he also knew the limits of rural law enforcement. He'd pushed the envelope before. They'd arrest his ass for dumping the body. Hell, he'd gladly confess to that. His excuse would be that he felt sorry for her or that she'd threatened him in some way. The time he'd do for hiding a dead man had to be less than the sentence he'd get for shooting the guy in the first place. Especially since it would be his second shooting. Besides, he thought, that second blast was the one that killed the guy. She was the real killer.

He flipped the headlights back on. He didn't want to pull too close to the shack and ding it up. He rolled next to it and put the truck in park. Punched off the lights, turned off the truck. Pulled the keys out of the ignition and dropped them in his jacket pocket. What did he need from inside the truck? He reached over and popped open the glove compartment. Fished out a flashlight and stuffed it in his jacket pocket. Anything else he needed would be in the dark house. He closed the glove compartment. Zipped up his jacket. Pulled his stocking cap tighter over his head. Flexed his gloved hands. Opened the truck door and hopped out. Looked inside the truck with his hand on the door. Thought about reaching across the seat and taking the guns and shells and casing with him. They could go down the hole with the body. No. He wanted to keep those cards until he was sure about the Pink Lady. The way she was—so hot for him one minute and a nutty, nosey bitch the next—he might never be sure. Who would have thought she'd be packing a pistol? Who would have thought she'd have the guts to use it? Why didn't she have papers for it? Felons and head cases couldn't get handgun permits in Minnesota. Which was she? He tried not to think about it. Thought about her breasts instead. She had nice ones. Liked having them squeezed. She'd wanted to do it right there on the floor. No time, he told her. Later. Even in the cold, he was getting hard thinking about later. Horny over a woman, and he didn't have a clue as to her real name. She only knew him by his nickname. He liked the way she said it. She hung on to that *ch* at the end. Made it last forever. Sounded like someone saying "shhh." *Catcchhh.* He slammed the door. A gust of wind sent snow flying against the back of his neck. He pulled his jacket collar up and walked over to his shack, limping as he went. He took the flashlight out of his pocket, flicked it on and shined it on the door. Shit. The padlock was hanging there, open. Did he forget to lock up? He'd used it the night before and was sure he'd locked up. Had someone messed around inside? He slipped off the padlock and shoved it in his jacket pocket. Put a foot on the step leading up to the door. He held his breath and pulled open the door. Ran the light around the inside of the shack. Stepped inside.

Everything was the way he'd left it. Built as solidly as an outhouse and twice the size of one, he was proud of the place. The shanty was made of lumber scraps and sat atop the ice on landscape ties. Inside, the interior walls were covered with wood paneling and the floor with sheets of plywood. He'd scavenged the works—lumber, paneling and landscape ties—from the dump, construction sites and neighbors' trash. His biggest expense had been nails. After that, spray paint. Every interior surface was covered with black. Ceiling, walls, floors, door. Cracks that emitted the slightest sliver of daylight were filled with black caulk. A couple of vents in the walls—necessary so he wouldn't suffocate when he used the heater—were covered with black rounds of wood that pivoted open. Sitting inside the shack, alone and surrounded by inky darkness, was like hiding in a closet. The rectangle cut into the ice offered the only light. A greenish glow. The eyes adjusted to the dark. Focused on the rectangle. He could see all the way down. He'd dump eggshells into the hole. They'd settle on the bottom and provide a background against which he could better see the fish. Dark silhouettes against a white canvas. He'd hover over the hole for hours, watching the decoy he'd lowered into the water and holding his spear poised in anticipation. Regular fish houses were loud party shacks. Anglers crowded into them to drink beer and watch television and tell stories.

Occasionally someone paid attention to the poles over the holes in the floor. Circles the size of dinner plates. Dark house spear fishing required a bigger hole. A rectangle the size of a window. More than that, it demanded quiet. Blackness. Patience. Solitude.

His furnishings were minimal. Leaning against one wall, a seven-tined spear. Resting next to it, a long-handled chopper like the kind used to break ice on sidewalks. An aluminum lawn chair. A propane heater that he hated using because it required that he open the vents. A cooler to keep his beer from freezing. For the rare occasions he needed interior light, a battery-operated lantern sitting on a card table. Stashed under the card table, a tackle box filled with decoys he'd carved himself, an ice scoop and an empty coffee can that served as a urinal when it was too cold to pee outside. Also under the card table: the chainsaw he'd used to cut the hole in the ice. The chainsaw would come in handy if Plan A failed.

He turned back around and closed the door against the wind and snow. He went over to the card table and set down the flashlight so the beam illuminated the lantern. He turned the knob on the lantern. Set it to low. The twin fluorescent tubes glowed white. He picked up the flashlight and went to the far end of the shanty. Using a rope handle, he lifted up a rectangle of wood. Underneath the trapdoor was the hole in the ice. At night, the green rectangle turned into a black pit. He imagined he could fall into it and never stop. Keep falling, falling, falling. The trapdoor was hinged. He pulled it open until he could loop the rope handle over a hook attached to the back wall. He walked to the side opposite the hinges and squatted next to the hole. Aimed the beam down the pit. The lake ice was better than a foot thick. It had taken some work to cut into it, even with a good chainsaw. He could see a new layer of ice had formed over the rectangle of water since he'd fished last. He stood up and grimaced.

His ankles didn't like the cold. He flicked off the flashlight
and set it on the table next to the lantern. His breath hung in
the air. He thought about turning on the heater but didn't
want to go through the trouble. Wanted this to be a quick
operation. He retrieved the ice chopper from its resting
place against the wall. Went over to the hole. Held tight to
the chopper handle with both hands and lunged down at the
black pit. A dozen jabs broke up the layer of ice. He pushed
the ice chunks to the side of the hole. Returned the chopper
to its place against the wall. Now comes the hard work, he
thought. He pulled his cap tight over his ears. Gripped the
knob with his hand and pushed open the shanty door. He
was hit by a blast of snow and wind. He left the door open
so he could work by the light of the lantern.

He went around to the back of the truck. Opened the
back gate. Eyed the snowmobile. A beauty. Yamaha Warrior. Silver and red. Looked like a bullet with a seat on it.
Better than that bastard deserved. Probably stole it. Catch
had kept the helmet with the sled. He'd contemplated hanging on to both. Now he told himself he couldn't. Not until
he saw how this mess played itself out. Too late to wrap the
helmet with the body, though. He didn't want to undo the
mummy. After getting rid of the body, he'd dump the sled
and the helmet in the woods. Come spring thaw, maybe
he'd come back for it. He gripped the rope and the folds of
the tablecloths. The frozen vinyl crackled in his gloved
hands. He slid the body toward him until half of it was
hanging over the edge of the gate. He hunched over, wrapped
his arms around the middle of the package and picked it up.
Hiked it over his right shoulder like a sack of flour. He
stumbled backward two steps and groaned. The weight
taxed his ankles. "Big mother," he mumbled. He regained
his footing, readjusted the body on his shoulder and headed
back to the shack. Carried the body up the step and into the
dark house. Bent over and let the body slide off his shoulder

and fall to the floor with a *thud*. He stood straight and used the back of his glove to wipe the snot running down his nose. He was panting, his breath clouding the small space. He rested his hand against the folding table and studied the bundle. Thought about how an hour or so earlier, this had been a living person. Big and mean and ugly, but alive. Reminded him of another bully. He kicked at the bundle with his foot. Half expected the checked mummy to sit up and swear at him. "I'm a gimp, but at least I ain't dead," he said. He turned around, went out the door, still leaving it open. Went to the back of the truck and shut the gate. Tried to look into the night and the blowing snow. Coming down so thick, it was hard to keep his eyes open. All he could see through the slits was black and white. He limped back to the shack. Fought the wind to pull the door shut.

He turned and looked down at the body. Prayed to God Plan A worked because Plan B would be so messy. "You'd better go down and stay down, you bastard. Otherwise I'm feeding you to the fish in chunks."

The head was at one end of the pit, perpendicular with it. He picked up the feet and pivoted the body so it rested parallel with the rectangle. He crouched down next to it and rolled it into the water. As he expected, the mess was too long. Filled the hole and stayed on top. He got the ice chopper. Held tight with both hands and pushed down on the lump of vinyl and rope. Steered it under the ice. Away from his dark house. Pushed and steered and tucked it under the ice. While he worked he tried to remember a number. What was it? Forty-five. Lake water needs to be at least forty-five degrees at the bottom before beginning the chemical reactions that make a body float. Forty-five degrees to make a body's innards rot and form gases that bring it to the surface. Up north, the lakes stay cold well into spring. Forty-five degrees was months away.

One last push with the ice chopper. The checked mummy

disappeared into the black water. "Good-bye, you son of a bitch." He put the blade on the ground and leaned against the handle with his left hand. Imagined the rectangle of water was a coffin. What would happen if he joined the bastard? What if he went down on his back like a vampire in the movies? Crossed his arms over his chest and let himself sink into the hole? He could float away. Be trapped under the ice. Die under the ice. A fitting way to go for a spear fisherman. Would facedown be better than faceup? He took a step toward the edge of the hole. The foot of the coffin. Another step. He closed his eyes tight. Took a third step. Felt the edge of the hole with the toe of his boot. Remembered another time when he'd walked to the edge with his eyes shut. That hadn't turned out the way he'd hoped. He opened his eyes and backed away from the rectangle. Inhaled deeply and exhaled slowly. With the back of his hand, he wiped his runny nose and congratulated himself on pushing down the yearning. Again.

HE walked into the bar through the back, the same door he'd used to drag out the body. He half expected her to be gone, or maybe curled up in a corner crying. She was up front, pounding on the front door with a hammer. A cigarette hanging from one side of her mouth. She didn't hear him stepping up behind her. "What are you doing?"

She turned with the hammer. Pulled the cigarette out of her mouth with her free hand. "Jesus Christ! You scared the shit out of me. Don't do that again."

He unzipped his jacket. "Sorry."

She stepped aside so he could get a better look at her work. Took a pull off her cigarette and blew a cloud of smoke out as she talked. "What do you think? See any holes?"

He pulled off his stocking cap, stuffed it in his jacket pocket. Studied the door. She'd moved one of the beer posters from the back wall. A knockoff of a vintage beer ad. The Hamm's bear in the middle of a lake, running on a floating log. At the bottom of the poster: *Born in the land of sky-blue waters.* His eyes went from the poster to the woman. He was freaked by how calm she appeared. In the last couple of hours she'd been threatened with robbery, plugged a guy in the back with a gun and cleaned up a bloody mess. Here she was standing with a hammer in one hand and a smoke in the other, asking his opinion on whether her poster covered holes from gunfire. She could have been asking him if the oil painting she'd hung was crooked or straight. He looked away from her and stared at the poster again. Tried to think of an intelligent question. One that would make him sound as in control as she. "So how bad is it under the bear? Do the holes go all the way through?"

She shook her head. "Checked. You lucked out on that."

"*We* lucked out," he said.

"Blood was tough, but I got a lot of it off. What I couldn't get off I covered with more red. Found a can in the closet." She took a drag off her cigarette. Exhaled.

He sniffed. "Thought I smelled fresh paint." He pulled off his gloves and shoved them in his pocket. "Maggie won't notice. She's always having me touch up her damn door. What'd you do with the bloody rags?"

"Soaking in the janitor's closet."

"We could toss them. Maggie has a pile of rags. Won't miss them."

"Better to toss clean rags than bloody ones. We'll throw them in a garbage bag. I'll toss it in a dumpster at the hotel."

She's really thought this through. She was scaring the shit out of him. He tried to think of another good question. "The floor?"

"Mopped it up. Rinsed off the mop. Took the runner from behind the bar. Threw it down in front of the door."

"Maggie might not like that. She likes it behind the bar.

Easier on the legs than the hard floor. Anything noticeable under the rug if she moves it back?"

"Same filthy floor. You'd have to be looking for it."

"Hopefully she won't be looking for shit. Nobody will be looking for shit."

She talked while she walked to the closet to put the hammer back. "How realistic is that? Someone's going to miss that guy. He was an asshole, but everybody has somebody."

"You remember what he said. He lost his pals on the trail. They'll report him missing. Search the woods. Who'd think of searching a bar? The storm will cover his outside tracks. We took care of the inside stuff."

She stopped in the open doorway of the closet and glared at him. Took a long pull off the cigarette down to the butt. Exhaled. "I took care of the inside stuff." She walked into the closet.

He heard water running. He ran his fingers through his hair and then looked at his hands. They were shaking. She was giving him the shakes. He tightened his hands into fists and willed them to stop trembling. Rammed his fists into his jacket pockets and followed her. He walked past the tables. All four were missing their checked tablecloths. It had taken that many to wrap up the mess. He was always threatening to get rid of the ugly things. Maggie will figure he finally went through with it. He got to the closet doorway. Stood watching with his hands in his pockets. She was standing over the slop sink, rinsing the rags under running water. Twisting and squeezing. She'd tossed her cigarette butt into the sink. "You'd make a good maid," he said, smiling. He hoped she wouldn't notice it was a nervous grin.

"I *was* a maid," she said. She held up one of the rags by its edges. Clean. She draped it over the side of the sink. Held up another. Clean. Draped it next to the other. "My parents' maid. Actually, more like a slave."

He pulled his hands out of his pockets and crossed his arms over his chest. "This that dark past you were going to tell me about?"

She held up a third rag. Still a little pink. She held it under the water longer. Stretched it out and ran it back and forth under the tap. Squeezed it and twisted it tight. Shook it out and held it up. Inspected it by the bare bulb hanging from the closet ceiling. Cleaner than it was before it served its bloody duty. She draped it over the side of the sink. Looked down at her shirt. Bloody drops on it and the smudge the robber had left over her breast. "I'm going to burn this shirt when I get home." She looked up at him. "What did you do with the bastard's body?"

"Under the ice."

"Whole or in pieces?"

"Whole."

She wiped her hands on the thighs of her jeans. "Too bad."

His eyes widened. She was mean, and maybe a little crazy. Those Popsicle eyes seemed too excited. Ready to pop out of her head. Her little-girl voice had gotten even higher and sharper. He'd have to watch her. Watch his back while he was around her. At the same time, he figured he could learn a few things from her. Cool, crazy Pink Lady. He wanted to make sure she understood how hard he'd worked as well. "Whiskey bottle went down with him. Dumped his sled and helmet in the woods, away from any trail."

She leaned one hand against the sink and with the other, pushed the hair out of her face. "The guns and the rest?"

Without pausing he answered: "Down the hole."

She took her hand off the sink and straightened her back. "Will the bar owner notice the shotgun missing?"

"She sure as hell will. The whole town knows she keeps it under the bar. I'll tell her someone made me an offer on it. Maggie's always up for more money. She'd sell the whole place if she could. I'll leave a note and some money so she doesn't freak when she opens on Sunday and realizes the thing is missing."

She put her hands on her hips. "Maybe you should make it a good-bye letter."

"What are you saying?"

"Tell her you're taking your friend's advice. Quitting this lousy job and moving away. Don't tell her where you're headed. Only that you're leaving. You're gone. I'll help you write it if you want."

"Good idea. I'm not much of a writer."

That didn't surprise her. "Does she owe you any pay? Is it more than the gun's worth?"

"Yeah."

"Tell her you took the gun in payment. You're even. Then you won't have to leave a forwarding address."

He leaned his shoulder against the door frame. "But where am I going?"

"Down to St. Paul. With me."

"Not a bad idea." He figured while he was glued to her, she couldn't turn him in. Couldn't turn on him. "I've got a brother in St. Paul."

"You live upstairs, right?"

She'd heard more of his conversation with Siggy than he'd hoped. She had big ears and a good memory. "Yeah. Upstairs."

"Grab some things and come with me now. Your truck. Can you leave it somewhere? Any furniture?"

"Ain't my truck. Maggie's. Furniture upstairs is Maggie's, too." The guns and shells and casing on the seat of the truck. He'd have to retrieve those. Hide them with his other stuff. "Got some of my own stuff in back of the truck, though. Tools and shit. Don't want to leave that behind. Otherwise I won't pack more than what'll fit into a duffel bag. Most of my clothes are shit anyways."

"We'll go to Giants Ridge. You get rid of the bloody rags while I check out of the lodge. We'll be in the Twin Cities before lunch."

"Still coming down hard. Roads are bad."

"My Explorer's out front. Four-wheel drive. It'll get through. Grab the keys out of my purse. Pull it around back and load up while I finish in here."

He stepped toward her and stuck out his hand. Was relieved to see it was steady. "Enda Clancy."

She wiped her palms on her pants again. Took his hand in both of hers. "Serene Ransom. I don't mind Pink Lady, though. Kind of like that."

FIVE

HE TOLD HER that night, on the way to the restaurant. Later, she wondered how she'd missed all the clues. The way he kept ditching her during their vacation. His excuses about meetings and errands. The folder he left on their bedside table. The phone call. His questions about whether she liked Arizona. Her keen senses and intuition—a combination that had helped her solve so many murder cases—had failed her in her personal life.

Jack was driving their rented Lincoln Continental. A light-rock station was playing James Taylor. "Fire and Rain." She was staring into the night, preoccupied with the twinkling. Christmas and New Year's Day had come and gone, but the Scottsdale hotels and resorts were still wrapped in lights. Instead of decorating pine trees, they strung lights around cactus plants. She saw one giant after another with lights wrapped around their trunks and arms. Maybe they were always illuminated and she'd never noticed on her previous visits. "Do they keep them on all year?"

"Keep what on?"

"Do the hotels keep the cactus plants lit year round?"

"You'll be able to answer that question yourself soon enough."

Her head snapped around. "What?"

Jack braked at a red light. He punched off the radio. "I have something to tell you, and I hope you consider it good news."

Doesn't sound good, she thought. "Go ahead."

"I've been offered a position with the Mayo."

Her stomach fell. She knew it wasn't the clinic in Minnesota, but she had to ask anyway: "In Rochester?"

He put his right hand over her left. "No, babe."

"Arizona," she said evenly. "You're moving to Arizona."

"*We're* moving," he said. "I want you with me. Perfect chance for us to get away from all the crap back home." The light turned green, but he didn't notice. He was studying her face, hoping for a positive reaction. The car behind them honked. He took his hand off hers, put it back on the steering wheel and accelerated. Looked straight ahead at the road and talked fast. "A great position. Opportunity to do some groundbreaking work. The Rochester and Scottsdale emergency medicine groups are planning a multicenter research project looking at the best medications for acute vomiting treatment in the Emergency Department. Their Phoenix facility is phenomenal. Do you realize it's the first hospital actually designed and built by the Mayo?"

She rested her head against the car window and shut her eyes. Felt as if she was going to vomit herself. She didn't understand why he'd dumped it on her like this. While in the car, driving to a restaurant. They couldn't even talk about it openly once they got there. Not with his folks sitting across from them. He'd probably told them already, and they were undoubtedly ecstatic. She opened her eyes and lifted her head off the window. Realized they were turning into the restaurant parking lot.

He pulled into a space, put the car in Park and shut off the engine. Yanked the keys out of the ignition and held them in his hand. Seemed to talk to them instead of her. "I know this seems out of the blue, but I've been thinking. Not about this particular job necessarily, but about getting the hell out of Minnesota."

She covered her face with her hands. Took a deep breath and released it. Dropped her hands in her lap and looked at him. "Why?"

He didn't answer. He stared straight ahead while his fist tightened around the keys in his hand.

"Why?" she asked again.

He hurled the keys against the windshield. They bounced off and landed on the seat between them. "Why do you think?"

The affair she'd had with Erik. "We put that behind us."

"Did we?"

"This trip was a mistake. I thought it would fix everything. We should've gone with the counseling."

"I don't want to tell our problems to some stranger just because he has some bullshit degree hanging on his office wall. We can fix this on our own."

"Where's the *we* in all this, Jack? *We* haven't talked about this moving stuff. You were keeping this to yourself. Sneaking around all week. In job interviews I suppose."

"Sneaking? Okay, let's talk sneaking." A car pulled up and parked to the left of theirs. Jack realized he was yelling and lowered his voice. "Let's talk about you and that piece of shit, Mason, sneaking around and fucking behind my back."

"How many times do I have to say I'm sorry? How many times for that one time?" She'd slept with Erik once, over the summer while she was struggling with one of her biggest cases. She suspected a wealthy plastic surgeon was a serial killer of prostitutes. Jack told her she was nuts. Erik worked with her in the investigation and supported her. She was proven right, but the doctor shot himself with her gun before she could arrest him. Months later, the case was casting a shadow over her life larger than the scar the doctor had given her. She wondered if she'd ever shake it. Ever repair the damage caused by the affair. "What can I do, Jack? It happened and it's over and done with."

He looked away from her and stared outside the driver's side window. "Is it over, babe?"

The way he asked the question. In a voice that was sad and fearful. She finally understood Jack's desire to move wasn't fueled by a quest for a new job and a fresh start. He wanted to get her away from Erik. He was worried she would gravitate back to her lover. She didn't know which made her more miserable—Jack's mistrust of her or his insecurity about his hold over her. She could think of only one thing to say. One reassurance: "I love you."

He scooped up the keys and shoved them in his pants pocket. Opened the driver's door. "My parents are waiting."

"They know about the Mayo offer?"

"You think I'd tell them before I'd tell you?" He slid out of the car, stood up and slammed the driver's door.

THE Japanese restaurant was as much about theater as it was food. A chef chopped and tossed meat and vegetables at a grill set in front of the two couples. She and Jack sat at opposite sides of the square table. His parents sat next to each other on one side. The cook and his supplies took up the fourth side. Murphy was grateful for the seating arrangement and the lively food preparation. Instead of talking to each other, she and Jack were able to talk to his parents and the cook.

She had to admit Douglas and Helen Ramier made a handsome couple in a tweedy, academic sort of way. Both were tall and slender and had the slightly bent posture of people who spent a lot of time at desks. His gray hair was a bird's nest of knots and tangles. Her brown hair was streaked with gray and cut into a pageboy that fell just short of her chin. They each wore narrow reading glasses to look at the menu and slipped them off to watch the cooking show. He tucked his spectacles into the front pocket of his short-sleeved oxford shirt. Hers hung from her neck by a pearl-and-gold-link chain. The chain was draped over a short-sleeved silk blouse. The shirt matched her slacks. Murphy recognized the outfit. They'd purchased it during one of their many trips to Japan. They were professors in the University of Minnesota's College of Liberal Arts. He was chair of the English Department, and she was head of the Department of Asian Languages and Literatures.

Helen sipped some sake. "How are your parents, dear?"

"Fine. Getting older." Murphy wondered if her face was going to crack from the smile she was forcing.

"Working on any interesting murders?" asked Douglas. He took a drink of Scotch.

"Not at the moment." Jack's parents always asked about her work. Murphy felt they didn't have a real interest in their daughter-in-law's life as much as a clinical fascination with the details of her cases.

"We read in the papers about that one you had," said Douglas. "That old high-school chum of yours from St. Brice's. Amazing story."

He was referring to a case she'd had in the fall. "We weren't friends," said Murphy. "Classmates."

Douglas: "So this Justice Trip fellow ran down a woman,

buried her body and planted her finger so he'd find it while with a search party. All to be lauded as a hero?"

"All to play hero." Murphy looked across the table at Jack. He was watching the cook sharpen his knives. He hated hearing about her work.

Helen: "He killed his father and his father's nurse as well?"

Murphy nodded. She suspected he'd killed others over the years, going back to her high-school sweetheart and three of his friends. She'd never get all the answers. Trip was dead.

Helen: "The papers said another officer was injured during the pursuit."

"Axel Duncan," said Murphy. "Commander in Homicide." She shot Trip while he was taking off in his truck, and then Duncan rammed the truck with his own car.

Helen took another sip of sake. "I hope it wasn't serious."

"Some broken bones. He made a full recovery." She never told Jack that after Duncan was released from the hospital, she spent a few days nursing her boss at his place and then at her houseboat. Although there was nothing between Murphy and Duncan, she figured Jack didn't need more fuel stoking the jealousy fire.

Douglas took another drink of Scotch, crossed his arms on top of the table and leaned forward, as if he was waiting for the punch line of a good joke. "How did he do them in exactly? His father and the nurse? I don't remember reading. Poison? Strangulation?"

Murphy: "Slit their throats."

Douglas nodded toward the cook, who was chopping vegetables so quickly his hands were a blur. "With a kitchen knife?"

"Something more exotic. Trip collected switchblades and swords and daggers."

Jack glared at his parents and then at his wife. "Can we

get off this subject? Dad. How's everybody in the depart-ment? How are you making out under the state budget cuts?"

"Horseshit," said Douglas. "Liberal arts are always the first to go. I'd like to see our friends in IT tighten their belts for a change."

"The engineers are the moneymakers, Douglas," said Helen. "Not the poets."

"A culture is remembered for the quality of its literature and art, not the durability of its sewer systems." Douglas emptied his glass and waved the waitress over for another drink.

Murphy sipped her wine and turned her eyes to the cook. He was squirting something on the grill, creating a steamy cloud. She wished they could eat and get out of there. She longed for the evening to be over. Wanted the en-tire vacation to be finished. Suddenly, the cop shop seemed the safest place in her life.

MURPHY claimed she had a headache so she and Jack could bail out before the waitress came by with the dessert cart. Helen and Douglas were in no hurry to leave and of-fered to pick up the check. Jack threw some bills down for the tip. The younger couple got up from the table. Douglas stood and clasped Murphy's right hand in both of his. "Come by the house before you leave."

"We will," said Murphy. "When do classes start up again?"

"The Tuesday after the MLK holiday," he said. "But we'll be flying home the week before, if not sooner. I've got to get back and train my successor. Teach him how to cut someone loose." Douglas released her hand.

Jack frowned. He'd met most of the English faculty through his parents: "Firing anyone I know?"

"Serene Ransom."

"Don't think I've met her."

"You'd remember her if you had," said Douglas. He sat back down.

"A victim of the budget cuts?" asked Jack.

"Not exactly." Douglas polished off his Scotch and set down the glass.

Murphy came behind her mother-in-law and bent over to kiss her on the cheek. She straightened and saw Jack was already at the restaurant door, waiting for her with his arms folded across his chest.

"He's in a big hurry," said Helen, looking over at her son. She raised her hand to wish him good-bye, and he saluted from his station at the door.

"I'm sorry," said Murphy. She grabbed her shoulder bag hanging from the back of her chair and went after him. He pulled the door open for her without a word. She stepped outside. He closed the restaurant door and walked ahead of her to the car. Yanked open the driver's door, got in and slammed it shut. She took a deep breath, let it out and pulled open the passenger's door. Slid inside and shut the door.

He shoved the key in the ignition but didn't turn it on. He put his hands on the steering wheel. Looked straight ahead and said: "I know I blindsided you on this Mayo deal. I didn't want to give us time to argue about it. I was hoping you'd enjoy yourself for a couple of weeks. Get in the mood. Then get excited about the idea when I told you. Surprised in a good way. Not a shitty way."

She fingered her purse strap. "We'll talk about it."

"Sure we will." He turned the ignition and backed out of the parking space with a squeal.

AS bad as the evening was, it got worse when they returned to the hotel. They didn't talk during the drive. Walked into their room without exchanging a word. He went straight into the bathroom and shut the door. She sat down on the edge of the bed and dropped her purse on the floor. She kicked off her pumps, crossed her right foot over her left knee and rubbed her toes. She'd worn a dress and heels for Jack's folks, but she was always most comfortable in jeans. She put her foot down and saw the red button on their room phone was blinking. She figured it was for him. Something about the new job. He could pick it up when he got out of the shower. She leaned back against the headboard and put her feet up on the bed. Grabbed the remote off the nightstand and turned on the television. Surfed until she got to the Weather Channel. Northern Minnesota was getting socked by a blizzard. The news made her homesick. She surfed some more. Stopped at an action flick with Bruce Willis. She tossed the remote on the bed. The shower stopped. The bathroom door popped open. Jack walked out with a towel wrapped around his waist. She looked at the beads of water dripping down his well-muscled chest and felt a stabbing sensation in her gut. She couldn't lose him. Not again. She tried to shake off the ache. She didn't want him to see her hurting. "Probably for you," she said, tipping her head toward the phone.

He picked up the receiver. Called the front desk. As he listened to the message, he looked at her. He took a pen off the nightstand and scribbled a phone number on hotel stationery. He set down the receiver, picked it up again and punched in the number. She looked at the pad and vaguely recognized the digits. Someone's cell. Someone in her family. She picked up the remote and shut off Bruce Willis. Dropped the remote back on the bed. Her eyes locked on Jack's face. His brows were knotted. Her heart fluttered. She instinctively wrapped her arms around herself and curled her knees up to her chest. "What is it?"

"Your dad's at Regions. His heart."

"How bad? Calling the hospital?"

"Pat and Ryan. They left their cell." Patrick and Ryan

were her older brothers. They were doctors—orthopedic surgeons with a practice together—and always took the lead when it came to family medical issues.

She thought about the phone she'd left at home. "I should have brought my cell. I'll bet they've been trying to call us on it."

Jack sat down next to her on the bed. Draped his left arm over her shoulders while his right hand held the phone to his ear. "Want to talk to them first?"

She shook her head. "You go first. Translate for me."

"Damn. Their machine." He paused. Said into the phone: "Guys. It's Jack. Call us back at the hotel." He hung up the receiver. Picked it up again. Cradled the phone between his right ear and shoulder while he punched in another phone number. One he knew by heart. The Regions emergency room.

She wrapped her arms around his warm, wet body. She was never more grateful to have him next to her. "We have to get home."

His left arm tightened around her shoulders while he waited for his ER to pick up. "We'll go home."

SIX

SHE LET HIM drive. Left her hands free for smoking. They exchanged life stories during the five-hour ride down to St. Paul. Each held back some details, and revealed some things wiser people would have left hidden.

BUTTERFLY pad saves. Pad saves. Stick saves. He was good at all of them. They called him Catch because he excelled at making glove saves. Shined at it from the moment he first pulled a goalie glove over his left hand. He liked how it was shaped like a fielder's mitt in baseball. Strange piece of equipment for the ice, he thought. With it, he executed catches that should have been impossible given the speed or angle or height of the shot. His arm would dart left or right or down or up. The fans in the stands would jump to their feet and scan the net behind him, sure the shot had gone in. He'd open his glove when the ref skated up. There it would be. The puck. Magic. Like producing a coin from behind someone's ear or pulling a rabbit out of a hat. The cheers. The praise. All for the catches. *Good catch, goalie! Good catch! What a catch!* Even praise from the other side. *Did you see that catch? Their goalie is damn good.* One voice was always silent when others were cheering. The voice he strained to hear praising and never did. The voice that offered only criticism. *We should've had a shutout. How could you miss those weak-ass shots? Is there a fucking hole in that glove? Don't let the win go to your head. Their shooters were wimps. Their goalie was better.* That voice. Harsh and cruel and loud. Embarrassing him in the locker room before the game and in the car after the game and at home. That voice. Grinding him down. Beating him. Wearing him down. Sometimes he'd hear it in his dreams. Calling him names. Swearing at him. Telling him he was shit. That voice. The voice of his coach. His father. Owen Clancy.

His dad was hard on the other players. Called the forwards ladies. *The ladies must be having their periods tonight. They're skating like they got cramps.* The center was a pussy. The defenders were sieves. The players on the other teams were crap. The coaches of the other teams didn't know the sport. The refs were idiots. *Don't know an offside from an ass wipe.* A few players and parents grumbled but most put up with Owen Clancy. He was a winning youth hockey coach. His teams took home a lot of hardware. The gruffness must be what the kids need out on the ice. He couldn't be all bad, they figured. They didn't have to go home with him. Listen to his abuse day and night. *Call that a shoveling job? Do it over. I don't care if you're sick. Lazy. Since when is a B good enough in this family? No television or that shit you call music until I see straight A's. Dummy. Only place you're going Saturday is the stockroom.* When he wasn't on the ice or at school, Catch was at his father's hardware store. Counting nails. Sorting screws. Hanging hammers.

Mixing cans of paint. Sharpening ice skates. Damn skates. Even at the store, he couldn't get away from hockey.

Catch's mother was aptly named, he thought. Damita, shortened by his father to Dot. That's all she was. A smudge of a woman. Short and skinny and brown and nervous. Clothes hung better on wire hangers than they did on her. Hair the color of coal. She kept it cut as short as a man's. A black dot on Dot's head. She was the daughter of Mexican migrant workers who'd labored in southern Minnesota sugar-beet fields. She never said how she ended up in northern Minnesota, married to a hardware-store owner. Catch liked his mother's Mexican accent. He wished she would teach him the language, but his father banned it from the house. *We speak English in this country.* Catch's older sisters, Eldora and Melisenda—shortened by their father to Dora and Mel—were duplicates of their mother. Right down to the skullcap haircuts. When Owen Clancy had one of his yelling fits, the three females tripped over one another to get out of his way. Ran and hid like pups that had been kicked. Scared and shivering. They didn't say a word when Owen Clancy shot the kids' pet rabbits for fun. They didn't protest when he forbid the family from going to church because he didn't like the new priest. They didn't even speak up when Owen Clancy beat the shit out of his sons because he didn't like the wax job they did on his pickup.

The oldest child, Robert—shortened by his father to Bob and then Bo—tried to teach his younger brother how to stay under their father's radar. *Don't say anything to him when he gets home from work. Hand him a beer and get the hell out of the front room. Don't talk during dinner. Eat and shut up. Don't give school a reason to call. Stop arguing with him. Jesus. Are you trying to die?* Catch envied Bo. He was smart. Got straight A's in school without trying hard. Without his father's threats. He was more popular at school. Both boys were good-looking with their mops of dark hair and dark eyes and muscular build. Bo got the girls, though. Knew how to sweet-talk them. Catch figured Bo had learned sweet talk after talking his way out of so many beatings from his father. Bo even talked his way out of hockey. Told his father it was interfering with school. Owen Clancy didn't let his younger boy off the hook, though. Enda Clancy was better than Bo in the net. Too good to stay off the ice. Bad grades or not. Sick or not. When he was twelve years old, he played an entire weekend tournament with a gut ache. His father told him it was nothing. A stomach bug. By the third period of the last game, he was bent in half. Furious that Catch had let in so many shots, Owen Clancy waited until the next morning to take his son to the hospital. The appendix had ruptured by then. Catch spent a week in the hospital. His father made him finish the season.

Catch thought he'd get away from his father by the time he was a teenager. High-school hockey was separate from the youth program. Had a real coach, not somebody's dad. Instead, it got worse. Frustrated because he had to sit in the bleachers with the other parents, Owen Clancy berated his son and the other players from the stands. Swore at the coaches and refs. The entire arena could hear him. When Catch made it on the varsity team sophomore year, his father got more intense. Louder. Catch knew it was time to do something.

That winter he was shoveling snow off the porch roof when he looked down and studied the sidewalk. He'd cleared it the way his dad insisted. Swept so clean the concrete could have been baking in summer sun. He remembered a story he'd heard the year before about a hockey player jumping from the bleachers after a game. He'd landed on the concrete floor. Broke an ankle. Stupid stunt. Kept him off the ice the rest of the season. It occurred to him if he jumped feet first, he'd do enough damage that he'd miss the rest of the season. He told himself another option would be to go all the way and dive headfirst. Miss the rest of his life. Unhappy life. As he stared at the cleaned surface, so much like a blank sheet of paper, he asked God for a sign. What kind of sign? He raised his eyes to the sky and then cast them to the ground. He saw his mother's bird feeder in the yard. A round dish hanging from a tree branch by some chains. A chickadee was standing on the lip of the dish, pecking at the sunflower seeds. He told himself if a second bird landed on the feeder before he could count to one hundred, he would jump headfirst. If two or more landed, feetfirst. If none landed, he'd resume his shoveling duties and forget the idea. He counted out loud. "One, two, three, four, five, six . . ." A second bird lighted on the edge of the feeder. Another chickadee. He paused in his counting. Resumed it in his head. When he reached ninety, he started getting nervous. Slowed down. Counted out loud again. "Ninety-one . . . ninety-two . . . ninety-three . . . ninety-four . . . ninety-five." A third chickadee touched down on the feeder, followed by a fourth. He stopped counting. No need to finish. He had his sign. He looked up at the sky. "Okay then." He looked down at the shovel. Held on to it with both hands. Figured falling with a shovel would make the accident more believable. He shut his eyes and started walking toward the edge. He felt air for a second, and then pain as he landed on his feet and crumpled to his knees. Fell forward on his face and howled. His feet and ankles were on fire.

On the way to the emergency room, writhing on the bed of his dad's truck, he imagined a winter without hockey. It made the pain tolerable. He didn't foresee the throbbing he'd feel for years. Whenever it snowed or rained or he did too much. He didn't foresee his father making him even more miserable. *Should have been more careful. Big dummy. Threw it all away. Could have played Division I. Gotten a free ride in school. Now you're fucking dead weight.* Had he been able to see all that in his future, he would have done things differently. He would have gone off the roof head-first, without waiting for the chickadees to land.

The following fall, he and his father went deer hunting on an overcast Saturday morning. Owen Clancy's idea. *Get your ass up and out of the house. Stop whining about how you hurt. Fresh air will do you good.* They drove to some public lands east of town, in Superior National Forest. They talked during the short drive. About an eight-point buck a neighbor brought home. About how the Vikings were doing that season. They pulled over and parked. Got out with their rifles. Each carried a Mossberg .30-06. They loaded their guns by the light of the car. One clip, five rounds in each. They hiked down a logging road to a spot where they'd hunted before. The edge of a clearing. His father took point. Their breath hung in the November air. Catch looked up at the sky and figured it was better than an hour before sun-rise. The deer were still bedded down. He'd noticed no other cars on the roads or hunters in the woods. His ankles were aching, but he knew he couldn't utter a word of complaint. The more they walked, the worse they throbbed. He stum-bled over a stump. Regained his footing without falling or dropping the rifle. His father stopped and turned. Looked behind him and said: *Watch your step, gimp.* He turned back around and kept walking. Said in a low voice just loud enough for his son to hear: *Gimp. Good name for you.*

The crunch of Owen Clancy's boots on the forest floor wasn't enough to mask the sound. The metallic scrape of the bolt being pulled back and shoved forward on Catch's rifle. The older man froze. Turned to yell at his son for be-ing reckless with his gun. The last words out of Owen Clancy's mouth: *You big dummy.*

SOME local reporters came by the house. Stood in the yard until Dot and the daughters came out for interviews.

Owen Clancy's sons stayed silent. The papers talked about the loss to the community. A fine father and winning hockey coach. The wake and funeral service were packed. His wife and daughters wept until dirt was thrown over the casket. They didn't cry after that. They never asked Catch about what had happened in the woods. Bo moved to St. Paul a year later; he'd gotten a scholarship to a private college. After Catch graduated from high school the following spring, Dot sold the hardware store and the house. She and her daughters moved to Duluth. Catch stayed behind to work at Maggie's joint. She let him drive her truck and live upstairs for cheap. Let him share her bed. For a long time, he heard the noises in his sleep. The bolt pulled back and rammed forward. Then the shot. Inexplicably, the order would be reversed some nights. The shot and then the bolt action. A nightmare played in reverse. Either way it would make him sit up in bed. If Maggie was with him, she held him. She never asked him for details. In northern Minnesota, accidents happened in the woods and on the lakes. Like most folks around town, Maggie left it alone.

Clancy admitted to Ransom that the law gave him a hard time over the shooting. Deputies questioned him again and again. They had no hard evidence it was anything other than an accident. Eventually stopped hounding him. Clancy told her he was happy to leave Hoyt Lakes. He didn't want to stay in a town where the cops had it in for him. Where they thought he was guilty of killing his father. He didn't tell her that while walking in the woods behind his father that morning, he'd run his hand over the length of the barrel. Wondered how hard it would be to use a rifle on himself. It had taken no chickadees to change his mind. Only his father's words.

SEVEN

IT DIDN'T SURPRISE him that her story was longer and stranger than his own. Parts of it he found hard to believe. She did, too.

She grew up off of West Seventh Street in St. Paul, the daughter of two CPAs. The neighborhood was speckled with ethnic groups and their churches. Polish and Bohemian Catholic. Czech-Slovak Congregational. German Presbyterian. None of these religions suited her conservative parents, however, so Jeremiah and Elizabeth Ransom started their own. Services were initially held in the basement. When the faithful numbered more than could be accommodated by the folding chairs, her parents moved out of their house and purchased a building in the neighborhood. A storefront downstairs and living quarters upstairs. Pews were rescued from a church being demolished on the other side of town. No crosses or religious statues—for budgetary reasons, not dogmatic ones. The windows were dressed up with lace curtains from Target. One of the windows displayed a small sign advertising INCOME TAX RETURNS FOR UNDER $200. The other window had a placard announcing 10:30 A.M. SUNDAY WORSHIP. Plastered on the front door were a PHEASANTS FOREVER sticker, a DUCKS UNLIMITED decal and a bumper sticker from the National Rifle Association declaring MY PRESIDENT IS CHARLTON HESTON. The storefront's previous tenant was a taxidermist who'd been operating without the approval of city zoning. He'd skipped town, leaving behind a closet filled with mounted fish and stuffed animal heads. Those were incorporated into the church's décor. Every so often an irate hunter or angler would walk into the church—sometimes in the middle of services—and pull a trophy off the wall. Tuck it under his arm and walk out. As a child, Serene would sit on a bench listening to her father while staring at the heads of the dead animals. She imagined she could see their mouths move and their eyes blink. A neighbor girl asked her the name of her church. Serene—a home-schooled child well educated in every topic except mainstream religions—didn't know what else to call it except the Dead Animals Church.

The tenets of her parents' religion were vague. Sunday-morning services usually started and ended with a Bible reading. Old Testament or New Testament. Didn't matter which. In between the readings, her father stood at the podium—another secondhand piece, a plaque on it said IN-DEPENDENT SCHOOL DISTRICT NO. 833—and railed against the liberality of the pope. After the final reading, there were donuts and coffee if someone brought the donuts. If not, it was just coffee. The three requirements for membership remained consistent. The first two: a weekly donation and bitterness toward the Catholic Church. Those with limited financial resources were sometimes forgiven the weekly donation if they demonstrated sufficient bitterness. Her parents had situated their church well. With all the houses of worship around them, there was no shortage of disgruntled ex-Catholics. A few disgruntled Lutherans were let in, but they didn't stay long. They had no beef with the pope.

The Ransoms' foray into religion would have been harmless if not for the third requirement: Members could never set foot in a hospital. Visits to a doctor's office and a dentist's office and an optician were fine. Clinic checkups were allowed. Day surgery was permitted and in fact encouraged as a way around spending the night in a hospital. Walking through the doors of a building labeled HOSPITAL or MEDICAL CENTER was forbidden. Even visiting patients in these places was disallowed. From his pulpit, Jeremiah justified the third rule with talk about the healing power of faith and hospitals being the houses of the devil. He tossed in some references to the hemorrhaging woman who was healed and the blind men who had their sight restored, miracles accomplished by Jesus without hospital stays. Behind their preacher's back, church members questioned the inconsistency of barring hospital visits but permitting other medical care. Still, most went along with the third rule because they didn't need to go to the hospital. Once a need arose, that member dropped out. Jeremiah's congregation was not devoted enough to him or angry enough at Catholicism to die for their new church. Being the obedient wife, Elizabeth never asked her husband about the third rule. Had she, her husband might have told her he hated hospitals because his grandfather had died in a psychiatric hospital. Strapped to a metal-frame bed. Drool snaking down the corners of his mouth. Gibberish spewing from his lips. By barring them from such institutions, Jeremiah figured he was doing a favor for his followers. He never anticipated what the third rule would do to his family.

SERENE worshipped her brother Ezekiel, her senior by six years. His hair was as blond and his eyes as blue as hers.

He was more athletic than she. He was the top scorer on his youth soccer team and a star forward in community basketball. While the other boys thought being home-schooled was weird, they overlooked it when it came to Ezekiel. Invited him to birthday parties and sleepovers. Made up a nickname for him. E.Z. They'd yell from the bench: "Easy basket, E.Z.!" As much as his athleticism, his clowning helped make him popular. He liked tucking his hand under his armpit and pumping his arm up and down. The fart noise got him kicked out of church. His sister ran upstairs after services and asked him how to do it. He could burp at will. Whistle by sticking two fingers in his mouth and blowing. He could also add columns of numbers in his head as quickly as a calculator and, by thirteen, was doing college-level math. His parents talked about turning their CPA business over to him before he turned twenty.

He never saw twenty. Hints of Ezekiel Ransom's illness surfaced the fall of his sixteenth year. He stopped bathing and brushing his teeth. His hair became matted to his head. He wore the same clothes for a week at a time. On the margins of his school notebooks, he sketched eyes. Hundreds and hundreds of eyes. The eyes started showing up at the breakfast table—on the edges of the daily newspaper and on the paper napkins. They spread to the pages of the phone book. Magazines. Books. The family Bible. His first psychotic episode was that winter. He woke in the middle of the night. Turned on every light in the house and pulled open closet doors, looking for the source of the voices. Warning voices. Voices that told him his life was in danger. His parents tore apart the house looking for an intruder or a radio left on. They found nothing, but he remained frightened. They let him sleep on the floor in their room. The second time it happened, days later, they tried to talk him back to bed. Reassured him there were no voices. This convinced Ezekiel that his parents were in on the conspiracy. They could read

his mind. They were trying to kill him. He climbed on top
of the dining-room table and stood in the middle of it. Told
his mother and father they would never take him alive. He
unscrewed the bulbs from the chandelier hanging over his
head. Lobbed them at his parents like hand grenades. When
he ran out of bulbs, he took his clothes off one piece at a
time. Balled up each item and threw it. Ten-year-old Serene
hid behind a couch in her pajamas. Fell asleep that way, hiding behind the furniture. When she woke at dawn, she saw
her naked brother curled up in a ball in the middle of the
table, surrounded by a field of broken glass. Her mother was
in the kitchen frying eggs. Her father was on the phone
telling the school district they could take their marijuana-
infested high school and shove it up their liberal asses.
Ezekiel had been home-schooled up until that year and had
just started attending the public high school. Jeremiah and
Elizabeth blamed their son's bizarre behavior on drug use.
They treated him by locking him in his room. All the furniture had been removed except for a mattress on the floor.
His father stood on the other side of the bedroom door and
read Bible passages to him. To Ezekiel's ears, his father's
words were a CIA manifesto. Further evidence his parents
were out to kill him. To block out his father's voice, and to
prevent anyone from reading his mind, he sang at the top of
his lungs. The same thing over and over:

> *Row, row, row your boat*
> *Gently down the stream.*
> *Merrily, merrily, merrily, merrily,*
> *Life is but a dream.*

When his father's voice increased in volume, Ezekiel
countered by banging his fists against the bedroom door
while he sang. *Bang.* "Merrily!" *Bang.* "Merrily!" *Bang.*
"Merrily!" *Bang.* "Merrily!" Serene and her mother fled

downstairs to the church. The girl sat on a bench doing her math while giving sideways glances to the animal heads. Her mother sat two pews ahead of her, struggling to keep her hands from shaking as she worked on her needlepoint. Every so often they'd hear an especially loud *bang* over their heads. The racket went all night. Serene and her mother slept on the church benches. The noise stopped at sunrise, when Ezekiel collapsed exhausted on the mattress. Elizabeth and her daughter found Jeremiah asleep in the hallway, his back propped against his son's bedroom door and an open Bible in his lap. Elizabeth threw a blanket over her husband and ordered her daughter to scrub the kitchen floor. The girl had mopped it the day before, but she didn't question her mother. Elizabeth Ransom's answer to every problem was to clean the house. Serene pulled out the bucket from under the kitchen sink.

"On your hands and knees this time," said her mother. "Make sure the water is good and hot."

Ezekiel's bizarre behavior continued for weeks. The house was never cleaner. Serene initially thought he was goofing around to get out of going to school. Then she noticed the way he looked at her, as if he didn't recognize her. Once he demanded her name and rank and badge number. Ordered her to stop reading his mind. She asked her parents not to leave her alone with him. The boy she'd idolized was a crazy stranger.

One of the church helpers—Jeremiah alternated between calling him a deacon and an altar boy—told the minister to send the boy to the hospital. The man had a nephew who was schizophrenic, and Ezekiel displayed the same nonsensical behavior. This was the last thing Jeremiah wanted to hear. All he could imagine was his son strapped to a hospital bed. He continued trying to cure his son with Bible verses. Ezekiel's lucid periods became fewer and briefer. He lost interest in eating and dropped twenty pounds.

Stopped wearing clothes. Hardly slept. Became increasingly hyperactive. He refused to cut his hair. Something to do with shielding his head from mind reading. When he spoke, it was to no one in particular. His language was rambling and disconnected. Finally, he jumped out of his bedroom window one night in an attempt to escape the CIA and the voices and his parents. He ran naked through the snow until he found some railroad tracks. He lay down on them and waited. The train whistled a warning but couldn't stop in time. Ezekiel was cut in half.

The Ransoms saw Ezekiel's illness and death as a punishment for failing to adequately educate and protect their son. They vowed to do better by their daughter. Serene's contact with the outside world was limited to church attendance and chaperoned social gatherings with other home-schooled children. When she wasn't being taught by her mother, she was scrubbing floors for her. All the while, her parents watched her. Waited for her to start drawing eyes or hearing voices or talking nonsense. The girl spent years anticipating her own mental illness. Looking forward to it in a way because it would be a sort of reunion with her brother. She'd join him in that strange world he'd imagined. Perhaps meet him there. More important, insanity would be a release from her parents. What finally freed her, however, was good handwriting.

Serene had always enjoyed putting a pen to paper. The family computer—purchased primarily for her parents' home accounting business—didn't interest her. She preferred writing essays and doing other homework by hand. Her greatest joy was in keeping detailed and voluminous journals. Their pages were the only private place her parents allowed her to go. Her allowance went to buy fresh journals. Cracking open a new book was a treat. She'd run her hands over the lined pages and inhale the new-paper smell. In no time, the blank pages were filled with her poetry and personal thoughts. All in a cursive that was graceful and classic. The slant was proper. The spacing consistent. The letter proportions correct. Each word sat perfectly on the line. A ballpoint pen company sponsored an annual cursive contest. For the first time, home-schooled children were allowed to enter. She took first place in her age category—by then she was sixteen—and won a college scholarship. A few years later, she was attending Princeton University. An English major. Her parents' nightmare. They'd begged her to stay in Minnesota. Take accounting at a community college. She supported herself by working a string of part-time jobs. She stopped calling her parents. Disassociated herself from them and their church.

Ransom told Clancy that once she discovered college life, she discarded her virginity with a vengeance. She slept with every man who had an interest and a condom handy, but gravitated toward younger men. She didn't confess to Clancy that some of those youths were less than her brother's age when he died. She left out that she'd been arrested for having sex with a minor, but was never charged because the boy and his family were embarrassed and refused to cooperate with police. She neglected to tell him that she'd fled the East Coast because of her problems with young boys. She didn't admit to Clancy—because she was having trouble admitting to herself—that her habit of sleeping with her freshmen English students was now endangering her teaching job at the university.

Ransom also failed to tell Clancy the true reason she carried a handgun. She saw no need to break the news yet. She'd reveal the information soon enough. Have him fix the problem inside her house. First she wanted him to take care of her university problems. Starting with the head of the English Department.

EIGHT

MURPHY AND JACK snagged a flight back to the Twin Cities late Saturday night. With the rest of the Murphy clan, they camped out at the hospital all day Sunday and the better part of Monday. The couple retreated to her houseboat to shower and sleep. Her place—tied up at the St. Paul Yacht Club across from downtown—was closer to Regions than his. By Tuesday afternoon, an angiogram had determined there were blockages in two of the three arteries feeding blood to Sean Murphy's heart. A balloon angioplasty was tentatively scheduled for Thursday, but the lesions were in a difficult location to reach with the catheter. The cardiac surgeon and the cardiologist were still debating whether the blockages would be amenable to the procedure or require bypass.

Murphy and Jack went back to the boat Tuesday night and returned to Sean Murphy's hospital room before the sun came up Wednesday morning. They found him asleep in his bed. Amira Murphy, head bent forward, was snoozing next to him in a recliner. "Imma," whispered Murphy, using the Lebanese word for mother. She touched her mother's arm. The older woman didn't stir.

"Let her sleep," Jack said in a low voice.

"She's going to get a sore neck." Murphy stepped closer to her father's bedside. Bent down and brushed his cheek with her lips. His familiar smell—Aqua Velva aftershave and cigar smoke—had been replaced by a hospital smell. Face soap and disinfectant. She stood straight and took a step back from the bed. Studied her parents. Found it hard to believe they had been hardy enough to run a bar along the riverfront a few years earlier. Her father's face so pale. His gray hair flattened against his head. His barrel torso and big arms seemed smaller in the hospital bed. Shrunken. An IV line and heart-monitor wires snaking from his body and oxygen tube snaking out of his nose. Plastic vipers attacking the withered old man. Her tiny mother slouched in the chair, wrinkled hands in her lap with rosary beads between her fingers. Dressed in one of her usual housedresses with the zipper up the front. Hair knotted in a bun behind her head, with tendrils escaping. Creating a silver halo around her leathery face. Her parents never looked older and more vulnerable to her. Murphy covered her mouth with her hand. Turned and ran out of the room. Leaned her back against a wall in the hallway. Jack followed her. He wrapped his arms around her shoulders. She buried her face in his shirt. She'd been holding her emotions in since she'd gotten word of her father's heart attack. The dam burst. She was glad her brothers weren't around to see her cry.

Jack rubbed her shoulders. "He's going to be fine, babe. You're wiped out. Go back to the boat and crash."

She lifted her head off his chest. Saw she'd made a wet spot on his shirt. Smoothed it with her hands. "What about you?"

He checked his watch. "Cardiologist will be making his

morning rounds soon. I want to talk to him. Amira should be up by then. I'll take her home if she wants."

"She won't go."

"You're probably right."

She wiped her eyes with her hands. "Don't tell Imma I fell apart."

"You and your brothers. Each one of you trying to be tougher than the other."

She reached into her purse and pulled out a tissue. "What's wrong with that? We're trying to be strong for one another. Hold it together."

"I got news for you. The Murphy Rock of Gibraltar is crumbling. You're all a mess. Your mother won't leave the hospital. Pat and Ryan are at each other's throats. Can't even agree on what day it is, let alone make a unified medical decision. Tyke is freaking out."

"What's wrong with Tommy?" He was the youngest sibling. Everyone in the Murphy clan referred to him as Tyke. He stood six and a half feet tall, weighed well over two hundred pounds and had just turned twenty-eight. "You guys are trying so hard to put up a good front, you can't see what each other needs."

"What's wrong with Tyke? Tell me, Jack."

"He's freaking out because he thinks Sean won't live to see his next grandchild baptized." Tyke and his wife were expecting their second child later that winter. "I told him he needs to calm down. Trust these doctors."

"God, Jack. What about us? We haven't even started. What if Papa dies?" Her eyes started welling with tears again.

Jack realized he'd said the wrong thing. "Nobody is going to die. I didn't bring up Tommy and the baby to upset you. I'm just saying you guys need to talk to one another. Pull together and stop acting like ten islands floating out there on your own."

She blew her nose and nodded. "I know." She looked at

him. Was thankful they were together. Couldn't imagine weathering this without him. "I love you," she sniffed.

"I love you, too." He kissed her on the forehead. "Go home. Get some sleep." He looked outside the hospital windows. "It's still dark out for God's sake."

She wanted to be somewhere other than home or the hospital. She drove to the one place she felt she had control over her life.

NINE

*ALMOST DAWN WEDNESDAY, and still no rest for
me. I listen to his breathing and wonder at how easily he
sleeps just days after taking a man's life and disposing of
his body. I don't think I've slept an hour since it happened,
and my role was minor. Thinking back, I'm now convinced
the bullet I fired made no difference. The fiend was already
gone. Sent to Hades. Still, I had to stay and clean up. I
couldn't abandon this boy. Sensitive, tortured boy. Untrust-
worthy boy. I know he would turn on me without a second
thought. I suspect he realizes I would likewise betray him.
The tension is delicious and makes the sex wonderful. The
sex. I've lost track of how many times we've made love. He
pushed me down on the floor the minute we walked into the
house. Made love to me while my babies padded around us.
We haven't worn clothes or set foot outside since Sunday.
My boy loves my nakedness, and I adore his. What do we
care? The neighbors can't see. The drapes are drawn. I ignore the phone when it rings. We revel in our secluded*

*house of passion. I will have to venture outside eventually
to buy groceries and go to my office. Dreaded place. I know
they are lying in wait for me. One of the snakes came knocking. My boy will take care of them. I will convince Catch it
is the right thing to do. The only thing he can do. I have
something I can hold over his head. Am I evil for plotting
like this? Am I Lady Macbeth's finest pupil?*

> *Naught's had, all's spent,*
> *Where our desire is got without content:*
> *'Tis safer to be that which we destroy,*
> *Than, by destruction, dwell in doubtful joy.*

Ransom stopped writing. Tucked her pen between the
pages. Closed the journal and set it on the nightstand. Picked
up her cigarette and took a last pull. Blew out a cloud of
smoke. Crushed the butt in the ashtray. Reached for the lamp
next to her bed and shut it off. Held her breath and listened.
Was it her imagination? The wind rattling the evergreens
outside her window? Her lover's breathing? No. She heard
it again. Definitely. She turned the lamp on again. With
trembling hands, pulled the covers up under her chin. Her
eyes darted around the room. Landed on the closet door.
Had she remembered to lock it shut before going to bed?
She forced herself to check. Damn. She'd forgotten to slide
the bolt, and the door was open a crack. She hopped out of
bed, padded over to the closet. Took a deep breath and closed
the door. She held it shut with one hand while pushing the
bolt into place with the other. Ran back to bed and slipped
between the covers. She again held her breath and listened.
This time, silence. She exhaled with relief. Said out loud
without realizing it: "Thank God."

Clancy lifted his face off the pillow. Turned his head
toward her and squinted in the light. "What'd you say?
What's wrong?"

Ransom fell back onto the bed. "Nothing. A nightmare. I'm sorry I woke you. It's still early. Go back to sleep, my love. Let me collect myself. I'll turn the light off in a minute."

"I've had bad dreams, too."

She reached out and touched his shoulder. "Tell me."

"Forget it." He sounded embarrassed that he'd brought it up.

"I want to hear."

He flipped onto his back and put his hands behind his head. Stared up at the ceiling. "I keep seeing that mean fucker's face floating in water. Not his body or even his head. Just his face. All flat and wobbly. Like one of those rubber masks from Halloween. Except he has eyes. They blink. His mouth moves, too, but I can never remember what he says. There're fish circling his face. Northerns mostly. Big ones. Swimming around and around. They've all got big hunks missing from their middles. You can see their guts and stuff. But they ain't bleeding or anything. Then I wake up."

She caressed his cheek with the back of her hand. "Sleep hath its own world."

"What?"

"Byron. The poet." She sat up. Took a book off her nightstand. Cracked it open. Turned a few pages until she found what she wanted.

> *Our life is twofold; Sleep hath its own world,*
> *A boundary between the things misnamed*
> *Death and existence: Sleep hath its own world,*
> *And a wide realm of wild reality,*
> *And dreams in their development have breath,*
> *And tears, and tortures, and the touch of joy;*
> *They leave a weight upon our waking thoughts,*
> *They take a weight from off waking toils.*

She closed the book and set it back on the nightstand. He didn't say anything for several seconds. She hoped he was absorbing the words. Thinking about them.

He asked with irritation in his voice: "What's that suppose to mean?"

She wished her new lover was more interested in literature. More literate. He hadn't once picked up a book or magazine in front of her. When he wasn't sleeping or eating or making love to her, he was watching television. *Baywatch* and *I Dream of Jeannie* reruns. She turned off the lamp and flopped back against the mattress. Sighed. "It means you should stop worrying and go back to sleep."

"I know what will take my mind off stuff."

Stuff. A key word in his vocabulary, she thought. Second in importance only to *ain't.* "What would take your mind off of stuff, my love?" Clancy rolled on top of her. "You are insatiable." He was already hard. She wondered if that was his natural state. She couldn't remember seeing him without an erection.

He reached over and turned the lamp on. Looked down at her face. "I like to watch you."

She looked into his eyes. So dark. Seemed to grow darker when they made love. Turned the color of charcoal. "Why?"

"You look like you're in pain sometimes."

"Afraid you're hurting me?" She reached up and ran her fingers through his hair. So soft. She wished she could burrow into those curls and hide from the world. Hide in the meadow of black grass. Even in winter, he smelled like grass. The outdoors. The perfect lover, as long as he kept his mouth shut. She brought her legs up and locked them around his lower back. Wrapped her arms around his shoulders. Smooth and muscled at the same time. She inhaled sharply when he entered her. She would never get used to his size. Every time, it was a shock.

He started with small thrusts. A rocking motion. "Am I?"

"What?" she asked breathlessly.

"Hurting you?"

"A little," she said. She knew he'd like that answer.

Clancy smiled and increased the force of his thrusts, all the while watching her face. He rolled onto his back so she was on top. He gripped her hips with his hands so he could control their rhythm. Unlike the other youths she'd had, he was a generous and disciplined lover. He didn't allow himself to climax until she had.

She collapsed on top of him. He stroked her back with both his hands. They felt like sandpaper against her skin. She liked the sensation.

"Was that okay?" he whispered.

"Better than okay." She kissed his chest and peeled herself off him. He turned his back to her and fell asleep. She rolled onto her side and stared at the closet door. It would be light soon, and then she'd feel safer. They'd never come out during the day. She reached over and shut off the lamp. Fell asleep as the sun was coming up.

TEN

MURPHY THREW HER purse in a drawer, hung her coat over the back of her chair and sat down. She eyed the top of her desk and frowned. Littered with newspapers, empty lunch sacks and foam cups. The insides of the cups had dried coffee in them. Her fellow detectives had been using her desk while she was gone, and it irked her that they hadn't picked up after themselves. "Bunch of slobs," she said. She pulled the wastebasket out from under her desk. Not a scrap of paper inside of it. She held up the basket and with her arm, swept the garbage into the can. Set down the basket. Saw an apple core under her desk. Bent down to pick it up and tossed it into the trash. Spotted a pair of Sorels pushed way under her desk. She dragged them out and set them next to her desk. Shoved the wastebasket back under her desk. She noticed a notebook propped against her phone. She picked up the pad and waved it at the only other detective in the room. Max Castro. "Anybody missing this?" He looked across the room at her and shrugged. She flipped it open. Scanned the writing. "Stabbing in Highland Park."

"That's Dubrowski's shit. He's out sick. I'll take it." Castro got up from his desk and walked over. Chuck Dubrowski was his partner. They'd worked together so long, they looked like brothers. Curly gray hair, bushy brows, big arms, big guts. Wore the same brand of jeans. Had glasses with identical wire-rimmed frames. Castro pulled the notebook out of her hand. Slid it into the back pocket of his jeans.

She nodded to the Sorels on the floor. "Those clodhoppers yours?"

"Dubrowski's." Castro sat on the edge of her desk. Sniffled. "Yo-Yo spread the word on your dad. How's he doing?"

Murphy had left a message on the homicide commander's voice mail over the weekend telling him she was back in town early because of her father. "He's cranky. Giving the nurses a hard time. Wants to get the hell out of there."

Castro coughed. Covered his mouth with his hand. Coughed again. Wiped his hand on his pant leg. "When they sending him home?"

"He's probably having a thing tomorrow. That deal where they stick a catheter in your groin and thread it through the artery to the heart. Expand a balloon to open stuff up."

"My brother had that done. Piece of cake. He'll be fine. Bet you're glad you've got a bunch of docs in your family. They can explain all that medical junk."

She was glad, especially for Jack. "Yeah. It helps."

"How's Amira handling it?"

"Ma's okay. Wants to take him home and feed him. Food is probably what landed him in the hospital."

"Murphy!" Duncan was standing in his office doorway. "Get your ass in here." Duncan turned around and sat down at his desk.

Castro got up from her desk. "Don't let Yo-Yo load you

up your first day back." He picked up his partner's boots. Walked back to his desk. Started hacking again.

She said after him, "I'm not really back." She stood up and headed for the commander's office.

The other detectives called Duncan "Yo-Yo" behind his back. He'd come to Homicide from Vice, where he'd worked as an undercover cop. He'd cut his long blond hair and ditched the tee shirts for dress shirts, but Duncan still acted like a renegade. He sent his people on bizarre assignments and called them at home at all hours. Didn't worry about crossing jurisdictions. Didn't care about search warrants. She and the other detectives initially thought Chief Christianson was crazy for tapping Duncan to head Homicide. Lately, however, they were warming up to him. Especially since he'd been injured working on the Justice Trip case with Murphy. A supervisor on the front lines. A few cops around the department even suggested Duncan should get the top job.

The previous summer, Christianson was accused of interfering with Murphy's investigation into the serial killer. It turned out the plastic surgeon was a cousin of Christianson's wife. The mayor wanted Christianson out and so did many of the officers on the street. Murphy didn't want Duncan wearing the chief's badge, however. She had a secret reason for opposing him: He knew she'd encouraged the surgeon to kill himself with her gun. The only other person who knew was Murphy's mentor, Gabriel Nash, and he'd retired. Gabe was the one who told Duncan. He'd once been Duncan's partner.

Murphy walked into Duncan's office. He was on the phone. He pointed to the chair in front of his desk. She sat down. He kept talking into the phone. "You betcha. Not a problem. We'll do a drive-by. Check it out."

His feet were on top of his desk. He was wearing athletic shoes with his dress slacks, shirt and tie. His usual footwear. She noticed the bottoms sported serious winter treads. Sand and road salt were packed in the grooves. She wondered if his doctor had given him permission to hit the streets, or if Duncan had started running again on his own. She told herself to keep her mouth shut about it. She'd cared for him after his hospital release because she felt bad he'd been hurt during her watch. That was back in October. He wasn't her responsibility anymore.

Duncan pulled his feet off his desk, knocking a stack of papers and a notebook to the floor. He cradled the phone between his right ear and shoulder. "What kind of car is the kid driving?" He grabbed a pen. Scanned his desk for a notebook. Murphy stood up, went behind his desk, plucked the notebook off the floor and tossed it in front of him. Went back around and sat down again. He flipped the pad open and started writing. "Spell that first name. Got it. Got it. Should we hold him for you?" He stopped scribbling. "Wait a minute here." Clicked his pen a few times. "What's the deal with that? You looking at him as a suspect or a victim?" He paused. Threw the pen down. "Bullshit. Makes all the difference in the world. Are my people going in to arrest his ass or break the news to his family that he got croaked?" He switched the phone to his left ear. Picked the pen up again. Clicked it repeatedly. "Sounds like you need to get your ducks in a row on this deal. Figure out what you're looking at here."

The guy on the other end of the line yelled so loud Murphy could hear it. She wondered how many people Duncan pissed off every day.

"Isn't my job to blow sunshine up your ass," he said into the phone. He looked at Murphy and rolled his eyes. Held the phone away from his ear while the guy yelled some more. Put it back to his ear. "Tell you what. E-mail the kid's mug and your notes. Anything and everything that would help. Straight to my detective. Sergeant Paris Murphy." Murphy looked at him and shook her head. He ignored her. Kept talking. "Paris like the city and common spelling on Murphy. The rest of the address is the same as mine. As a favor—a fucking favor—we'll send someone over to the brother's place. Give me that street again." He scratched in the notebook. "We'll call you either way." He hung up the phone and dropped the pen on his desk. "How's your old man?"

"Still in the hospital." Murphy folded her arms in front of her and crossed her legs. "Duncan. I'm not back yet."

"What do you mean? You were gone two weeks. That's long enough for a vacation."

"You gave me three weeks."

"I don't remember signing off on three weeks. Shit. Come to think of it, today is Wednesday. You should have been back at work two days ago. You owe us two days."

Murphy glared at him. "I had three weeks of vacation left and I had to use it before the next cycle."

"Is that in the contract? Fucking union."

"That's your rule. Use it or lose it."

"Well fuck me, then." He waved her away with his hand. "Get out before I give you something to do. We're so shorthanded around here it isn't funny. Dubrowski's out with the flu." He paused and listened to Castro coughing on the other side of the office. "Castro just got back from having the flu. I've been paying that piece of shit Bergen so much overtime it makes me sick to my stomach."

Evans Bergen was the night man in Homicide. Murphy considered him a lazy turd. He had a habit of coming in late and leaving early. When Bergen was working overtime, things were desperate. She unfolded her arms and uncrossed her legs. "If you really have something for me, I'll punch in. There's not much I can do at the hospital right now. But you still owe me a few more days of vacation. None of that *use it or lose it* crap. Plus it looks like my dad's having that balloon thing done tomorrow."

"Balloon angioplasty."

"Yeah. I'm at the hospital for that."

"You've got it, Potato Head." He picked up the notebook and threw it at her.

She caught the pad. She wished he would stop using her nickname. Only her family and a few close friends used it. She started to chastise him. "Duncan."

"What?"

She decided to skip it. "Nothing." She looked down and read his writing. "I'm going to this address to do what?"

"Here's the story." He put his feet back on his desk.

Murphy couldn't contain herself. Pointed to his feet. "I sure as hell hope you got your doc's okay before you started running again."

"Who says I'm running?" He flashed his Robert Redford smile and winked.

He knew how to use those blue eyes, she thought, but it wasn't going to work with her. She'd seen him in dirty sweats, hobbling around with crutches and his arm in a sling. "Turn off the charm, Axel."

He patted his flat gut. "Worked too hard to let it get flabby now. So what if I'm running again? My doctor doesn't know shit."

She paused. Glanced down at the notebook in her hand. She and Duncan had been doing this too much. Meddling in each other's business. Attacking each other's personal and work decisions. They'd had loud confrontations in his office, she questioning whether he'd used drugs while undercover and he bringing up the surgeon's suicide. He'd walked in when Erik and Jack were slugging it out and broke up the fight. He knew too much about her—*Potato Head* was evidence of that—and she was too involved in his life. Unprofessional—and dangerous. She looked up. "You know what? Never mind. It's your call. Fill me in on this deal."

"They've got two missing men up on the Iron Range. One was tearing around on his sled solo last Saturday. During that kick-ass blizzard they got up there. He met some local guys at a watering hole along the trail. They tipped a few and went out together. The lone ranger falls behind. His new buds double back and can't find a trace of him. Not even his sled."

Murphy: "They'll find his frozen carcass in the woods or at the bottom of a lake."

"Thing is, this dude is a mean son of a bitch."

"A mean s.o.b. can't freeze to death?"

"That's not what I'm getting at here. His riding partners weren't all that fond of his drunken butt. They were more concerned that he'd made good on some of the shit he was talking. Tough guy was bragging about how he'd done time at Stillwater. He was getting bored with life on the outside. Maybe he'd knock off a liquor store on his way outta this hick town. Pick up a few women. Party hardy before the cops catch up with him."

"Any women or cash registers reported missing?"

"Here's where our second missing guy comes into the picture. Bartender. Local kid. Enda Clancy. Reliable employee. Works hard. Shows up on time. Blah, blah, blah. The joint's owner opens up the place Sunday. Finds this long letter from the bartender taped to the cash register. Full of big, pretty words, but it doesn't really tell her much. Basically says, *I'm outta here*. Taking off is not like this kid at all."

"So he quits his job and takes off. Big deal. Not against the law to act out of character."

"If that's all there is—the kid taking off—you're right. But there's some other weirdness related to this. For one thing, the cash is missing from the register."

"Employee dips into the till and takes off."

"The sawed-off she keeps behind the bar is missing. Kid says in the note that he took her piece in place of his last paycheck."

"I'm still not hearing anything more than thievery."

Duncan pulled his feet off the desk and sat straight in his chair. "The kid shot his old man a few years ago. Killed him. Deer-hunting accident."

"He hates guns."

Duncan nodded. "The broad who owns the bar wasn't excited about turning in a report. Wasn't a ton of money. She likes the kid. He's been fucked up since he shot his old man. His family moved and left him behind. Kid's older brother is in St. Paul. His mother and his sisters live in Duluth. The bar owner has been his family—and then some."

"The kid and his boss are supposedly involved?"

"Like bunnies. Anyway, this gun thing really bothered her. She was worried about him. She goes upstairs—the kid lives above the bar—and checks his stuff. Looks like most of his clothes, if not all, are still there. Not that he has shit to begin with. She calls the sheriff. He sends a deputy. Local guy. Been in her joint a million times. Maggie's Red Door. He looks around. Notices some changes. Nothing huge. The plastic tablecloths are missing. A beer poster that was hanging in back of the bar is now tacked over the front door. He asks her when she did the redecorating. She tells him the bartender must have done it Saturday. He was always trying to spruce up the place. Treated it like his own. So the deputy asks her what other changes she noticed Sunday morning."

Murphy leaned forward. Petty thievery was turning into a good tale. "And?"

"A rug had been shifted from behind the bar to the front door. The front door had been freshly painted."

Murphy raised her brows. "Shit. Please tell me the cops up there looked under the rug and behind the beer poster."

"If the Hamm's bear could talk, he'd tell us someone got blown away at Maggie's Red Door. In front of the fucking red door."

Murphy: "Scenario A says the felon emptied the till and wrote the note—or forced the kid to write it—to cover his tracks. He shoots the kid. Cleans up. Wraps the body in tablecloths. Dumps it. Takes off on his sled with the piece and the cash. A lot of work for a little bit of money and a shotgun. Your average scumbag would have emptied the till and shot the kid. Forget the note and the cleanup. On the other hand, this guy said he was looking for some excitement. Maybe he tried to get creative."

Duncan: "Scenario B says the kid took off with the gun and the money. For some reason, someone got nailed in the process. Maybe it's our tough guy snowmobile rider. Could be someone else, though no one else has been reported missing. Regardless, the kid cleans up, dumps the body and the sled and takes off with the booty."

Murphy: "Scenario A works if everyone stays in character. The good kid stays the good kid, and the felon acts like a lowlife."

"Pretty boring, but it works. The cops up there called Stillwater with a description of the snowmobiler. Had a snake tattoo crawling up his ugly puss. The prison was able to ID the guy right off the bat. Van Hogan. Did time for a couple of armed robberies. Liked to wave guns around, but never shot anyone. Maybe this time his trigger finger couldn't resist."

"I think the kid did the killing," said Murphy.

"Why?"

"Expect the unexpected."

"The sheriff thinks the kid did it, too. The BCA boys are doing their thing," said Duncan, referring to the crime-lab guys from the Bureau of Criminal Apprehension. "They'll see if the forensics back up the sheriff's gut. Meantime, this whole thing is under wraps. They're keeping it out of the papers and all that until they know what they're dealing with. Two missing guys. Maybe two dead guys. One of each. None of the above."

"Why's the sheriff like the kid for this thing?"

"Seems that deer-hunting accident didn't smell right."

"I'd love to know more about that," she said. She looked down at the pad in her hand. "In the meantime, I'll check out the brother. Robert Clancy."

"While you're doing that, the law up there's talking to the kid's mother and sisters. They've already interviewed some of Maggie's regulars. A few closed up the joint Saturday. They're trying to get ahold of another customer. Regulars said she was still there when they left. Sheriff thinks she's a St. Paul gal. She'd written a check that night. Damn near the only thing left in the till. Her name is in there." He tipped his head toward the notebook. "She's not answering her phone."

Murphy flipped through the pages. "Serene Ransom." She looked up at Duncan. Frowned. "I know that name. I've heard it. Where?"

"Don't worry about her," he said. "Work the brother angle. Maybe Bobby boy is hiding young Enda."

She paged through the notebook some more. "I don't see a plate. What's the kid driving?"

"Doesn't own any wheels. Sheriff says nothing's been reported stolen up there. The kid's boss-slash-girlfriend says he used her truck to get around town. She found it parked in back of the bar."

"So if he's here, he probably hitched a ride down. Interesting." She stood up to leave.

"One other thing." He bent down to pick up the papers he'd knocked to the floor. He set them on his desk. "That task force we talked about is off for now. Federal funding went down the crapper."

He wasn't looking at her. He was shuffling the papers around. She could tell he was trying to hide his disappointment. A few months earlier, he'd invited her to join a major crime task force that he was helping organize with other homicide chiefs from around the Midwest. "I'm sorry," she said.

"Don't be. It'll happen eventually. When it does, I want you for the team." He looked up from the papers. "You probably heard what *is* on."

"We're getting a new building." On her way to the station, Murphy had heard the news on the radio. The City Council was pushing ahead with plans to relocate police headquarters from its longtime downtown home down the hill from the State Capitol to a spot on the East Side.

"When you get time, start throwing away the shit you don't need. Moving day will be here before you know it."

"I'll bet the chief is pissed." Christianson had opposed the proposal.

"He doesn't give a shit anymore." Duncan leaned back in his chair and put his feet back up on his desk, again knocking the papers to the floor. "He knows his days are numbered."

Murphy was about to ask him who the next chief might be, but instead turned and headed for the door.

"Take Castro with," Duncan said. "He's sitting around itching his ass. Blowing his nose. Fill him in. Check if the sheriff's e-mail made it across. Then the two of you take off."

She stopped in the doorway and turned to face him. Duncan knew she preferred working solo. He was her last partner of sorts, and that was months ago. She sensed he was being overprotective. What was that about? She didn't need another Jack hovering over her. "I don't want help."

"The kid has a twelve-gauge. A fucking sawed-off shotgun."

"I've got a fucking Glock." She turned back around and walked to her desk.

"Take Castro," he yelled after her. "That is not a request."

ELEVEN

MURPHY HATED CASTRO'S driving, but she let him take the wheel anyway. Easier than arguing with him. They pulled out of the station parking lot in an unmarked car. A Ford Crown Victoria. He had a classic-rock station cranked high. Van Morrison. "Bright Side of the Road." She reached over and turned it down. "Are you going deaf or what?"

He sniffled. "My ears are plugged."

"Slow down," she said as he headed for Interstate 94. "Roads are slippery."

"You sound like my old lady." He weaved around the car in front of them and steered onto the ramp. "I've been driving longer than you've been alive. Let the master do his thing."

Castro and Dubrowski were the office experts in surveillance. They prided themselves on their ability to tail suspects without spooking or losing their prey. Even when they weren't following someone, they always drove as if they were. They'd sit slouched in the front seat. Dart in and out of traffic. Make squealing turns. Bolt through intersections to beat the lights. They had desk drawers and car trunks and coat pockets filled with gadgets and tools. Cameras. Binoculars. Lock picks. Glass cutters. Screwdrivers. Tape recorders. Microphones.

He came up on a rusty Volkswagen Beetle in the far left lane, driving slower than the speed limit. A sticker on the back bumper: VISUALIZE WORLD PEACE. "Get that hunk of shit off the road." He weaved around it and darted back in the left lane. "Seriously. You're thinking the little brother is the killer? Not the asshole with a record as long as his arm?"

She picked up the computer printout of Enda Clancy's photo she had sitting on her lap. Studied it. Handsome young man. Curly dark hair. Dark eyes. Reminded Murphy of her brothers. "I'm probably full of shit." She folded the photo. She reached for her purse sitting on the floor. Put it on her lap. Slipped the photo inside.

"The big brother. The one we're watching." He coughed. Cleared his throat by making a guttural noise. Swallowed. "What's his name again?"

"Robert Clancy."

"We're watching Robert Clancy to see if the kid is with him?"

"Right."

"If he doesn't have a new roommate, then little brother is missing—maybe even croaked—and big brother doesn't know the kid is history."

"*We* don't know the kid is history. We don't even know the snowmobile guy is missing. The kid could be looking for work somewhere and Hogan could be sleeping off a drinking jag. All we know for sure is the till got emptied at this bar and some poor soul got blown away."

"Lots of holes in this thing." He slowed down behind a semi in the far left lane, got impatient and passed it on the right. "Sounds like one of Yo-Yo's dizzy deals."

"Isn't his fault. I heard him on the phone with the St. Louis County sheriff. Duncan told the guy this was a lame fishing trip." Traffic was jammed up ahead of them. "Watch it. You're gonna rear-end that minivan."

"Yes, dear." He veered to the far right lane and took the Lexington Parkway exit. Took a left. Headed south on Lexington. "Where's he live again?"

"Apartment on Grand Avenue. Fourteen-hundred block."

They stopped at a red light. "Shit. Did I get off too soon? Should've taken Snelling. My head's plugged from that flu bug. Not thinking straight."

"You're still good. Take a right on Grand. It's about a half mile up."

The light turned green. He stepped on the gas. Veered around a slower car. "It's late in the morning."

"So?"

He accelerated to make it through an intersection with a yellow light. "I assume big brother works."

"In the same building as his apartment."

"How's that? He the caretaker or what?"

"He's a massage therapist. Works for a couple of chiropractors with offices on the first floor of the building."

He took a right on Grand Avenue. Headed west on the stretch of road filled with homes, apartments, restaurants, boutiques and small businesses. "So the guy rolls out of bed and he's at work. How easy is that?" He coughed hard. Swallowed.

"I knew you'd appreciate it."

"Hell yeah. Think I'll turn in my badge and become a back cracker."

"I wouldn't let you touch my back."

They stopped at another red light. He put his hand over his heart and looked at her. "I'm insulted. I give really good back rubs. The old lady says so. Good foot rubs, too."

"With those big meat hooks?"

He flexed his right hand in front of her face. "It's not the size of the appendage. It's what you do with it." He wiggled his fingers. "These are magic digits."

The light turned green. She pushed his hand away. "Pay attention to the road, magic fingers." He put his hand back on the steering wheel and accelerated.

They surveyed the addresses on the buildings as they went. "There it is," he said, nodding toward a building across the street, on the south side of Grand. He made a U-turn in the middle of Grand and almost collided with a pickup going east. The truck driver honked and passed him. Castro flipped him the bird.

Murphy shook her head. "You are nuts. You know that?"

"I've been told that on more than one occasion." He pulled up in front of a stucco apartment building. Sniffled. "Double-check your notes. This it for sure?"

She pulled Duncan's pad out of her purse. Flipped through the pages. Looked up at the building. "Yeah. For sure." She tucked the pad back in her purse.

Castro made another U-turn, nearly smacking a delivery van traveling west on Grand. They were back on the north side of the avenue. He put the car in park.

Murphy: "What the hell are you doing?"

He shut off the engine, pulled the keys out of the ignition and dropped them in his pocket. "We can't sit right in front of the damn building. Who taught you surveillance? Dubrowski?"

Murphy saw a new tool sitting on the seat between them. She picked it up. Held it in both hands. Pointed it at the windshield and looked through the lens. "What's this gizmo?"

"Careful with that." He reached over and pulled it away from her. Set it back on the seat. "You said we're watching, not apprehending. I like watching with that. Makes it more interesting. What if we see a Kodak moment? The little brother drags the body of this snowmobile guy down the front steps for us. We'll want him to smile for the camera. Capture it on film."

She eyed the gadget on the seat. "That looks like binoculars on steroids." It had three lenses instead of two. "Where's the camera come in?"

He picked it up again. Held it in front of her face. "Integrated binocular and digital camera. You can capture anything from a distance of fifty feet to infinity."

"Infinity?"

"Well. That's what the box says. Infinity might be pushing it. Stores up to a hundred images. Downloads to a PC. Then you can print or e-mail the pictures."

"So the middle lens is the camera lens?"

"You got it. This black box thing that sits over the camera lens—between the barrels of the binoculars—is the part with buttons that work the camera." With his left hand, he pointed to a couple of buttons in back of the box, on the top. "The one on the left turns on the camera. The one on the right snaps the picture. There's some other stuff involved, but I'm not gonna get into it because I'm not letting anyone else touch this baby."

"Selfish."

"Sick of replacing batteries. People borrow my shit and they leave stuff on and I gotta run out and get new batteries." He looked across the street. Eyed a sign in the chiropractors' window. He lifted the binoculars to his eyes. Looked through them at the apartment building. "Take this down."

She pulled out Duncan's notebook again. Rummaged around in her purse. Pulled out a pen. Wrote as Castro fired off some numbers. "Got it."

He lowered the binoculars. Looked at her. "Your back's been bothering you for weeks. The pain is in your lower back. Shoots down the front of your left leg. No. Wait. Your right leg. Shoots down the front of your right leg. You don't know what caused it. Too much shoveling maybe. A skiing accident. Too much sex. Those weird positions your husband's been trying. Whatever."

She pulled her cell phone out of her purse. Looked at the number on the pad. Punched it in and held the phone to her ear. "Yes. Could I get in today? As soon as possible. My back is killing me. I can hardly walk straight." She winked at Castro. "No. I can't wait that long. Can't you squeeze me in sooner?" She paused and listened. "Sure. I can make that. See you then." She turned off the cell and tucked it back in her purse. Flashed Castro a grin. "I'll be on the road to recovery in twenty minutes."

"Good. I was worried sick about you." He turned his head back around. Lifted the binoculars to his eyes and studied the apartment windows. "Got a phone number?"

She checked Duncan's scratches. Just the address of the building. She reached into her purse and pulled out some notes she'd printed from the sheriff's e-mail. Address again. No phone number. She took the phone out of her purse again. Punched in a number and lifted the phone to her ear. "Robert Clancy in St. Paul. On Grand Avenue." She scribbled in the notebook. Hung up. Dialed. Listened. It rang three times before an answering machine kicked in.

This is Robert. If you're selling stuff, I don't want any. If you're asking for money, I don't have any. All others leave a message at the tone.

"His machine is on." She hung up and dropped the phone back in her purse. She checked her Glock. When she didn't want to wear a belt or a shoulder rig, she carried her gun in her bag, slipped inside a special sleeve. "What about a search warrant?"

He was looking down. Fiddling with the binoculars. "What about it?"

"Never mind. Forget I asked."

"Asked what?"

She closed her purse and glanced at the office across the street. "By the looks of the chiros' door number and this guy's apartment number, I'd say Clancy lives above the office. Directly above it. So you gotta be quiet."

"Castro the ghost." He lifted the binoculars up to his eyes again. Coughed. "Take your time in there. Your back is really, really messed up."

TWELVE

RANSOM'S EYES FLUTTERED open. She sniffed the air. Something fried. With onions. She kicked off the covers. Threw her legs over the edge of the bed and sat up. Ran both her hands through her hair. She'd finally gotten a couple of hours of sleep and felt better than she had in days. Clancy stepped into the bedroom doorway wearing a barbecue apron—I KISS BETTER THAN I COOK—and nothing else. "Nice outfit," she said. "Very attractive."

"Come and get it before it gets cold." Two cats walked into the bedroom. Brushed against his legs. He kicked them away.

"My babies are being friendly," she said. "They love people. They hate when I'm away. Didn't you see how they rushed us when we came through the front door? They'd probably been sitting in the windows every waking moment. Waiting. My poor babies."

"Who watches your *poor babies* when you're gone? Who feeds the fur balls?"

"I leave out lots of food and water dispensers."

"I noticed," he said.

"If I'm gone more than a few days, I have neighbor boys with keys."

He cracked a smile. "I'll bet you do." The plumpest of the two cats came back for more. Stepped on his feet. He cranked his right foot back, ready to give it a boot. "Leave me alone, you lard ass."

"Don't," said Ransom. "She isn't fat. She's pregnant. Due any day now."

He lowered his foot. "More cats. Great." He turned and went down the hall. Went through the living room into the kitchen, and they followed.

She stood up and yawned. Stretched her arms over her head. Contemplated pulling on some clothes. One of them had to break the run of nudity, she thought. She stepped up to the closet door and glanced at the bolt. Slid the bar open. She pulled open the closet and yanked her robe off a door hook. Closed the door.

"Got any Tabasco?"

She started. He'd stepped back into the doorway. "The cupboard to the left of the stove."

"Why do you have locks on all your closets?"

"What?" She avoided meeting his eyes. Slipped her arms into the sleeves of her robe and tied the belt around her waist.

"What's with all the locks?"

"Original to the house," she said. "I never bothered taking them off."

He came up behind her and twined his arms around her waist. Her robe was pink and dotted with kittens. More little-girl clothes, he thought. He buried his face in her hair. Inhaled the herbal smell. Her shampoo. He turned his cheek. Pressed it against the silky curtain. The best part of her. "I could take them off. I'm handier than hell. Remember. I grew up in a hardware store."

"No. Too much trouble." She untangled his arms from her body and stepped around him. Scooped her cigarette pack and lighter off her nightstand. Headed for the kitchen. "Come, babies," she said to the cats at her feet.

"I'm gonna pull on some sweats," he said after her.

Clancy waited until she left. Put his hand on the knob. Opened the closet door. Saw nothing but a wall of clothes. Rack of pumps and sneakers on the floor. Most of her stuff was pink. Even her shoes. Strange woman, he thought. He closed the door and looked at the bolt. Her house was a 1920s bungalow. She'd updated the kitchen and bathroom and had all the wood floors stripped and refinished. Otherwise most of the interior was original, and needed a lot of work. Behind the flowery wallpaper, the old walls were crumbling. The shiny brass locks on the closets sure as hell didn't come with the house, however. "Original, my ass," he muttered.

A cat walked between his legs. He started. Fucking cats. Always brushing up against his legs. Jumping next to him on the couch. How many did she have? How many more were pregnant? They were already all over the place. He couldn't tell them apart. She talked to them like they were people. *My babies.* They'd started creeping him out even before she'd opened the front door to her house. The things had been waiting for her to return from skiing. They'd lined up along the radiators under the front windows. Pushed back the drapes and looked outside. A row of furry spies. The cat slithered through his legs again. He bent over, picked it up by its scruff. Looked at its underside. It had nipples. It was nursing. He wondered where the kittens were hiding. Under some furniture? In a food cupboard? He didn't want to think about the possibilities. "Yuck," he said, and tossed it into the hall. It landed on all fours and yowled.

At that moment he decided he wasn't going to stay around much longer. All of it was giving him the creeps. The locks on the closets. The pink clothes. The poetry readings. Cats. Place stank of cigarette smoke and cat litter and cat food. That little-girl voice. *My love. My love. My love.* Like listening to somebody's sappy kid sister. She did more yapping in an hour than his mother and sisters combined did in a year. She kept the thermostat cranked so high, he was sweating even without clothes. She perched cake pans filled with water on top of half the radiators, adding to the humidity in the house. Uncomfortable furniture with skinny legs and flowery upholstery. Flowers on the wallpaper and flowers on the bedspread. Curtains and rugs and towels with flowers. Flowers and heat and humidity. Might as well live in a hothouse, he thought. Whenever the phone rang, she ignored it. Someone knocked once. She ignored that, too. Closed the drapes tighter and cracked a joke about nosey neighbors. He didn't know what else to do but laugh with her. Worst of all was her constant scribbling in her journal. She told him it was poetry and short stories. He didn't believe her. He'd caught her staring at him. He was her bug in a jar.

He went over to the window over her nightstand. Opened the drapes. The sunlight bouncing off the snow shocked his eyes. A camera flash going off in his face. He lifted up the window and the screen behind it to let in some cold air. Inhaled. It felt and smelled good. Invigorating. It made him want to get out of the hothouse even more. His eyes fell on the phone on her nightstand. He searched his memory. Remembered Bo's home but not his work number, and he was pretty sure his brother worked on Wednesday mornings. Clancy picked up the receiver. Punched in the home phone. Got the machine. Waited for the tone and left a message. "Bo. It's me. I'm in town. Staying with this woman I met at the bar. A babe, but kind of goofy. Probably won't hang out much longer. Her weird shit's starting to get on my nerves. I'll call back. See if you can put me up." He hung up. He turned and went over to his duffel bag sitting on the floor, at the foot of the bed. He kneeled next to it and unzipped it. Dug around until he found some boxers and a pair of sweatpants and a tee shirt. He pulled them out and threw them on the end of the bed. He peered into the bag. Felt the lumpy pillowcase at the bottom. The guns and shells and casing were still there. He wondered how long he'd have to hang on to the insurance policy. There'd been nothing on the television news about a missing man up north. The guy had probably been lying about being with a group. Could be he didn't have anybody who gave a shit about him. Clancy suspected his own mother was relieved that his father was gone. Whole family was happier. Maybe the asshole on the snowmobile was another Owen Clancy. A cold wave washed over him. He didn't want to think about his father. He zipped the bag shut.

THIRTEEN

A PLAQUE ON the waiting room wall: CHIROPRACTIC FIRST. DRUGS SECOND. SURGERY LAST.

"May I have your insurance card?" asked the receptionist. "I assume your policy requires a co-payment."

Murphy read the sign nailed to the front of the counter: YOUR CO-PAYMENT IS DUE AT THE TIME OF YOUR VISIT. THANK YOU. "I'm paying cash. My insurance won't pay for this."

"You sure? We could send it through. See if they cover it. Most do these days."

"They won't. Don't bother." Murphy pulled some bills out of her wallet and paid the woman. She handed Murphy a receipt. As Murphy stuffed the paperwork in her purse, she smiled at the thought of turning in an expense report for an undercover chiropractic visit.

The receptionist handed Murphy a set of forms on a clipboard and a pen. "Both sides, please."

Murphy put her left hand on her lower back and walked
over to the row of chairs. They'd squeezed her in over
lunch, and there was no one else in the office. She turned
and lowered herself into a seat. Grimaced. Unbuttoned her
coat. Crossed her legs and set the clipboard on her knee.
Glanced around the office. The walls were painted the color
of moss. A tabletop fountain bubbled in one corner. Harp
music drifted out of a CD player perched atop a table in another corner. Smoke from smoldering incense wafted up
from a dish on the receptionist's desk. She inhaled. Sandal-
wood. Murphy couldn't remember the last time she'd gotten such a cushy assignment.

She looked down at the forms. The first one asked basic
information. She filled it out using her married name and
her old address. Under *Occupation* she wrote *Chef.* She
loved to cook. *Have you had chiropractic care before?* She
circled *No.* That was the truth. She hated going to any sort
of doctor—even though her husband was one—and she had
never set foot in a chiropractor's office before. The second
form required more creativity. *Describe your symptoms
and how they began.* She thought about it. In college, she'd
stepped into a pothole while running. Her knee had suffered for it, not her back. Still, it sounded like a good story.
Pulled a muscle while jogging on uneven road. She stopped
writing. Examined her lie. Not elaborate enough. *Then
slipped on the ice and fell on butt.* Believable, she thought.
What describes the nature of your symptoms? She had her
choice: *Sharp. Dull ache. Numb. Shooting. Burning. Tingling.*
She circled *Dull ache.* Then the form had four drawings of
a nude male—minus the penis—from the front, back, left
side, right side. *Indicate where you have pain or other
symptoms.* She drew a star on the figure's lower back and a
line down the front of the right leg. *What activities make
your symptoms worse?* She wrote *Housecleaning.* She hated
cleaning the house. *What activities make your symptoms*

better? Jack would like this answer: *Sex.* The last question: *What do you hope to get from your visit/treatment?* Her options: *Reduce symptoms. Resume/increase activity. Explanation of condition/treatment. Learn how to take care of this on my own. How to prevent this from occurring again.* A blank space allowed her to list her own goals. She wondered what they'd think if she wrote the truth: *Determine if there's a killer hiding in the building.* She circled *Reduce symptoms.*

"I can see you now, Mrs. Ramier."

She lifted her eyes from the form and saw a tall man with broad shoulders standing in front of her. He looked very much like his brother. Dark eyes. Dark hair. Not as curly as his brother's mop. She expected he'd be in some sort of medical garb, but he was wearing khaki slacks and a polo shirt with the name of the clinic embroidered on the right side: BACK TO NORMAL. He extended his hand. "Robert Clancy. I work with the doctors."

She slipped the pen under the clip and took his hand. Nearly as big as Castro's mitts, she thought. She let go of his hand.

He eyed the board on her knee. "Finished?" He picked it up. Scanned the top sheet. Lifted it and read the one underneath. "A runner, huh? Not the best thing if you've got a bad back. Swimming is better." He read some more. "Pain down the front of your leg?"

"Yeah."

"Most folks feel it behind their legs."

She should have called Jack before making up symptoms. "I feel it there, too."

"Okay." He took the pen off the clip. "Right or left or both?"

She paused. Wondered what the hell the right answer would be. Decided to stay consistent. "Right."

He drew a line down the front of the naked man's right leg. "Sounds like you've got something going on with that right leg." He kept reading. "And sex makes you feel better? That's another new one. Lucky you."

Murphy stood up and hiked her purse strap over her shoulder. Pressed her hand to her lower back. "Sure hope this helps." She heard a creak over her head and resisted the urge to lift her eyes to the ceiling. "Which way?"

"Follow me," said Clancy. He slipped the pen back under the clip, turned and went toward the hall with the board. Another creak. He stopped walking and frowned. Glanced up.

She stepped ahead of him and went down the hall. Put her hand on a door marked PRIVATE. "In here?"

He looked down. "No, no. That's the doctors' break room." He followed her down the corridor and stepped up to a door on the opposite side of the hallway. "We'll put you in here." He dropped the clipboard into a holder on the wall and opened the door for her. She stepped inside, and he stood in the doorway. "I saw on the form you've never visited a chiropractor before. My job is to loosen you up so the doctor can do the adjustment."

"Sounds good," she said.

"Gown is on the table. Hooks for your coat and clothes and purse are against the wall. I'll give you a few minutes and come back."

She looked at the square of cloth in the middle of the bench and wrapped her coat tighter around her body. "What?"

"If you don't want to disrobe, we can get started right now. I can work around your clothes. Just loosen your jeans and lie facedown on the table."

She heard another creak over her head. Thought she heard a cough. She had to get him out of the room. She went over to the hooks. Pulled off her coat and hung it up while still holding on to her purse. "I'll put on the gown."

"Be back in a bit." He left the room, shutting the door behind him.

Another noise above her head. She wished Castro were a thin man. She turned and looked down at the material on the table. Same fabric as her dad's hospital robe. She didn't want to take her clothes off. Even when she'd worked as a decoy in vice, playing the role of a hooker, she'd never taken her clothes off. It was one thing to dress sexy. To start undressing—to undo even a single button—would have been cheap and desperate. Then last fall, the serial killer surgeon had forced her to remove her shirt at gunpoint. Put his hands on her. The thought of disrobing for her job now—even when acting the part of a patient—unnerved her. She hadn't anticipated she'd have such a strong reaction. The medical setting didn't help. She noticed a poster on the wall next to the clothes hooks. A dozen black-and-white blocks were pictured, each containing an X-ray of a spine. At the bottom of the poster: SUBLUXATION DEGENERATION. She looked at the purse in her hand. She didn't want to be separated from it. Separated from her gun. This assignment was looking less and less cushy. She longed to be upstairs snooping around. Why couldn't Castro be the one dropping his clothes? Getting poked and prodded and adjusted? She berated herself for thinking that way. For being a coward. *Don't be a chickenshit. A guy wouldn't think twice. I shouldn't think twice.* She heard a knock at the door. "One minute," she said. She looked up at the ceiling. Didn't hear anything more. Maybe he was done. What to do with her purse? She saw a shelf under the head of the table. The padded ledge was designed for patients to rest their arms while they were on their stomachs getting treatment. Perfect spot. She could reach her purse, even keep her hands on it most of the time. She set her bag on the ledge. She kicked off her boots. Picked up the gown and threw it on a chair. Lay facedown on the table. Put her hands on her purse. "Okay," she yelled. "Ready."

Clancy opened the door and walked in. Shut the door behind him. Eyed his patient. "Decided against the gown?"

"Too drafty."

"That's fine. Half the patients don't bother with them."

Murphy exhaled with relief. Turned her head and watched him. He went over to a machine sitting on a bed stand at arm's length from the table. The gizmo was the size of a car battery and looked like a futuristic bread machine. A control panel on one side bore numbers arranged in a block like the numbers on a telephone. He put his hand on a switch. "What's that?" she asked.

He held up four round pads the size of silver dollars. Each pad was attached to the box by a length of cord. "They deliver a mild electrical stimulation that relaxes the muscles. I'm going to place them on your lower back over the area of pain and leave you alone for ten minutes to relax and let the machine do its thing."

"No you're not."

"What?"

"Let's skip that part."

"Okay." He set the pads back down. "Ultrasound?"

"I'd rather not. I have this thing about gadgets touching me."

"Acupuncture then?"

"Needles?"

"I can see you're tense, Mrs. Ramier. We've got to loosen you up. How about a massage? No gadgets involved. Only hands." He held up his palms.

She paused. If she didn't hear Castro over her head, he was either in the car or in another part of this guy's apartment. To play it safe, she decided to occupy him a while longer. "Sure. A massage."

"Can you loosen your jeans? I need to reach that lower-back area that's been bothering you."

She silently cursed Castro's suggestion that she go with lower-back pain. Should have gone with neck pain. She told herself she could do this. Her hesitation was stupid. She rolled on her left side, unbuttoned her jeans and pulled down the zipper. Rolled back onto her stomach. "How's that?"

"Can you hike your sweater a little, up to your bra strap? Can you reach or does that hurt?"

She paused. "No. I can manage." She reached behind her and pulled up her sweater.

"Good." He took a bottle off the bed stand and squirted something in one of his hands. Set down the bottle and rubbed his palms together. "Massage lotion. Shouldn't stain your clothes but I don't want to take any chances with wool."

"I suppose I'm one of your more difficult patients." She put her face down into the padded slot at the head of the bed. The opening was ringed with paper. She felt as if she were looking through a crack in a padded fence. She rested her hands on top of her purse.

"You'd be surprised. I've had all sorts."

"How long have you been doing this?" she asked into the crack. He put his hands on her back. Slid them just under the waist of her panties.

"A couple of years. Since I got out of college. Working on my master's now. In human development. I'd like to open my own clinic some day. Do massage therapy. Acupuncture. Other therapies."

He pressed down on both sides of her lower back and pushed up toward her bra strap. He moved down, still pressing. Feels good, she thought. Stay on track, she told herself. Get him talking about his brother. "Two of my brothers are orthopedic surgeons. They recommend massage therapy for some of their patients." She had no idea if that was really true.

He pressed down on her lower back and with his palms, stretched the muscles out toward her hips. "Two doctors in one family. Impressive. How many brothers you got?"

"A bunch. What about you?"

His hands moved up and down along her back. Tight ovals on each side of her spine. "One brother."

"Older?"

"Younger. He's a bartender. Smart kid. He could be doing something better than pouring beers, but he didn't want to go to college."

"He live around here? My brothers are all right here in town. Drive me nuts."

"I wish he lived in the cities. Might see more of him. Maybe talk him into getting more schooling. He's up north. In Hoyt Lakes. Where we grew up."

"That's on the Range, right? Your dad a miner?"

His hands went down to her lower back. With his thumbs, he pressed down and rubbed in circles. Walked all the way up her back with his thumbs doing circles. "No. Owned a hardware store in town."

"Owned? He retired?"

"No." His hands stopped moving. Rested in the middle of her back. "He's dead."

"I'm sorry."

"That's how it goes." Clancy peeled his hands off her skin and turned back to the bed stand.

"My dad's in the hospital right now. Heart attack."

"Too bad. Hope he comes out of it okay." He picked up the lotion and squirted more into his left hand. Rubbed his palms together.

"Was it your dad's heart? You seem awfully young to have a parent gone."

He turned and put his hands on her back again. Rubbed gently on her lower back. Sloppy, distracted circles. "No. Wasn't his heart. Deer-hunting accident." He stopped moving his hands. "A . . . rifle."

The way he said it. *Rifle*. Like he was going to gag on the word. Her hands instinctively tightened around her purse.

She and Castro had to get a look at the report. Talk to the sheriff. "God. I'm so sorry. I hunt myself. Birds mostly. Gotta be careful out in the field."

"Yeah," he said in a low voice. "Careful." He took his hands off her. Turned to the bed stand. Opened a drawer and took out a towel. Wiped his hands. "How was that, Mrs. Ramier? Paris? Unusual name, Paris. You French or something?"

"Lebanese and Irish."

"That's quite a combo." He folded the towel and set it on top of the bed stand. Turned and saw she was sitting up on the table, zipping up her jeans. "You'll want to leave your clothes loose so the doctor can do the adjustment."

She slid off the table and stood up. Buttoned the top button of her jeans. Pulled down her sweater. "You know what? I feel so much better, I'm going to skip the adjustment."

He crossed his arms over his chest. "I've never had a patient do *that* before."

She didn't want to make them suspicious at the clinic. Especially this guy. "You're probably right. I'm nervous." She unbuttoned her jeans again, unzipped them and went back down on her stomach. "Will you stay here until the doctor comes?" she asked through the crack.

"Sure." The door popped open. "Here's Dr. Johnson now."

She lifted her head and looked at the chiropractor. He was built like a professional wrestler. Stood well over six feet. Head shaved bald. Thick neck. Shoulders nearly as wide as the doorway. Hands the size of hams. Murphy felt her body tense. She buried her face in the crack.

"How are you feeling, Mrs. Ramier? Robert got you all loosened up?"

Clancy: "She's a little nervous, doctor."

Johnson: "We'll fix you right up."

Clancy put his hand on Murphy's shoulder. "I'm going

to leave now, Mrs. Ramier. Nice meeting you. Good luck to your father." Clancy walked out. Murphy heard the door close behind him.

Johnson stepped over to the side of the table. "Going to have a look at that back. See what we're dealing with here." He bent over her and hiked her sweater halfway up her back. "Let me know if this hurts, or if you feel it more on one side than the other." He started at the base of her back. Pressed along both sides of her spine with his thumbs until he got to her bra strap. "You are really tense."

"I know," she mumbled into the crack.

He pulled her sweater back down and stood straight. Walked to the end of the bed. "Do you stand on one foot more than the other? Is one running shoe more run-down?"

She thought about it. "Actually. Yeah."

"You're favoring one side."

"Really?"

"One leg is shorter than the other because your pelvis is misaligned. That's causing you problems. We should be able to fix that." He lifted Murphy's left leg straight up. Bent her heel back toward her butt. "Where does that hurt?"

"The front of my thigh."

"Good. That's where we want you to feel it."

He straightened her leg and set it down. Picked up her right leg. Lifted it straight up. Bent her heel back toward her butt. "And this one. Where does that hurt?"

"Thigh again."

"Very good." He straightened her leg and set it down. "Inhale. Deep breath."

She sucked in a breath.

"Let it out. Quick puff."

As she did, she felt the doctor throw his torso on top of her back. She heard a *crack*. He got off of her. "Wow. That felt good."

"Surprised?"

"I guess."

"Now roll onto your right side and cross your arms over your chest." She did. He grabbed her left ankle and curled her left leg up to her chest. "Inhale and then let it all out." As she was exhaling, he threw his body over the left side of her torso. Another *crack*. He slid off of her.

"Cool," she said.

He straightened her bent leg. "Now onto your left side. Fold those arms over again." She rolled over. Crossed her arms. He went around to the other side of the table to face her. Bent her right leg up to her chest. "Inhale deeply and exhale." As she blew out, he threw himself over her right side. *Crack*. He stood up. Pulled her right leg straight and patted her calf. "We're not through yet. On your back."

She went on her back. He went to the end of the table and wrapped his hands around her right ankle. Yanked it straight out. *Crack*. He grabbed her left ankle. Pulled. *Crack*. "One last adjustment. Stay straight. Cross your arms over your chest." She did. He went around to the side of the table where he'd started. "Going to give you a bear hug here." He wrapped his arms around her shoulders. "Inhale and blow out hard." As she blew, his torso landed on top of hers. *Crack*. He stood over her. "How was that?"

She uncrossed her arms. Laid them at her side and stared up. For the first time, she noticed a poster of a snow-covered mountain taped to the ceiling over the table. "That was great. I feel great."

"Good. You could use a couple of more visits. You are very, very tense. Wound tight. I could feel it in those muscles."

"Yeah. My whole family could use some cracking. My dad's in the hospital. We're all going nuts."

He put his right hand under her shoulder and gave her his left hand to hold while she sat up. "I'm going to give you some stretching exercises to do before running. I'll leave them at the front desk."

She swung her legs over the edge of the table and hopped off. "Thanks, doctor."

Johnson went to the door, pulled it open and stepped into the hallway. Turned and said: "Make an appointment with the receptionist. I'd give it a couple of days and come in again."

"You betcha."

He shut the door behind him. She went over to her coat, took it down and slipped it on. Took her purse off the ledge and hiked the strap over her shoulder. Stepped into her boots. She had her hand on the doorknob when she realized her pants zipper was still down. She zipped up her jeans and buttoned the top button. She opened the door and stepped out of the exam room. Rotated her shoulders as she walked. Bent her head from side to side. She'd never been so relaxed and limber. She felt as if she could run another marathon the minute she stepped outside the office.

FOURTEEN

RANSOM WALKED INTO the bedroom while Clancy was pulling on his sweats. She had a champagne glass in each hand and three cats at her heels. The flutes were filled with something orange and fizzy. "I made us mimosas."

He pulled the tee shirt over his head. "Kind of early, ain't it?" Since they'd arrived, she'd been pushing the booze. Bringing him beers. Mixing him cocktails. For a single woman, she had a lot of liquor in her house. The other night she even came up with some pot. Kept it in her refrigerator, in the butter compartment. She took a pull off the joint. Gave him the rest. She told him it was from one of her students.

"Never too early for mimosas, my love." She took a tiny sip out of the glass in her right hand. "Besides. I'm still off school. This is my vacation." She noticed the drapes and window were open. "My babies will catch a chill, Catch." She laughed at her double use of his nickname.

She walked over to the window. Set the flutes on the nightstand. Reached over and closed the screen and the window. Shut the drapes. Picked up the glasses and turned around. He noticed that with all her stretching, the belt around her waist was starting to come undone. Her robe was opening on top. He could see her right nipple. A pebble on the beach. Hard and round and salty. He found that peek at her breast every bit as alluring as the eyeful he got when she paraded around the house naked. He could feel himself getting hard again. Maybe he was being too hasty. Wasn't so bad here, after all. Unlimited booze and sex. Free food. An occasional toke. Run of the house. His brother would charge him rent and make him pay for food. Make him get a job. He'd have to find work eventually—he was flat broke—but not yet. He didn't mind taking it easy after years of busting his ass working. He'd put up with her creepy crap a bit longer. Put up with the poetry and flowers and heat and cats. He'd wait awhile before calling Bo back.

She took another sip from one of the flutes and smiled. "Don't keep me waiting, my love." She headed back to the kitchen, the cats slinking behind her.

"My love," he snarled under his breath. He glanced over at the nightstand. The journal was there next to the phone. Under the poetry book. He'd have to take a look when she wasn't around. Read what the Pink Lady professor had to say about her bug. He followed her into the kitchen.

She was sitting at the table, a pack of cigarettes, a lighter and an ashtray on one side of her. A pile of mail and magazines on the other. In front of her, a plate of scrambled eggs and onions. She picked up her fork and poked at the eggs. Studied them. Looked up at him. "Aren't you eating?"

He patted his stomach. "Got six eggs in the belly already."

She lifted a forkful of egg to her mouth and nibbled. Set it back down.

"What's wrong? Too dry?" He went to the cupboard next to the stove. Opened it and scanned the contents. "I don't see the Tabasco. They taste great with Tabasco."

"They don't need a thing. I'm not a breakfast eater."

He closed the cupboard. "Breakfast? This is lunch."

"What's in them? I'm not much of a cook. Your mother's recipe?" She started rifling through the stack of envelopes.

He turned around and leaned against the counter. "Maggie taught me how to cook. She told me I should at least know how to make eggs."

She dropped the mail. Took a sip of the mimosa. Set down the glass. Picked up her pack. Fished out a cigarette and set it between her lips. Flicked on the lighter. Lit up. Took a long pull and exhaled, sending a cloud over the kitchen table. "Sit down with me."

He started for the table, but suddenly realized the blinds were closed again. He'd opened them so he could see while he was cooking. He walked over to one of the windows and put his hand on the cord.

"Don't open it," she said. She took another drag, exhaled and set the cigarette in the ashtray.

He dropped his hand from the cord. Turned his head and looked at her. "Why?"

"I like it dark. So do my babies." She picked up an envelope and held it in both hands. Stared at it. Grabbed a butter knife, inserted it under the flap and ripped it across. She dropped the knife and paused. Frowned.

"Bad news?"

"Bills, my love. Bills." She reached inside the envelope and pulled out a letter. Unfolded it and read.

He turned his head back to the window. Lifted the blind away from the pane and glanced outside. Two cardinals—a male and a female—danced on the branches of a bush outside the kitchen window. A squirrel ran across the top of her back fence. "How close are you to the lake? Can you see Como from your front yard?"

She looked up from the letter and laughed dryly. "Hardly. Couldn't afford a house with a view on my pay."

"Your neighbors across the street. Can they see the lake?"

"No. The neighbors behind my neighbors. How's that for obstructed seating?"

"It's close enough. Let's go for a walk around the lake after breakfast. I want to check out the neighborhood. The zoo. We could walk to the zoo."

She folded the letter in half. Dropped it on top of the pile of mail. Picked up her cigarette. Took another drag. Blew smoke over the table. Set the cigarette back in the ashtray. "What about your ankles?"

"They're fine." He let go of the blind and turned to look at her. "Let's get out. I want some exercise. Fresh air. Staying inside. Drinking. Eating my own cooking all day. I'm gonna get fat."

She took a sip of the mimosa, set down the glass and picked up her cigarette. Took a couple of puffs. Tapped a tube of ash into the tray. Patted the chair to her left. "Come drink your drink before it goes flat."

He walked over to the table. A cat jumped up on the chair ahead of him.

"Chaucer," she said, setting down her cigarette. "No."

He brushed the animal off the chair. "Go."

"Chaucer's my old-timer. I think he's jealous. Be nice to him."

"Sure. Nice." He sat down next to her. He was thirsty. He guzzled the champagne and orange juice. Felt something on the tip of his tongue. He picked it off and looked at it. A cat hair. He wiped it on his pant leg.

"Sorry. My babies shed."

"Why do you have so many? What good are they? They're not like dogs. Can't hunt and fetch and stuff."

"My babies have talents."

He took another gulp out of his glass. "Yeah. Like what? Making more babies?"

"They're wonderful mousers."

"Poison does the same thing."

She paused. She didn't like that he'd brought up the word *poison*. She had some under the sink. He'd been snooping around her house. "I tried poison. It didn't work. Besides, poison doesn't purr and hop on your lap."

He took another drink. Set down the glass. "What kind of death would that be? Poison?"

She frowned. She didn't like his fascination with this topic. She stopped herself from looking at the eggs. "What?"

"Haven't you ever wondered what it would be like to die a certain way? In a car accident or by drowning? With a gun?" He paused and put his hand on the stem of the glass. Looked at the bubbles. "Haven't you ever wondered which would hurt less? Be more like falling asleep or blacking out? Wouldn't it be better to pick how you clock out?"

"Have you forgotten that's how my brother died?" She took another puff. Held the smoke in as long as she could. Exhaled. "I'd never entertain suicide."

He ran his thumb and forefinger up and down the stem of the flute. "Entertain suicide." He picked up the glass, brought it to his lips and emptied it. Set the glass down but held on to the stem. Said in a low voice: "That's exactly what it's like. Entertaining the idea. Having a party for two. Would you like to put your feet up, stay in my head awhile? Would you like some cold water? How about a bullet? A spoon of poison? No? Maybe later then. Let me know when you're hungry."

"Stop talking like that. Morbid." She reached over and refilled the flute with straight champagne. The top of her robe loosened.

"Trying to get me drunk?" He took a long drink while staring at the V of skin between her breasts. Pulled the glass away from his lips. He'd never had champagne before. Never even served it to anyone at the bar. He liked the taste, but it was stronger than he thought it would be. Kind of snuck up on him. He could feel his head growing light and his face getting hot. A comfortable, lazy feeling. He finished the glass. Set it down. She emptied the rest of the bottle into his flute. "You *are* trying to get me drunk."

She smiled and took another sip of her drink. Set down the glass. Stood up. Went around behind him. Untied her robe so it fell open. Leaned over him and ran her hands down the front of his chest. Nibbled on his neck. Her hair fell on either side of her head and dusted his shoulders. "I've got more bottles in the fridge. Let's take a couple of them back to bed with us." She leaned into him and pressed her breasts into his back. Reached down and rubbed his crotch over his sweatpants. She slipped her hand under the waist. Rubbed him over his boxers. Slipped her hand under the boxers. Ran her fingers through his tangle of hair. He leaned his head back and moaned.

They spent the rest of the afternoon in bed. Drinking champagne. Making love with the shades drawn and the heat turned up. He fell asleep on top of her, sweat beading his back.

FIFTEEN

"SO YOU GET a nice massage and cracking while I'm tiptoeing around upstairs. Collecting cooties from this guy's flophouse."

She was thankful Castro let her drive back to the cop shop while he fiddled with his recorder. She turned the car onto the freeway ramp. "A real pit?"

"Actually wasn't too bad." The tape finished rewinding and clicked to a stop. "Imagine Dubrowski's desktop multiplied to the size of a one-bedroom apartment."

Bruce Springsteen was vibrating the dashboard. She reached over and turned off "Born to Run." She looked at the box in his hands. "What did you get?"

"Didn't find anything suspicious in the apartment, but check this out." He pushed the Play button and held up the recorder. A young man's voice: *"It's me. I'm in town. Staying with this woman I met at the bar. A babe, but kind of goofy. Probably won't hang out much longer. Her weird shit's starting to get on my nerves. I'll call back. See if you can put me up."*

"The St. Paul woman the cops up north were trying to reach."

He hit Rewind. "Sounds like she took a liking to little brother. Brought the puppy home with her. Wonder if she knows he might be rabid."

Murphy steered around a slow-moving minivan. "Serene Ransom. Damn. That name. I know her somehow. Can't think how."

"Maybe this'll knock something loose in your head." Castro pushed the Play button again. Turned up the volume. *"It's me. I'm in town. Staying with this woman I met at the bar. A babe, but kind of goofy. Probably won't hang out much longer. Her weird shit's starting to get on my nerves. I'll call back. See if you can put me up."* Castro clicked it off. "I wonder what the 'weird shit' is about."

"And why did he wait so long before calling his brother? This is Wednesday. He ditched the bar over the weekend."

Castro rewound the tape a third time. "Maybe the two bros don't get along."

"Robert Clancy likes his brother. Said he wishes he lived closer. He'd try to get him to go to school. College. Do something better than tending bar."

Castro punched Play again. *"It's me. I'm in town. Staying with this woman I met at the bar. A babe, but kind of goofy. Probably won't hang out much longer. Her weird shit's starting to get on my nerves."* He hit the Stop button. Rewound part of the tape. "Could be little brother doesn't want to get big brother involved in a big fucking mess. Think the woman had something to do with the mess?"

"I don't know. If she's home, why hasn't she been answering her phone? Cops up north have been calling her house." She took a downtown exit and steered the car off the interstate.

He hit Play again. *"Her weird shit's starting to get on my nerves."* He stopped the tape. "Maybe the kid did something to Ransom. Sounds like he's fed up with her."

"No. I don't think that's it. He sounds too calm in that tape. Aggravated, but not agitated." She braked at a red light. "Say the kid shoots somebody in the bar after closing time Saturday. Even though the bar owner says Clancy hates guns, let's say he picks one up and blasts away."

Castro sniffled. "Who is the unfortunate target?"

The light changed. She accelerated. "For the sake of argument, let's go with the snowmobile guy. Van Hogan. He's the only one missing so far. DNA will confirm it, but that's gonna take awhile."

Castro wiped his nose with the cuff of his jacket sleeve. "Motive?"

"I don't know." Murphy turned the Ford into the station parking lot. Pulled into a space and shut off the engine. "The kid and the snowmobile guy don't have a history together. The kid spent his whole life in Hoyt Lakes, and Hogan is one of our fine felons grown in the Twin Cities."

"How about a dumb-ass bar fight?" Castro coughed twice. Covered his mouth with his hand. Coughed again. Wiped his hand on his pant leg. "Bar fight's always good for a killing or two."

"Dumb-ass bar fight doesn't seem a good enough reason for a guy with a gun phobia to pick up a piece again." Murphy pulled the keys out of the ignition.

He sniffled. "Maybe the gun-phobia stuff is bullshit."

"No. Older brother sounds shaken up still, and he wasn't the one who pulled the trigger."

"Go with the dumb-ass bar fight for now."

She tossed the keys back and forth between her hands. "Then what? Kid dumps the body. Cleans up. Empties the till. Takes the gun. Leaves a long good-bye letter that doesn't really say much."

Castro held out his hand. She dropped the keys in his palm. His turn to jiggle them. "Kid takes off with the weird babe. Hides out at her place down here for a while. Gets sick of her. Calls big bro, who apparently doesn't know about all the shit that went down with little bro." Castro dropped the keys in his jacket pocket.

She put her hand on the driver's door. Opened it. "Something's missing. There's more to it. I know there is."

"You and your intuition." He popped open the passenger's door. "Let's go inside. I'm freezing my nuts off." He slid out of the car with the tape recorder and the binoculars. Stood up and stuffed the gadgets into his jacket pockets. Slammed the door shut. Buried his hands in his pockets and came around to her side of the car.

She slid out with her purse, stood up and shut the door. Slung her purse strap over her shoulder. A gust of wind made her shiver. She buttoned her coat up to her neck and eyed the sky. The sun had clouded over. Looked like snow. Her gloves and hat were in her pockets, but she didn't want to bother with them. The station entrance was a few steps from the lot. She rammed her fists into her coat pockets. Her insulated black leather covered her past her knees, but it wasn't heavy enough for serious weather. She'd been putting off buying a down jacket because she thought most of them looked like marshmallows. "For sure one thing isn't right," she said to Castro. "This long-good-bye thing."

"What isn't right about it?" He coughed twice. Sniffled and wrinkled his nose.

The pair walked across the parking lot, their shoulders hunched against the cold. The wind blew puffs of snow against their backs. She pressed her arms close to her sides. "Duncan said it was a long, flowery letter. From a boy bartender without much of an education? A kid who didn't want to go to college? Someone who's hanging around town, working the taps at the local tavern?"

"I see where you're going with that." He pulled the door open for her, and she stepped into the station. He followed her inside. The plate-glass door closed behind them. A blast of wind curled a snowdrift against the glass. They stomped their feet on the doormats and walked to the elevator. She unbuttoned her coat, and he unzipped his jacket. Castro pushed the Up button. His eyeglasses were fogged. He took them off, wiped the lenses with the hem of his jacket and slipped the spectacles back on. "You think someone helped him write it? The woman?"

"Yeah." Murphy sniffled. Fished some Kleenex out of her purse. Castro held out his hand. She passed him a sheet. She blew her nose. Balled up the tissue and dropped it in her purse. "We gotta get a copy of the letter. Check it out. Check out Serene Ransom. See what her story is."

He coughed into the tissue. Blew his nose with it. Folded the Kleenex and slipped it in his jacket pocket. "The woman has to know what happened. She was still sitting in the bar when the regulars took off. That's what you said, right? She didn't leave and the kid blows someone away and then she comes back. Doesn't make sense."

The elevator doors opened and Murphy stepped on, followed by Castro. The doors closed. She pushed the button for their floor. "I suppose Ransom and the kid could have made arrangements to meet later. The regulars leave. She leaves. The snowmobile guy walks in. It's just him and the kid. This thing happens, whatever the hell it was. Bar fight or whatever. Afterward, the kid hooks up with Ransom outside the bar. Maybe he tells her what went down. Maybe he doesn't." She paused. "I don't know, though. That's a lot of work for one person. Getting rid of a body and cleaning up. Plus there's this letter business. I think if she helped him write it, she had to be right there in the bar with him when it happened. When he blew this guy away. She didn't help Clancy write it somewhere else and then he comes back and slaps it on the register."

"I agree with that," said Castro. The elevator doors opened. The pair stepped out and headed down the hall. "Dumb shits who return to the scene of their crime wait a day or two. They don't kill someone, clean up, take a hike and then come back while there's still gunsmoke in the air. Not unless they leave something really important behind, like their home movies. Remember that one idiot?" A few years back. A woman was found hours after she was strangled, a camcorder on her dresser. Castro and Dubrowski were standing outside the victim's house, watching the camcorder's screen. A man materialized at their elbow and asked if he could have his property back. They slapped the cuffs on him. He was the killer; he'd recorded her strangulation for his archives. "Too bad all our cases don't come with their own documentaries."

They walked into Homicide. Castro went straight to the water cooler. Started coughing again. Pulled a paper cup from the dispenser and poured a drink. Hacked while he drank. She went to her desk. Dropped her purse on top. Took out the notebook, Enda Clancy's photo and the printout. Opened a drawer and dropped her purse into it. Peeled off her coat and draped it over the back of her chair. Sat down. Started paging through the printout. Found the sheriff's number. She put her hand on her phone. Thought she'd better tell Duncan what she was doing first. She took her hand off the receiver. Got up and headed for his office.

The door was open. He was at his desk rifling through a stack of papers. At the bottom, what looked like an architect's rendering. She poked her head inside. "Got a minute?"

"A minute's about all I got, Paris." He looked up. "Murphy." She walked through the door. He hadn't called her Paris since he camped out at her place during his recovery. A slip, she thought. Nothing more. She sat down at the chair across from his desk. Nodded toward the paperwork. "What's all that?"

"Bullshit related to the new building." He dropped the papers on his desk. "Don't know why I got saddled with it."

She knew why. So did he, she thought. They're looking at Duncan for the top job. "Can I get a desk with a window? Always wanted a window."

"Take a number," he said. He heard coughing outside his office and tipped his head toward the sound. "Castro and Dubrowski already put in a request. So did Sandeen, and he beats all of you when it comes to seniority."

Pete Sandeen was in his early fifties. The most senior detective since Gabe retired. A longtime union activist and a steward. He'd guided Murphy through the internal-affairs investigation that followed after the surgeon shot himself with her gun. Murphy figured Sandeen deserved a window more than anyone. "I can live with that. Just make sure I get dibs on a window before Bergen."

"Bergen. That weenie called in sick on me. Too damn short around here." He picked up the pile of papers and tapped the bottom against his desk to even out the stack. "We gotta fill Nash's job. Another thing I gotta get to sooner than later."

She couldn't imagine replacing her mentor. "I keep thinking he'll get bored with retirement. Tired of fishing. Come back."

"I wish." Duncan set down the stack of papers. Ran his fingers through his hair. "I'm glad you're back on the job. Appreciate you cutting your vacation short. Don't know if I said thanks."

"You didn't." She crossed her legs. "Is it okay with you if I call the sheriff? I want to ask about that hunting accident. Get a fax of that letter the kid left in the bar."

"Good idea. Go for it." He leaned back in his chair. "Got some ideas? What'd you two get from the older brother? Anything?"

"Didn't talk to him directly. Didn't know what we'd say to him. Whether he'd be truthful. So we took the indirect route."

He put his hands behind his head. "I like your style."

She uncrossed her legs and leaned forward. "Sounds like little brother is shacked up with that woman."

He lowered his arms and sat straight in his chair. "Serene Ransom?" Duncan drummed his desk top with his hands. "The plot thickens. I love it."

Castro walked in behind her. Coughed. She turned her head and looked at him. "Got the tape?" Castro held it up in his right hand, like a trophy. Hit Play. *"It's me. I'm in town. Staying with this woman I met at the bar. A babe, but kind of goofy. Probably won't hang out much longer. Her weird shit's starting to get on my nerves. I'll call back. See if you can put me up."* Castro clicked off the tape. Stuffed the recorder in his pants pocket. Stepped next to Murphy. Sniffled and put his hand on the back of her chair.

Murphy looked across the desk at Duncan. He was all grins. She thought he belonged out on the street, not stuck in this office shuffling papers. "What do you think? Think she's got something to do with what happened at the bar?"

"Maybe she's the cause of what happened," said Duncan. He picked up two pens. Held one in each hand. Started tapping on his desktop. A drummer in a band. "Maybe the two studs went at it because of a woman."

Castro wiped his nose with the back of his hand. "That's a thought. The guys who closed up the place? What did they have to say? They see any heavy-duty flirting going on between Clancy and Ransom? I'd like a little more before we go banging down her door."

Duncan stopped tapping the pens. Dropped the one in his left hand. Started clicking the one in his right. "The sheriff didn't say. I haven't touched base with St. Louis County since this morning. I could call him back myself if you two are swamped."

Murphy eyed the paperwork on Duncan's desk. By the looks of it, he was going to be there all night. "We can do it."

"Go ahead." Duncan sounded disappointed. He dropped the pen on his desk. "Regardless, sounds like we should haul Romeo's ass in to answer a few questions. The woman, too."

Castro: "Is that our call?"

Duncan: "No. It's *my* call."

Murphy: "What about the sheriff?"

"Don't worry about him," said Duncan. "In fact, don't mention it to him when you guys talk to him. I'll deal with it."

Murphy raised her eyebrows. Duncan recognized jurisdictional lines only when it suited him. She told herself it wasn't her problem. She was following her commander's lead. She stood up. "Come on, Castro. Let's work the phones."

Castro turned and walked ahead of her through the office door, hacking as he went. Murphy looked at Duncan and thumbed over her shoulder. "He's still sick. He's gonna make the rest of us sick."

Duncan raised his palms like he was surrendering. "I can't send him home. We got no one. Two out sick. Two more out of town on that Chicago case. Sandeen just left for vacation. I send Castro home, and it's you and me."

"So what? We'd do okay." She turned on her heel and walked out of his office.

He watched her go. Said under his breath, "I would do better than okay with you, Paris." He sighed and lifted the top sheet from the stack of papers under his nose. "I hate this shit."

SIXTEEN

MURPHY'S PHONE RANG the minute she sat down at her desk. Jack, and he wasn't happy: "What are you doing there? I send you home to get some rest, and you go back to that place."

"They're short. People out sick. People out of town."

"You punched in? Jesus Christ. You're on vacation. Your dad's in the hospital."

Murphy heard hospital noises in the background. A doctor being paged. A cart rattling down the hall. Jack was still at Regions. She felt bad she'd left him there and hadn't stayed herself. "Thank you for hanging around the hospital. Dealing with all the medical crap. You're suppose to be on vacation, too."

"You're my wife," Jack said. "He's your dad. I'm a doctor. Where else should I be?"

You're my wife. She liked that simple statement of fact. She smiled to herself. Her marriage was going to work despite her job and her family and her affair. She'd make sure of it. "How's he doing? What'd the cardiologist say? Castro says his brother had that balloon thing done. He says it's not a big deal."

"Which medical school did Castro attend?"

"Don't be snotty. He was trying to make me feel better. What about my dad?"

"He's still on for the balloon angioplasty tomorrow. Don't bother visiting him after work. He's a bear. They're giving him a sleeper so he gets some rest before the procedure."

She liked that word better. *Procedure.* Sounded less serious than that other word she associated with hospitals. *Surgery.* "Spend the night at my place again? Have a nice dinner. Crash early. Shoot over to the hospital in the morning for the procedure."

"What about work? Will they let you take some time off from your job so you can be with your dad? While you're on vacation?"

"I told them I was off-limits tomorrow. Duncan's fine with that."

"That's generous of him." Jack sighed. "Your place is good. I'm going to give your mom a ride home. Then I'll pick up some groceries. Some beer. You want some wine?"

She realized she was exhausted. "I could use some wine."

"When you going to be home?"

"I've got some calls to make," she said, looking at the sheriff's number on her desk.

"Me, too. My folks. They're back in town."

"Already?"

"Dad's got a lot to do. Turns out getting ready to retire is hard work."

Jack's dad. Murphy remembered where she'd heard Ransom's name. "Are your folks home right now? At the house?"

"Yeah. Why?"

"We were at that Japanese restaurant. He mentioned a

woman in the English Department. She was going to be fired."

"Remember him saying something like that. Don't recall her name."

"Serene Ransom. She might be involved in a mess."

"What kind of mess? A police mess?"

"Don't call your dad right now. Let me call first. We can talk when I get home."

"Sure. Love you, babe."

She couldn't hear that enough. "Love you, too." She hung up. Turned and yelled to Castro, "I know how I know Ransom."

He got up from his desk and walked over to hers. Sat on the edge of it. Took a sip from the water cup in his hand. "You know everybody in this town. I suppose she's one of your one million relatives. She from the Irish gang or the Lebanese?"

"No. She's not a relative, but a relative knows her."

"Who is this relative?" He coughed and took another drink.

"Jack's dad. Douglas."

"How's Jack's old man know this woman?"

"He's head of the English Department at the U. She's a prof there. Would make sense that she dictates some flowery good-bye note."

"A poet."

"Not a very talented one, I guess. They're getting ready to fire her ass."

"No shit?" He polished off the water and crumpled the cup. "Maybe her weirdness is getting to the job, too."

"What would an academic type want with a bartender? A kid from up north with minimal education?"

"Could be all she wants from the kid is a fuck. Could be this whole deal is what Duncan said. A sex thing. The two morons fight over her in the bar. One moron ends up dead. The other ends up with the woman. Comes down here with her."

"Could be." She remembered Douglas had uttered something cryptic when Jack said he'd never met Ransom: *You'd remember her if you had.* Something told her Ransom wasn't a bystander in this affair. Murphy thought about the shootings and stabbings and fistfights she'd been called to as a uniform and a detective. When women were the prize, they were rarely blameless trophies standing on the side lines. The clever ones were good at manipulating. Instigating. A college professor—especially a beautiful one—would be in a league of her own.

Castro sniffled and slid off her desk. "I'll take St. Louis County. You give your relative a call."

"I'M sorry, Paris. It's an employee matter. I'd be violating university policy and breaking I don't know how many laws."

Murphy was disappointed in Douglas's response to her query, but not surprised. He followed the rules. Like his son. Unlike Jack, however, he was interested in her police work and might be persuaded to bend the rules to help her with one of her cases. She switched the phone to her left ear. "You can tell me something. What's the *official* word on why she's getting the boot?"

"Is this an *official* police investigation?" He was excited about the prospect. "What sort of trouble is she in? Doesn't involve young men, does it?"

Murphy thought that was a telling question. "Let's say it does."

"Wouldn't surprise me."

"She messed around with a student? Is that why she's being fired?"

Douglas didn't answer right away. Then: "It's one reason. One of many."

Murphy leaned back in her chair. "What kind of behavior are we talking about? Was it just once she did this?"

Douglas laughed dryly. "Once a month."

"Since when? How long has this been going on? With how many kids?"

He paused. "We don't know with any certainty."

She sat up in her seat. "Take a wild guess." She picked up a pen and flipped open a notebook.

He took a breath. Let it out. "It's been going on for years, we think. Possibly since she started here. How many lovers? Who knows?"

Murphy's jaw tightened. She scribbled in the notebook. Ransom sounded like a sexual predator. "How young are the students?"

"She seems to prefer freshmen."

"What's the age difference? How old is she now?"

"She acts as if she's over the hill. She's always pulling out compacts. Checking her face in the mirror. Running her fingers over her neck. The sort of behavior that makes her seem ancient. But she's around your age. Mid-to-late thirties."

Murphy tried to imagine sleeping with teenagers herself and shuddered. She switched the phone back to her right ear. "So she's messing around with boys half her age?"

"Yes."

Her hand tightened around the receiver. "And it's *one* of many reasons she's being fired? Not the main one?"

"You have to understand something, Paris. University policy doesn't say faculty members can't sleep with students. These are adults, after all. What the policy does do is warn against the abuse of power. Not so much an age thing as a rank thing. Bad idea to have someone who controls the grades sleeping with the person who needs the grades."

"So as long as the instructor doesn't have that student in her class, it's okay?"

"No. Even then it's strongly, strongly discouraged. If you have a moment, I'll read from the policy."

"Fine." She heard a file drawer open and close. Paper shuffling. She looked over at Castro. He was hanging up his phone. She wondered what he'd gotten out of the sheriff.

"Here it is. Under *Nepotism and Consensual Relationships.* Subdivision Three. *Relationships with Current Students.* And I quote: *Personal relationships between faculty members or advisors and their current students are very unwise and may violate other university policies, even when prohibited activities have been avoided, because of the trust accorded to faculty members and advisors by students, the power differential inherent in academic associations, the difficulty of making alternative arrangements for grading and evaluation, and the risk of real or perceived favoritism toward the student in the personal relationship and the potential harm to this student and other students.* That's it in a nutshell."

"Say a teacher screws around with a student regardless of the policy, and you find out. Then what?"

"As a department head, it would be my responsibility to send both of those involved—faculty member and student— to talk to the vice president of human resources."

"After that?"

"The instructor is warned that a sexual-harassment charge is possible. That the student could make such an accusation."

"That's it?"

"No. Then we create a 'work around.' We reconfigure the individuals' school relationship so that one is not overseeing the other's work." He paused. "This is of course difficult even in situations involving one affair."

"Let alone Professor Ransom's serial sleeping around."

"She's not a full professor, which brings us to the second cause for termination."

Castro came up to Murphy, folded his arms over his chest and leaned against the edge of her desk. He had a slip of paper in his mitts. "Go on," Murphy said into the phone.

"Off the record?"

"Off the record."

"Serene Ransom was full of promise when she landed on our doorstep out of graduate school. Master's and doctorate in English language and literature from Princeton University. Twenty-seven years old and on the tenure fast track. She published some solid work exploring the conflict between science and religion in late-eighteenth-century and early-nineteenth-century literature. Nothing wildly groundbreaking, but it added nicely to the work already out there. I've got one of her books on my kitchen table as we speak. *Romance or Reality? How the Divided Soul Pains the New Prometheus.* She blazed through the rank of assistant professor and, at the age of thirty-two, became an associate professor."

"How did she do socially?"

"Every man in the department and half of the women had a crush on her. She was beautiful and intelligent. When she walked into the faculty lounge, it was like driving an ice-cream truck past a playground. Ringing the bell. They followed her around with their tongues hanging out. But she didn't seem to care for close human contact. Refused to date anyone, male or female. Didn't attend even the most benign social functions. Faculty picnics. Holiday potlucks. Nothing. Didn't take long before the fascination with her evaporated." Douglas paused. Added: "Children know to stop chasing the ice-cream truck if the driver never stops."

"What was her problem?"

"She seemed one of those academics for whom the work is their life. Would always be their life. That's all well and good, as long as the work is flourishing. When the work goes to hell, you've got nothing left. A void."

Murphy couldn't believe how much Douglas was giving her. He'd obviously wanted to unload all this on someone. "What happened?"

"She stalled. Burned out. Hit a wall. She stopped publishing, and publishing is essential if you want to continue up the ladder. Make full professor. Publish or perish, the saying goes. Last school year we started receiving complaints about her classroom performance. She was late. Seemed disorganized. Even confused at times. About the same time the first student came forward, making noise about her advances. She'd tied his performance in the sack to his English grade. He thought he deserved better than a C on both counts. A second student knocked on my door. Another freshman. Word got out around campus that it was safe to tell. We had a line snaking from my office. Some cases were years old."

"She'd been having close human contact all along. Of the peach-fuzz variety."

Douglas: "That isn't the end of the story. Last month, shortly before winter break, she delivered a bizarre lecture to two hundred students. An introductory literature class."

"Bizarre?"

"She drew comparisons between the female quest for orgasms and the theme of pursuit between creator and creature in Mary Shelley's *Frankenstein*. Certainly sexual themes abound in *Frankenstein*. Victor Frankenstein's desire to penetrate the secrets of nature and all that. But Serene took it upon herself to model her thesis."

"How do you mean?"

Douglas: "She stripped."

Murphy blinked. "Whoa. She took off her clothes?" Castro's eyes widened. He unfolded his arms and got off the edge of her desk. Looked at her.

Douglas: "Yes."

Murphy: "All her clothes?"

"The 'full monty,' as they say."

Murphy looked up at Castro and raised her eyebrows. Wrote in the notebook. "When does she get the pink slip?"

"Friday. Spring semester is breathing down our necks. We tried to reach her earlier during break, but without success. She didn't answer her phone. We know she's home. Another faculty member drove by her house Monday and spotted her car. Stopped and knocked. She wouldn't open the door. He got an eyeful before she closed the drapes tighter. She was buck naked—and in the middle of the day. Probably there with another one of her freshmen."

"Did he hear anything unusual through the door?"

"The two of them laughing. God knows what she was doing with him. A private strip show perhaps."

Murphy wasn't ready to tell Douglas it wasn't one of Ransom's students getting the attention this time. "So how'd you reach her?"

"We sent her a letter informing her that she has a mandatory meeting in my office. Seven in the morning. We wanted the meeting early enough so there's no one around, in case she makes a scene."

"*We*? Is this a group firing?"

"I'll be in attendance, but my successor gets the honor of handing Professor Ransom her walking papers. You've probably met him at a cocktail party or some other to-do at our place. He lives right across the street. Kipp Henry. I told him getting rid of her will be his first official act as the new chair of the English Department."

"Tough duty. How will she take it?"

"If a homicide detective is asking about her, we're obviously the least of her problems. Can you tell me what sort of trouble she's in now?"

"I can't. Not yet. I promise I'll fill you in as soon as I get a handle on it myself. You've been terrific."

"Should I flag Kipp?"

"Don't know what you could tell him at this stage of the game. Let's wait on that. Go ahead with your meeting."

"Fine. How's your father, then? Jack said he's having surgery tomorrow."

"A procedure. Balloon angioplasty."

"We'll be thinking about him. May he have visitors?"

"Thanks for asking. Hold off awhile. I'll let you know." Castro passed a fax under Murphy's nose. She pulled it out of his fist. Ran her eyes over it. "Douglas. One more thing before I let you go. What was the title of that book again? The one on your kitchen table?"

"*Romance or Reality? How the Divided Soul Pains the New Prometheus.* Why?"

She wrote down the title. "Curious."

"Come see us."

"I will. Thanks again. Tell Helen I said hello."

"Will do."

Murphy hung up, dropped the pen and closed the notebook. Looked at Castro. "What did the sheriff have to say?"

Castro sat on the edge of her desk. Crossed his arms over his chest. Sniffled. "Locals didn't notice any hanky-panky going on between the kid and the woman that night in the bar. In fact, the kid's buddies thought she was weird. They're pretty sure the kid thought the same."

"So the sheriff doesn't think there's any romantic connection between the two of them?"

"I didn't say that." Castro coughed twice. Cleared his throat. "Sheriff thinks the kid is one of those guys who likes to go after older women. What do you call them?"

"Lothario?"

Castro frowned. "Never heard of the guy."

"Don Juan?"

"Isn't that a restaurant?"

"You're thinking of Don Pablo's."

"Oh, yeah. Good food. But that ain't it."

"Casanova?"

"No. Jeez. How many nicknames are there for horny gold diggers?"

"Gigolo?"

"There you go. One of those guys. Mister Iron Range Gigolo was screwing the bar owner. Maggie. She was letting him drive her truck. She gave him a break on the rent. Gave him furniture."

"So maybe he's sponging off this professor woman?"

"Could be."

Murphy tried to imagine someone taking advantage of Jack's mother. Couldn't conceive of it. "Wouldn't Ransom be too smart for that?"

"Sheriff said Clancy's a good actor. Said the kid was never charged in his dad's shooting even though there were problems with his story."

"Such as?"

"Such as the angle of the shot wasn't right for the sort of accidental firing the kid described. Why was the kid walking with the safety off in the first place, and with a bullet in the chamber? All the Clancy guys were experienced hunters, sheriff said. Knew better."

"Why didn't they charge then?"

"County attorney didn't believe it was intentional. The boy was so broken up. And his story was believable. Hunting accidents happen all the time, even with seasoned shooters. Blah, blah, blah. Sheriff said the biggest reason they let the kid off the hook is the whole town has a soft spot for him. He used to be a big hockey star. Could have taken his school to state."

"Could have?"

"He fell off the roof. The winter before the shooting. Fucked up his ankles." Castro unfolded his arms. "What did Jack's old man have to say about the hottie professor?"

"If Clancy is a gigolo, she's a cradle robber. She's been

screwing freshman boys. Stood in front of a class and whipped off her clothes as part of her English lecture."

"Never had an English teacher do that for me." Castro smiled. "Might have taken a greater interest in nouns and verbs and all that other shit."

"She gets her notice first thing Friday morning."

"Jack's dad is doing the firing?"

"Along with the prof who's taking over as head of the department."

Castro hopped off her desk. "I say we start watching the place. When she leaves her house to go to her meeting, we knock on the door. Grab the kid for questioning. Search the place."

"When should we start the surveillance?"

"Day before. No emergency. Cops up north still aren't sure what they're dealing with. Murder. Missing person. Plain old employee theft. Who knows?"

She looked outside the station windows. Still daylight. Snow was falling. "Let's have another quick meeting with the commander. Update him. Then I'm going to leave for home early. Swing by Ransom's house before it gets dark. Get a look at where she lives."

Castro coughed and cleared his throat. "Sounds like a plan."

She picked up the piece of paper he'd given her. "Can I keep this?"

"I don't give a shit." He turned and went back to his desk. "I'll grab my notes."

"Okay. Be right there." She looked at the fax from the sheriff's office one more time. Clancy's letter. Beautiful words rendered in sloppy script. One sentence stood out from the others. A flowery, romantic phrase: *My divided soul pains me.*

SEVENTEEN

HE WOKE LATE in the afternoon. Rolled off of the mattress. Stood by the side of the bed and yawned. Couldn't believe it was still Wednesday. Time was standing still inside the hothouse. While he ran his fingers through his hair, he studied her. She was passed out or asleep or both. She called it *napping.* On her back with the covers pulled up to her mouth. One leg sticking out and resting on top of the sheets. Gold hairs running down her thigh and knee and shin. Dotting her toes and the top of her foot. She shaved her armpits but he'd never before noticed she didn't do the same to her legs. He couldn't decide if she looked exotic at that moment, or old and ugly and hairy. The shadows in the room didn't help him with his decision. For a second, he thought she had a mustache, too. He raised his hand to flip on the bedside lamp, but stopped himself. Lowered his arm. He didn't want to rouse her. He enjoyed his waking moments without her, when he could be up and about by himself. He rubbed the back of his neck and bent his head side to side.

He was starting to sober up, and he didn't want to. He stepped over to his bag, crouched down, unzipped it and rummaged around. Took out some jeans and socks and boxers. A sweatshirt with the sleeves cut off. He stood and dressed while studying her nightstand. Contemplated finally snatching her journal off the top and reading what she'd been writing. Decided he was too tired to read. Words always exhausted him, and slogging through someone else's handwriting was even more work. Maybe later, he told himself. He hunkered down and felt over the pillowcase for the guns. He zipped the duffel shut and stood up. Paused and glanced over at Ransom. Still out. He went back down. Opened the bag. Reached inside the case and pulled out her gun. Zipped the duffel closed. Stood up and looked at the pistol in his hand. All his life guns had called to him. Followed him. As much as he tried to hate them or fear them or distance himself from them, they were always there. Presenting themselves to him with open, alluring mouths. Unwanted whores tagging after him. *Pick me, Catch. Take me. Use me.* Whenever the yearning tugged on him, he imagined a list of ways he could satisfy it. Drugs or a car or the water. Even a rope. Guns were never at the top of his wish list. Yet they kept appearing at the right time. Like now. He slipped the Ladysmith into the pocket of his jeans and told himself to be patient. Wait. Get something to eat. Think about it on a full stomach. Sometimes food crowded out the yearning.

He went down the hall and into the living room. Picked the remote off the coffee table, aimed and pushed Power. Flipped through the channels with one hand while scratching his crotch with the other. He stopped surfing when he got to *The Brady Bunch.* He sat on the edge of the coffee table. He'd seen the episode three times before. Greg and his football buddies steal a rival team's mascot, a goat named Raquel. Greg hides it in his room, and the other Brady kids think he's got a girl with him. A good episode.

He'd watch it a fourth time. He set the remote on the table and stood up. Went into the kitchen.

He surveyed the counter. He wouldn't touch the bowl of oranges and bananas and apples. Not with the cats licking it. One brushed against his calves and he kicked at it. "Get away from me." He spotted a bag of bread. He undid the twisty and reached inside. Pulled out a couple of slices to make a sandwich. Saw green fuzz on the crust. "Gross." He dropped the slices on the floor. "Here, kitty." He laughed to himself as two of the cats padded across the floor to sniff the moldy stuff. He pulled two more slices out of the bag and tossed them down. "Here. Go wild." He brushed his hands on his pants and went over to the refrigerator. Yanked it open. Saw a quart of skim milk. Wondered how anyone could drink that watery stuff. He grew up on whole. Carton of eggs. He was sick of eggs. A head of lettuce. A couple of Tupperware containers. He didn't want to mess with those. Whatever was inside was probably furrier than the bread. He spotted a package of individually wrapped American cheese slices on the middle shelf. He pulled out the cube and tucked it under his arm. An uncorked bottle of champagne sat on the top shelf and a corked bottle next to it. The way they'd been drinking, he was surprised there was any liquor left in the house. He wondered if the open one was flat. He picked it up by the neck. Almost full. He brought it to his mouth and chugged. Took the bottle from his lips and burped. Plenty of bubbles left. He tipped it back again. Another long drink. Shut the fridge and carried the bottle and the cheese into the living room.

Clancy sat on the couch with the bottle between his legs and the plastic package on his crotch. He decided to make a game out of finishing the wine and cheese. Took a drink and peeled open a slice every time someone said "Marcia." The champagne was done after four Marcias. The cheese made it to the tail end of the episode. He dropped the empty bottle on the floor and brushed the cheese wrappers off his

legs and onto the couch cushion next to him. That light
feeling was returning. Energized by a fresh drunk, he took
the remote off the coffee table, aimed it at Greg's head and
punched off the television. He dropped the remote back on
the table and stood up. Swayed and looked at the windows.
Cracks of light were seeping through the closed drapes. He
touched the hard profile of the gun pressing through his
pants pocket and felt the urge boiling in his gut. Churning
and rolling. He decided he wouldn't die in her dark house,
with her cats padding over his body. He could imagine
them licking his face. Lapping up his blood. He'd do it
while inhaling fresh air. Standing in front of an ice-covered
body of water. Frozen lakes seemed to have their own natural light. On the darkest nights, they shined like the surface of the moon. He'd do it as soon as the sun went down,
so he could enjoy the glow. Take that vision with him.

He pulled on his winter gear. Boots and jacket and gloves.
No hat. He wanted to feel the cold against his brain. He transferred her handgun from his pants pocket to the inside breast
pocket of his jacket. More comfortable and accessible. While
he dressed, he thought about how he'd go about it. Decided
he'd make a game out of it. Like the Marcia drinking game.
He'd do it after counting so many women. They all had to be
pretty like Marcia. All had to be visible before the sun went
down. Then he'd take it as a sign. A message from God. *Pull
the trigger, son. Do it.* How many women? Seven seemed a
good number. Six wouldn't do it. Six would send him back
to the house. He'd sneak inside. Put the gun back in his bag.
Never tell the Pink Lady he'd gone outside. Seven would be
another story. If seven pretty women crossed his line of sight
by sunset, he'd open his jacket. Slip it out of his pocket. Put
it in his mouth. Taste the metal. Pull the trigger. Die while
standing on the edge of the moon. Maybe he'd do it in front
of the last one. The seventh Marcia would have one hell of
a tale to tell when she went home that night.

EIGHTEEN

MURPHY SPIED HIM from the road. He was sitting on a bench, tossing slices of bread to the Canada geese. She pulled into the Como Lakeside Pavilion lot and parked. Shut off the Jeep. Pulled out the keys and dropped them in her purse. Fished out his photo and examined it to make sure. Definitely him. She stuffed the photo back in her purse and checked her Glock. Closed her purse. Pulled her cap snug over her head and her gloves tight over her fingers. Popped open the door and slid out. Shut the door and locked it. Stood next to the Jeep for a moment while she cooked up a ruse. She bent over and untied the laces of her boots. Stood straight and surveyed the area. Two other vehicles in the lot. A sedan covered with snow. Battery was probably dead. A station wagon with a light dusting on its windows. Probably belonged to someone who'd driven to the lake to walk or run around it. She spotted a trio of female joggers. They were using the path that followed the shoreline and snaked behind his bench. His head turned as he watched them go by. She headed for the path, looking up at the sky as she walked. Daylight was retreating and the snow was coming down steadily.

She left the path and stepped over to the bench. Looked at him and smiled. "Hey."

He looked up and nodded. Seemed disappointed to see her, like he was hoping she'd be someone else. "Hey." He threw another slice to the geese, making the bread fly like a Frisbee.

Murphy noticed he smelled like booze and his eyes were bloodshot. She sat down on the opposite end of the bench, to his right. She slipped her purse off her shoulder and set it on the bench to her right. Pressed it close to her thigh. She bent over to tie her left boot lace. "Don't let the geese police see you." She moved her hands to her right lace. "They'll ticket you."

He paused with another slice in his hand. "What?"

She sat up. "There's a ban on feeding."

"You gotta be shittin' me." He ripped the slice down the middle. Tossed one hunk to the right and the other to the left. A dozen birds chased after them before they hit the snow. "Why should they care?"

"They're trying to clean up the goose crap." She paused. Leaned back against the bench. "But you're right. Stupid rule."

"All right." He reached into the plastic and pulled out another slice. Handed it to her.

"Thanks." She took the bread. Broke off a piece the size of a quarter.

He tipped his head toward a sign along the shoreline, posted several yards from where they were sitting. "Is that what those orange things say? DON'T FEED THE GEESE. Can't read them from here."

"No." She tossed the piece of bread to a bird in front of her. "The feeding ban is a city thing. Those are DNR postings. They're aerating the lake and want people to stay off. Thin ice and open water."

His eyes locked on the lake. Narrowed. "Where is it exactly?"

"What?" She broke off another bit of bread.

"The thin ice. Open water."

"All over the place probably. Aeration or not, it's been such a bad year for the ice." She paused. Wanted to get him talking about home. His life. "Unless you're from up north. I guess the lakes up there are solid."

"Yeah," he said, staring at the lake. "I guess."

She tossed a triangle of bread to her left. A goose snatched it off the snow. "I've got a couple of these fellas in my freezer. They look a lot bigger with their feathers on."

He returned his attention to the waterfowl. Took a cue from her. Started breaking the bread into smaller pieces before tossing it. "Your husband a hunter?"

Murphy figured he'd find it easier to talk to an unattached woman. "No husband. We're split."

He tossed a corner of crust. Three waddled after it. "Sorry."

"That's okay." She paused. "He wasn't much of a shot anyway."

He laughed. "Sounds like you hunt, though."

"Every chance I get." She threw her last piece overhand and almost hit one of the birds in the head. "What about you?"

He took out another slice and handed it to her. "I used to hunt. Haven't been out in a while. Pheasant used to be my favorite. Pretty birds and good eating." He took the last piece—the heel—for himself. Dropped the bag on the bench between them. Nodded toward some geese at their feet. "What do you go after besides these guys?"

"Grouse. Pheasant. A little duck. I'm not a big duck eater. They say if you know how to prepare it, then it's good. Tried a bunch of different recipes. Wrapping it in bacon. Cooking it with apples and onions. Just don't like it. The texture or something."

"Know what you mean. Too much like liver." He tore a piece of bread off the slice and hurled it to the birds.

She ripped off a corner of crust and tossed it. "I try to go out deer hunting with my brothers once in a while. With my dad when he's feeling up to it." She paused. Waited to hear his reaction.

"Not a venison fan," he said in a low voice. He leaned forward and rested his elbows on his knees. Stared at the ground with the square of bread in his right hand. "And my dad's gone."

"I'm sorry."

"Thanks." He sat up and flung the remainder of the heel into the air. It landed in the middle of a circle of birds. They swarmed around the food.

She ripped off a piece of bread. Made it smaller than the last. She didn't want to run out too soon. She threw it to her right. "Was he big on hunting?"

"Big on hunting. Even bigger on hockey."

Two hikers went past, walking side by side on the path. Young women with long brown hair poking out from under their stocking caps. The one closest to the bench smiled at Clancy as he turned around and looked at them over his shoulder. "Hello."

He nodded back. "Hey." He followed their backs with his eyes.

Murphy watched him watching them. Clancy wasn't ogling them like a young man with an eye for the ladies. His brow was furrowed, and his mouth was turned down. He seemed depressed. Even a little fearful. What was he afraid of? She broke off another dot. Noticed it was moldy. "You skate?"

The hikers stopped at the station wagon. Got in. He

pulled his eyes off them and looked straight ahead. Studied the lake again. "Past tense. Busted up my ankles."

"Too bad." She threw the moldy dot to the right. A fat goose snapped it up.

He shrugged his shoulders. "That's how it goes."

She tried to think of something wise to say, and the only thing that came to mind was her mother's favorite in times of strife: "They say God only gives you as much as you can handle."

His back stiffened as he continued staring at the lake through the falling flakes. His angry words seemed directed at the frozen water. "The Lord must have a fucking high opinion of this boy. He's handed me a truckload of pretty shit over the years." He turned his head and looked at her. Lowered his voice. "Sorry. Shouldn't swear in front of a lady." His eyes dropped to the snow at their feet. "Besides, you don't know me. Don't need to hear my life story."

She felt bad for him. He was a screwed-up kid. She told herself that didn't make killing right. At the same time, she wondered: Is he really a killer, or was his father's death truly an accident? Was the bar shooting not what it appears? Had the woman who'd guided his letter writing also manipulated his trigger finger? Maybe if she brought up the subject of bars it would shake something loose. "My girlfriends wanted to meet me at a bar off the park. I'm not sure where it is. Can you give me directions?"

"I'm not from around here," he said distractedly. Clancy had returned his attention to the walking path. He unzipped his jacket. Reached inside with his right hand while turning his head to the left and then the right.

Murphy thought he looked as if he was waiting for someone in particular to come by. He had something for him. A surprise buried in his jacket. An unpleasant one. She wanted to draw him away from the path. "Did you notice a pay phone around here?"

Clancy didn't answer. Another jogger was headed their
way, coming from their right. He squinted like he was trying to see who it was. His hand started pulling something
out of his jacket. She gave him a sideways look. Was he carrying drugs? Money for drugs? The sawed-off shotgun
would never fit in a jacket pocket. Had he gotten his hands
on a pistol? Whom was he after? She picked up her purse
and set it on her lap. Opened it and put her hand inside
while watching Clancy's right arm and then his face. As
her fingers touched her Glock, his expression changed.
Softened as the jogger came into view. Her eyes followed
his gaze. The runner was an older man. Not a drug buyer or
dealer or quarry. She looked at Clancy's arm to make sure.
It seemed relaxed. He pulled his hand out of his jacket.
Nothing in his glove. She kept her hand in her purse, in case.
The jogger chugged past them.

Clancy turned back around and slouched back in the
bench. Zipped up his jacket to his chin and crossed his arms
over his chest. Stretched his legs out in front of him. Looked
out at the lake with a smile. "Looks like the surface of the
moon, don't it?" He uncrossed his arms, stood up, snatched
the bread bag off the bench and shook the crumbs onto the
snow. The geese had already waddled away. He headed for
a garbage can between the path and the bench. Lifted the lid
as another stroller came by. Seemingly out of nowhere. Another young woman. This one blond. He stared at her. She
smiled at him and kept walking. He dropped the lid back on
the can while the plastic slipped from his fingers and
floated down to the snow. He looked at Murphy sitting on
the bench. Said one word to her: "Seven." He turned and
headed for the lake.

Murphy took her hand off her gun. Closed her purse and
got up off the bench. Hiked her purse strap over her shoulder
and went after him. She didn't like the expression on his face.
A combination of surrender and sadness and determination.

The captain of a sinking ship watching the last lifeboat splash down without him. She thought back to what Castro had said about Enda Clancy. That *accidental* fall off the roof. A suicide attempt? "Stop," she said to his back. He stepped onto the ice and she followed. She could see a patch of open water yards in front of him. "You'll go through."

"That's the idea," he said over his shoulder. He kept going. Yelled and waved her away with his hand while he walked. "Go away, lady. I don't want to take you with me."

Murphy ran to try to catch up to him. She heard a crackle under her boots and stopped. Clancy was ten feet ahead of her. He had also stopped. She looked down at her feet. The smooth coating of snow was deceptive. Underneath it was corrupt, creaking ice. Her instincts told her to go down on her stomach and spread out the weight, but she couldn't talk to him while on her belly. Couldn't meet his eyes. Another crackle. She looked up and said to his back: "Don't take another step."

He looked up at the sky. "A few more feet and it's over." He was talking as much to God as to the woman behind him.

The sun had gone down. The snow was coming down heavier, and the wind had picked up. Streetlights speckled the road around the lake, but the glow of the lamps couldn't punch through the snowfall. Murphy wondered if anyone onshore could see the drama. She weighed pulling out her cell phone and summoning help. Turning her head and shouting for help. That could screw up the case. Worse, he could panic and run into the open water if squads and rigs showed up. If any new actors showed up. She'd seen it happen before with jumpers, and those were people who didn't have the additional burden of murder. Clancy had more reason than most suicidal people to flee from his saviors. She had more reason than most cops to rescue him.

She tried not to yell. Worked to speak in a voice loud enough to be heard, but low enough to sound reasonable:

"Whatever is going on with your life, this isn't the answer. Killing yourself isn't a solution."

He turned and squinted at her through the thickening curtain of white. Took a step toward her. "How do you know? You don't know me. You don't want to know me." He waved his arms around like a crazy man chasing away phantom crows. "Go away. Forget we ever talked. You never saw me." He turned back around and started walking again. Toward the open water.

She took a step toward him. Heard a creak but told herself to keep going in his direction. The ice had held him. She was lighter. It could hold her. She took another step. Heard another creak and felt it, too. A movement under her feet. Rocking and heaving. Up and down and up. She felt as if her legs were straddling the middle of a seesaw. She didn't want to look down. Couldn't let him leave her sight. She was his lifeline. What could she say that would stop him? Make him believe she gave a damn? What could a stranger offer him? She thought of one thing. The truth. "I saw someone commit suicide. Didn't stop it. Sort of caused it." She paused. "I did cause it. Encouraged it. I can't watch another one. I won't."

He stopped. Turned and looked at her. Flakes crusted his eyelashes. "What?"

She lifted her right foot and planted it a step closer to him. Lifted her left. Felt the ice under her right moving. She set her left foot back down. Stayed standing with her legs apart like a pair of scissors. "I knew this rich guy." She paused. The surgeon's case had been a big story. She tried to think of how she could word her confession to Clancy. She didn't want to reveal specifics that would tip him off and tell him that was the suicide she'd assisted. "You'd think money could solve anything, but it couldn't take care of his problems. His life was messed up. He couldn't see a way to fix it. I had a gun. He got his hands on it. I told him to go for it."

Clancy was taking an interest in her tale. He took a step toward her and another. Felt rocking under his feet. Looked down at his boots and up again. At her. "He kissed the gun right in front of you?"

Kissed the gun. What a horrible expression, she thought. It beautified suicide. Drained all the blood out of it. That's what Clancy was doing. Romanticizing the act. He probably thought he'd look down from heaven and watch his own funeral. That's how lots of people visualized their own deaths. Their life stories wouldn't end with a mess that needed to be cleaned up. The last chapter would take place in heaven. They'd be riding the clouds. "Don't try to make it sound so pretty. The rich guy didn't kiss shit. He blew his head off. Blood and bones and brains all over the wall and the floor."

Clancy's eyes widened. He didn't expect to hear the gruesome details. At the same time, he used her description of the shooting to rationalize his own plan. "I never really liked the idea of killing myself with a gun anyways. This will be better."

"How will it be better? It doesn't make a damn bit of difference how you off yourself. Dead is dead."

He looked down at the ice. Talked to the lake as if he had a business deal for it. A proposal. If only it would listen. Cooperate. Buy into the partnership. "I'll walk into a hole. Or maybe the ice will give way. Separate like a crack in the earth. I'll fall in. I won't splash around or yell. Shut my eyes and lie back and go down. I've heard drowning is like falling asleep. Especially drowning in cold water."

"Your family. Think about how heartbroken you'll leave them."

He was still staring down at the frozen water. His head was turning white from the snow. The stuff was coming down hard. "My family doesn't give a rat's ass. Not my mother. Not my sisters. I used to think Bo cared. Not anymore. He stopped calling months ago. Too busy, I guess. Or maybe I'm too much work. A lost cause."

She hoped getting him to talk about his closest sibling would snap him out of it. "Who's Bo?"

"My brother."

"I've got a bunch of brothers. They act like assholes most of the time, but that doesn't mean they don't love me. I'm sure Bo cares more than you realize. What's he like? Older or younger?"

"Older. Smarter. Better-looking. A better human being." He peeled his eyes off the ice. Glared at her. "You don't know me. I'm a bad person. You shouldn't even be out here with me. Go away."

He started to turn back around. She was afraid she'd lose him for good. "Stop. Please. I swear to God I'll follow you out there. Drown right along with you. Want that on your permanent record?"

He pivoted back around. "What do you care? This isn't your problem."

"Too late. We talked. I know you now."

"What do you know?" he snapped. "We shared a bench and a bag of bread."

She spoke quickly. She needed to get it all out before he turned around again. "You used to hunt birds, especially pheasant. You don't like duck or deer meat. You've got an older brother and a mother and sisters. You lost your father. You're from outside St. Paul."

He took two steps toward her. "Stop talking."

"You used to play hockey, but not anymore. You got hurt. You're kind of a renegade. A rule breaker. You like to feed the geese."

He took another step toward her. Lifted his hands. Covered his ears. "Stop."

She raised her voice, so he had to hear her through his gloves. "You're handsome and polite and friendly, but you've had a hard life. You think nobody cares, but they do."

"Stop it!" He took his hands down. Walked closer. Stood a yard from her. Two feet. A foot. Tears were running down his face. "Nobody cares! Nobody gives a shit!" He bobbed and rocked in front of her. Looked down. A popping noise.

Murphy reached for him. Locked her hands on his wrists. "Go slow. Glide." She slid backward while he skated forward. Awkward dance partners on the ice. She knew they'd have a better chance if they separated—the weight wouldn't be so concentrated—but she was afraid he'd turn and bolt to the open water. She decided to take a different way back. North of where they'd gone in. Farther from the aerator.

He was crying and hiccupping like a little kid, but he let her lead him. "I'm sorry."

"It's okay. Keep going." The back of her left boot bumped against a ridge. She stopped and held her breath. Wondered if she'd screwed up in the route she'd selected back to shore. Hoped her next step backward wouldn't be into a hole. She looked over her shoulder and down. Couldn't tell in the dark and through the falling snow. She exhaled and raised her right boot. Set it behind her, toes first. The ice was stable. She put the rest of her weight on it. She heard another pop.

He was looking down as they went. He whispered, as if the sound of his voice would make the sheet open up. "Leave me here. Go on. Do it. I'll make it back."

"No," she said. Her hold tightened around his wrists. "I know this lake. It's still over our heads here. But a few more feet and we're home free."

He chuckled low. Sniffled. "I thought you couldn't find your way around the neighborhood."

"So I lied. Sue me." She took another step backward.

He followed her. "Why did you lie? What were you trying to do?"

"Pick you up. Get in your pants."

His mouth dropped. He looked up at her. She was grinning. He laughed. "Wouldn't have minded. You *are* hot."

"I'm old enough to be your . . ."

"My what?"

She felt another ridge behind her right boot. Froze in her tracks. "Older sister."

They both felt the movement. Rocking and heaving. They stood still. A passerby would have mistaken them for two lovers holding hands on the ice. "Fuck," he breathed. "You think we can make it?"

She loosened her grip on his wrists. "I've got a cell in my purse. Let me use it before we end up in the water."

He pulled his wrists out of her hands. Locked his hands over her forearms. "No. Please. Don't call anyone. We can do this." He squeezed Murphy so hard it hurt her. "I have to get off this lake without anyone else knowing what happened. Got to be a secret. Our secret."

The bobbing stopped. "Fine. Forget the phone. Don't freak on me now." She lifted her right foot. Set it down behind her. Behind the ridge. Put her weight on it. "Okay. It's okay."

He skated toward her. Took a step. Skate. Step. "We're good. We're gonna make it." Skate. Step. He slipped and fell into her. Wrapped his arms around her shoulders. They heard a crack. He yanked her toward him and kissed her hard on the mouth.

She pulled her mouth off his. He tasted like sour wine. "What the hell are you doing?"

He untwined his arms. "I thought we were punching out. Had to kiss you good-bye."

Her turn to laugh. "You're a piece of work. What's your name?"

"Catch. Call me Catch." As if his name had the power to shatter, they heard a crack. They screamed as they went through. Two human torpedoes shooting through the surface.

NINETEEN

THEY STOOD WHERE they fell, in waist-high water. The cold was stunning. Neither one of them moved or talked for several seconds. "Jesus," he gasped.

Their heads and shoulders and chests were dry. Murphy's purse had fallen from her shoulder and was resting on a bobbing wedge to her right. The leather was dry. She reached out with her numb hand—their arms were soaked to the elbows—and grabbed the edge of the ice chunk. Pulled it toward her. Snatched her purse by the strap. Held it up and out of the water.

"Don't." He sounded breathless. "Don't call."

"I won't. We've got to get out before we pass out." She waded toward shore, to the edge of the hole they'd made. Tossed her purse ahead of her. Threw her arms over the top of the ice and tried to hop onto the surface. The edge cracked and separated. Made a bigger hole. He waded over to her, wrapped his arms around her midriff and lifted her up. Pushed her up onto the ice. She stayed on her belly. Wiggled over to her purse. Grabbed it with both hands. Pulled it toward her. Pivoted around and swung the strap into the hole. "Hold this. I'll pull you out."

"Son of a bitch it's cold." He locked both his fists around the strip of leather.

She got up on her knees. Prayed the ice wouldn't give way again. Clutched the purse with both hands and pulled as hard as she could while he walked his hands up the strap. He slid out. A big fish pulled out of a hole and dragged onto the ice. He stayed facedown on the ice with his arms stretched over his head and his hands still clutching the leather.

"Roll toward me," she said.

He moaned. "Fuck it's cold."

"Keep moving." She tugged on the strap to rouse him, and it slipped through his fingers. Came back to her. She looked over her shoulder, through the falling snow and the dark. Saw no one on the walking path or on the road beyond. The closest homes were better than a block away. She crawled to her feet with her purse still pressed to her chest. She stood for a moment, testing the ice. Solid. She couldn't feel her feet or her fingers. Realized her boots were waterlogged. She didn't think she could unlace them if she wanted to.

He got on his knees. Propped himself up with his left hand. Wrapped his right arm over his gut. "I'm gonna puke."

"No you're not." She skated over to him. Grabbed his shoulder with her left hand and pulled on his jacket. "Get up. Goddammit to hell, Catch. Stand the fuck up. Get off the ice before it goes again."

He laughed and then coughed. "You swear like a sailor, lady." He got on his feet. Stood for a moment. Swayed side to side. Folded. Went back down on his knees. "Let me take a breather."

She ran her eyes around the perimeter of the lake. Through the white curtain, she saw a red blur under the parking-lot lights. Her Jeep. She wrapped her arms around her purse and clutched it to her chest. Told herself to imagine it was a hot brick. She skated to the edge of the lake. Climbed over a snowbank and crunched through the snow. She wanted to run, but her legs and the clothes over them were starting to stiffen. All she could manage was a limping trot. She got to the driver's side. Shaking, she opened her purse and pulled out her keys. The keys and the purse fell from her fingers. She lifted her right glove to her mouth and bit down on the fingertips. She snapped her head back and yanked off the ice-coated leather. She spit out the glove. Shook her right hand until she could feel something. "Come on. Come on." She crouched down and picked up the keys. Shook off the snow. Scooped up her purse and cradled it in the crook of her left arm. Stood up and blew hot breath on her hands and her keys. Her leather jacket felt stiff from the waist down. She wished she could pull it off but told herself her body needed the insulation. With her thumb, she pushed the Unlock button on the remote attached to her key chain. She prayed it worked. She'd never bothered using the thing before, preferring her key instead. She transferred the keys to her left hand. Clawed on the door handle with her right hand and yanked. Still locked. She pressed the Unlock with her left thumb. Heard a *click*. She pulled on the handle again. The door opened. She hopped inside. Felt her pants and coat crackling with ice. She dropped her purse on her lap. Jammed the key into the ignition and turned. "Start. Please start." It turned over. "Thank you, God."

She reached for the door to close it and found she couldn't bend the fingers of her left hand. The other glove was rigid with a coating of ice. She brought the fingers to her mouth, pulled the leather off with her teeth and spat it out. It fell to the ground. She reached over and snagged the door handle. Pulled the door shut. Rested her head against the steering wheel for a moment. "Don't pass out. Don't fall asleep." She lifted her head up and reached into her purse. Thought she felt her phone, but wasn't sure. Pulled it out. Fumbled with the buttons. Wished she had voice dial. Frustrated, she dropped it back in her purse. "I don't need help." She dropped her purse on the floor of the passenger's side. Shoved the Jeep into Drive and rumbled over the snowbank. Pulled up to the edge of the lake and slammed on the brakes. Clancy had rolled onto his back and was sprawled with his arms straight out. A crucifixion on ice. "Dammit." She eyed the running path again. No one. Not a soul. She wasn't surprised. Only idiots would be out in this storm. She couldn't leave him there. He could get up and stumble back in a hole. Fall asleep and never wake up. She rammed the Jeep into Park and threw the door open. Jumped out and slammed the door shut. She remembered she had a blanket in the backseat. She pulled open the back passenger door and grabbed the blanket. Draped it over her shoulders and shut the door.

She alternated between sliding and walking to get to his side. Got down on her knees. Put her hands on his shoulders and shook him. "Don't you die on me."

He opened his eyes a crack. Blinked from the flakes falling into them. "Let me rest." He shut his eyes again.

She leaned over and hooked her right arm under his neck. Lifted his head. Brushed the snow from his eyebrows with her left hand. "Catch. I can't carry you. You've got to get up, or we're both going to freeze to death."

His eyes fluttered open. "Okay." They started to shut again.

She slipped her arm from his neck to behind his shoulders. "Do you have to be so big?" She heaved him into a sitting position.

His eyes popped open. He threw his left arm over her shoulders. "I'm okay."

They stood up together. He swayed backward. She

couldn't tell if it was from the booze or the cold. Decided it was a little of both. She steadied him with her arm. Pulled off her blanket. As she was draping it over his shoulders, she looked at his jacket and wondered about the bulge over his chest. Decided against asking about it or trying to take it away—whatever it was. Her most immediate worry was getting to land. The wind picked up and slammed into their backs. She shivered and wrapped one arm around his back. "Let's glide to the edge. Use some of those hockey skills." They stepped and slipped together. "What position did you play? Big guy like you. Bet you skated defense."

"Goalie. You know. *Catch*. Glove catches."

"Were you any good?"

His teeth started chattering. He pulled the blanket tighter around his body. "F . . . f . . . fuck yeah."

She felt movement under their boots. Held him back. "Stop." She eyed the surface in front of them. Couldn't see anything telling through the dark and the falling snow. Regardless, she steered him to the right. "This way."

He limped as they went. "God they h . . . hurt."

"Did you break something?"

"Ankles act up in this sh . . . shit."

"I'm sure the ice bath didn't help," she said. They got to shore. She let go of him after they stepped over a snowbank. Clancy had either sobered up or warmed up from the hike. He was still limping, but walked upright. Seemed in no danger of collapsing. They got to the Jeep. "N . . . n . . . nice wheels," he said, and leaned against the side with both hands.

She stepped up to the driver's door. Her teeth started chattering; she willed her jaw to stop vibrating. "Get in," she said. He dropped his hands from the side of the Jeep but didn't move to open the door. Stood like a statue. "Jesus Christ," she said. She went around to his side, yanked open the passenger door. Held it open while he crawled in. She slammed the door and went back to the driver's side. Pulled open the door and got in and shut it. She held up her hands. Flexed them. Her skin looked blue and red at the same time. She reached over and turned up the heat. Held her hands in front of the dashboard fan. Her heater was kicking in; the air coming out of the vent felt like a blast from a furnace. She took her hands down and glanced over at her passenger. The blanket had fallen off his shoulders and was crunched behind his back. His chest and shoulders and head seemed dry except for a dusting of snow. His jeans and gloves were crusty with ice. She tipped her head toward his hands. "Pull those off and put your hands in front of the heater."

He peeled off his gloves and dropped them onto his lap. Leaned forward and held his hands in front of the blowing vent. His skin was red. He took his hands down and put his face in front of it. Shut his eyes. His teeth stopped chattering. "That feels good." He opened his eyes and leaned back in the seat.

She reached over and pulled the blanket from behind his back. Threw it in a heap over his thighs. "Wrap it around you."

He unfurled the blanket and draped it over his front. Held it up to his chin. He stared straight ahead. Avoided meeting her eyes. Said in a low voice, "Sorry I'm so helpless."

She put it in Drive and steered out of the parking lot. "Want to talk about what happened?"

He poked his right hand out from under the blanket and held it in front of the vent. He lowered his eyes to the dashboard. "No."

"Maybe I should take you to the hospital. Have you checked out for frostbite. Have those legs looked at."

"Doctors can't do shit for my ankles. Home. If you could take me home."

"Where do you live? Is there someone there? Don't want to leave you there alone."

He pulled his hand away from the fan and tucked it back under the blanket. "In case I try to off myself again?"

"In case you start getting sick."

He looked outside the passenger window. "Yeah. There's someone home."

She stopped at an intersection. "Tell me where to turn."

"Here," he said. "Hang a right."

After a few more turns—the dazed Clancy led them down the wrong street at one point—they pulled up in front of Ransom's house. The both of them were still wet, but warmer. Murphy wished she didn't have to leave the snug Jeep, but she saw a chance to snoop around Ransom's house. "I think I'd better walk you inside."

"No," he said quickly. "I'm fine."

Murphy punched on the interior light. Turned her head and studied his face. His skin looked gray, and he had dark smudges under his eyes. "You look like shit." She put the back of her hand on his forehead.

He let go of the blanket. Reached up and wrapped his fingers around her hand. Took her hand down and brought it to his lips. He kissed her open palm. She pulled her hand away. He looked over at her with wide eyes. "Did that make you nervous?"

"Yes," she said.

He smiled and kept his eyes locked on her face. "I'd love to make love to you. The woman I'm staying with, I'm not making love to her. I'm fucking her. But you. I could really go for you." He put his left hand on her right thigh. He started shivering again and his teeth resumed their chattering.

She pushed his hand off her leg. Reached over and shut off the Jeep. Pulled the keys out of the ignition. Dropped them in her purse. "I think you're delirious. I'm walking you inside."

"F . . . f . . . fine." He put his hand on the passenger's door and popped it open. "You c . . . can meet the scary

b . . . b . . . bitch." He dropped the blanket onto the floor
and stepped out of the Jeep. Slammed the door hard.

Murphy opened her door and got out. Grabbed her purse
and hiked the strap over her shoulder. Shut the door and
went around to the sidewalk where Clancy was standing
and shivering. The snow was still coming down hard. A
gust of wind chilled her wet legs. She tipped her head
toward the house. "This it? Don't see any lights on inside."

"She likes it d . . . dark," he said tiredly. He went ahead
of her, walking stiffly. A tin man.

Murphy followed him, holding her coat tight around her
body. "We're going to scare the hell out of her, walking in
wet like this."

He walked up the front steps and stood in front of the
door. Said to Murphy without turning around. "She's p . . .
probably still asleep. N . . . napping. We both n . . . nap a
lot." He pushed the door open and stumbled inside.

Murphy was on his heels. She inhaled sharply as soon as
she stepped through the doorway. The sight of all the cats.
The odor of kitty litter and booze. No wonder they nap all
the time, she thought. They were drunks. Murphy turned
and closed the door. When she spun back around, she saw a
blond woman standing on the other side of the living room.

TWENTY

PINK SLACKS. PINK jacket pulled over a pink sweater. Pink scarf curled around her neck. Pink gloves pulled over her hands. Murphy thought Ransom looked like an Easter bunny. The only things that weren't pink were her boots. White Sorels trimmed with white fur. An Easter bunny dressed for winter.

"Who are you?" snapped Ransom.

The woman's words startled Murphy more than the smells and the cats and the pink. Ransom's voice sounded as if it had been transplanted from someone else's body. A child's body. "We had a little accident," said Murphy.

"Accident?" Ransom continued glaring at Murphy from across the room, but addressed the next question to Clancy. "Where have you been, Catch? I was about to get in the truck and go looking for you."

Clancy limped across the room and sat on the couch. Kicked off his boots. "Went for a walk. Fell in. This lady pulled me out." He lifted his right foot. Crossed it over his left knee. Peeled off his right sock and dropped it on the floor. Set his right foot down on the floor with a groan.

Ransom took her eyes off Murphy and locked them onto Clancy. Pulled off her gloves and stuffed them in the pockets of her jacket. "You're lying."

The bunny has sharp teeth, thought Murphy. She took two steps into the living room. "He's telling the truth. Look at us."

Ransom's eyes went from Clancy to Murphy. Back to Clancy. He had his left foot across his right knee and was yanking off the sock. He held it up. Dripping. He dropped it on the floor.

Ransom: "You're soaked."

"No shit." Clancy coughed. Brought both his feet up onto the couch and curled into a ball on his side. Rested his head on a throw pillow.

Ransom took off her coat and threw it over the back of a chair. "I'm sorry I didn't believe you at first. He's such a . . ." Her voice trailed off.

"Such a what?" Clancy pulled down a knitted afghan that was on the back of the couch and gathered it around him. "Come on. Let's hear it."

Ransom frowned. Unraveled her scarf and tossed it on top of the jacket. "Never mind, my love."

My love. These two aren't lovebirds, thought Murphy. How had Clancy put it? *I'm not making love to her. I'm fucking her.* A stranger could see they couldn't get along. What was tying them to each other? Murder? Murphy decided she had to spend some time in the stinky cat house. She started to unbutton her coat. "I've got to get this thing off for a while. Feels like a lead weight around me."

Ransom crossed the living room and went over to Murphy. Stretched out her hands. "Let me take it."

Murphy unbuttoned the last button and hesitated. She mentally inventoried her pockets. Anything inside that would reveal she was a cop? No. Her badge and gun and identification were in her purse. The only things in her coat were Kleenex and Chap Stick. Murphy set her purse at her feet and pulled off the coat. Handed it to Ransom. Realized for the first time the woman was about as tall as she. "Thank you."

Ransom looked down at Murphy's jeans. "Want a pair of sweats?"

Murphy picked up her purse and tucked it under her right arm. "No. If you could let me warm up for a few minutes. Pull off these boots and socks."

Ransom nodded. Pointed to a chair on one side of the couch. "Sit."

"I don't want to get your furniture wet."

"Pull that blanket off the arm and tuck it under you. Around your legs." She looked over at Clancy curled up on her couch. "He doesn't give a damn about my house. Why should you?"

Murphy walked over to the chair. Flowery like the couch and the throw pillows and the drapes. She took the blanket off the arm. Shook it out. More flowers. She draped it over the cushion. Sat down. Wedged her purse in the seat next to her. "Thank you."

Ransom held the wet coat in front of her face. "Leather. I'll try to dry it out a bit. But I'm sure it's ruined."

"It'll get me home." Murphy kicked off her boots.

Ransom laid the coat over a radiator. "Do you live close? I don't recognize you from the neighborhood."

"I live downtown." Murphy bent over and pulled off her socks. Dropped them in a heap on the floor. Sat up. Folded the ends of the blanket over her legs. Sat with her hands resting on top of the wrap.

Ransom paused. Looked pointedly at Murphy's left hand. "Need to call anyone? Tell them you're on the way home?"

"I'm divorced." Murphy twisted her wedding band back

and forth with the fingers of her right hand. "Haven't been able to give up the ring. Security blanket I guess."

Ransom nodded and flashed a tight smile at Murphy. "Want me to take your hat, too?"

Murphy had forgotten she had one on. She reached up and pulled it off. Dropped it in her lap. Ran her hand through her hair. Brushed her bangs with her fingertips. "That's okay. Hat's dry. We fell in up to our waists."

Ransom stared at Murphy for a moment. Eyed her hair. Her face. Didn't like what she saw. Too beautiful. She looked over at Clancy. "Catch, my love. How did you end up going for a walk on the lake? Who would do such a thing?"

"A dummy would," he said into the pillow. A cat sprang from the floor onto the couch and padded across Clancy's legs. He kicked at it through the blankets, and it jumped off.

Ransom walked over to Clancy. Sat on the edge of the couch near his head. Combed his curls with her fingers. "Shall I run you a bath?"

"Later," he breathed into the pillow.

Ransom rubbed the back of his neck. "You should get out of those wet things. At least take off the jacket."

"In a minute," he muttered.

Murphy watched Ransom touching him. Her movements were mechanical. Phony. She was putting on a show for her female visitor and maybe for Clancy, too. Ransom felt threatened by the presence of another woman in her house. She didn't even want to know her guest's name. She just wanted her out. Murphy knew the type. Other females were the enemy at the office and in social settings. Men were an opportunity to score—or an obstacle to advancing—in either venue. Ransom had no close friends. No gal pals. No male confidants. She had cats.

Murphy wanted to stretch out the visit. "I don't suppose I could trouble you for some tea."

Ransom got up off the couch. Flashed Murphy that tight

smile again. "Let me get the both of you something hot to drink." Her smile flattened as she added, "You can fill me in on the details. Tell me how this happened exactly. Then I'm sure you'll want to be on your way." She turned on her heel and went into the kitchen through a swinging door.

Clancy moaned under his cover.

Murphy: "You all right?"

"I'll live," he said into the pillow. He sat up and shrugged the blanket onto the floor at his feet. He shuffled his seat to the end of the couch closest to Murphy. He tipped his head toward her and said in a low voice: "Stinks in here, don't it?"

"Yeah."

"Ever seen so many cats under one roof?"

Murphy: "I'm a dog person myself."

He leaned closer to her. Whispered: "She's a regular head case. A nut."

Murphy looked toward the kitchen. Heard pots banging and the woman clomping around in her boots. Murphy looked back at Clancy. Bent her head toward him and asked in a low voice, "Why are you staying with her then?"

"Long story. Can't get into it right now."

"She holding something over you? Owe her money? What?"

The muscles in his neck tightened. He said in a louder voice, "Pink Lady doesn't have dick over my head. I've got stuff on *her*."

Murphy wondered how much of that was true. Had the woman instigated the mess that went down in the bar, whatever it was? Had she done more than help Clancy pen a good-bye note? Murphy had to ask, even though she knew he wouldn't give her the entire story. "What kind of stuff? What did she do? She in some sort of trouble?"

He lowered his voice again. "Damn right." He looked toward the kitchen door and back at Murphy. "Big trouble."

"How serious? She commit a crime? If she did and

you're hanging out with her, you could get nailed by the cops. You'd be what they call an *accessory* to the crime."

"You sound like someone who's had her own problems with the law. It have anything to do with that suicide you told me about out on the ice?" He grinned and reached over. Tucked a strand of her hair behind her ear. "Or was that a bunch of crap you made up to get me interested? What's your name, anyways? Bet it's something hot." The kitchen door swung open, and he withdrew his hand.

Ransom walked into the living room carrying a clear glass coffee mug in each hand. The liquid was copper colored and steaming. As Ransom got closer, Murphy could smell the whiskey. Ransom looked at Clancy sitting up, planted on the end of the couch closest to Murphy. She didn't like it. "You're better," she said, and handed him the drink. He took it. She handed the other to her female visitor.

"Thank you," said Murphy. She raised the cup and inhaled the steam. The alcohol was so strong it stung her nostrils.

Ransom sat down on the couch next to Clancy. Bent over and pulled off her boots. Sat up and rested a palm on his leg. Rubbed his thigh up and down and up again. Nearly to his crotch. "Now tell me what happened out there on the lake, my love."

Clancy ignored her hand. Blew on his drink, sipped and set it on the coffee table. "Told you, Serene. Went for a walk. Broke through. This lady was walking by. Saw me. Tried to help. She went through."

"How did you two get out?" She looked over at Murphy. Asked dryly: "Swim to shore?"

Clancy picked up his drink and held it between his palms. "I boosted her up onto the ice. She lay on her stomach. Tossed me her purse strap and pulled me out of the hole."

Ransom took her hand off his thigh. Crossed her right knee over her left. Folded her hands together and rested them on her right thigh. The tight smile snapped into place. "You must be very strong. What do you do for a living? Some kind of physical labor?"

"Sort of." Murphy decided to come up with a job that would rattle Ransom. "I'm a masseuse."

Clancy grinned. "Cool. My brother does the same thing. At a chiropractors' office. I'd never let my own bro do me, but I wouldn't mind a back rub from you."

Murphy smiled at Clancy. "Maybe later. After my hands warm up." She lifted the mug to her lips and blew on it. She didn't trust Ransom enough to sip. She lowered the cup. Looked past Clancy at Ransom. "What do you do, Serena?"

Ransom uncrossed her legs. "Serene."

Murphy knew that would bug her. "Sorry. Serene."

Ransom sat straighter in her seat. "I'm a professor of English."

Murphy wanted to take another jab. The woman sounded like a snob. "An English teacher. How nice. Elementary school? Junior high? Or the big kids?"

Ransom crossed her arms over her chest. "Very big kids. At the University of Minnesota."

Clancy: "Sounds boring, don't it?" He stood up. Headed for the hallway. "I'm gonna get out of this stuff."

Ransom glared at his back as he went. "Don't sit on the bed with those wet pants." She uncrossed her arms. Looked at Murphy. "Why don't I get you some dry socks, and then you can be on your way."

Murphy reached over and set her cup down on the coffee table. Dropped her hat on the floor next to her wet socks. Peeled the edge of the blanket off her legs and stood up with her purse. Hiked the strap over her shoulder. "Mind if I use your rest room before I leave?"

Ransom stood up. "This way." She walked ahead of Murphy, across the living room to the hallway. She pointed to an open door. "Help yourself." Ransom kept going.

Headed for the bedroom. Clancy had shut the door behind him. Ransom turned the knob. Locked. She knocked. "My love. It's me. Open up."

My love, thought Murphy. Never heard of lovebirds locking each other out of the bedroom. Murphy stepped inside the bathroom and gasped. Instinctively put her hand over her mouth. With her other hand, felt for the light switch against the wall. Flipped it on. She ran her eyes around the room and spotted the source of the odor. A litter box tucked into a corner. A Persian brushed against the back of her legs, and she started. The animal padded over to the box, stepped into it and squatted. "Yuck," Murphy said, and turned her head. She waited until the cat finished its business and scooted into the hallway. Murphy shut the door and locked it. Breathed through her mouth while looking around the room. She wondered if Ransom had genuine mental-health problems. If so, she'd probably have medication. Murphy flushed the toilet and turned on the bathroom tap. While the water ran, she opened the medicine cabinet over the sink. Aspirin. Cold meds. Mouthwash. Toothpaste. Birth-control pills. Otherwise no prescription meds. She shut the cabinet. Opened and closed the vanity drawers and cabinet. Tons of makeup. Brushes. Tampons. Perfumes and colognes. Toilet-paper rolls. She closed the last drawer. Shut off the water. Heard a knock at the door.

Ransom: "I have some socks."

Murphy unlocked the door and opened it. Stepped through the doorway and took the socks from Ransom. "Appreciate it." Murphy paused outside the bathroom. Wanted an excuse to see the rest of the house. At least the bedroom. She glanced up and down the hall. Floral paper on the walls and the ceiling. Murphy turned toward the bedroom. The door was open. "You've got a wonderful eye for decorating."

Ransom stepped in front of her. Blocked her way.

"Thank you." She motioned toward the other end of the hall with her hand. "This way."

Murphy pivoted around and walked ahead of Ransom into the living room. Clancy was in the kitchen. Murphy heard cupboards opening and closing. She sat on the edge of the chair. Dropped her purse on the floor. Put her right foot over her left knee. Pulled on a sock. Noticed it was pink. "Thank you. This feels so much warmer."

"You're quite welcome. I appreciate everything you did for my boy."

My boy. Condescending and creepy, thought Murphy. She set her right foot down. Put her left foot over her right knee and pulled on the other sock. Noticed the pink was covered with cat hair. "You two make a very attractive couple. It's obvious he's very devoted to you." Murphy set her left foot down. Looked up.

Ransom was standing over her with her hands on her hips. "I'll get your wrap." She went over to the radiator and pulled off the coat. Held it up with one hand and felt the hem with the other. "A little dryer. Like you said, it should get you home."

Murphy pulled on her boots. Picked her hat up off the floor. Tugged it over her head. Stood up. Ransom was standing in front of her, holding out the coat. "Thanks." Murphy took it and pulled it on.

"Your socks," said Ransom.

She's in a big hurry to kick me out, thought Murphy. She picked her socks and purse up off the floor. Stood up. Shoved the socks in her coat pocket and threw her purse strap over her shoulder. Buttoned the coat up to her chin. Shoved her hands in her pockets.

Ransom ran her eyes around the room. "Did you bring gloves?"

"Lost them in all the commotion."

Ransom's eyes narrowed. "He really did fall in, didn't he?"

Murphy blinked. "Yes. What did you think happened?"

The kitchen door swung open, and Clancy walked through. He was dressed in sweats. Carrying a plate stacked with sandwiches. He set the platter on the coffee table. "Don't go yet. Made us something to eat."

If Murphy didn't trust Ransom enough to take a drink from her, she sure as hell didn't trust her boyfriend enough to take a sandwich from him. "No thank you. I really have to go." She headed for the door with Ransom at her heels. She pulled open the door and stepped outside. Turned around to thank Ransom one more time. The door slammed in her face.

AFTER Clancy's rescuer left, Ransom poured each of them a tall whiskey. She took her booze into the bedroom. Shut the door behind her. Clancy guzzled his while sitting in front of the television. A *Star Trek* episode. When the drink and the sandwiches and the show were done, Clancy punched off the set and flipped off the lights and limped to the bedroom. The door was shut. He jiggled the knob. Locked. "How do you like it?" she said from the other side of the door.

He couldn't crash on the couch. He was sore all over, and a night on her fluffy furniture would make him feel worse. "I didn't want her walking in on me."

"Bullshit," she hissed. "You were trying to embarrass me in front of Florence Nightingale."

He rested his forehead against the door. "Who?"

Silence on the other side of the door. Then a snicker. The door popped open. She stood in front of him, naked. "You're a goof," she said. She wrapped her hand around his wrist and pulled him into the bedroom.

He went to his side of the bed. Stripped. Slipped naked between the covers. Collapsed on his back. She crawled be-

tween the sheets and rolled close to him. Ran her foot up
and down his leg. "Your skin is still like ice." She slid out of
bed. "I'll get you another whiskey."

"More whiskey would be good," he said. She left the
room. He put his hands behind his head, shut his eyes and
sighed. He was grateful she hadn't questioned him further.
He didn't want to tell her why he'd really locked the door;
he was putting the gun away. Miraculously, the Ladysmith
had stayed dry. He vowed not to take it out again. The temp-
tation to go through with it had been too great. He opened
his eyes and took his hands down. Rolled onto his side.
Pulled one of the pillows from under his head and held it in
front of him. Curled his body around it. Closed his eyes
again. Thought about what had taken place earlier that
night. How it could have ended with him shot in the head
on a park bench, or at the bottom of the lake. He thought
about the dark-haired woman. He wished she was the one
carrying a whiskey to his side. Naked.

JACK was taking a nap on the living-room couch when
Murphy finally got home. He woke when he heard the shower
running upstairs. Fell back asleep until Murphy roused him
for a late dinner. While she was cooking, Castro called. Asked
how her drive-by went. Had she observed anything weird in
front of the Ransom house? Did they have to start the surveillance immediately? She told him it could wait until morning. The snow was coming down hard. No one was moving.
She hung up without telling him that she'd gotten inside
Ransom's house. She wanted to talk to him about it in person. She'd have to tell Jack at some point, too. If he found
out some other way, he'd be furious. Both men would think
she was reckless for going inside a killer's home alone. What
would Castro and Jack think about how she'd saved Clancy?
She could never tell them why she was compelled to act.

TWENTY-ONE

THREE IN THE morning and rest again eludes me. My boy sprawls next to me; I envy his drunken coma. No amount of whiskey can dilute my fury. It interrupts my sleep like a thunderstorm. I've been summoned to the Star Chamber. I received the notice yesterday. I won't even have the dignity of being beheaded by the king in private; his heir apparent will be present. I cannot let this happen. Will not. Friday will be a fateful day. My boy shall repay me for the attentions I've lavished upon him. I will not ask for much; time is all I require. I need to delay this inquisition so that I may pull my defenses together. I am not so foolish as to trust my boy, so I shall accompany him on this errand.

My boy. Devious devil. Cruel. I hate the way he treats my babies. Mean and dismissive. His morbid fascination with death is disturbing. And those eggs! Thinking back, I now know what he was trying to do. Poison me. I won't let him touch the food again. This incident with the woman. I have no idea what really happened out on that ice. But I

*must lean on someone. I am running out of friends. All the
while, I hear the scratching in my closets. In the walls.
Scratching. Scratching. Scratching. Something is trying to
get at me. Claw out my eyes. My heart. Soon all I will have
left to protect me are my babies.*

SHE tucked the pen into the crack of the book and
snapped the journal shut. Set it on her nightstand. She
reached over to turn off the lamp and paused with her hand
on the switch. She held her breath. Strained to listen.
Looked at the closet. Locked tight. Good. She clicked off
the lamp and fell back against her pillow. Pulled the covers
up to her chin and shut her eyes. She flipped from one side
to the other and on her back. Couldn't sleep. She opened her
eyes and slid out of bed. Walked out of the bedroom, closing
the door behind her. Padded down the hall, brushing past
two cats as she went. She went into the bathroom, closed
the door, turned the lock and flipped on the light. Looked at
her reflection in the medicine-cabinet mirror. "I look like an
ancient hag," she muttered. A pair of frosted-glass sconces—
one on each side of the cabinet—illuminated the bathroom.
Each light fixture contained three bulbs. She reached over
and unscrewed one bulb from each sconce. Tossed them in
the wastebasket. She looked in the mirror again. Better. She
went over to the tub. Plugged the drain and turned on the tap.
Felt the water. She didn't want it too hot. Hot water dried
out the skin. At the same time, she'd heard warm, moist air
in a house preserved the flesh. She adjusted the tap temper-
ature. Lukewarm. She reached over to a wire basket hanging from the far side of the tub. Grabbed the bath oil with
vitamin E. Squirted a golden stream of the stuff into the
water and swished it around with her hand. She put the bottle back and stepped into the tub. Lowered her body into the
water. Pulled another bottle off the basket. Another greasy

concoction that promised to restore youth. She poured a
puddle into her hand, put the bottle back. Rubbed the oil into
her knees and elbows, where her skin felt like sandpaper.
Another sign of age. Soon the boys would lose interest. She
had no desire to go after the men. They wanted too much
from her. She didn't seek female friends. They expected her
to open up. Tell them things.

She knew her inability to socialize hurt her at the university. She didn't care. She felt like an outsider among them.
A skinny girl with no coins trapped in a candy store filled
with rich cherubs. They had normal families. No mental
illness in their backgrounds. No odd parents with bizarre
religions. Her mother and father. Last she'd heard, they'd
moved down south to start a church. Same goofy religion,
warmer climate. They'd sent her a postcard, and she'd thrown
it away. She never wanted to see them again. The older she
got, the more clearly she was able to analyze the past. See
they were completely responsible for the death of her
brother. Beloved brother she saw in every boy who shared
her bed. She bent forward and shut off the tap. Leaned
against the back of the tub. Thought about him. Each day,
her memory of Ezekiel grew less distinct. Lost its sharp-
ness and color. His bright blue eyes faded to the color of
the winter sky. His yellow hair dulled. Turned to wheat. A
fragile watercolor portrait left out in the sun. She had no
photos of him. Her parents had never bothered with photos.
They were the trappings of an ordinary life. The ordinary
life she and her brother would have devoured. She shut her
eyes and tried to see his face. Reached up and kneaded her
breasts with her hand. The right breast first, then the left.
Smooth and slippery from the oil in the water and on her
hands. Ezekiel had died before ever having sex. She rea-
soned she was somehow helping her dead brother discard
his virginity by sleeping with all those inexperienced youths.
She rubbed her nipples with the palm of her hand. The left

nipple, then the right. Her nipples hardened. She rolled each of them between her thumb and forefinger. That's what she was doing, she told herself. Helping her poor brother.

She spent nearly an hour in the tub. Uncorked the drain and stood up. Decided not to rinse off. Her skin needed the oils. She toweled off and went back to bed. Slipped between the sheets. She turned her head toward his breathing. Rhythmic inhaling and exhaling. He was still asleep. She wondered what Catch would think if he knew she imagined making love to her brother while he was on top of her. Inside of her. While all her boys were with her. She smiled and shut her eyes. Finally nodded off.

Two cats padding over his naked body woke him. He brushed them off his chest. They thumped onto the floor. He sat up on one elbow. He clicked on the lamp next to his bedside. Looked over at Ransom. Asleep. Buried in covers, even in this sauna. Last night he'd been grateful for the heat. With morning, he was back to hating it. He eyed the clock on her side of the bed. Nearly seven. Early still. He eased back against the mattress and put his hands behind his head. Shut his eyes. Struggled to remember what day it was. Thursday, he thought. He had a headache. A dull ache that stretched in a band across his forehead. Champagne and whiskey. He'd never drink both of those in the same twenty-four-hour period again. Beer and whiskey never gave him a headache.

He swallowed twice. The inside of his mouth tasted bad. Worse than his usual morning breath. What was that taste? Whiskey? No. Tobacco and kitty litter? His body was absorbing her house smells. He felt something in back of his throat. Worked it to the front of his mouth. Picked it off his tongue with his fingertips. Opened his eyes and looked at it. Long and yellow. He couldn't tell if it was cat fur or human hair. Either way it disgusted him. He flicked it onto the floor. Saw more cats slinking around the bedroom. Lay on

his side and counted them. Six. Six in the bedroom alone.
More were undoubtedly in the kitchen. Jumping up on the
counter. Licking the fruit. Sending more fur floating into
the air. He wondered how much cat hair he'd swallowed
since he walked through her door. He'd be crapping the
stuff out. Fur balls coming out of his ass.

Every time he thought about leaving, however, he suddenly felt tired and lazy. Drunk almost. A deeper drunk
than the one he'd been floating in and out of since Sunday.
He'd never been spoiled like this before. Allowed—no,
encouraged—to sleep until noon. Served booze until he
had to put his hand over the glass and say "enough." Sex
whenever he wanted it, and he always wanted it. She talked
about buying groceries, but hadn't asked him to kick in.
Good thing, too. He didn't have a dime on him. Maggie had
been much more demanding. Dragged him out of bed to
mop the bar floor, paint the front door before the place
opened for the day. Then pouring drinks all night. Maggie
was stingier with the sex, too. That had been fine with him.
Maggie hadn't been much to look at, especially without her
makeup. First thing in the morning, she looked tired and old.

He rolled onto his other side and looked at Ransom.
Sometimes she looked beautiful to him. Young, too. Other
times she looked as old as Maggie. Funny how women
could change like that. Look good one minute and bad the
next. Chameleons with tits. He rolled back around, reached
over and clicked off the lamp. Threw his legs over the side
of the bed and sat up. A cat brushed against his shins.
Stepped on his feet. "Get away." He kicked at it and stood
up. Felt pain in his ankles. Probably from that dip in the
lake. A strange trip he would never discuss in detail with
the Pink Lady or anyone else. That woman who'd helped
him off the surface of the moon. A real beauty. Not like
Ransom, who seemed to change with the light. After sleeping on it, he didn't know if he appreciated what she'd done

for him or hated it. The sense of relief and purpose he'd felt
as he'd walked toward the open water was unlike anything
he'd ever felt before. Looking back, he'd even enjoyed the
intense panic when they'd fallen through. A roller-coaster
ride. He told himself to forget the whole thing. Pretend the
ride was a bad dream. Pretend the woman was a fantasy.

He shook his head hard like a dog shaking off water. He
ran both his hands through his hair. His mop felt gritty. He
limped toward the door, a parade of cats trailing behind
him. He turned and closed the bedroom door behind him to
contain the animals. Two scooted out before he could shut
it. He went down the hall. Stepped into the bathroom. Lifted
the toilet seat and yawned. Closed his eyes while he peed.
He sniffed. Did his urine smell like kitty litter? He opened
his eyes. Noticed a litter box tucked into a corner. He finished relieving himself and took a step backward. Felt fur
against his right calf. He was not going to shower with
these things crawling all over the place. He herded out three
of them by pushing them along with his feet. He picked up
the fourth by the scruff and threw it into the hall. Closed
the door. Sniffed. With the door shut, the stink was unbear-
able. Made his eyes water. He picked up the litter box,
opened the door and set the box in the hall. One of the cats
tried to squeeze by and get back in the bathroom. "No you
don't." He tried to shut the door and slammed it on the cat's
head. It howled and collapsed onto its side in the threshold.
He picked it up by its middle and held it in front of his face
to see if it was hurt. He thought it was that old cat. What did
she call it? Chaucer. "You're fine, you stupid thing." The cat
batted his chin with a front paw. "You fucker."

He dropped the cat on the bathroom floor and cupped
his chin with his hand. He looked down. The thing was
brushing against his legs and purring, as if nothing had
happened. That pissed him off even more. Clancy shut the
door so it couldn't get away, and so Ransom wouldn't hear.

He bent down and wrapped both hands around the animal's middle. Stood up and lifted the cat over his right shoulder like a man winding up to drop an ax. Split some wood. He brought its head down on the marble counter. It howled and squirmed and ran its legs in the air. A crazy cat in a cartoon. He turned and faced the wall opposite the counter. Wound his arms back. A batter getting reading to take a swing. He slammed the thing's head into the tiled wall. Once. Twice. The cat went limp. Clancy found the twin *thud*s satisfying. He yanked open the door and flung the cat into the hallway. Shut the door. He'd tell the Pink Lady the old thing looked like it was having a seizure. Knocked itself dead. She'd buy it; selling stories to her seemed pretty easy. For a professor, she was damn stupid. He wished he could kill all the fur balls. Bash in every single one of their heads. If only he could think up a big-enough lie.

He stepped over to the tub. An old claw-foot. A shower curtain—decorated with fat flowers—hung from an oval rod. The rod was suspended from the ceiling by chains. The showerhead—a flat one the size of a dinner plate—was attached to the tub faucet by a six-foot-tall gooseneck pipe. Still, it wasn't tall enough for him. He'd have to duck when he stood under the spray. He didn't feel like doing that today. Not with his headache. He plugged the tub drain and turned on the water. Put his hand under the faucet. Good and hot. While the tub filled, he cleaned up the cat blood. He unraveled a wad of toilet paper from the roll, dipped it in the tub and wiped the blood off the wall and the counter. Blotted a few drops from the floor. Tossed the dripping paper into the toilet and flushed. He watched the bloody tissue circle the bowl. The act of cleaning up disconnected him from the dead cat. Sent the feelings down the toilet. He used to get the same feeling after field-dressing a deer. Gutting the animal finished the hunt. Disengaged him from the kill.

He wished he'd gotten that comfortable disconnection

after they buried his father. Owen Clancy was in the ground, and the thing was done. Still, he had nightmares for a long time. They'd only recently stopped. Now the snowmobile rider. Dumping the body should have finished the killing for him. Should have disconnected him. Instead, he was having bad dreams about the asshole. Those stupid floating-face dreams. Maybe those would stop with time, like with his father. Maybe he'd have to kill again. Replace one nightmare with another. Perhaps it would only end when he finally killed himself. He shook off the thought. Beat down the yearning that was burning his belly. Rising up in his throat like a bad bowl of chili. He studied his reflection in the mirror. Dim lighting in the bathroom, like in the rest of the house. He thought it made him seem older. He ran his hand over his cheeks. He should shave, but didn't want to go to the trouble. He took his hand down. Shadows under his eyes. Under his brows. He didn't like that. Made him look like his father. Steam started fogging the mirror. Now he was his father floating on a cloud. He wiped the mirror with his hand, turned and went to the tub. Shut off the water and stepped into the bath. Hot. The burn felt good on his ankles. He sat down. His knees poked out of the water. He leaned his back against the sloped end of the tub and sighed. What would his father think of him now? Living off a woman. Drinking her liquor and smoking her dope and eating her food. Doing her whenever he wanted. Not bad for a dummy. A gimp.

TWENTY-TWO

IN THE HALLWAY, Ransom knelt over the Persian. The animal's eyes were wide, and its mouth was open a crack. Blood matted the fur against its head and neck. She put her hand between its front paws, over its chest. Waited. No heartbeat. She cupped her hand and held it close to the cat's nostrils and mouth. No breath. She sealed her mouth over the cat's mouth and nose and blew. Lifted her mouth off and looked at the animal's side. No movement. No effort to take in air. She tasted something salty and wet on her lips. Didn't know if it was her tears or the cat's blood. She wiped it off with the back of her hand and looked. Red. She slipped her arms under the cat's body and lifted it off the floor. Held it tight to her naked body while she stood up. Cradled it like a baby. Rocked it side to side in her arms. She convinced herself that the rocking motion would restart its heart. "Wake up," she whispered while looking down at the bloody head. "Wake up, Hamlet." The animal's head slipped off her arm and flopped to the side like a rag doll's head. She stopped rocking the cat and stood frozen. Statue of a nude and a cat.

Not since her brother had Ransom lost a companion to death. Some of her cats were old, but they'd never been sick a day. She took good care of them. Brushed their teeth. Brushed their coats. Bathed them. Fed them the best cat food. Only took them out of the house for checkups at the vet's. She'd had most of them fixed. The few that weren't, she let reproduce. The kittens came into the world wherever they wanted, be it under her bed or in her closet or on her furniture. She kept as many as she could. Gave the rest to good homes. People she knew. She'd told herself that when the first one started dying of old age, she could handle it. She'd wrap it in blankets and feed it warm milk and help it go comfortably. She'd been unprepared for this. A violent death. Not even like her brother's death; that had been suicide. This was murder. She'd assisted the killer; she'd brought him into her house to walk among her babies. She turned her head and stared at the closed bathroom door. Hissed under her breath, "Monster."

She carried it to the kitchen. Laid it on the table. She bent down and kissed its bloody muzzle. She stood up straight and looked down at her own body. Saw the animal's blood smeared over her breasts. She went over to the refrigerator and pulled a towel off the handle. Reached up to wipe away the blood, but couldn't bring herself to do it. She carried the towel over to the cat and draped it over the still body. She felt fur brushing against her calves. A Siamese jumped up on the table and padded over to the towel. Put a front paw on the edge of the rag. "No, Chaucer." She scooped up the living cat, bent down and set it back on the floor. Scratched behind its ears. She stood up. Looked at the mound. She couldn't leave Hamlet on the kitchen table. The other babies would be all over him the minute she left the room. The backyard? She'd never get a shovel into the frozen ground to dig a proper grave. She'd have to put him outside until she could think of something. She bent over the rag and tucked its edges around the dead animal. Lifted it in her arms and carried it to the back door. Held it close to her body with her left arm while pulling the door open with her right hand. She crouched down and set the bundle on the back stoop, just outside the door. She stood up and closed the door. Rested her forehead against it. "For in that sleep of death what dreams may come."

She lifted her head off the door. Turned and surveyed her kitchen. She'd know what she needed when she saw it. Her eyes locked on the knives resting in the wooden block. She stepped over to the counter and wrapped her hand around the tool with the longest blade. She pulled it out and held the blade in front of her face. She could see her reflection in the stainless steel. Blood colored her chin and mouth and nose. Soon blood would cover the knife, she thought. His blood instead of her baby's.

She walked out of the kitchen. Through the living room. Stepped into the hallway and went up to the bathroom door. Put her ear to it and listened. Splashing and humming. What was he humming? That tune from *I Dream of Jeannie*. He was humming a television theme song after killing one of her babies. "Monster," she said under her breath. "Moron." Her right hand tightened around the knife handle she held at her side. She put her left hand on the doorknob and turned. Pushed the door open. He was sitting in the tub. The shower curtain was pushed to one side and blocked his head and shoulders from her view. All she could see were his knees poking up. Big, hairy knees.

"Serene?" he asked from behind the curtain.

"Yes, my love," she answered, and took a step into the bathroom, holding the knife behind her back, blade pointed down.

"You saw in the hallway?"

"Yes, my love." She took another step toward the tub.

"I think Chaucer had a seizure or something. Ain't unusual. Stuff happens when an animal gets old."

"That wasn't Chaucer, my love." A third step.

"What?"

"Hamlet was a kitten. Not even a year old."

"Shit. You should get a refund from the pet store then."

"I didn't get him from a pet store. He was a gift from one of my boys. One of my *good* boys." A fourth step.

"I'm not one of your *good* boys?"

"No. You've been bad. Very, very bad." She stepped next to the tub. Brought the knife out from behind her back. Raised it over her shoulder with the blade pointing down. She could envision pushing the curtain aside. Bringing the knife down on his back. She could see the steel going all the way in. Only the handle sticking out. "You murdered my baby."

"I didn't. It was an accident."

She put her left hand on the curtain. Gripped the edge. She raised the blade higher. Over her head. "Like shooting your father was an accident."

He stood up and yanked the curtain aside. Saw her with the blade raised and pointed down. He reached up and wrapped his left hand around her right wrist and squeezed. "Drop it."

Her eyes narrowed into Popsicle-blue slits. "No."

He squeezed harder. "Drop it or I'll break your arm."

She grimaced. "No."

The tip of the blade was pointed down, just above him. For an instant he considered relaxing his grip and letting her do it. A quick way to go, he thought. He imagined the blade sliding into his heart as easily as a carving knife slices a turkey breast. He didn't trust her enough to leave her with his body, though. That image again. Cats licking his blood. "Drop it," he repeated. She didn't answer. Her upper lip was curled into a snarl. A red stain ran from her nose down to her mouth and chin. He knew what it was: a cat's blood. She'd kissed the dead cat. That more than the knife infuriated him. He balled his right hand into a fist, cocked it back and rammed it into her stomach. She gasped and opened her hand. The knife plummeted down, hit the edge of the tub and splashed into the water. Clancy pushed her backward and she fell onto the floor. Curled up in a ball on her side, facing the tub. He bent down and fished the knife out of the bathtub. Stood up with the dripping tool in his hand. Stepped out of the tub and walked toward her. "I am so sick of your shit, Pink Lady." He stepped over her and walked out of the bathroom. Limped a bit as he went. Thumped down the hall into the bedroom, kicking a cat out of the way as he went. He slammed the door behind him.

She coiled her body into a tighter ball. She folded her arms over her head and wept. Not from the pain; it was subsiding. She realized she'd made a mistake. If he left, she'd have no one to help her. The villains at the university would win. They'd fire her. Word would get out about why she was let go. She'd never find another teaching position. She had almost no money in the bank. She'd eventually lose her house. She'd have to give away her babies. She'd be out on the street. Alone, except for the scratching. She was sure the scratching would follow her no matter where she went. It had already migrated from the closets and walls. Sprawled on the floor, she could hear it under the tiles.

TWENTY-THREE

MURPHY ROLLED ONTO her side and looked outside the sliding glass doors of her bedroom. Seven in the morning and the sun wasn't up, but at least the snow had stopped. She loved Minnesota in the winter but wished the daylight lasted longer. Some days she left for work in the morning in the dark and went home in the early evening in the dark. Still, it was nice waking up to the lights twinkling downtown. Streetlights along the Wabasha Bridge. Christmas lights decorating the trees dotting Kellogg Boulevard. The sparkle of the Radisson Riverfront Hotel. The illuminated windows of the St. Paul City Hall and Ramsey County Courthouse. The glow of the office buildings behind them. She heard a loud *thud*. The ice cracking on the Mississippi. It took her a couple of winters on the river to get used to it. Took her a couple of winters, too, to get used to the isolation. Not nearly as many people lived on the river in the winter as in the summer. Most houseboats weren't built for freezing temperatures. The live-aboards who toughed it out had to winterize their crafts. Some wrapped the exterior in what resembled giant shrink-wrap. Others—Murphy included—insulated their boats like regular homes.

Another *thud.* Jack rolled onto his side and molded his front against her back. Draped his arm across her breasts. "How can you stand that racket?"

"I love it. It's like the river is talking."

"What's it saying?"

She rolled over and faced him. Kissed him on the mouth. Pulled her lips off of his. "It's saying we should get our butts out of bed. Get to the hospital."

He went onto his back. "I think it's saying we've got plenty of time." *Thud.* "And that one was saying you should be on top this time."

She crawled on top of him. Buried her face in his neck. Nibbled on his shoulder. A fourth *thud.* The loudest. She lifted her mouth off his skin. "You could be right." She straddled him and rubbed her pelvis against his.

"I'm definitely right." He entered her.

THEY showered and dressed and went down to the galley, the nicest part of her houseboat. She'd upgraded the kitchen before making any other repairs. While Jack flipped through the *Pioneer Press*, Murphy made them scones.

One and three-quarter cups all-purpose flour
One-quarter cup sugar
Two and one-half teaspoons baking powder
One-half teaspoon salt
One-third cup butter, cut into cubes for easy blending
One-half cup dried cranberries
One-half cup chopped pecans
One large egg, beaten

Six tablespoons half-and-half
Sugar for sprinkling

Heat the oven to 375 degrees. Thoroughly combine the
flour, sugar, baking powder and salt in a large bowl. Using
a pastry cutter, cut the butter into the flour mixture until it
is crumbly. The butter should be the size of peas. Using a
wooden spoon, stir in the cranberries and pecans. In a
small bowl or cup, mix together the egg and half-and-half.
Stir into the large bowl of ingredients with a fork. Tip the
dough onto a lightly floured cutting board. Knead lightly
six to eight times. Pat into a ball. Roll the ball out into a circle about six inches in diameter. Using a large knife, cut the
circle into eight pie-shaped wedges. Sprinkle with sugar.
Place the pieces, spaced apart, on a cookie sheet. Set the
sheet on a rack set in the middle of the oven. Bake about
twelve to fifteen minutes, or until light brown. Remove immediately from the cookie sheet and eat warm.

They sat together at the table nibbling on the scones.
Jack had his head buried in the sports section. The Wild
were having another good season. "We should try to get
hockey tickets," Jack said in between sips of coffee.

"Hard to come by." Murphy set down her coffee cup,
picked up her scone, took a bite and dropped the triangle
back on the plate. Chewed and swallowed without tasting it.
She'd made the scones for Jack; he loved them. She was too
nervous about her dad's procedure to enjoy eating. "Want to
finish mine?"

"Sure," Jack said from behind the paper.

She pushed her plate toward him. Stood up. Took her cup
over to the counter that separated the galley from the living
room. Glanced through the living-room patio doors. The sun
was finally coming up. The river looked like a desert covered by white sand. She missed the barge traffic. Pleasure

boaters speeding by, rocking her boat with their wake. The Minnesota Boat Club's rowing teams cutting through the water in their narrow shells. She put her cup to her lips and tipped it back. Finished it off. Went over to the dishwasher. Opened it and loaded her cup inside. Set some other breakfast dishes in the rack. "Let's put the rest of the java in some travel mugs and hit the road."

Jack lowered the paper and looked at her. "A little early." He folded the paper. Set it down on the table. Picked up her scone. Finished it in a couple of bites. Washed it down with the last of his coffee. "Won't be much to do before the procedure except sit around."

She shut the dishwasher. Opened a cupboard over the counter. Pushed some cups around while trying to find the mugs. "I don't care. Let's go. I can't stand this waiting stuff."

JACK held her mug and his own while she locked up. He noticed she had a short jacket on. A wool peacoat. "Wimpy winter gear. What happened to the long coat?"

Murphy had it hanging in the laundry room, drying. "It's dirty. Gotta have it cleaned. Besides, the leather wasn't warm enough either. Might have to break down and get a down jacket this winter."

He surveyed the dock in front of her door. Almost shin high after the snowfall the night before. "You need to break down and shovel."

"Tell me about it. I haven't had time." In the middle of the river, some mallards splashed and honked in a patch of open water. The sight of them made her shudder. She knew what the icy water felt like.

Jack spotted the birds. "Ducks are the only sign of life I've seen out here. Are your neighbors all dead or what?"

She took her mug out of his hand. Took a sip while they walked down the dock toward shore. "We see each other.

We had a yacht club Christmas party last month. Later this month is the annual midwinter potluck. Gotta make a pan of baklava for that."

"Who stayed this winter?"

She tipped her head toward the barking coming from one of the boats. "Tripod and his master." Tripod was a three-legged dog that belonged to Floyd Kvaal, a garage-door salesman and musician. During the warm-weather months on the river, Kvaal paddled his canoe around the neighborhood with the dog and played the sax. Over the long winter, live-aboards took turns having him play at their houses. "I didn't think they would because Floyd bitched so much about his heating bill last winter. Three hundred a month."

"Jesus," Jack said. "That is steep. Especially for such a small space." They stepped onto shore and walked to the parking lot.

"That wildlife artist and his wife stayed. She's a photographer. They like the winter scenery for their work. The architect stayed. He's got a well-insulated boat. Hell. He's even got a Jacuzzi in the master bath. I'd love a Jacuzzi."

"On your dinky one-bedroom?" Murphy's boat had a master bedroom and master bathroom with a shower upstairs. The galley, living room and guest toilet made up the downstairs. "You'd better worry about some basic maintenance before you launch into Jacuzzis."

She took another sip of coffee. Already turning cold. "I know. I've got a list." The bedroom and living room had sliding patio doors leading to faded decks with wobbly railings. The boat's exterior was flaking and needed painting. She'd finally repaired the leaky showerhead and replaced the failing hot-water heater earlier that winter. Again the thought occurred to her: *Sell the boat and move back in with Jack.*

They stepped next to Murphy's Jeep Grand Cherokee, parked next to Jack's BMW. She opened the driver's door.

Tossed her purse on the front seat. Got in. Set her coffee mug in a holder between the seats. Slipped the key in the ignition. Turned on the Jeep and cranked up the heater. A blast as cold as that from an air conditioner blew from the vents. She leaned over and snatched an ice scraper off the floor of the front passenger's side. She slid out the driver's side and slammed the door. Jack opened the front passenger's door, set his mug in the other holder, reached down and took another scraper off the floor. Slammed the door shut. While the interior warmed, the two scraped snow and ice from the Jeep's windows. Steam rolled out of their mouths while they worked and talked.

"You should have waited inside while I did this," said Jack, scraping a layer of ice off the front passenger's side window. "No sense in both of us freezing our asses off."

Murphy scraped the front driver's side window. "Too late now." She thought to herself: *This is nothing. Try wading through Como in the winter.*

Jack moved to the back passenger's window on the right side. Scraped. "So you prefer this shit to sunny Arizona?"

She moved to the back passenger's window on the driver's side of the Jeep. Wiped her nose with the back of her glove. Another thought popped into her head: *Sell the boat and move away with Jack.* She pushed the idea aside and started scraping the glass. "Can we put off this discussion until my dad's procedure is done? One big deal at a time."

"Fine." Jack walked around to the back window. Scraped. "Speaking of your dad, you realize this could turn into an even bigger deal, right?"

Murphy stopped working and looked at him. "What? What do you mean?"

Jack went around to her side. "Patrick and Ryan didn't tell you? They didn't call you at the shop? They told me they'd talk to the family. I offered to, but they said they'd do it."

"They didn't tell me shit. You tell me."

He went around to the windshield. Started scraping. It didn't take much muscle. The heater had softened the snow and ice. "Here's the thing. If the balloon angioplasty doesn't work, he may have to have an emergency bypass. That isn't a little procedure. It's surgery. They're going to have to open up his chest and operate on his heart. Change out the plumbing."

She walked around to the front of the Jeep. "They'll wait a couple of days, won't they? Give us all time to prepare for it?"

"It'll happen while he's already on the table. Prepped and ready." Jack stopped scraping. "I'm sorry, babe. They said they'd talk to you. I guess the Murphy communication lines broke down."

"Those lines were never up." She walked to the driver's side of the Jeep. Jerked open the back passenger's door. Tossed the scraper onto the floor. Slammed the door shut. She yanked open the driver's door, hopped in, slammed the door shut.

Jack opened the front passenger's door and tossed the scraper onto the floor. He looked over at his wife. Her hands were wrapped tight around the steering wheel. Her lips were set hard. She looked ready to cry or punch someone. "You want me to drive, babe?"

"No. I'm fine."

Jack got in and shut the door. He noticed for the first time that her hands were bare. "Where are your gloves?"

She paused. "Lost them."

"Want mine?"

"No. I'm good. I've got another pair somewhere. I'll dig them out."

He reached over and turned the heat down a notch. "Great heater in this thing. It's actually too hot in here."

"It's probably me." She pulled out of the parking lot and headed for the hospital. Crossed the Wabasha Bridge over the river. Drove north through downtown. She braked at a light. She picked up her mug and drained the rest of the coffee. She set down the mug and clicked on the radio. Bob Dylan was in the middle of being "Tangled Up in Blue." The light changed, and she accelerated. Weaved around two cars in front of her. Ran a yellow light.

Jack reached over and turned off Dylan. "Smacking up the Jeep isn't going to help, my desert flower."

She stopped at another light. "I'm pissed off. Pissed they didn't call me. Pissed Papa is going through this. Pissed at the whole thing."

"We'll get through this." He brushed her cheek with his gloved hand.

"I'm glad you're with me for this." The light turned green, and she didn't notice. A driver behind them honked. She returned her attention to the road and accelerated. She hung a right on Eleventh Street.

She looked to her right as they drove past the cop shop. They stopped at another red light. She glanced at the station again and thought about Castro. Felt guilty. He was still sick but agreed to watch Ransom's house all day. They were going to drag Bergen in—sick or not—to take the overnight surveillance.

Jack saw her staring at the station. As if he'd read her mind: "Hey, what's the story on that woman from the English Department."

"Serene Ransom. She's mixed up with a guy who might have gotten into some trouble up on the Range."

"What kind of trouble?"

"It's complicated. Cops up north are trying to sort it out. Regardless, the bad guy is shacked up with her as we speak. Your dad and another guy are going to fire her butt first thing tomorrow morning."

"For sleeping with a felon?"

"For a long list of other junk. She's been taking students

to bed with her. Young guys. Freshmen. Showing up late for work. Acting weird." The light changed. Murphy took a left onto Jackson Street.

"Does my father know about this woman's boyfriend? Is he safe meeting with her?"

"Don't worry about it. The guys are watching Ransom's house today and tonight to make sure she and her new squeeze stay put. When she leaves her place to collect her pink slip tomorrow morning, we swoop in and grab the boyfriend for questioning. Grab her before she crosses the border into Minneapolis. Execute a search warrant on the house. We didn't want to get them together. We don't know yet if they're partners in crime or what. Don't want to put her in danger or let her get in the way."

"What's this *we* talk?" asked Jack. "You're not doing it, right? You're not picking up the sleaze-bag boyfriend? You've got enough on your plate the next couple of days."

She paused. She and Duncan hadn't discussed who was going to pick up Clancy. Regardless, she decided to avoid a fight. Give the answer Jack wanted. "No. I won't be doing it." She crossed Twelfth Street and took a quick right into the Regions parking lot. She pulled into a space, put it in Park and turned off the Jeep. Pulled the keys out of the ignition and dropped them in her purse. Put her hand on the door and looked at her husband. "Here we go, then."

"It'll be fine." He leaned over and kissed her on the mouth. Opened the passenger door and got out. Closed the door.

"Fine," Murphy repeated. She opened the driver's door and hopped out with her purse. Shut the door and hiked the purse strap over her shoulder. Jack took her hand in his, and together they walked across the parking lot. A gust of wind blew curls of snow around their ankles. Her hand tightened around his. Her mind was a mix of work and personal worries. What would happen to her papa? Would they have to open up his chest? What would happen to her marriage? To save it, would she have to sell the boat and move away? What was happening with Castro in front of Ransom's place? What was going on inside that house crawling with cats and decorated with flowers? Even after saving the boy's life and spending time with the woman, Murphy couldn't answer the most chilling question scrolling through her head: Was Enda Clancy a killer or a victim?

TWENTY-FOUR

RANSOM WIPED HER eyes with her hands. Crawled to her feet and shuffled to the vanity. Felt dizzy. Feared she was going to fall backward. She clutched the edge of the counter with both hands to steady herself. Looked in the mirror and blinked. Hair a tangled mess. Red eyes. Flushed cheeks streaked with tears. A red T of emotion stretching across her forehead and shooting down her nose. A reindeer nose. Another red took over after that. The blood. She turned on the cold water, bent over the sink and cupped her hands under the water. Splashed her face five times. Stood straight. Pulled a towel off the bar next to the sink and patted her face dry. Held one end of the towel under the cold water. Wrung it out. Wiped under her left armpit. Under her right. Ran more water over the towel. Twisted it and scrubbed the cat's blood off her breasts. She dropped the towel on the counter. Opened a drawer to the right of the sink and took out a brush. Started stroking her mane. Static electricity made her hair fly. She passed the brush under the cold stream.

Turned off the faucet. Ran the brush through her hair. Her hands were shaking. Vibrating like when she was trying to steady her gun in the bar. She concentrated on counting the strokes. That would calm her. "Twenty-five, twenty-six, twenty-seven, twenty-eight . . . " She stopped at forty.

She dropped the brush on the counter. Grabbed a fistful of cosmetics from the drawer and dropped them on the marble. She needed something to counteract the red in her face. She picked up the round compact. Popped it open. Green pressed powder for complexion correction. She picked the brush out of the compact, stroked the tip of the brush over the powder. Dusted the brush over the red splotches. She set the brush back in the compact, snapped the case shut and dropped it in the drawer. Picked through the pile. Found her favorite shade of lip color. Saucy Mauve. She pulled off the top and twisted the tube until the pink stick rose from the silo. A stroke over the top lip. A stroke over the bottom. She pressed her lips together. Smiled and checked in the mirror to make sure there was no pink on her teeth. There wasn't. She relaxed the grin. Twisted the tube down and snapped the top on. Dropped the lipstick in the drawer. What else? She picked up a thin tube. Mascara. She drew the brush out of the tube. Two strokes to the top set of lashes. Two to the bottom set. She slipped the brush back in the tube and dropped the mascara back in the drawer. She picked up a red quilted case the size of a pencil case. Unzipped it. Four perfume bottles in a row. All by Estée Lauder. White Linen. Beautiful. Dazzling Gold. Pleasures. She lifted the Beautiful bottle out of the case. Yanked off the top. Sprayed the hollow at the base of her neck. Sprayed the inside of each elbow. Reached down and sprayed the inside of each thigh. She pressed the top back on the perfume bottle, set the bottle back in the case, zipped the case shut and dropped it in the drawer. She looked in the mirror again. If her face had been too red, her nipples seemed faded. She took a square compact off the counter and flipped it open. Blush. She rubbed her right index finger over the pressed powder. Rubbed pink over her right areola. Rubbed her finger over the blush again. Rubbed pink over her left areola. She snapped the compact shut and dropped it in the drawer.

Ransom looked in the mirror. Said his name. Softly. "Catcchhh." She smiled at her reflection. "I want you, Catcchhh." She stopped smiling. Said even more softly: "I hate you, Catch. But I need you." She swept the rest of the cosmetics back in the drawer with her forearm. He'd told her he hated seeing her cosmetics all over the place. Seeing her paint her face. He said it was like watching surgery; he'd rather not know the messy details. She put her hand on the drawer to close it when she spotted the scissors in back. She used them for trimming split ends. She bunched a handful of hair in her hand and checked the ends. They were good. Even and shiny and smooth. She let go of the hair. Had an idea. Reached in back and fished the scissors out of the drawer. Held them in her hand by the blades. Looked in the mirror again. He admired her hair. Enjoyed combing it with his fingers. He'd told her he'd hated that his mother and sisters kept their hair short. She liked her hair, too. Knew he'd appreciate the offer. The sacrifice. A show of trust. An opportunity for revenge.

She closed the drawer. Walked out of the bathroom and down the hall. Stopped at her bedroom. The door was closed. She put her ear to it. Didn't hear anything. She switched the scissors to her left hand. Held them at her side. Put her right hand on the knob and twisted it. Pushed the door open.

He was in his sweatpants. Crouched over his duffel bag, his back turned to her. He didn't bother looking up. The knife was on the end of her bed. "I'm outta here."

She leaned against the door frame. "Where are you going?"

He pulled a sweatshirt out of his bag. Dropped it on the floor next to the bag. "My brother's place."

"How are you going to get there?"

"Hitchhike. Walk. I don't give a fuck." He fished out a pair of socks. Dropped them on top of the sweatshirt.

"Catch. I'm sorry. Don't go. Please stay."

He kept rummaging in his bag. "Stay so you can stab me while I'm sleeping? No thanks."

"I was upset. Seeing Hamlet dead like that. Bloody and dead. I lost control. I didn't expect him to die so suddenly." She took a breath and silently let it out. Couldn't stand the words coming out of her mouth. "That seizure and stuff."

He started closing the bag. The zipper caught on a tee shirt. "How in the hell can I sleep next to you knowing any second you could lose it again? Not my fault the damn thing died on you. You could have hurt me big time with that fucking big knife." She took a step toward him. Then another. Stood behind him and pressed her crotch into the back of his head. Put her right hand on his right shoulder. "That won't work this time," he said. He reached inside the bag and pulled the tee shirt off the zipper. Shrugged his shoulder to get her hand off it.

She brought her left hand around to his face. "Hurt me, then. We'll be even. Just stay."

The hardware startled him. He snatched the scissors out of her hand. She took a step back. He stood up and turned to look at her. Wondered for a second if she'd intended to stab him with the scissors and then chickened out. His eyes narrowed as he studied her face. No. She was serious. "What are you saying?"

"Cut my hair." She put her hands on the sides of her head. Ran her fingers up and through her hair. "It's the prettiest part of me. You've said that more than once."

He looked down at the scissors in his right hand. His fist tightened around the blades. He looked back at her. She'd cleaned herself up for him. He liked the effort. She looked beautiful. Smelled nice. Doesn't matter, he told himself. She'd tried to stab him because of a stupid cat. He'd have to exact some payment. Make sure she knew he was in charge. The boss. He could only trust her if he could keep her down. Turn her into an obedient puppy. The way his mother and sisters had been around his father. He took a step toward her. Brought his left hand up to the back of her head. Buried his fingers in her mane. Grabbed a handful of hair and pulled hard so her chin tipped up. "No." He flung the scissors at her dresser. They clattered into some perfume bottles. "That's not how I'm going to hurt you." He brought his right hand up. Bunched her left breast in his hand and squeezed. She gasped and bit her bottom lip, but didn't protest. "Shit. I think you like it this way. Ain't no punishment. Not for you." He let go of her hair and breast. Put his hands on her shoulders. Pushed her down onto her knees. "I'm a dog lover myself." He took her from behind. Sodomized her.

HE fell asleep on the floor, sprawled on his back. She stretched out on her side and rested her head on her bent arm. She scrutinized his face and figure. Tried to pretend she was seeing him for the first time. Tall and broad shoul-dered and well muscled. Black curls on his chest, but not a carpet of them. Black curls around his face. High eyebrows. Long, thick lashes. A woman would die to have those lashes. Olive skin, but it seemed to be fading a bit. Turning pale. Not enough sunlight perhaps. Finely drawn nose. Full lips. Almost a pout. The stubbly beginnings of a beard shadowing his cheeks. That night in the bar she'd imagined he had the face of a gentle poet and the body of a noble Titan. He'd turned out to be neither, she thought. He was closer to Frankenstein's monster. She feared she'd had a role in assembling him. What if she hadn't urged him to fire that shotgun? Would she be sleeping with a different boy? A kinder one? She recalled the monster's words of self-loathing from the closing scene in Mary Shelley's Gothic work. A novel she'd studied and committed to memory:

> When I run over the frightful catalogue of my sins, I cannot believe that I am the same creature whose thoughts were once filled with sublime and transcendent visions of the beauty and the majesty of goodness. But it is even so; the fallen angel becomes a malignant devil.

Was Catch the fallen angel or she? Which was the maker and which the monster? She closed her eyes and moved her head off her arm. Rested the side of her face against the floor. Felt a cat brushing against her leg. Reached down and stretched out her hand. Let the animal lick her fingers. She thought she heard something under the floorboards. She held her breath. Heard the scratching again. She fought the urge to shake the devil awake and send him after the noise. Send the big monster after the small one. She opened her eyes and told herself to be patient. Handle the university problem first. The scratching could wait. She'd be safe as long as it stayed in the walls and under the floors and in the closets.

She crawled to her feet and walked out of the bedroom. Hobbled down the hall to the bathroom. Glanced in the mirror. Good. The mascara had stayed in place. She didn't think she'd cried during his assault, but couldn't remember exactly. Parts of the ordeal were a blur, and she wanted to keep it that way. Didn't want to dwell on it. A bad dream. She opened a drawer to the left of the sink and pulled out the cold cream. Unscrewed the top and set the jar and cap on the counter. Used her fingertips to smear the white stuff over her face. It felt cool and light. She wished she could smooth it over her heavy heart. Another look in the mirror. A ghost face with blue eyes. She screwed the top back on the jar. Set the cold cream back in the drawer. Shut the drawer. Reached into a ceramic jar she kept on the counter, pushed into a corner. A sitting cat with a hole in its back. She took some cotton balls out of the cat's back. Wiped off the makeup, dropping each ball into the wastebasket as it was soiled. She went over to the tub. Leaned in and turned on the faucet. Felt the water. This time she'd allow herself a hot shower. When it was scalding enough, she stepped in, pulled the curtain closed and turned on the spray. She held her face up to the burning stream and wept. Wondered if saving her career and her house and even her babies was worth the pain and humiliation. She grabbed a bar of soap out of the basket. Dragged it over her arms and shoulders and breasts and thighs. Rubbed it between her legs and but-tocks. She wanted to scrub away the memory of his body invading hers. She worked the bar between her hands until she had a thick lather. Dropped the bar back in the wire bas-ket. Scrubbed her cheeks and forehead with her hands. Shut her eyes and held her face up to the spray. She heard his heavy steps in the bathroom. Stood straight. Braced herself for another assault. He pulled the curtain back and stepped behind her into the tub. Closed the curtain. Twined his arms around her midriff. She felt his erection in her back. Her body tensed. Stiffened. She kept crying. Was glad she'd kept the bedroom and bathroom doors open, so he could hear and come to her.

He kissed the curve of her neck. "I'm sorry. Didn't mean to hurt you so much. Only enough."

"Enough?"

He kissed her right shoulder. Scraped her skin with his teeth. "Enough so you'd know you can't pull any more shit. So you'd behave."

Big, hiccupping sobs. "I'll behave."

"Good." He brought his hands up and cupped her breasts. Squeezed.

She rested her hands over his. Her shoulders shook. "No more. I hurt all over."

He dropped his hands. Put them on her waist. "Stop crying, then."

"I can't."

He hated seeing her cry. Made him feel too much like his father. A bully instead of a boss. "What can I do? How can I make it up to you? Tell me. I'll do it."

The words she'd been waiting to hear. She stopped crying. Took a breath. "I'll think about it."

HE wrapped the towel around his waist. Ran his fingers through his damp hair while looking in the mirror. "Gonna open a can of soup or something for lunch," he said as much to his own reflection as to her. "Want anything?"

She rubbed her head with a towel. "No thank you."

"Suit yourself." He walked out of the bathroom. Headed for the kitchen.

She hung her towel over a bar. Pulled open the drawer to the left of the sink. Took out some moisturizer. Squirted a puddle of the stuff into her palm. Smoothed it over her face and down her throat. The lotion promised to lessen the appearance of fine lines, but it didn't seem to be doing her skin any good, she thought. She dropped the bottle back in the drawer and shut it. Studied her neck in the mirror. A washboard. She walked out of the bathroom. Went down the hall to the bedroom. Headed for her closet. On her way there, she noticed his duffel on the floor. Wide open. He'd been careful about keeping it zipped. What did he have in there that was so important? She stood over the bag and looked down.

Noticed a flash of metal. Poking out of a pillowcase at the bottom of the duffel. She glanced up at the door to make sure he wasn't standing there. She dropped to her knees next to the bag and reached inside with her right hand. Used her fingertips to slip it out of the pillowcase. She pulled it out of the bag and held it up by the end of the barrel. She gasped and almost dropped it. Cradled the butt in her left hand.

Her gun. He'd lied to her. He'd kept it. Her eyes darted back to the door. She listened. Heard him opening and closing cupboards in the kitchen. She set the handgun on the floor next to the bag. Lowered both hands into the duffel. Pressed down on the outside of the pillowcase. Ran her hands over something longer. The shotgun. Small lumps around it. The spent shells. She withdrew her hands from the bag and sat back on her heels. He'd kept everything. Had he been too greedy to discard perfectly good firearms? No. That wasn't it. Why would he have kept the empty shells as well? Was he going to frame her using the weapons? How could he? Both of them had left prints. Was he that stupid? Maybe. Regardless, he was up to something. She'd think about it later. No time now. He was already done cooking. She heard the television on in the living room. He was probably sitting at the coffee table. Slurping soup while surfing with the remote. Searching for another episode of *Baywatch*.

She picked up her gun and held it by the butt in her right hand. Checked the side. No red dot. The safety was on. She didn't want to touch the other items in the bag. The shotgun was a mystery to her. A length of metal with parts that slid back and forth. Besides, he'd notice right away if it was missing. Such a large profile under the cloth of the pillowcase. He might not miss her gun right away. She'd hide it. She knew how to use it. He couldn't question her about it. That would reveal he had the guns in the first place. She'd shut her mouth about her discovery. See what he'd say or do. At least now they were on even footing. One gun each. One chance to kill each.

She stood up with it. Ran her eyes around the bedroom. Between the mattress? He might feel it. He thrashed all over the place, especially when he napped in the bed by himself. Her dresser? She didn't trust that he wasn't going through her drawers. One place he never went was near her cosmetics. She walked to the doorway and listened. He was laughing. She'd been wrong. No *Baywatch* this time. *I Dream of Jeannie.* She went down the hallway and into the bathroom. Stood in front of the vanity and scanned the possibilities. The drawers on either side of the sink would be good. They were filled to the brim with her makeup. She could bury the pistol under an inch of compacts. Blush and eye shadow and face powder. Appropriate for a gun called Ladysmith, she thought. In the cabinet below the sink? In a half-empty box of tampons? Cumbersome if she needed it instantly. She surveyed the countertop. Spotted an even better place. Quickly accessible to her if she needed it. She switched the gun to her left hand. With her right, pulled the cotton balls out of the ceramic cat. She set the gun inside the cat and dropped cotton balls over it.

He poked his head through the doorway. Picked at his teeth with his fingernail while he talked. "What're you doing in here for so long? Thought you fell in."

She looked at him and smiled. Plucked a cotton ball out of the cat. Lifted it to her cheek. "Putting on my face, my love."

"You know how much I like to see that." He turned and went down the hall. Back to the living room.

She dropped the cotton back into the cat.

SHE sprang it on him that night. She wore clothes and minimal makeup. Thought he'd find the change appealing.

She squeezed into her tightest jeans and a pink cashmere sweater that had pearl buttons all the way up the front. She undid the first few buttons so he'd get a peek of her pink bra underneath. A pat of blush on her cheeks and a couple of strokes of clear gloss on her lips. A shot of perfume behind each ear. White Linen. She found a steak in the freezer. Thawed it out and fried it with onions. Fried diced potatoes with onions in another pan. He liked fried things with onions. She served it to him in the living room so he could eat in front of the television. She brought him a beer. A second and a third and a fourth. She curled up next to him on the couch with a glass of Chablis and a cigarette. Watched him eat. He sawed the steak into six pieces the size of matchbooks. He stabbed the first piece, dipped it into the puddle of A.1., popped it into his mouth. Chewed three or four times. Swallowed. She turned her attention to the screen. A movie. *Excalibur.* A 1981 version of the Arthurian legend. Better than his usual picks. "This is based on a piece of literature, you know."

"I didn't know." He stabbed another piece, dunked it in sauce and put it in his mouth. Chewed while keeping his eyes on the movie.

"Sir Thomas Malory. *Le Morte d'Arthur.*"

He swallowed. "Sounds boring."

"It's not boring. Do you find this movie boring?"

"A little. Too much talking. Not enough fight scenes." He impaled a square of steak. Skipped the A.1. this time and forked the meat directly into his mouth.

A tabby jumped on the couch between them. Ransom picked it up and set it back on the floor. "No, Ophelia."

"Thank you," he muttered in between chews.

She picked her cigarette out of the ashtray, took a drag, blew smoke over the coffee table. Set the cigarette back in the ashtray. Lifted her glass of wine, took a sip. Held it between her hands. "You don't like my babies, do you?"

He swallowed. Dropped the knife and fork on his plate. Picked up a bottle. Took a long drink of beer. Set the bottle on the table and burped. "I can't stand eating while they're all over the place. It's like any minute one of them is going to land in the middle of my plate."

She took another sip of wine. Set her glass on the coffee table. Reached over and ran her fingers through his hair. Brushed the back of her hand against his cheek. Felt the scrape of his beard. "I know you killed Hamlet, my love."

He turned his head and pushed her hand away from his face. "Was an accident."

"The hell it was." He opened his mouth to respond. She put her fingertips over his lips. His mouth was greasy, and the corners were stained with steak sauce. "Don't deny it, my love. I know. It's okay. I can forgive you." She took her hand off his mouth. "I can forgive you everything if you do two things for me. I'll even pay you for them. For the chores. I know you're lacking funds."

He closed his mouth. His eyes were wide. The money had his attention. He opened his mouth again. No words came out. The sound of clanging swords filled the air.

She took the remote off the coffee table, aimed it at the set and lowered the volume. Dropped the box back on the table. "Well?" she asked.

The question that finally came out of his lips wasn't the one she expected to hear first: "How much money?"

TWENTY-FIVE

SEAN MURPHY'S TWENTY-MINUTE balloon angioplasty went to a four-hour emergency bypass surgery. The operation was successful; the family meeting in a hospital lounge that night was a disaster.

"Both of you can go straight to hell!" Tyke was furious Patrick and Ryan had failed to warn the rest of the family about the possibility that their father could have heart surgery. "Some doctors you are. Might as well hike over to the soup kitchen. Tap one of the bums on the shoulder. Ask him to come over here and explain shit to us. He'd be more help."

"I second that," said Dominick Murphy.

"Ditto," said Randy Murphy. Dominick and Randy were thirty-one years old and the siblings closest in age and temperament to Tyke. Dominick was a plumber, and Randy owned a landscaping and snowplowing business. They were the shortest in the family, the most muscular, the only ones with green eyes, the only redheads. When they were mad, the twins' faces flushed and their brighter coloring gave the illusion of spreading to their Brillo-pad tops. Murphy called it "mood hair." That night in the lounge, their heads seemed ready to burst into flames.

The calmer members of the clan crowded on the chairs and couches that lined the room's walls. The agitated ones—Tyke, Patrick, Ryan, the twins and their sister—stood. Jack wasn't agitated, but he stood as well. He wanted to be ready to step between brothers or between brother and sister—a task he'd taken on during other contentious Murphy gatherings. Amira Murphy wasn't in the room. She was in the hospital's Chapel of the Divine Healer with her rosary. She'd herded a contingent of daughters-in-law with her with cries of *"Yalla! Yalla!" Let's go! Let's go!* When she was stressed, her Arabic flowed easier than her English.

Tyke stepped up to Patrick and Ryan. The pair stood next to each other, shoulder to shoulder. They could have been twins as well. Over six feet in height. Wavy hair the color of ink. Blue eyes. Fair skin. Both in their early forties. Their arms were folded over their chests, and their eyes were unblinking. Two horse thieves staring down a lynch mob. Tyke poked Patrick in the chest with his index finger. "You thought we couldn't handle the information or what? Fucking elitists." Tyke, a carpenter, was the tallest in the family and towered over his surgeon brothers. He was always ready to jump on them at the slightest sign of snobbery— and he always saw snobbery. The twins usually joined him. Before either doctor could answer, Tyke snapped his head around and pointed the attacking finger at Jack. "And you, Jacko." Tyke knew Jack hated the nickname the Murphy boys had long ago assigned him. "You knew about this? When were you gonna let the rest of us in on the big secret? When Papa went home with a seam down his front? Or did you think we'd be too stupid to notice that?"

"That's enough," said Murphy, who was glued to her husband's side.

Jack touched her arm. Tipped his head toward her and said in a low voice: "Let it go."

"Don't blame Jack," Patrick said to Tyke's back. "We told him we'd handle it."

Tyke spun back around to face his older brother. "You handled it, all right. You kept the big secret from everyone."

Ryan unfolded his arms. Held out his palms. A poker player showing he had no hidden cards. "We didn't see the need to alarm everyone. That's all there is to it." He dropped his arms. Shoved his hands in his pants pockets. "Honestly. We didn't think this was going to happen. All indications were . . ."

Dominick stepped up to Ryan. Stood inches away. Put a finger in his face. "All indications are you're an elitist jerk."

Jack slipped his body in between the two brothers, his back to Ryan and his front to Dominick. He put his hand on Dominick's shoulder. "Give it a rest."

Dominick shrugged off Jack's hand and took a couple of steps backward. "Doctors. You all stick together. Kiss my ass, Jacko." He turned and went toward the door with Randy on his heels.

"Where are you going?" Murphy was afraid they were going to hit the bars. Get drunk. A coping mechanism the pair had used before. "Get back here."

"What do you care?" Randy flipped her the bird over his right shoulder.

Amira Murphy stepped into the doorway with her fists on her hips. Her rosary was wrapped around her right hand like a set of brass knuckles. "Sit down," she said to the twins.

Dominick and Randy froze in front of her. All Randy could get out of his mouth was one word: "Ma."

She shook her right fist at her two sons, rattling the rosary tangled around her hand. "I catch any of you boys giving your sister the finger again, I'll break it off. So help me God I will."

The twins backed away from the door.

"Mrs. Murphy," said a voice behind Amira. The siblings suddenly noticed there was a priest standing behind their mother. The Reverend Peter King, an old family friend. He was African-American, as short as Amira and half as wide. Dressed head to toe in his black religious garb, including a black brimmed hat, he looked like an exclamation point. He stepped around Amira and went into the lounge. Faced the twins. Took off his hat. The exclamation point was bald. "You children need to stop fighting. This isn't what your mother needs right now. She's got enough on her mind."

"Father Pete. You don't know what's been going on." Dominick turned and looked at Murphy and the three doctors. "They've been withholding information."

Amira walked into the room. Stood next to the priest. Nodded toward the accused group. "Good for them. I'm glad they kept their mouths shut."

"Imma," said Randy. "Why?"

Amira: "Why should all of us lose sleep? I worry enough for all of you put together."

King put his hand on Amira's arm. "You know what they say, Mrs. Murphy. If you pray, don't worry. If you worry, don't pray. Can't do both."

She patted the priest's hand. "The hell you can't."

Murphy smiled. She couldn't remember the last time her mother swore. Never in front of a priest. She thought her Lebanese mother was sounding more and more like her Irish father.

Tyke: "Why should half of us be in the dark? We're a family!"

Amira: "So what? Everyone doesn't need to know

everything. You think my parents told me everything? It's better this way. Less said, less suffering."

Dominick: "That makes no sense."

The ring of a telephone. Murphy turned and went to an end table in a far corner of the room. The nurses had been transferring calls to the room. Friends and relatives inquiring about her father. She picked it up while the voices continued behind her.

Duncan: "How'd it go?"

Murphy: "Horseshit. Thanks for asking. The little procedure turned into a big deal."

"Bypass?"

"Yeah. He's okay. Resting. We're in here taking off each other's heads."

"Sounds like you need a break. Up for a little fun?"

She sat down in a chair next to the table. "Now what?"

"Sheriff called. It's Hogan's blood in the bar."

She heard Tyke and Patrick going at it behind her. She pressed the phone tighter to her right ear and covered her left ear with her hand so she could hear Duncan more clearly. "How's he know? The DNA stuff can't be back already."

"A guy tromping through the woods on snowshoes found Hogan's sled under a pile of brush. Far from any trail. Someone had dumped it there. Someone who knew the area. Along with the snowmobile, they found Hogan's helmet." He paused. "Pocked with shot and dotted with blood. Like the front door of Maggie's Red Door."

She leaned forward in the chair. Told herself not to regret saving Clancy. She'd had to do it—as much for herself as for the boy. "What are the cops up north gonna do?"

"The kid has a fish house. They're gonna get inside. Check it out."

"And what are *we* gonna do?"

"Arrest Romeo at the house."

Murphy checked her watch. Already six. Like the rest of the clan, she'd been at Regions all day. Had eaten lunch and dinner there. "When do we go in?"

"I say we stick to the plan. Wait until the woman leaves the house in the morning. Keep it low-key. Send you and Castro in. Forget the men in black with the big guns."

Murphy knew Duncan hated calling in special teams to help. It meant a loss of control, and he wanted complete control over his operation. Whether the sheriff liked it or not, this had turned into Duncan's production. "Sure. We could do that." Shouting behind her. She turned her head. Saw Jack stepping between Ryan and Dominick. She turned her head back around. Stared at the blank hospital wall. Decided Duncan was right. She needed a break. "Tell Castro to swing by my place tomorrow morning and pick me up. We'll head on over from there. Watch Ransom leave. Go in and get Clancy. Who are we gonna send after Ransom?"

"I'll take care of the lady prof."

Murphy wasn't crazy about Duncan working on another case with her. "We could get help from another unit."

"I'll take care of her. It'll be good to hit the streets for a change."

She remembered her husband's father. "Maybe I better call Jack's dad. Warn him about what's going down."

"Why? We're gonna grab Ransom before she crosses the city line. The fewer who know about this ahead of time, the better. You can call him after the fact. Tell him why he didn't get a chance to fire her ass."

Douglas was going to be mad she left him out of the loop, but she had to agree with Duncan. More than once, Jack had warned her university faculty could be gossips. If Ransom got the slightest hint the police were looking at her and her new boyfriend, it'd be a disaster. "You're right, Duncan."

"I never tire of hearing that. So we're all set, then. What time should I tell Castro to pick you up?"

"Five-thirty sharp. None of his usual late crap."

"Good. I'll meet you guys outside her house at six. Should give us plenty of time. When she pulls out, I'll follow her. You guys take Clancy."

Murphy didn't know what Clancy would say when he realized his savior was a cop. She'd have to tell Duncan about what had happened out on the ice and in the house. She held the phone closer to her mouth. "Axel. I have to tell you something."

She rarely used his first name. It jarred him. Signaled she was about to spill something big. "What?"

"I did something last night. I don't know what you're going to think of me." She paused. "I drove by the Ransom woman's house."

"Castro told me you were going to do that. So?"

"So I did more than drive by the place." She looked over at Jack. He was preoccupied with her brothers. "I got inside."

"How in the hell did you do that?"

Here comes the really tough part, she thought. "I had to bring the kid home. He was trying to kill himself. He walked out on the ice. On Como. I saw. Went after him. We both went through."

"Holy shit."

"We only got wet up to our waists. The kid didn't know I was a cop. He thought I was some Good Samaritan. I took him back to Ransom's. He let me inside to warm up. I snooped around. Talked to her."

"I have so many questions about this deal, I don't know where to start. First one: Why did you risk your ass to save a murderer?" He paused, then answered the question himself. "You think this makes up for that freak who managed to off himself with your piece."

She gasped. How did Duncan read her so well? At the same time, she was relieved. Someone to talk to. "The head case didn't *manage* to off himself with my piece."

"I know the story. Wish I didn't. Irregardless, Paris, lives aren't interchangeable like that. You can't shuffle souls around. Trade them like baseball cards. What were you thinking?"

"Axel." She didn't know what else to say.

"Does Castro know any of this?"

"No. I was going to tell him later. Have a face-to-face. Not tell him *why* I saved the kid, just that I did it. Tell him I got inside the house."

"Anything come of that? See anything useful?"

"Not really. The bartender and the prof like their wine and whiskey. She's got a houseful of cats. He thinks she's Looney Tunes. I'm pretty sure she thinks he's an idiot. They're lovers, but they can't stand each other."

"Sounds like me and my ex. What else?"

"Something's gluing the two of them together. Clancy told me she's in serious trouble. I think they're *both* in it up to their eyeballs."

"In what? Did he give you any specifics about what went down in the bar?"

"She walked in while we were talking. Could hardly wait to get me out of the house. Clancy wouldn't have given me any details anyway. He's not as thick as Ransom thinks."

"Did you see any guns?"

"Not in the house. The kid might have been carrying a piece out on the lake with him. I decided it wasn't the time to take it away."

"Let's assume guns, then." He paused. Cleared his throat. "I'm gonna wear a shield. How about I have Castro throw a couple of vests in the car for you two?"

All the uniforms wore the vests as a regular part of their gear, but plainclothes cops saved the shields for risky situations. While the Kevlar provided an extra layer of protection against the wind in the winter, it could be a burden. Each vest weighed about five pounds. An extra load to carry. Duncan once told her he never wore the stuff. She wondered if his new caution was a holdover from the case they'd worked together. The killer took a swipe at Duncan with a knife. Nicked him on the chin. A shield wouldn't have helped in that situation. Still, maybe it had spooked Duncan. She decided to go along with it. "Vests would be good." Shouting behind her. A *thud*. She didn't want to look.

"What the hell is going on over there?"

She rubbed her forehead. Felt a headache coming on. "Murphy family meeting."

He laughed. "Should I send a squad over?"

"Not yet. I'll let you know."

Another *thud*. Murphy heard her mother yelling to King and breaking into more Arabic. *"Shoof! Shoof! Abouna!"* Look! Look! Father! Murphy turned and looked. Jack had pushed Dominick up against a wall and was holding him there by the arms.

"Gotta go." She hung up the phone and got up off the chair. Went to her husband's side. Put her hand on his shoulder. "Let's go."

Jack let go of Dominick's arms and backed away. "Good idea. I've had enough fun for today." He turned and went to a chair where he and his wife had their jacket and coat. He scooped both up and stomped out the door. Murphy grabbed her purse. Rushed past her mother and the priest.

King saluted her. "Nice seeing you, Paris. I'm sorry for the circumstances."

"Me, too," Murphy said over her shoulder and ran out the door.

TWENTY-SIX

MURPHY AND JACK went back to her boat. He kicked off his boots and dropped his jacket on the kitchen table. Went straight to the refrigerator, yanked it open and pulled out a St. Pauli Girl. "I could use a case of these tonight," he said, shutting the door.

"Don't hate my family," she said as she stood inside the front door, pulling off her boots and peeling off her coat.

"I don't." He shut the refrigerator and scanned the front of it. Plastered with bills and notes. The magnetic bottle opener was holding up the mass schedule for the cathedral. He looked for another magnet. Spotted her miniature police badge. He slapped that over the schedule and took down the bottle opener. Popped off the beer cap and dropped the cap and the opener on the kitchen counter. He lifted the bottle to his mouth and chugged. Wiped his mouth with the back of his hand. He walked into the living room and plopped onto the couch. Put his feet up on the coffee table, grabbed the remote and surfed. Stopped when he got to a hockey game. The Stars were playing at Colorado. He took a bump off his beer. "Babe. Good game. The Avalanche were up by two. Just scored again with two minutes left in the period."

"Be right there," she said from the kitchen. She draped her coat and purse over the back of a kitchen chair. Took his coat off the top of the table and draped it over another chair. She went to the refrigerator. Opened it. Decided to leave the beer for Jack. She pulled out a bottle of wine. Rested her free hand on the open refrigerator door while scrutinizing the label. French. Blanc de Lynch-Bages 1995. Jack must have bought it. She checked the price. Forty-five dollars. She looked toward the living room and opened her mouth to yell at Jack, but stopped herself. That's something her father would do. Complain about how much someone had spent on a bottle of wine. She and her mother seemed to be taking on her dad's habits while he was laid up in the hospital. Murphy found that both amusing and disturbing. She set the bottle back in the refrigerator. Jack had already started on beer, and the wine looked too good to enjoy alone. She pulled out a St. Pauli Girl and closed the door. Took the bottle opener off the counter, popped off the bottle top, dropped the cap on the counter. Slapped the opener back on the fridge. She snatched her cell phone off the counter and went into the living room. She sat down next to Jack. Took a long drink of beer. Set the beer on the table and put her feet up next to it.

Jack eyed the phone in her hand. "No yapping until the period ends."

"Yes, sir."

The second period ended. Murphy stared at the cell phone, trying to remember. Jack looked at her. Knew what she wanted. Recited the number for Regions. She punched it in. Asked for her father's room. Her mother picked up.

"Imma. How is he?"

"Good. How are you, daughter? How's that tough husband of yours?"

Murphy could hear the pride in her mother's voice. Amira Murphy was pleased that her son-in-law could stand up to the Murphy men. Get them in line. "We're both good, Ma. Tired."

"Get off the phone and go to sleep then. We can talk tomorrow."

"About tomorrow, Ma. I gotta work for a few hours. Do you mind? I've got to tie up some loose ends on a big case. They're short at the shop." Jack looked at his wife. Put the bottle to his lips and took a sip of beer. Murphy looked away from him. Didn't want to meet his eyes. He was pissed.

"Go to the station," said her mother. "Papa will still be here when you get off work."

"When will he be out? What did the surgeon say? The cardiologist?"

"The doctors. The nurses. They come in and they look at him and they leave. I don't know what the hell is going on."

Murphy suspected the cardiologist did tell her some things, but she'd tuned him out. Whenever someone in a medical uniform talked to her mother, she had trouble understanding them or chose not to understand them. Sean Murphy was pretty much the same way. "Want me to have Jack stop by in the morning during rounds? Have him talk to the cardiologist?" Jack looked at her again. Took another drink of beer.

"Sure, honey. That would be nice. Did you and Jack eat today? You want to go to the house? You know where we keep the key. I've got cabbage rolls in the fridge. Still good. Warm them up. Flat bread in the freezer."

"No thanks, Imma. Aren't you going home tonight?"

"Why should I? What's there? My husband is here."

Murphy looked over at Jack. Third period had started

and he had returned to watching the game, but with the mute button pushed. His eyes were locked on the action. His mouth was set hard. Hand wrapped around the beer bottle. He ran his other hand through his hair. His eyes and hands and mouth and hair. All things she'd missed while they were apart. *My husband is here.* That's how she felt. If Jack wasn't there, it wasn't home. Would Minnesota stop being home? Would it become a place that meant nothing, like an empty house? If Jack moved to Arizona, she'd have to go with him. She felt a lump rise in her throat. Swallowed it. A bitter pill taken without water. "You're right, Ma. Stay where you are. Should I send anything with Jack?"

"I'm fine. Brought plenty of underwear."

"Good. Jack wouldn't want to be hauling your underwear around with him." Jack raised his brows but kept his eyes on the television. "Okay, Imma. See you when I get off of work. Love you."

"Love you too, daughter."

Murphy shut off the cell and set it on the table. Picked up her beer and took a long drink. Held the bottle on her lap, cradled between her hands. "What's the score?"

Jack took the remote off his lap. Turned the sound back on, but lowered the volume. Dropped the remote on the couch between them. Finished off his beer and set the bottle on the table. "What's this about you working tomorrow? Don't those bastards up at the station give a shit that your father had a coronary bypass?"

"It's a big case." She took another sip of beer. Set the bottle on the table.

"So I heard. Is it that English professor and her boyfriend? I thought you weren't the one making that arrest. Sounds dangerous."

She regretted telling him anything about the case. Decided to lie. "There's some other stuff I gotta do. They're short."

He picked up the remote and shut off the game. Dropped the box back on the couch. "They're always short. It's always a big case. You always jump when they snap their fingers. Nothing ever changes up there. Jesus Christ. Get your priorities straight. Your father comes first. Your family. I come first. Fuck that shitty job."

His voice was hoarse. He'd had too much of her family the last few days. Maybe too much of her. This discussion about her work could easily turn into a big blowup. She wanted to avoid it. Tried to think of a compromise. "I've got to do a couple of things in the morning. Paperwork. Then I'm done, okay? I'll take off the rest of the time they owe me."

"Sure you will," he said dryly. He picked up the remote and held it in his right hand. As if he were weighing it. Set it back on the couch. Not between them. On his side. He put his right hand on her left thigh.

Here it comes, she thought. Might as well let him know it's okay to talk about it. "What else, babe? Let's hear it."

"What about the Mayo offer? They called again today. Want a commitment. We've been so busy with your dad. Your work. We haven't had time to sort this out. I know there's a lot going on, but we really need to talk."

She inhaled and blew out some air. Braced herself. "We could talk now. I've been thinking about it." Her eyes were drawn to the patio windows. Snowing again. Come morning, the frozen river's surface would be blanketed in yet another layer of smooth white. White over white over white. She'd miss the Mississippi, but not as much as she'd miss her husband. She couldn't stay behind, and she couldn't hold him back.

"Yeah?" He rubbed her thigh through her jeans. Studied his hand and her leg instead of her face. "What do you think?" He stopped rubbing. Waited for her response.

She pulled her eyes away from the window. Looked at him. His eyes were down. He was anticipating the worst. No support. No encouragement. Just the word *no*. She felt guilty that she'd conditioned him to expect that out of her. "If you really want to do it, we will. We'll move. I'll find something in Phoenix or Scottsdale. Hell, it's the Wild West out there, right? It's not like the Twin Cities has a lock on homicides."

He raised his eyes and stared at her. Smiled. "Seriously? That's it? No big fight? You'd move?"

She put her left hand on top of his right. Enjoyed the heat and weight and familiarity of his hand on her leg. "Yeah. I wouldn't be thrilled. But for you, for your career, I'd move. That's what married people do. Make changes for each other." She lowered her eyes. "Besides, you did a really big thing for me. You forgave me. Put it behind us."

He slipped his hand from under hers and brought his right arm up behind her. Wrapped it around her shoulders. Turned toward her and kissed her on the mouth. Pulled his lips off hers. "This means a lot. You have no idea."

"Yes I do," she said, lifting her eyes. That lump was fighting its way up her throat again. She swallowed hard.

TWENTY-SEVEN

HOW QUICKLY AND thoroughly this relationship has deteriorated! The passionate teacher and eager student have undergone a hideous metamorphosis. Witness now the desperate old whore struggling to control the sodomizing, sadistic devil. My sexual charms are fading for him. He wouldn't lay a hand on me after dinner, not even with a half dozen beers and a juicy steak lubricating his libido. The monetary seduction was successful, however. It's amazing what someone will do for a bag of coins. Thomas Hood:

> *Spurn'd by the young, but hugg'd by the old*
> *To the very verge of the churchyard mould;*
> *Price of many a crime untold:*
> *Gold! Gold! Gold! Gold!*

My boy didn't spurn my gold. Far from it. He cared not what the tasks were, as long as they paid well. He insisted on a down payment and I was in no position to argue. The

clock is ticking, and I have run out of options. When my tar-
nished knight has completed his first quest, he must return
to my castle and slay the dragons within these very walls.
Only then will he receive the second bag of coins. Catch is
my last hope. If he doesn't perform well tomorrow, I shall
suffer. So shall he. I shall make sure of it.

RANSOM tucked the pen in the crack of her journal.
Closed the book and set it on her nightstand. She reached
over to shut off the lamp and stopped herself. She looked
over at the empty pillow next to her. They'd both gone to
bed early. He was sleeping on the couch. His choice, not
hers. Regardless, she told herself she could leave the light
on all night if she wished. She held her breath and listened.
The scratching seemed to be getting louder. More insistent.
Her eyes fell on the closet door, even though she'd checked
the bolt a dozen times already. Yes. Still locked. She left the
lamp on. Fell back against the pillows, pulled the covers up
to her chin and willed herself to fall asleep. It was an un-
easy rest. She dreamed of flying dragons; all the monsters
had Clancy's face.

CASTRO camped out across the street from Ransom's
house into the evening. Bergen pulled up behind him a little after ten Thursday night. Castro spied him in his rearview mirror. Got out of his car and went over to talk to
his relief. Each detective drove an unmarked Ford Crown
Victoria. Castro's was silver, and Bergen's was dark blue.
Bergen rolled down the window. He didn't want to get out
and talk. Too cold and windy and snowy.
Castro leaned into the driver's side. Sniffled. His glasses
were steamed up. "I feel like shit."

"I feel worse." Bergen felt a sneeze coming on. He cupped his hand over his nose. The urge dissipated. He took his hand down. "What's the story? Any action?"

Castro shook his head. "They're both still in there." He stood straight. Pulled a gadget out of his pocket. Held it up. "Saw them through a crack in the curtains."

Bergen reached for it. Castro pulled it away. Buried it back in his jacket. "Get your own."

"Those are department binoculars."

"The hell they are. I paid for them myself." He took off his spectacles and wiped the lenses on the hem of his jacket. Slipped them back on. "And they ain't binoculars. It's an integrated binocular and digital camera."

Bergen gave him a dismissive wave of his hand. "Don't need special shit to watch a house anyways. Thought I'd get a gander at some titty is all. Watch the happy couple do the nasty on the couch."

"You're a sick fuck." Castro sniffled. Spotted the box of tissues on Bergen's car seat. Nodded toward it. "Give me a wad of that."

"You won't let me use your junk and you want my Kleenex? Use your sleeve." To rub it in, Bergen reached over, pulled a sheet out and blew his nose. Put his hand through the window and dropped the tissue at Castro's feet.

"You're a dick." Castro wiped his nose with the back of his glove. Moved the phlegm to the front of his mouth by making a growling noise in the back of his throat. He spat twice into the street. Wiped his mouth with the back of his glove. "I'll be back with Murphy in the morning. Duncan is meeting us here, too. We'll all get here six or earlier. The kid and the woman shouldn't be pulling out until six-thirty or so. Keep your eyelids open."

"Yeah, yeah." Bergen rolled up the window. Castro walked back to his car, got in and pulled away.

Even doped up with cold meds, Bergen was used to the third shift and had no trouble staying awake. As he covered the car seat next to him with snot-filled tissues throughout the night, he repeatedly told himself coming in sick was worth it. They'd agreed to pay him overtime. He'd be that much closer to his dream ride. He had his eye on a sweet Corvette. The color of ripe banana skins. Another cop was selling it. A guy in Vice who was getting married and needed some cash for the honeymoon. Bergen swore to himself he'd never let a woman take precedence over a hot car. He imagined himself riding around with the top down and the wind blowing in his hair. In his imaginings, he had better hair. Still blond, but thicker. Not thinning on top. He was also a foot taller in his driving fantasy. When that dream played itself out, he switched to watching Ransom's windows and imagining he could see a bare female breast or a bare female leg or a bare female bottom.

Fantasies aside, nothing involving his job ever got Bergen's pulse racing. He couldn't see why the other detectives in Homicide got worked up over this case or that. It all paid the same, unless there was overtime involved. He could get excited about cash. Not so much the money itself as what it could buy. Bergen liked to have fun, and every paycheck he received brought him closer to his latest toy. Over the summer it had been a new motor for his bass boat. The summer before that, it had been the boat itself. Bergen was in his thirties. Didn't have a wife. Didn't own a house. Didn't like kids. Rented an apartment downtown in a complex that was populated by singles. His place was so close he could walk to work. For some reason, however, he always found himself arriving late.

Halfway through his shift, Bergen checked his Dick Tracy wristwatch. Hours to go before he could go home and crash. He dipped his fingertips into the tissue box next to his thigh. Felt cardboard on the bottom. He looked over at the mound of dirty tissue on the passenger's seat. Started picking through it to find some that were less soiled, or at least dry. He found one, put it to his nose and blew. The snot went through the tissue and wet his hand. He dropped the Kleenex on the floor and wiped his hand on his pants. Should have brought another box with him, he thought. Going to be a long night.

TWENTY-EIGHT

RANSOM LOCKED HER door, turned and walked down the steps leading from her front stoop. She held on to the handrails as she went. The steps were covered with six inches of snow, and under the snow was a glaze of ice. She hadn't shoveled or put down salt since winter break had started. She paused after the last step. Looked up and studied the sky. Five in the morning and as black as night. Flakes were falling. Had been falling all night. "Cloudy out. That's good."

Clancy stood waiting for her on the sidewalk that ran in front of her house, between her yard and the boulevard. He pulled his gloves tighter over his fingers. "There'll be street-lights." He zipped his jacket up to his neck. Shoved his hands in his pockets. Hunched his shoulders in the wind. "That's not good."

"You'll have to be quick then. Quick and quiet like a cat." She stepped next to him and eyed the sidewalk. Knee-deep snow, while the neighbors on either side had only a few inches of white. She told herself she'd have to shovel soon.

She tromped ahead of him. Crunched across the boulevard to the curb. Both sides of her street were solid with unfamiliar parked cars—typical after heavy snows. To make way for the first salvo of plows, residents living on the busier roads had to move their cars to quieter blocks like hers. She stepped into the street and went around to the driver's side of the Explorer. Yanked open the door and tossed her purse on the front seat. Hopped in next to it. He opened the front passenger's door. Got in. Slammed it shut. She winced. "Try to make a little less racket." She closed her door. Put the key in the ignition. Started the Ford. Cranked up the heat. The fan slammed cold air into their faces.

"Should have started the thing and waited inside while it warmed." He felt something hard on the floor, under his boots. He looked down and saw a scraper. Brush on one end of the stick for snow and sharp edge on the other end for ice. He reached down and grabbed it. Sat up and put his hand on the door.

"Where are you going?"

"To clear off the windows." He popped open the door. Stepped out. Closed the door. Crossed in front of the truck to the driver's side. Leaned over and brushed snow off her side of the windshield. Flipped the stick and scraped off the ice. He looked through the swath of cleared glass. She was breathing hard. Fogging up the inside. He didn't like her looks this morning. Eyes too wide. Too blue. Excited. The sound of her voice. High-pitched with an edge of anger. Reminded him of that night in the bar. *Shoot him! Don't let him go! Shoot the bastard!* Here she was, telling him what to do again. At least he'd be making some money this time, he told himself. She'd already given him some cash. A wad was stuffed in the front pocket of his jeans.

He went around to his side of the Explorer and shivered. Wouldn't be so bad if not for the wind, he thought. The wind seemed to blow right through his clothes. Through his skin. Straight into his bones. He imagined that it felt even sharper since that dip in the lake. That the dunking had somehow made him more vulnerable to the cold. He set the scraper down on the hood for a moment while he pulled the cap tighter over his head. The hat was too small and kept riding up. It belonged to her. A black ski cap that could be pulled down as a face mask. He picked up the scraper with his left hand. With his right, he reached inside his jacket pocket. Felt the knife. The big one. The one she'd tried to use on him. He'd picked it out himself. Found some weird justice in turning around and using the thing on another man. He took his hand out of his pocket and wrapped it around the scraper. Brushed the snow off the hood and then worked on scraping snow and ice from his side of the windshield. While the shaves of ice curled off the glass, he thought about what they'd planned to do that morning. What she'd planned in an effort to save her job. She didn't tell him why she was being fired. He guessed it had something to do with all the students she'd been bringing home. He didn't care. Not as long as he got paid.

She said the professor lived close. She'd drop Catch near the front of the house or in the alley. She wasn't sure where the guy usually parked. She just knew it would be outside. Every winter, he complained his garage was too packed with junk to handle his Volvo wagon. She'd wait a couple of houses down, with the engine running. Catch would stab the guy's tire or tires. They hadn't yet decided if one or two would be good. One flat could be blamed on something sharp on the road. Two flats would send a message. She said he was a wimp who wouldn't know how to change a tire. One flat would rattle him. Make him miss his meeting with her and the other boss prof. Give her the weekend to come up with a way to fight the firing. Two flats would send the chicken shit into hiding for a week. Buy her even more time. She said he'd never figure she did it. If the guy happened to look out his window or if a neighbor noticed, they'd see a big man in a ski mask. Not a woman. The two of them would be long gone by the time anyone called the cops. The only question: One flat or two? They'd talk it through on their way to the guy's house. Make a decision by the time they got there.

Clancy went around to the passenger windows on his side of the Explorer. He brushed and scraped while his breath rolled out of his mouth in cottony puffs. He stopped and wiped his dripping nose with the back of his glove. Went around to her side of the truck. Worked on the windows. She looked at him through the glass. The inside must be warmer, he thought. Her breath had stopped steaming out of her mouth. Maybe she was so worked up she was holding her breath like an overexcited kid. Crazy bitch. As soon as this tire stuff was done, he was through with the Pink Lady and her crap. He hadn't told her that. She had one other thing she wanted him to do. Something back at her place. *Housekeeping chore,* she called it. God knew what she had in mind. A pile of bodies in the basement she had to get rid of. Lovers who hadn't dodged her knife. He didn't care what it was or how much more she'd pay. She'd already given him enough for a Greyhound ticket. He'd get back to her place. Grab his bag and leave. Hop a city bus to the station. Forget about seeing his brother. Bo didn't give a shit about him. He'd go as far south as the cash would take him. Get a job when he ran out. Earn some more travel money. Head south again. Keep going until the snow was gone and the sun was strong.

Clancy went around to the back window. Lifted his arms to start brushing. Realized the rear defroster had melted the snow and ice. He lowered his arms and looked at the back of her head through the glass. Dumb cunt. She'd yelled at him for slamming the door and here she was with the interior lit up. The truck looked like a lighthouse. The whole neighborhood would notice. Her hands were buried in her purse. She was probably digging for something important. Her makeup or a brush or more of that stinky perfume. She was so fussy about her hair she didn't want to wear a hat. Stupid. Her ears were going to get frostbite. He didn't care. He was sick of her shit. Let her freeze to death.

He went around to the front passenger's door and pulled it open. Tossed the scraper on the floor and got in. Shut the door. "Let's roll."

She pulled her hand out of her purse and looked at him. "Ready?"

"Yeah."

She flipped off the interior lights and turned on the headlights. Put the Ford in drive and pulled away from the curb. Activated the wipers. Punched on the truck's four-wheel drive. "Coming down heavier all of a sudden."

He stared outside the passenger window. The flakes were a solid sheet of white. "Might be in for another storm. Want me to drive?"

She took her right hand off the wheel and reached inside her purse again. Felt the hard outline through her gloves. She withdrew her fingers. Closed the purse and pushed it tighter against her thigh. Put her hand back on the wheel. "I can handle it."

WHEN Ransom and Clancy stepped out of the house, they didn't give the Crown Victoria a second glance; there were so many cars jammed onto the street. They didn't see Bergen slouched in his seat. The detective tried calling the station. No one picked up in Homicide. When the pair pulled away, Bergen checked his watch. They'd taken off a good hour earlier than expected. He wasn't supposed to do the tailing. He wasn't good at it, and he knew it. Everybody in the unit knew it. He pulled out and followed the truck while calling the commander. He caught Duncan as he was leaving his house.

Duncan: "I'll get ahold of Murphy and Castro. Stay on their asses. Keep calling in. Let me know what the fuck is going on."

Bergen went through a red light to keep up with the Explorer. Narrowly missed getting hit by a van. The van's driver honked at him. Flipped him the bird. "Shit."

Duncan: "What's wrong?"

Bergen: "Nothing. Where do you think they're headed?"

"The university still. Lind Hall. The woman probably has some paperwork she wants to pull together before her meeting. Some sort of defense or whatever."

The Explorer braked at a red light and Bergen stopped behind it. Slouched in his seat. "Yeah. Testimonials from all the freshmen she's done."

"I don't like it that Clancy is with her. Screws up our plan to get him home alone. Plus it makes me wonder what else they could be plotting. Why in the hell is she taking the bartender boyfriend with her?"

"Maybe he's going to be her character witness." Bergen sniffled. "Should I pull them over? You could send some squads."

"I want to see what they're up to. Don't lose them. I'm gonna hop in my car and head your way."

The light changed. The truck moved forward and Bergen followed. "What happens when I cross the city limits?"

"Don't worry about it. I'll give Minneapolis the heads up."

"Gonna have them send some backup?"

"Fuck no. This is our show."

TWENTY-NINE

SHE STEERED THE truck onto Lexington Parkway and headed south for University Avenue. It wouldn't be the most direct route, but Lexington and University were major streets and would be plowed. Besides, she only knew how to get to his house from University Avenue. She'd taken that way after school, when she'd dropped off classroom paperwork.

Clancy's head snapped back and forth as he took in the homes and businesses along both sides of the parkway. They stopped for a red light at Energy Park Drive. He pointed to the right. "What's down there?"

"Apartments. Offices. Some old railroad buildings converted into shops and restaurants."

He stared at the glow of lights to the west. "We should have gone for walks. Gone to the zoo. Bo told me once that Como's got a giant greenhouse open even in the winter. A place with a glass dome for a roof. Ponds with goldfish as big as your arm. Fountains and stuff."

"The conservatory. We passed it back there." The light turned green. She accelerated. The tires grabbed, and they lurched forward. "We could go this weekend."

He turned his head and looked at her. "We could."

She didn't like the way he said that. The voice of an adult humoring a child. The Explorer crossed a bridge that humped over some railroad tracks. They kept going. Went through a residential area with a mix of bungalows and large homes. She hung a right when they got to University. She'd been right. The avenue was plowed. She braked at a red light. The Ford slid a couple of feet before stopping. "The house is on a block with old-fashioned streetlights. They aren't as bright as regular lights. That could help."

Clancy turned his head and looked at her. Pushed the ski cap back from his brows. "So what's the magic number. How many tires?"

"Two. Even three. With three, there'd be no question that someone did it on purpose. For that matter, why not four?" The light turned green and she accelerated.

He nodded as he kept staring at the sights along the avenue. "Four ain't no accident. That's for damn sure."

They kept heading west on University. They drove past a shopping area with grocery and department stores. Car dealerships. Fast-food restaurants. She braked at a red light at Snelling Avenue. Despite the snow and the early hour, the intersection was busy. A Suburban rolled by, headed north on Snelling, followed by a pickup truck and a station wagon. A taxi. They all kicked up snow as they went. Two southbound minivans followed each other on Snelling. They were fishtailing. A string of other cars followed in their wake, slipping and sliding. A Metro Transit bus heading east on University was waiting for the light to change on the other side of the intersection. Clancy's eyes locked on the bus. The light turned green, and she stepped on the gas. They rolled through the intersection. His head turned as he watched the bus passing them, going in the opposite direction. She glanced at him as she steered. "Care to share your travel plans?"

"What?"

"Never mind," she said in a low voice. She told herself she was being paranoid. Catch was a country boy taking in the big city. She stopped at another red light.

He pointed to the left side of the road. "What's with the pig's head?"

"Porky's. A drive-in."

"Cool." He turned his head back around. Looked down at the dashboard. Punched on the radio. Started pressing buttons until he found a rock station. Cranked up the volume. Screeching guitars vibrated the inside of the Ford.

"I have a headache." She reached over. Punched off the radio. Put her hand back on the wheel, tightening her grip.

"Thought it would relax us."

"You thought wrong." The light changed, and she accelerated and veered from the left lane into the right in preparation for a turn a few blocks up ahead. Traffic had gotten heavier.

"It's an oven in this truck. Like your house." He reached over and turned down the heat.

"Turn that back up. It's still freezing in here," she snapped.

"Crabby." He turned the heat up again. Pulled off the ski cap and the gloves. Stuffed the gloves inside the hat. Unzipped his jacket.

"Don't get too comfortable. You've got work to do outside."

"Yeah. Yeah." He dropped the hat in his lap and stared out his window. Scratched his forehead. The tight cap left lines on his skin. His head whipped to the right.

She knew which sign had caught his eye. The one with the arrow pointing north. AMTRAK STATION ONE BLOCK. She came up behind another Metro Transit bus; it braked at the red lights at Vandalia Street. She stopped behind the bus. Turned her head and looked at Clancy. The Popsicles had melted into blue slits. "You'd better not be getting any ideas, mister."

He turned his head back around and looked at her with wide eyes. "What ideas? What?"

"You've still got *stuff* to do at my house."

He fingered the cap in his lap. "I know."

"Stop shopping around for a ride."

"I wasn't. Looking at junk. That's all." His eyes went to the road. The lights had changed, and the bus was moving. "Light's green."

Ransom didn't budge. She sat with her hands wrapped around the wheel and her eyes slicing a hole in his head. She said in a low hiss: "I'm serious, my love. Burn me and you'll regret it." Another Metro Transit bus had pulled up behind them. It honked. She returned her eyes to the road and accelerated.

Clancy stared straight ahead. Told himself not to freak because he was in a truck with a crazy woman. He'd dominated her once, and he could do it again. His palms were sweaty. He bunched the hat in his hands so the material would absorb the dampness. He briefly wondered if he could fling open the door and roll out of the truck at the next light. Make a dash for it. Head for the train station. He told himself that was a stupid idea. He couldn't run worth shit with his bad ankles. The nutty bitch would probably chase him down. Roll right over him. He concentrated on keeping a flat, expressionless face. *Dead-rabbit face.* That's what Bo called it. The face all the Clancy children put on after their father shot their rabbits. They knew if they cried, he'd beat them. They all worked at showing no emotion. They later learned the face came in handy whenever Owen Clancy was in a rage. The girls had been the best at it. Bo caught on eventually. It had taken Catch the longest, but he'd mastered it. *Dead-rabbit face.* Catch told himself that stabbing the guy's tires wouldn't take long. He'd go back home with her and take care of her chore and then take her money. Take off. She wouldn't need him after that. He could tell she was as sick of him as he was of her. He wished she were as afraid of him as he was of her. He told himself not to be afraid. He had a knife. She had nothing. No weapon. Only those razor Popsicle eyes.

WHEN they got to Raymond Avenue, she turned right. Steered the Explorer into a neighborhood of curving streets lined with restored Victorians. Most of the homes were still strung with blinking Christmas lights and evergreen garlands. The decorations were wrapped around porch columns and ran along rooflines and outlined windows. "Fancy area," said Clancy.

"Douglas and Helen have a nice home, but Kipp's place is a pit."

"Kipp? That's his last name?"

"First name. Kipp Henry. As I was saying, he let it go to hell after his wife left him. She was a silly woman. Ran off to work a dig in Israel with an archeologist. Now they're living in a kibbutz."

"What's that?"

"Forget it."

She steered the Explorer to the right and then to the left as she navigated the winding streets. "I never asked you. I guess it doesn't matter. I'm curious. Do you have any intention of ever returning to school?"

"You think I'm a dummy because I don't know what a kibble is?"

"Kibbutz. It's a collective farm. Everyone works together and all that."

"Big deal." The truck slid to the right as she braked at a stop sign and finally came to a halt in the middle of the intersection. "Nice stop. You sure you don't want me to drive?"

"I can handle it." She straightened the truck's tires and accelerated. Rolled out of the intersection. "Let's talk about this tire-slashing business."

"What's to talk about?" He fished the gloves out of the cap and pulled them on. "You drop me off at the dork's place. I cut his rubber. We take off." He pulled the cap over his head and zipped up his jacket. "No big deal."

BERGEN told himself it was no big deal when he lost site of the Explorer between Vandalia and Raymond. Bergen had been going too slowly, and a bus took advantage. Cut in front of him. A semi pulled up in the left lane before Bergen could steer around the bus. He was trapped behind two metal walls. He couldn't see shit up ahead. He didn't panic, however. He sat back and waited for traffic to start moving again. He knew where the woman was headed. He'd catch up.

After Ransom turned north, Bergen could have looked to his right and spotted the Explorer rumbling down Raymond. Instead, he looked to his left as he drove through the intersection. Eyeballed the coffee shop on the southwest corner of Raymond and University. Wondered what time it opened and if he could get a cup of French Roast on his way back to the station. When he straightened his head and looked in front of him, he saw the bus. The SUV had pulled away. He steered around the bus and scanned the lanes ahead. Didn't see his quarry. The snow was coming down hard. He figured they were a block or so up, on their way to the university. By the time Bergen pulled in front of Lind Hall on the east bank of the Minneapolis campus, he realized he'd figured wrong. He called the commander.

CASTRO had just pulled into the yacht club parking lot when Murphy got the call from Duncan. She held the cell phone to her ear with one hand, and with the other, grabbed her purse and flung the strap over her shoulder. "Where did he lose them?"

"University Avenue."

She pulled open her door and stepped out. Slammed it shut. Jack would have to lock up. She thumped down the dock. "University and what?" She couldn't hear Duncan clearly. He was on his cell. She stepped onto shore and ran for the parking lot. "Duncan. You still there? University and what?" She got to the Crown Victoria, yanked open the front passenger's door, tossed her purse on the seat and hopped in. Shut the door.

Castro eyed Murphy. "What's up?"

She pressed the phone tight to her ear. Held up her free hand to quiet Castro. "Duncan. University and what?"

"He thinks somewhere around Raymond."

"Son of a bitch," she breathed. Ransom and Clancy were after Douglas or his successor. "I know where they went. The St. Anthony Park neighborhood."

Castro looked at her. Asked in a low voice, "That where we're headed?" She nodded. He pulled out of the parking lot.

Murphy said into her cell: "A bunch of university faculty live in that area. I'm worried about two in particular. The two she was suppose to meet with this morning. Ransom may be after them."

Duncan: "Clancy's her hit man."

"Yeah." Murphy started digging through her purse. Found her personal address book. Gave Duncan her in-laws' address. "We need backup there and at a home across the street. A prof named Kipp Henry lives there."

Castro steered the car through downtown. Asked Murphy, "Should I slap on the lights?"

She nodded. Kept talking into the phone. "Duncan. I'm gonna hang up and call my father-in-law. I want to make sure he locks his doors."

Castro looked at her with wide eyes. He steered the car onto Interstate 94 heading west.

"I'm meeting you and Castro over there," said Duncan. "How many vests did he bring?"

Murphy turned around and scanned the backseat. Nothing. She looked at Castro. Held her hand over the phone so Duncan wouldn't hear. "Where are the shields?"

"At the shop."

She took her hand off the phone and said to Duncan, "You'd better bring some shields with you."

Duncan: "Too late. I'm already on the road. Which exit for St. Anthony Park?"

"Take Cretin-Vandalia. Duncan. Be careful. No cowboy stuff. Call for backup."

"Don't worry about me. Call your in-laws."

"Call for backup. I mean it. Duncan?" She took the phone away from her ear.

"You lose him?"

"Hung up on me. Stubborn jackass." She punched in a phone number. Chewed her bottom lip while she listened. It rang five times before the answering machine picked up. Douglas's recorded voice: *"You've reached the home of Helen and Douglas Ramier. We're unable to take your call at the moment. At the tone, please leave your name and phone number. We'll get back to you as soon as possible."* She left a message. Strained to make her voice sound calm. "Douglas. Helen. Serene Ransom might be headed over to your place or to Henry's. She's got a dangerous guy with her. He may be armed. We're sending over some squads. Lock your doors and stay inside. Stay away from the windows." She hung up. Dropped the phone in her purse. "I was worried my own father was going to die this week, not my father-in-law."

Castro steered around a slow-moving minivan. "Murphy. Holy shit."

She was digging in her purse again, this time to check her Glock. "I'm sitting here praying to God that Ransom is going after the other guy. Not Jack's dad. Isn't that horseshit?"

THIRTY

CLANCY'S BACK WAS turned to the professor's house as he hunkered down to stab the tire on the front passenger's side of the Volvo. He'd already sliced the front tire on the driver's side and as far as he was concerned, he was finished. Two flats seemed enough, he thought. She could do it herself if she wanted more. She couldn't see what he was doing anyway. She was parked two houses up. She'd wanted to keep the engine running, but he'd insisted that she shut it off. Then he'd reached over and pulled the keys out of the ignition. Shoved them in his jacket pocket.

"You don't trust me," she'd said.

"Fucking right," he'd responded.

As Clancy worked, the ski cap kept crawling up. He could feel his head sweating under the hat. He wished he could yank the thing off and run his hands through his wet mop.

*　　*　　*

PROFESSOR Kipp Henry would have envied Clancy's mop. Henry's thirty-something wife, a part-time art instructor at a community college, left him for a younger man with lesser academic credentials but a thicker head of hair. Since then, Henry had taken to standing in front of the bathroom mirror and scrutinizing his hairline. He imagined it receded a little more every morning. He'd tried quantifying it once by using a ruler and measuring the distance from the top of his right brow to the beginning of his hairline. His left brow suffered a nervous twitch and was useless as a consistent starting point for his calculations. After a month and three days, he lost the ruler under a pile of junk on the kitchen table. He told himself it was becoming a depressing exercise anyway. His life was already packed with depressing rituals.

Every morning he rose at a quarter past five, rolled from his back to his side and shut off his bedside alarm clock before it could go off. He kept it set to ring at half past five. He never overslept. Without the security of a bedmate to wake him, however, he needed the clock to reassure him he would never be late for class. He'd slide out of bed and shuffle to the bathroom. Bend to lift up the toilet seat even though it was already up. There was no longer a woman in the house to leave the seat down. After urinating, which lately was taking longer and longer, he'd go over to the tub and turn on the tap. Feel the water to make sure it was hot enough. Turn on the shower. Step into the tub. Close the vinyl curtain. Tell himself the mold at the bottom of the curtain was natural. A form of plant life. After a seven-minute shower—ten minutes was a waste of water, and five minutes wasn't enough to rinse the shampoo from his hair— he'd turn off the shower and step out of the stall. Wrap a towel around his thickening waist and stand in front of the medicine-cabinet mirror. He'd run a fine-toothed comb— like the kind used in barbershops—through his damp hair.

After eight strokes, from front to back, he would examine the plastic teeth. Count each gray hair as he pulled it off and dropped it down the drain.

He'd wear the same thing to school every day. Khaki slacks with elastic on the sides and a white polo. The only variation would be the length of the shirtsleeves. Winter dictated long sleeves; all other seasons required short. Breakfast was always two slices of toasted white bread spread with apple butter. The toast was washed down with two cups of strong coffee, two teaspoons of sugar per cup. One teaspoon wasn't sweet enough, and three made the molars on the bottom left side of his mouth ache. He'd leave the dirty plates and cups in the sink until there were no more left in the cupboard. Then he'd wash them by hand because he didn't want to touch the dishwasher. His wife had interrupted the rinse cycle the day she left him. Corrine had needed to grab her retainer case out of the top rack. She'd had a perfect bite since high school because she'd followed her orthodontist's instructions and continued to wear her retainer to bed. Whenever he approached the dishwasher's control panel to restart the rinse cycle, it reminded him. Corrine was gone. She'd left behind his broken heart and a dishwasher full of plates that still needed to be rinsed. She'd also left behind the retainer itself. Forgot it on the bathroom counter in her rush to catch a flight to Tel Aviv. Anyone else would be mystified by how someone could remember a retainer case but forget the retainer itself. Henry could explain it perfectly, however. He knew his wife inside and out. He'd long ago discovered there was no inside of any substance. Corrine was an airhead with perfect teeth who, as luck would have it, was incredible in bed. He missed her terribly and kept her retainer under his pillow.

While Henry's personal life was a mess, he'd succeeded in keeping his professional life tidy. He always arrived at Lind Hall at 6:45 so he could squeeze in an hour of work before his first class. Over lunch, he brought food back to his office so he could correct papers and meet with students in between bites. They'd all gotten used to seeing the twelve-inch Subway Cold Cut Trio on their professor's desk. They didn't mind his fondness for extra onions. More than any other professor in the University of Minnesota English Department, Kipp Henry was adored by students. His lectures were so riveting, his undergraduates would set their pens down and forget to take notes. His comments scrawled on the margins of their essays were tough, but tempered by good humor. He'd stop on the mall to talk to kids about anything and everything. The poor use of dialogue in modern fiction. The poetry of William Blake. The demise of outdoor baseball stadiums.

He was as respected by his colleagues as he was loved by his students. Before joining the University of Minnesota English Department thirty years earlier, he'd served as a professor of English and American literature and language at Harvard. He'd been an exchange professor at the University of Dublin and a Fulbright lecturer at the University of Southern Denmark. He was the recipient of the University of Minnesota College of Liberal Arts Distinguished Teacher Award. He had four books under his belt—two modestly successful mystery novels, a well-received set of poems and a textbook used in senior-high literature classes around the country. His current projects were writing a review of Jewish-American poetry for *American Literature* and contributing a chapter to a book chronicling the deterioration of proper punctuation in twentieth-century newspaper writing. His chapter was on the misuse of the parenthesis—a suitable topic, he thought, for a precise man trapped in imprecise times.

In the end, it was Henry's precision—along with the dishwasher—that proved his undoing. While sitting at his kitchen table Friday morning, he glanced over at the pile in the sink and determined it was time to do the dishes again. This conclusion was reinforced by the fact that he was sipping coffee out of a juice glass and eating toast off of a square of toilet paper. At the same time, it struck him that he was spending too much time washing dishes relative to other household duties. He theorized that if he could more evenly distribute his limited morning minutes among a variety of domestic tasks, he could dig himself out from the squalor. To that end, he decided to start using the dishwasher. He set his cup down and stood up. Picked up the last piece of toast from the toilet paper and rifled it into his mouth. Chewed and walked over to the appliance. He took a breath and reached his hand down. Pushed the Resume button on the control panel in an attempt to continue the rinse cycle that Corrine had interrupted so many months earlier. Nothing happened. He pushed it again. Nothing. Perhaps if he opened and shut it again, he thought. He tried pulling open the door. It wouldn't budge. He needed a tool, he thought. A crowbar. He'd used it recently, but couldn't remember for what purpose. He leaned one hand against the counter and frowned. If he could remember why he'd used it, he might be able to recall where he'd left it. It came to him. He'd taken down a painting that Corrine had given him as a birthday gift. A hideous watercolor of a bowl of fruit. He'd used the claw end of the crowbar to remove the nail from the wall. The watercolor had been hanging in the front room. Ergo, the tool had to be in that vicinity. As he left the kitchen and walked across his front room floor, stepping over copies of the *New York Times* from the previous four Sundays, he glanced through his bay windows. That's when he saw a masked man on the boulevard, crouched next to his station wagon.

Henry was not only a precise man; he was a brave one. At least braver than anticipated by Ransom and Clancy. He was also fed up. His block was being tormented by teenagers. A

couple of new families had moved into the neighborhood a
year earlier. Their children tore up and down the street in
their trucks. Over the summer they snatched planters off
porches. Broke them in the street. Over Christmas, they'd
taken the illuminated Nativity scene from a corner house.
Stuffed the plastic Baby Jesus in another neighbor's basketball hoop. Henry was sure the person crouched next to
his car was one of the delinquents. "Vandal," he said under his
breath as he stared at the figure on his boulevard. "I'll teach
you a lesson." The professor ran his eyes around the floor for
his boots. Couldn't see them for all the newsprint. He kicked
at Sunday Travel and spotted his slippers underneath.
Stepped into them. He looked for his coat. Found it thrown
over a ladder-back chair painted to look like an obese nude
woman—another of Corrine's masterpieces. He scooped
the coat off the chair and pulled it on. Didn't bother but-
toning it up. Found the crowbar on the seat of the chair—in
the folds of the nude woman's belly. He grabbed the tool
with his right hand. It felt sturdy and dependable. He swung
it once to the left and once to the right. Satisfied he'd mastered the finer points of wielding a crowbar as a weapon, he
yanked open his front door and marched out of his house.

CLANCY cranked his right arm back and up. Brought the
blade down into the side of the tire. He adjusted his grip.
Wrapped his fist tighter around the knife handle to pull the
blade out. The thing was stuck. Jammed into the rubber just
above the curb. "Great," he muttered. He pulled harder.
Wiggled the blade handle side to side. Up and down. Pulled
again. The knife came out, slipped through his gloves and
dropped into the gutter. "Terrific." His ankles were aching.
He leaned his left hand against the side of the car while he
reached down to retrieve the knife. As he stretched out his
right arm, the ski mask crawled up his face. The eyeholes

were over his eyebrows. He pulled his hand out of the gutter and reached up. Tugged down on the hem of the mask until he could see again. Reached down for the knife. Felt the handle before he saw it. He picked it up and held tight to it with his right hand. He didn't want to drop it again. He groaned as he stood up, sliding his left hand up the side of the Volvo for support. He pivoted around and faced the owner of the station wagon standing on the sidewalk.

Henry raised the crowbar over his right shoulder, took a step forward and paused with his mouth open. The person in front of him was not a teenager. This was an adult male six inches taller than he with broad shoulders and big arms. He wore a ski mask like the kind robbers donned to disguise their identity. In his hand was the biggest knife Henry had ever seen. This man was not a minor annoyance, but a real criminal. Henry cocked his arm back to emphasize he intended to use the bar in his hand. "Drop the knife." The eyes staring out through the ski mask were wide. Shot up to the crowbar raised in the air. Henry took another step forward. "Drop it."

If only it was another knife or even a gun, thought Clancy. He'd gladly drop his knife and let the old man do him in. A crowbar wouldn't do it, though. It'd be messy and bloody and wouldn't finish the job. Maybe it'd just leave him goofy in the head. A goofy gimp in prison. Clancy decided he couldn't let that happen. His eyes darted down to the knife in his own hand. The blade was pointed down. He told himself if he relaxed his grip on the handle, the knife would slide from his fingers and plummet to the ground. Stick straight up in the snowbank. Excalibur embedded in a rock. He looked up at the man standing in front of him. Clancy noticed there were crumbs on the man's lips; the guy had been eating breakfast. He was smaller than Clancy had imagined he'd be, and older. Clancy wondered what would happen if he tightened his fist around the knife handle instead of loosening it. Aimed the blade straight ahead like a lance and charged. Excalibur embedded in a man's chest. Henry took a third step. Started bringing the crowbar down. Clancy raised the knife so the blade stuck straight out. He lunged toward the professor's torso. A white target under the brown coat.

The blade pierced Henry's chest. Henry dropped his arm, and the crowbar fell into the snow. The professor clamped both his hands over the knife handle. He looked down at the thing sticking out of his body. Saw the red spreading around it. Still clutching the handle, he looked up at his assailant. The man had pulled off the ski cap. Henry's eyes were drawn to the thick head of hair. Henry opened his mouth to say something. What came out was a gurgle. Henry stumbled two steps forward. Swayed as he stood less than a foot from his assailant. The professor made another sound. Like air escaping from a balloon. He swayed forward and back and forward again. His hands dropped from the knife handle. He collapsed on his back on the boulevard. His hands at his sides. His legs sticking straight out. His feet inches from the killer's feet.

Clancy took a step back. Felt the side of the Volvo against his back. Dropped the ski mask in the gutter. "Fuck. Mister. You okay?" Clancy poked at the bottom of the man's feet with the toe of his boot. Saw the old guy was wearing slippers. That made him feel worse than seeing the crumbs. "Fuck, mister. Why'd you have to have a stupid crowbar?" Clancy leaned his back against the Volvo and stared. Couldn't pull his eyes off the figure sprawled at his feet. For an instant, the old man dead in the snow became Owen Clancy. A middle-aged man dead in the leaves. Clancy shut his eyes and opened them again. He was relieved to see his father was gone. A dog barked in the distance. Then another. The noise snapped him out of his trance.

Clancy didn't want to step near or over or around the body. He pressed his back against the station wagon and slid until he was clear of the dead man. He turned and ran across the boulevard and into the street. Headed for the Explorer. She had the interior lights on again. This time he was glad. The Ford was a lantern in the falling snow. As he ran, he shoved his hands into his coat pockets. Found the truck keys. Pulled them out. During the seconds it took him to reach Ransom, Clancy didn't worry about the body he'd left behind. His only concern was whether she was going to bitch at him because he'd stabbed two tires instead of three or four. It didn't occur to him until he reached the Explorer and put his hand on the door handle that it didn't matter how many tires he'd stabbed. Professor Kipp Henry was not going to be firing anyone today.

Clancy yanked open the front passenger door, threw Ransom the keys and hopped in. He slammed the door shut while she plugged the key into the ignition and started up the Ford. She reached over to the dashboard and turned off the dome light.

He said: "Waiting for a fucking invitation? Go!"

She put the Explorer in drive and rolled down the snow-clogged street. "What happened?"

He stared straight ahead. "Nothing. Flattened a couple of his tires and left."

"Liar. I saw through my rearview mirror."

"You didn't see shit." He thumbed over his right shoulder. "You went through a stop sign back there. You want us to get picked up on a stupid traffic violation?"

"I'm not the one who should be worried. I didn't stab a man to death." She braked at another stop sign. Smiled and looked at Clancy. "He is dead, right?"

Clancy stared back at her and blinked twice. The crazy bitch from the bar shooting was definitely back. "He's gone." He looked down at his jacket and gloves. Wondered if there was blood on them. The thought made him feel like vomiting. He pulled off the gloves and tossed them down to the floor. He unzipped his jacket. Noticed his hands were trembling and his palms were wet. He wiped his palms on the thighs of his pants. "I'm sweating like a stuck pig." He reached over to the dashboard and turned down the heater. Put his trembling hand on the passenger door buttons and lowered his window. The fresh air smelled good. The urge to throw up was dissipating.

She steered the Explorer around another curving street. "I couldn't see exactly. What did he have in his hand? A small bat or something?"

"A stupid crowbar." Clancy wrapped his arms around his middle and tucked his fists under his armpits. Maybe that would stop his hands from shaking. "Looked ready to take my head off with it."

"I didn't give him enough credit. Didn't think he'd do something like that. Go after another man. Courageous."

"Stupid is more like it." Clancy untangled his arms from his body. Wiped his nose with the cuff of his jacket sleeve.

"No one saw?"

"Nope. Quiet outside. No passing cars. No neighbors out. Not yet at least. Couple of dogs barking is all." Clancy ran his fingers through his hair. Looked at his right hand. Still shaking, but not as violently. He tucked both his hands under his legs. "Now what?"

She stopped at an intersection. "We go home, clean off the knife and open a bottle of champagne."

His mouth dropped open. "The knife!"

"You left the knife?"

He pulled his hands out from under his legs. Held out his palms. "Do you see it on me?"

"My prints are on the knife! Your prints!" Her eyes went to his mop of hair. "Where's the ski mask?"

He felt like puking again. Swallowed twice to keep it down. Braced himself for her reaction. "Dropped it I guess."

"You guess? We have to go back!" She did a U-turn in the middle of the intersection.

He grabbed the steering wheel. "Stop!"

She slammed on the brakes. The truck skated to a halt. "We have to go back! We can't leave evidence behind! Our prints are on the knife! Our hair inside the hat!"

Her voice was so high-pitched it was hurting his ears. He told himself he'd have to be the calm and cool one this time. "We can't go back there," he said evenly.

"You said nobody saw anything!"

"Not while I was doing it." He took his hand off the steering wheel. Looked through the windshield. Nodded toward a house on the corner. A man in a bathrobe had opened his front door and was bending over his front stoop. "Neighbors are getting up by now. Flipping on their porch lights. Taking their newspapers off their steps. Leaving for work. For sure someone's already seen his body. They're on the phone to the cops."

"We could check. We could drive by."

"No way."

"Where are we going, then?"

He looked through his open window. Some snowflakes wafted inside. Along with them, the sound of sirens. He hadn't expect them so soon. "Shit."

"Catch. Where should we go?"

He turned his head and looked at her. "Away from here."

THIRTY-ONE

"TURN HERE!" YELLED Murphy.

"Got it." Castro took a right. The Crown Victoria fish-tailed. He straightened out the car, and they rumbled down the street.

Murphy ran her eyes up and down both sides of the block as they went. Spotted the body sprawled on the boulevard. Pointed at it through the windshield. "Son of a bitch."

"I see it." Castro pulled up next to the Volvo and braked. Shoved the car into Park and radioed for an ambulance. Murphy pulled her gun out of her purse and slipped it in the pocket of her coat. She threw open her door. Was reassured to hear sirens in the distance; Duncan had called for backup. She jumped out of the car and ran to the figure in the snow. She fell to her knees next to the body. His eyes and mouth were open. A round stain colored the front of his shirt. As snow hit the bloody circle, the flakes melted into the wetness. In the middle of the red, a knife handle. A dart stuck into the bull's-eye. She pulled off her right glove and cupped her hand over his nose and mouth. No breath. She pressed her fingertips against his neck. Nothing. She pulled her glove on and sat back on her heels. "Son of a bitch." She scanned the area around the body. Saw the crowbar in the snow. Guessed the professor had used it to defend himself. Was his attacker still around? She looked up and across the street. Douglas and Helen. She jumped to her feet and ran.

Duncan pulled up behind Castro. Saw the body on the boulevard. Castro on the radio. Murphy dashing across the street. He pushed open his car door and went after her. "Murphy!" he yelled to her back. She was running up the porch steps. "Don't go in without backup! That's a fucking order!"

She yanked open the screen door and ran inside the porch. Duncan came up behind her. She pounded on the front door with one hand and jiggled the knob with the other. "Helen! Douglas!"

Duncan pushed her aside. "Get back!" He turned sideways and kicked the door. His leg bounced off the wood. "Fucking old-world craftsmanship." He stepped back to get a running start and try it again.

The door popped open. Helen Ramier stood in the doorway, dressed in a bathrobe with a towel twined around her head and slippers on her feet. "Paris! My God! What is it?" She eyed the man standing next to her daughter-in-law and pulled the robe tighter around her body.

Murphy grabbed the older woman by the shoulders. "Douglas?"

"Upstairs in the shower." Helen heard the sirens. She looked past Murphy and the unfamiliar man. Saw a string of squads pull into the street. "What is it?"

Murphy took her hands off her mother-in-law's shoulders. "You didn't pick up my message."

Helen pulled her eyes off the squads. Looked at her daughter-in-law. "We heard the phone ring." Her eyes were drawn to the street again. "What happened?"

Castro stepped onto the porch. Duncan turned and told him: "Put Mrs. Ramier in a squad while we search the house."

Helen's eyes widened. She stared at the man giving orders on her porch. "Our house? Why?"

Douglas stepped into the doorway and stood behind his wife. His hair was wet. He was dressed in a water-spotted tee shirt, slacks and moccasins. Half ready for work. He eyed the trio standing in front of his wife. Looked past them into the street. Brushed strands of damp hair off his forehead. "What in God's name?"

Murphy looked over her mother-in-law's head to her father-in-law's face. Felt a knot in her stomach loosen. Her husband's dad was alive. She said to Douglas: "You and Helen need to wait in a squad while we go through the house. Professor Henry has been murdered."

Helen gasped. Clapped her hand over her mouth. Douglas's mouth fell open. Castro trotted back outside and held the porch door open for them. The couple stepped out of the doorway and walked through their porch and down the steps. Murphy watched their backs as they left. She saw Douglas take Helen's hand in his. Castro let go of the screen door and followed the couple down the sidewalk.

Murphy and Duncan drew their guns. They peered through the open doorway into the house. "I'll take point," said Duncan. He stepped inside, and Murphy followed.

*   *   *

BY the time Duncan and Murphy stepped back outside, the sun had started to come up, the snow had stopped falling and the street had turned into a parking lot. Six squads. Three unmarked police cars. The Ramsey County Medical Examiner's hearse. Two paramedic units. Police tape blocked off both ends of the street. More ribbon blocked both ends of the walk that ran in front of Henry's house. The boulevard containing the body was squared by yellow, as was the dead man's house and yard. Across the street, more ribbon was staked in a straight line on both sides of the Ramier house— from the alley behind it to the boulevard in front of it.

Except for the gap created by the taped-off sidewalk in front of the Ramier home, a solid wall of neighbors lined the walk across the street from Henry's house. A ragtag firing squad. Some gawkers were dressed in pajamas with down jackets pulled over their nightclothes and boots on their feet. Others shivered in their robes and slippers. A man wearing a dress coat and carrying a briefcase stood on his tiptoes for a better look. Several people, including a few children in Catholic-school uniforms, stood in the front yard of the neighbor to the right of the Ramier place. The yard was elevated a bit and offered a prime vantage point from which to watch the action. The media had also figured out which yard had the best view. Mixed with the parochial plaid and pink bathrobes were television crews and newspaper reporters. In one corner of the yard, a female reporter talked while a cameraman filmed her. In another corner, a male reporter interviewed a sobbing woman while a photographer snapped pictures.

"Look at this shit," sneered Duncan as he pushed open the porch door and walked down the steps. He heard a roar and looked up. Television news helicopters dotted the sky. He looked over his shoulder at Murphy. "Circus has come to town."

Murphy shut her in-laws' front door, turned and followed

Duncan off the porch. "No surprise." She knew the murder of a professional in an upscale neighborhood would be big news.

The two of them stepped into the street. She stopped and rubbed her forehead with her fingertips. She finally had time to think about what had happened to Henry. What had almost happened to her father-in-law. How it all could have turned out differently had she let Clancy keep walking toward the open water. She needed to talk to someone. The only one who knew the whole story. He was standing by her side. "Axel . . ."

He put his hand on her shoulder. Turned her toward him. "Don't. What's done is done."

She bent her head down. "You were right. Lives aren't something you can trade. My stupid thinking cost a man his life. Could still cost others theirs."

He bent his head toward hers. "Listen to me, Paris. After we talked about what happened on the lake, I started thinking. It boils down to this: You stopped a man from committing suicide. Period. You saved a life. Nothing wrong with that. Any one of us could have done that. Should have done it. What happened here this morning, this isn't your fault. This is Bergen screwing up and Clancy and Ransom doing their thing. It has nothing to do with you. Stop thinking everything is your fault."

She looked up at him. "If I hadn't saved him, this wouldn't have happened."

He squeezed her shoulder. "You don't know that. If Clancy had died, Ransom might have done the job by herself. She might have sucked in another patsy to help her. Someone with a gun instead of a knife. Could have taken out half the neighborhood."

"Okay," she said. "You're right."

"Stop saying that so much. You're scaring the shit out of me."

Murphy glanced around to make sure no one had stepped into earshot. She said in a low voice: "What I did out on the lake. Can we keep it between us?"

He raised his brows. "You didn't tell Jack?"

She shook her head. "No."

"Fine. We'll keep it our secret as long as we can. We'll see what Clancy and Ransom say when we haul them in. If they recognize you, if they bring it up, we'll cook up some bullshit about you working undercover."

She grinned. "That's what I was doing, more or less."

"More or less my ass." He put his mouth closer to her ear. "That makes two secrets I'm keeping for you, lady. You owe me." He looked down the street. "I gotta check in with the ME. You go find your relatives. Take care of them." Duncan dropped his hand from her shoulder and walked over to the hearse.

She watched him go. *You owe me.* Was Duncan serious? She took a deep breath. Exhaled. Told herself to stop thinking so much. She ran her eyes from one police vehicle to the other until she found a squad with the older couple huddled in the backseat. She went over to the car, parked in the middle of the street. Murphy pulled open the back passenger door. Rested her hand on the top of the door and leaned inside. "How are you two holding up?"

Her in-laws looked up at her. Both had red eyes and tight lines around their mouths.

"Don't worry about us," said Helen. She'd pulled the turban off her head and had the towel folded on her lap. Her hair hung flat and damp. She sniffled and tightened the belt around her robe. "We're fine."

"The hell we are," said Douglas. His hair had dried into a carpet of tight, gray rings around his head. He folded his arms over his chest. "What the hell is going on? No one is telling us anything. What happened to Kipp?"

Murphy: "We're still figuring it out."

Douglas: "Serene did it. That's what you're thinking."

Murphy took her hand off the door and stood straight. "We're interviewing neighbors in case they saw anything. Collecting some evidence we found at the scene."

Douglas: "A murder weapon? How did she do it? We didn't hear a gunshot. Even with the doors and windows closed, wouldn't we have heard?"

Murphy didn't want to tell them too much. "It wasn't a gun."

Douglas shook his head. "I should have terminated that witch years ago."

Murphy's eyes widened. She was surprised to hear her father-in-law talk like that. "It's not your fault."

Helen patted her husband's thigh. "You and Kipp were both meeting with her this morning." She leaned forward and glanced out the door, at the scene beyond Murphy. "That could be you."

Murphy turned and looked. The ME guys were wheeling a gurney over to their hearse. On top of the gurney was a bagged body. Murphy turned back around. Rested her arm on the door. "The two of you spend the night at Jack's place."

"In case she comes back to finish the other half of the job?" asked Douglas.

Helen inhaled sharply and squeezed her husband's leg while addressing her daughter-in-law. "You can't let her go after Douglas."

Douglas's upper lip curled into a sneer. He said to Murphy, "I'd like to see her try. I'll take care of her myself. Save the justice system some time and money."

Murphy stifled a smile. She'd never seen this side of her father-in-law—and she liked it. He reminded her of Jack whenever he got backed into a corner. A Boy Scout slipping on the brass knuckles. "I'll have a couple of uniforms keep an eye on your house while you're gone." She patted her coat pockets. Realized her phone was in her purse, in the Crown Victoria. "I'll get my cell and call Jack. You two stay here and stay warm."

Helen fingered the towel in her lap. "I'd like to get dressed, dear. May we return to the house? Pack a few things?"

"Sure," said Murphy. "Let me send a couple of officers to accompany you inside."

"Is that necessary?" asked Douglas.

Murphy eyed the crowd. The onlookers were respecting the tape that was keeping them off the Ramiers' sidewalk, but she was afraid there were some reporters mixed in with the regular folks. They could start firing off questions, and Murphy didn't want her in-laws saying anything that could jeopardize the case. She didn't want Helen or Douglas in the news at all. "How about I have two of our guys walk you to the front door and then wait for you on the porch?"

"That would be satisfactory," said Douglas.

Murphy waved over two uniformed officers. Big women who didn't take any crap. "Carter. Boone. Escort the Ramiers up to the house and wait for them on the porch. They've gotta throw some things into a suitcase. Lock up."

"You betcha," said Carter, a husky blonde.

"Keep the media away from them," said Murphy.

"Don't worry," said Boone, a tall African-American woman. She folded her arms over her chest. "We know how to handle those assholes."

Helen and Douglas slid out of the car, glanced nervously at the crowd outside. They followed Boone to the house while Carter walked next to them. A man broke from the sidewalk throng. Hopped over the tape and onto the sidewalk. Cody. The *Pioneer Press* cop reporter. His shoulder-length hair hung out of his Elmer Fudd cap. Murphy could see his signature Hawaiian shirt poking out from under his down jacket. Notebook in hand, Cody stepped between Boone and the Ramiers. "Do you know who did it? What did you see this morning? Can I get your names?"

Boone turned around and stepped behind Cody. Bent down and said into his ear, "Back behind the tape. Now."

Cody turned around and looked up at her. "Trying to do my job."

"Me, too," said Boone. She pointed. "Back behind the tape."

Cody lowered his pen and notebook and shuffled back to his place with the rest of the crowd. The officers continued walking Helen and Douglas to their house.

Satisfied her in-laws were taken care of, Murphy headed for Castro's car. Was glad to see her temporary partner wasn't inside the vehicle. She wanted to talk to Jack about this without an audience. She opened the front passenger door and hopped in. Shut the door. Pulled off her gloves and hat and stuffed them in her coat pockets. Reached down for her purse. Plopped it on her lap and opened it. Took her Glock out of her coat pocket and returned the gun to its customary sleeve inside her purse. Pulled out her phone. Checked her watch. He probably left for the hospital already to check on her dad. She punched in the number for home anyway. As it rang, it suddenly occurred to her that he could have been watching all this commotion on television. She hoped he hadn't had time to turn on the morning news.

He had. Jack: "Is my father all right?"

"He's fine."

"Television said Professor Henry is dead."

Murphy: "Television got it right."

"Who did this? Tell me who did this. That Ransom woman?"

"She's at the top of our list, along with her latest boyfriend. I don't know if television has figured that out yet. We're not ready to name them as suspects, so don't say anything."

Jack laughed dryly. "The way you didn't say anything to me about what you were *really* doing this morning? Paperwork my ass."

She rubbed her forehead. "I'm sorry."

"About what? Lying to me?"

She didn't need a fight with her husband this morning, when she was already filled with guilt. "Jack. Please. Stop for a minute."

Castro opened the car door and slid behind the wheel. Shut the door. He eyed the phone she was holding to her ear, but didn't say anything. He reached over and turned the key in the ignition. Started up the car. Cranked the heater. Pulled off his hat and gloves and dropped them on the seat next to him. His glasses started to fog. He took them off and wiped them on the sleeve of his jacket. Slipped them back on. Took a notebook out of his jacket pocket and started flipping through the pages.

Murphy continued talking to her husband. "Your folks are spending the night at your place while we look for the people who did this."

Jack: "Should I come and get them?"

Murphy: "I'll have an unmarked car take them. We'll post some uniforms outside your house, until all this settles down."

"It never settles down with you," Jack said.

She switched the phone to her other ear. "Any word on my papa?"

Jack: "I was about to head on over there. My folks know where my spare house key is. Tell them to make themselves comfortable. I'll check on your dad and then come right home. Hold my own dad's hand for a while."

Murphy: "Tell Imma I'll get over to the hospital this afternoon."

"Sounds a bit optimistic, don't you think?" said Jack. "Looks like a regular cluster fuck over there."

"It is," she said.

"I don't like how this went down, Paris. What happened? Thought you had people who were gonna pounce on Ransom and her boyfriend."

Murphy looked through her passenger window at Bergen, who was leaning his back against a squad while getting chewed out by Duncan. "One of our guys had problems tailing them."

"I'll say." He paused. "Hey. I want you to know I'm not blaming you personally, babe. I know you wouldn't lose someone like that. As much as I hate your job, I have to admit you're good at it. Damn good."

"Thank you," she said. Coming from Jack, that was high praise. It made her feel worse about saving Clancy—and terrible about keeping it from Jack. She'd tell him someday. Not today, though.

Jack said in a low voice, as if someone could overhear: "Feel like a heel for saying so, but I'm glad she picked poor Professor Henry to nail instead of my dad."

"Me, too," she said. She didn't want to say it out loud, but she had a particularly selfish reason for wanting her father-in-law spared: Had Jack's dad been killed, it would have ended her marriage for good. She was certain of it.

Jack: "Want me to call you from the hospital? Give you a report?"

"Not unless there's some problem. In fact, skip my dad today. Go straight home. Meet your folks there."

"I wish you had room on your boat," said Jack. "Feels more like home these days than that big house."

Murphy smiled. She enjoyed hearing that. "They could

take our bed and we could crash on the couch. It opens up."
Castro stopped flipping through his notebook and looked
over at her. Raised his eyebrows. Murphy knew what he
was thinking. *Bad idea.*

Jack didn't answer right away. He was thinking about it.
Then: "You know what? I think they'd get a big kick out of
that. Being out on the river, especially in the winter. A new
experience for them. An adventure."

Murphy ran her fingers through her hair. Thought about
how different his folks were from hers. Her mother couldn't
swim and feared she'd drown if she set foot on the houseboat. "Good. I'll have our guys drop them off." Castro
shook his head grimly. Murphy frowned at him. Continued
talking into the phone. "It'll be fun. Save the department
some overtime, too. Won't need any uniforms hanging
around if they're at my place."

Jack: "God knows I always worry about saving the
St. Paul Police Department some money. What about
food?"

"I've got stuff in the fridge. Plenty for four. We'll have a
nice dinner."

"I'll straighten up around here. Wait for them."

Murphy: "Are you implying I'm a lousy housekeeper?"

Jack laughed. "Not at all, my desert flower."

"Do me a favor, though. Call my papa's room and tell
Imma you won't be coming. Tell her I'll stop by tonight."

"It's gone from this afternoon to tonight, huh?"

She looked through the windshield. Duncan was march-
ing toward the Crown Victoria. His eyes were locked on
her. She figured her hands were going to be full. "Yeah.
You'd better tell Ma I might not make it in at all today."

Jack: "Will you be back in time to make dinner tonight,
or should I plan on ordering a pizza?"

Duncan pulled open the back passenger door on the
driver's side of the car and hopped in. Slammed the door

shut and leaned forward. Poked his head between Castro and Murphy. Looked from one detective to the other. His face was lit up like a Christmas tree. She knew that excited expression too well.

"Pizza," Murphy said into the phone.

THIRTY-TWO

CLANCY SLAMMED HIS right shoulder into the door.

"Again. Harder this time," whispered Ransom. She stood behind him in knee-deep snow, a flashlight in her right hand and her purse tucked under her left arm. "But try to be quieter about it."

"How can you quietly knock down a door?" He stepped back and got a running start. Galloped through the snow. Rammed it again. The impact left a dimple in the wood, but the door stay closed. He backed away from the building and stood next to Ransom. Wiped his nose with the back of his sleeve. Unzipped his jacket. The snow had stopped hours earlier. The sky had cleared, and the moon was out. It felt warmer than it had during the day. He looked down at the light in her hand. The beam was illuminating the white at their feet. Two actors standing onstage, in the middle of a spotlight. Clancy said in a hoarse whisper: "I told you. Shut that fucking thing off."

"Fine." She clicked it off. The yard turned dark except for the glow provided by the moon. Neighboring lots were lit. Every other house on the block had a floodlight illuminating the back.

He stepped over to the building again. Turned his left shoulder to the door this time. His right was sore. He slammed his body against the door twice in a row. The door popped open.

"Excellent," she said.

He stepped through the doorway, and she followed. Clancy turned and closed the door behind them. "Now some light would be good."

She flicked on the flashlight and aimed it at the door. It wouldn't shut squarely in the frame; he'd knocked the hinges loose. He wrapped his fist around the knob and tried to lift the door while closing it. "Forget it," she said. "It's good enough."

He let go of the knob. They both turned around. Stomped the snow off their boots. Kept their backs against the door while she shined the light into the room. He eyed the closest pew. Pointed at it. "Those screwed down?"

"No," she said. She remembered squirming on the hard seats as a kid. Scrubbing them clean while her mother stood over her. Nodding off in them during services. She hated them. "They're heavy, though."

"Good." He walked over to the bench, picked up one end by the arm and started walking backward with it. Dragging it toward the door. It squeaked against the floor.

"What are you doing?"

"I don't want someone walking in. Surprising us," he said.

"Want some help?"

She'd probably drop it on his foot, he thought. "I'm good. Keep the light on me." He set the bench down. Took a breath. Walked to the other end of the pew. Maybe pushing would be easier. He saw her standing against the door. A pale statue. He motioned her to one side with a wave of his hand. "Move." She stepped away from the door. He planted both his hands on the arm of the bench. Pushed until the other end bumped up against the door. He took a breath. Bent over and picked up his end again. Pivoted the pew sideways until the back of the bench was flush against the door and the wall. He stood straight and grimaced. His ankles. He plopped down on one end of the bench. She sat on the other end. Ran the light around the room. Along every wall and at varying heights, dead things with glassy eyes glared back at them. A half dozen deer with massive racks. An antelope. A ram with curling horns. Elk and moose. Walleye and large-mouth bass. She ran the beam past a snarling specimen on the wall to their right. "Stop," said Clancy, leaning over and grabbing her wrist. He pulled the flashlight out of her hand and trained the light back on the head. "Wild boar," he said. "Ugly spud."

"Always wondered what that one was. Boar. Basically a big pig."

"Basically." He shined the light ahead of them. He saw the backs of row after row of church pews with an aisle running between them. At the front of the church, a podium. Beyond the podium, boarded-up storefront windows. He lowered his arm and clicked off the light. "You weren't kidding. What a weird place to grow up."

"This isn't the half of it," she said.

They heard a creak over their heads. He clicked the light on. Kept the beam down but looked up at the ceiling. "Sure your folks are gone?"

"They're gone. Building is condemned. I suppose squatters could be living upstairs. Kids messing around. Squirrels. Rats. Who knows?" She switched her purse from under her left arm to her right. Held it tight. "We'd better stay down here."

He took his eyes off the ceiling and looked at her. "This might not be the best place to hide."

"I couldn't think of anywhere else to go. I'm new at this fugitive business."

"What about your Explorer? Cops have got to be looking for it."

"Truck's fine until we figure out where to go next. And once again, I have to disagree with you, my love. We have no idea if they're onto us. These aren't rocket scientists." She'd driven them north from St. Anthony Park. Looped through the northern suburbs. Falcon Heights. Roseville. Maplewood. Took residential streets to get back south and onto West Seventh Street, a working-class neighborhood west of downtown St. Paul. Her old neighborhood. She'd pulled her Explorer into the detached garage that sat behind her parents' old place. The truck just fit. The garage leaned to one side. Looked ready to fall over with a good push or a strong wind. They'd waited inside the shack for night to fall. With no room to sit or stand in the shed, they'd sat cross-legged on top of the Explorer's hood. She'd run out of cigarettes and worried out loud about her cats. He'd talked about needing a beer. A few times they'd crawled back in the truck and started it up. Turned on the heat and the radio. Heard news about the murder, but not whom the police were pursuing. With every report that left out a description of suspects or a car, she'd looked at him and smiled smugly. "See?"

Clancy shut off the flashlight with one hand. Rubbed his gut with the other. Stood up. While they were hiding in the garage, they'd gnawed on frozen Hershey bars they'd dug out of her glove compartment. It wasn't enough to keep his stomach from growling. "I'm starving. There a chance in hell you've got some food around this place?"

"There's a kitchen off to the side. My mom used it as a second pantry, and for Sunday donuts." She got up off the bench and stepped into the aisle. A crack in the boarded windows let in a strip of white from a streetlight. She headed for the front of the church, following the band of light. In her mind's eye, she saw her father standing at the podium, banging it with his fist. Her mother sitting in the front row, nodding in agreement with her husband. No matter what the sermon's message. Was that coffee she smelled? She stopped walking. Put her left hand on the arm of a pew. Felt something carved into the wood. She traced it with her index finger. Two initials. *E.Z.* Her brother's handiwork. She was there when he scratched it into the wood on a gray Saturday afternoon. They were bored. Ezekiel had found a cache of rusty hunting knives. The taxidermist's abandoned treasure. She could still hear the scratching sound the knife made as her brother dug into the wood. Like the scratching noise in her house. In her walls. Under her floors. Scratching. Scratching. She yanked her hand away from the pew. "I don't like it here," she said to the darkness.

"Me either."

She was startled by the male voice. For an instant, it was her brother. "Ezekiel?"

"What?"

Ransom wanted to get away from the ghost. She took two steps forward. Tripped over something. Almost fell. Put her left hand out in front of her and steadied herself by grabbing the back of a pew. She remembered who was behind her now. Not the adored brother. A hated fool. "Dammit, Catch. Turn it back on."

"Trying to conserve the batteries." He clicked it on. Walked toward her and shined the beam down the aisle in front of her to see what she'd stumbled over.

She yelped and jumped backward. "What is that? A dead rat?"

He stepped around her and walked over to it. Looked down. Kicked at it with the toe of his boot. Laughed. "Rat with fins." He bent down and picked it up by the tail fin. Turned around and dangled it in front of her face. Stiff as a board. Missing both of its manufactured eyes.

"Stupid stuffed fish." Still, she took another step back. In case it sprang back to life.

Clancy dropped it on the seat of the closest bench. It landed with a sharp *thump*. He walked down the aisle ahead of her. Ran the flashlight from one animal head to the other. "This place reminds me of every other bar up north. Trophies all over the place. Wood floors. Paneling on the walls." With his free hand, he unzipped his jacket.

"You look like you belong here with all these dead beasts. Dressed in that big hunting coat."

He stopped walking. Turned and looked at her standing behind him. Her comment angered him. He knew it wasn't meant as a compliment. "This ain't no hunting jacket," he said in a low voice. "Got rid of my hunting stuff after the accident. This is just a good, heavy coat. At least it covers my ass better than your stupid little outfit." He shined the light on her jacket. As pink and as shiny as a neon flamingo. "Always meant to ask. Why do you dress like that?"

"Like what?"

He raised the flashlight so it shined in her face. "Like a little girl."

She turned her head to the side. "Get that out of my eyes."

He took the beam off her face. Brought the flashlight under his chin so it shined up at his face and made it appear shadowy. Monstrous. "What's wrong, Pink Lady? Forget to trowel your makeup on this morning?"

She walked toward him. Pulled her gloves off her fingers as she went. "I've got a question for you, my love. Why do you keep calling that thing with your father an accident? Huh? We're alone. Both on the run. Let's be honest here.

Call it what it was." She shoved her gloves in her jacket pocket.

The face in the flashlight tightened with anger. "You weren't there. How in the hell should you know?"

She stopped walking and stood in the aisle. Six rows of pews separated them. She put her hands on her hips and opened her mouth to say something more. Hurl another insult. She closed her mouth. Decided she didn't want to fight with him. Not yet. Not until she was ready. She reached up and unzipped her jacket. "Whatever you say."

"Where's this kitchen?" barked Clancy.

She stepped closer. Raised her arm and pointed to the left. "There."

He shined the flashlight into an open doorway in the middle of the wall. Saw cupboards on the other side. "Great." He kept the light trained on the door. Walked down the aisle and stepped into a pew to cut across. Stopped and turned. Shined the light on her. She was still standing in the aisle, holding tight to her purse as if it could protect her. "You coming?"

She walked over to his pew and sat down on the end of the bench closest to the aisle. Pulled her scarf off her neck and dropped it on the seat next to her. Set her purse in her lap. Twined her arms around it. "I want to sit here for a minute. This place doesn't have the best memories."

"Suit yourself." He turned and finished cutting through the pew.

As soon as he disappeared through the doorway, she held her breath and opened her purse. Slipped her hand inside. Exhaled when the tips of her fingers touched the hard lines. She withdrew her hand. Reached into her jacket and fished out her gloves. Pulled them tight over her fingers. She dipped her hand back inside the purse. Pulled it out by the butt. Used her scarf to wipe it clean.

THIRTY-THREE

PATROL OFFICERS HAD driven past the house earlier that day. Tried the doors. Peeked inside. Found nothing amiss. Castro put the place at the bottom of the list of possibilities. He figured Ransom would never hang around town. Never return to an empty, dilapidated building she hadn't seen for years. A home once occupied by parents she'd disowned. He bet Ransom and Clancy were headed back to the Range. Duncan agreed with him. Murphy wasn't so sure. The two detectives spent the day on the phone with cops up north. They'd tracked down Clancy's family in Duluth and Ransom's parents in Florida. They'd driven around town chasing false sightings phoned in by other agencies. They'd crafted a description of the suspects and their vehicle. Duncan would feed the press release to the media at the right time. When something needed to be shaken loose.

After a twelve-hour day, Murphy walked home from the cop shop. It had warmed up, and she enjoyed the hike. She popped her head inside to greet her in-laws. She told Jack she was picking up her Jeep to go to the hospital and then go grocery shopping. She turned around and went back outside. Instead of heading to Regions, she drove to West Seventh Street.

The streets and sidewalks were jammed. She braked at a light. A man with a hockey jersey squeezed over his down jacket walked in front of her Jeep. He held his homemade placard over his head as he crossed the street, so the drivers waiting for the light could see it. NEED TICKETS!!! The Wild were playing Pittsburgh at Xcel Energy Center. She tapped her index fingers impatiently on her steering wheel. Willed the light to turn green. It did. She accelerated. Came up on a traffic snarl. Braked again. She had a knot in her stomach. Her instincts had put her on West Seventh Street; they told her to try Ransom's childhood home on her own. Now her gut was telling her to make it fast.

The knot of cars and trucks untangled. It took ten minutes, but she got past the worst of it. Kept heading west. The trendy bars and restaurants gave way to neighborhood joints. She hung a right. Turned into Ransom's old neighborhood. Steered down a freshly plowed road. Parked her Jeep across the street from the place. She pulled her keys out of the ignition, dropped them in her coat pocket. She put her hand on the driver's door to open it. Looked across the street. Through a gap in the boards covering the windows, she saw a glint of light.

CLANCY ran the beam around the kitchen, the room was the size of his fish shack. The back wall had a service door. He guessed it led directly outside; a dusting of snow peeked through the threshold. He wanted to know for sure. It could serve as his escape route later. A way to get away from Ransom. He walked across the floor, the wood creaking under his boots. He put his hand on the knob, turned and tried to pull it open. Stuck. He pulled harder. Heard boards groan. It opened a crack. He set the flashlight on the floor. Slipped his hands in the gap and pulled on the edge of the door. It popped open and slammed against the inside wall. He stood in front of the opening. An *X* of boards blocked the way outside. He looked over the top of the *X*. Saw a wall of weathered cedar a few yards away. The neighbor's privacy fence. He pushed the door closed. Locked it. He didn't want any surprises from the neighbors. Any visitors.

He picked his flashlight up off the floor, turned around and inventoried the room. Cupboards lined the walls to his right and left. The laminated countertop under the cupboards was warped. Had mounds and waves rippling through it. On one side of the kitchen, in the middle of the span of counter space, was a double-sided sink. He went over to it and peered down. Shined the flashlight into it. Both sides were stained and dirty and littered with dead flies. He switched the flashlight to his left hand. With his right, he reached over and turned on the cold tap. Nothing. He licked his lips. They'd have to find some water. He stepped to the opposite side. Shined the light on the counter. Nothing but warped laminate. He used his index and middle fingers to draw two lines down the counter, from back to front. He rubbed his soiled fingers against his thumb. Dust and grit. With the index finger, he drew a smiley face. As big and round as a dinner plate in the middle of the length of counter. He lifted his finger off. Wiped it on his pant leg. Set the finger back down. Drew lashes on the face's eyes, fat curls around its head. He lifted his finger off again. Not quite right yet. He set his finger down one more time. Drew eyebrows over the eyes. Mean dashes that jutted down toward the button nose. He took his finger off and wiped it on the front of his jacket. Shined the flashlight over his handiwork. Perfect. A scary female smiley face.

Below the counter were cabinets. He squatted down and

pulled open the first cabinet door. Shined the flashlight inside. Nothing but cobwebs. A dead mouse surrounded by droppings. Dead flies. He shut the door. Followed the cabinets around the room. Open. Close. Open. Close. The last cabinet had a can opener. The old-fashioned kind that had to be stabbed into the top of the can and worked around the rim by hand. He snatched the opener off the shelf, shut the door and stood up. "Fuck," he muttered. He tossed the opener onto the counter. Gripped the edge of the counter with his hand and took a deep breath. Blew it out. His ankles hadn't ached this bad in a long time. As if they were in a vise and someone kept screwing the jaws tighter and tighter. "Shake it off," he breathed. He yelled without turning to face the doorway. "Found an opener." He reached up and opened and closed cupboards. Shined the light inside each. Nothing. Dead mouse. Nothing. An aluminum pie tin next to a dead mouse. Nothing. A few empty canning jars. The sixth one had a collection of cans on the middle shelf. The cylinders were warped and swollen from freezing and expanding, but he didn't care. "Good deal," he said. He wrapped his hand around the first one, took it down. Blew the dust off the top and held it close to his face. Shined the light on the label. A picture of beans in a pot. BUSH'S BEST. ORIGINAL. SEASONED WITH BACON & BROWN SUGAR. "Great," he muttered. He set the can on the counter. Reached for another. Took it down. Read the label. HORMEL FOODS. MARY KITCHEN CORNED-BEEF HASH. Even better, he thought. He set it on the counter next to the beans. The third can was a bust, unless he got desperate. Cherry pie filling. He put it back on the shelf. Paused. Picked it up again, blew the dust off the top and set it on the counter. He'd eat the good stuff. Save the sweet shit for her. He turned his head and looked over his shoulder. Listened. Didn't hear anything. He returned his attention to the counter. He set the flashlight down on its side. Enough to provide a dull illumination for the room. He locked his left hand around the beans and with his right, picked up the opener and jabbed the top of the can.

While he worked the opener around, he thought about the Pink Lady. How he hated her. How he regretted ever getting involved with her. Ever drinking her booze and eating her food and sleeping in her bed. The sex. It had been good, but he regretted that, too. She'd let him cross a line other women had never allowed him to step near. He feared he'd have trouble finding another partner like that. He didn't want his bedroom memories of Ransom to crowd out other women. Beyond the sex, he found nothing good about the Pink Lady. During the drive down, they'd fought about who was to blame for the sloppy killing. He'd bitched at her for thinking up the lame plan in the first place, and then for misreading Henry. Wimps didn't charge after people with crowbars. She'd yelled at him for dropping the hat. For bolting before retrieving the knife. At one point she'd demanded her money back. He'd refused. She didn't complain that he'd stabbed Henry to death, however. She was glad. Almost giddy about it. She'd chanted the same thing over and over: *O, snatched away in beauty's bloom! O, snatched away in beauty's bloom!* She'd stop for a while and stay silent and then start up again. As if a favorite song were on the radio again and she had to sing along. Only the radio was off. *O, snatched away in beauty's bloom!* He'd snapped at her. Told her to knock it off. Her response: *Byron, my love. Byron. You should read more.* Then she'd be at it again. She scared the hell out of him. He swore to himself he'd get away from her. Go into hiding. The police would have a hard time finding a guy traveling alone and on foot. She'd be an easy target for the police. A description of her, her Explorer and the truck's license plate had to be circulating around town, even if the cops weren't broadcasting it publicly yet. Even if she didn't believe they were wise to her. So much left behind at the murder scene. The police had to figure out who did it. The biggest thing would be the motive. He remembered that from his ordeal with the cops up north. The police in St. Paul would have no trouble figuring out who had a motive for targeting Henry.

He finished running the opener around the can. Used the opener's pointed tip to pop off the round top. He dropped the opener on the counter. Wiped both his palms on his pants legs. He wrapped his left hand around the can and brought it to his lips. With the tips of his right fingers, he scooped up the frozen beans and shoveled them into his mouth. He'd never tasted anything better. He got to the bottom. Ran his index finger around the inside of the can, pulled the finger out and licked it clean. Tipped the can toward the light and peered inside. A few beans. He lifted the can to his lips and tipped it back. Tapped the bottom to make sure he got all the beans. He took the can away from his mouth. Set it on the counter. Wiped his mouth with the back of his hand. Looked at the empty. Decided he didn't want her to see it. He opened a door below the countertop and set the can and the top inside. Shut the door. Burped. "Good eats," he muttered. He slid the hash toward him. Wrapped his fist around the can. Picked up the can opener and stabbed the top. His mouth was watering. He could taste the salty potatoes and meat already.

MURPHY reached inside her purse. Pulled out her cell phone. Punched in Duncan's number. He answered after two rings.

"They're here," Murphy said into the phone while keeping her eyes on the windows. "At her old house."

"You sure? Castro's chasing what sounds like a solid lead."

"Saw a light inside."

"How do you know it's them?"

"My gut." She waited for Duncan to respond. She knew he wasn't sure about this one.

"I don't know," he said.

She was getting mad. "Send backup!"

"Where are you?"

"In my car. Parked across the street."

"Stay put. I'll pull Castro off what he's doing. Round up some squads."

"Make it quick." She dropped her phone in her coat pocket. Murphy eyed the shuttered windows. No more light. She feared they were taking off. She reached inside her purse. Pulled out her Glock and slipped it inside her right coat pocket. Dropped her purse on the floor of the Jeep. She threw open her door and stepped out. Dug under the driver's seat and fished out a flashlight. Shoved it in her left pocket. Closed the door. Ran across the street. The front door had slats of board nailed across it. No way they got in that way. She decided to cut through a neighbor's yard and go down the alley. Enter through the back. Murphy ran between two houses. Stepped into the alley from a backyard three houses away. Jogged down the alley toward the backyard of the Ransom place.

RANSOM stood up. Hiked her purse strap over her shoulder. She walked between the pews, her sights set on the lighted doorway. She stopped at the end of the bench and reached down with her free hand. Flipped the safety off. *Red means fire.* She stepped from between the pews and walked toward the kitchen. Heard a faint noise. Stopped to listen. Metallic grinding. He'd found something to eat and was opening a can. Probably gorging like a pig, the way he always did. She continued walking. Wondered what made up his last meal. Tuna fish? Soup? Stew? She didn't care. She'd had enough of him. The boy with a poet's face and a Titan's body and a monster's heart. Bringing him into her life had been a mistake. She had to correct it. She raised her right hand and stepped through the doorway. His back was turned. He spun around and gaped at her. His mouth hung open with food inside of it. How appropriate that he die the way he lived, she thought. As a slob. She brought her left hand up. Locked it around the gun along with her right.

His eyes widened and went to the pistol. The Ladysmith. She'd gotten it back. How? When? He raised his arms up in the air as he had for the bar robber six days earlier. A lifetime ago. He looked at the Pink Lady. Her face was red and contorted with hate. Deep lines around her mouth and between her eyebrows. Grooves he'd never seen before. Not in her worst moments. Was it the shadowy room? His former lover had pulled a devil's mask over her head. "Serene. Please."

"Too late to make nice, my boy." She raised the gun higher. Took a step closer. Aimed for the center of his torso.

She was less than six feet away. She'd never miss. He tensed his body for the impact. Felt something in his left hand. The can. He cranked his arm back and flung it at her. "Fuck you, bitch!"

The can bounced off her forehead and clattered to the floor. She screamed one word. "No!" She stumbled backward, and her arms flew up. The gun went off. A bullet blasted through a cupboard. She dropped the gun and her purse and slapped both hands over her forehead.

MURPHY was one house away. Heard the gunshot from the alley. "Son of a bitch." She bolted to the Ransom place. Ran through the backyard and up to the door, pulling out her gun as she went. She wrapped her left hand around the knob. She turned the knob and pushed. The door opened a crack and stopped. Jammed. She turned sideways and pushed her hip against the door. It moved an inch. She took a step back, curled her right leg up to her chest and brought her foot down on the middle of the door.

THE gun clattered on the floor between them. He dropped his body on top of it. He heard someone at the back door. So did she. She didn't care. All she wanted to do was get her gun back. Kill him. She fell on top of him. She kneeled on his back and buried her hands in his hair. Pulled and yanked. "I hate you!" She let go of his hair and felt around his body for the gun. Pushed her hands under his belly.

"Get off me, you cunt!" He bounced her off of him. A bronco throwing a rider. She fell against the cabinets. Stayed on her hands and knees. Blood snaking down her forehead and between her eyebrows. Dripping down her nose. Devil's snot. He heard more banging. Who was it? Should he call out for help? The gun was in his right hand. He didn't need help, he thought. He slapped his left hand up on the counter and gripped the edge to pull himself up. He raised himself to a crouch. His ankles gave way. He folded on his knees. Dropped the gun.

Ransom heard the *thud* of the gun hitting the floor. Saw the dark outline on the floor between them. She stretched out her arm and dove for it. Snatched it off the floor and crawled to her feet. Backed up until she felt the counter behind her. She aimed at the man kneeling on the floor. "Get up! I need a clear shot!"

"Fuck you!" he said. He raised his left hand and rested it on the counter but didn't try to pull himself up. "Do it! Come on! Pull the trigger!"

THE door was loose, but there was something propped behind it. Keeping it closed. There had to be another entrance.

A side door. Murphy slipped her gun back in her pocket
and ran around the house. Found it. Two thick slats of wood
crisscrossed it. She lifted her right foot and planted it
against the door frame for leverage. Hooked both her hands
over the top board. Tugged. It wouldn't budge. She heard
voices on the other side of the door. Took her hands off the
board and stepped back. She couldn't make out the words.
They were screaming at each other. Murphy wasn't going
to force her way in through that door. Announce she was a
cop. Dropping between two feuding murderers would be
worse than walking into a domestic. She needed to sneak
up on them. She stepped back and eyed the side of the
house. Pulled her flashlight out of her pocket, snapped it on
and shined it up and down the building. Saw no other en-
trances. All the windows were boarded solid. She clicked
off her light. Shoved it in her pocket. Ran for the back door
again. She pulled her cell phone out of her pocket as she
went. Hit Redial. Duncan picked up on the first ring. "Shots
fired inside."

"Where are you?"

"Back door. Where in the hell is my backup?"

"On the way. There's a hockey game on, you know."

The traffic. She'd forgotten. "Hurry." She hung up and
dropped the phone in her pocket.

HER upper lip curled into a sneer while blood dripped
off the tip of her nose. "You want this!"

"Sure I do!" He grimaced and pulled himself up to a
standing position. "If it makes you feel better. Helps you
sleep better tonight. Sure. I want you to blow my head off!"

"Don't have the balls to do it yourself. A man who kills
his own father doesn't have the balls."

He swayed and wobbled. Clutched the edge of the

counter for support. "Fuck you! It was an accident! I didn't mean to!"

With the back of her sleeve, she wiped the red from the end of her nose. "You don't mean to do anything, do you? Poor Catch. Shit keeps raining down on your head. Life is one fucking accident after another."

"Shut the hell up!" He couldn't look at the devil's face anymore. Focused on the devil's jacket. The pink. The devil's hands. They weren't shaking like in the bar. They were gloved, too. She'd probably wiped the pistol clean of prints. She'd thought this through. Learned some things in a week. Learned too much. Maybe she knew them all along.

"Shooting your father. The guy in the bar. Killing Henry. Hamlet. Hurting me. Going through the ice so that woman could rescue you. Accidents. Accidents. Did you stick your cock in her ass, too? Was it an accident?"

Her language stunned him. He'd never heard a woman use words like those. A devil's voice. His hand tightened over the counter edge. "I didn't touch her."

"You wanted to. Good thing for her you didn't. Your life is a train wreck."

"Shut up! I know it is! You think I don't know?" Tears running down his face, striping the dirt on his cheeks. "What about you? Screwing boys all over the place. Boozing it up. Getting stoned. Getting fired. Living with a bunch of cats. Your only friends. Cats."

Her turn to cry. She shook the gun at him. "Stop it!"

"Yeah. I killed that one cat. Picked it up and slammed its head against the counter. I hope you think about that every time you go in there and slather on your makeup. This is where Catch killed my baby."

"I hate you," she hissed. The banging against the door had stopped. Had they gone to call the police? Ransom figured she had to finish this and get out. She steadied the gun.

"Is that the best you can do? Where's your poetry now? Your pretty rhymes. Don't I get any pretty rhymes before you do me?"

"I hate you!"

"Yeah. So I've heard." He leaned his head against a cupboard. Wished it were already over. He closed his eyes. He wondered if Bo would miss him. If his mother and sisters would still cry years after his death, or if their eyes would stay dry as they had for his father. He wondered if there was a hell. Whether he'd meet his father there.

She wrapped her left hand around the gun, under her right. Raised her arms straight out. Took aim at the man clutching the counter. That's what he was, she told herself. He wasn't a boy. He was a man. Cruel man. Her first mistake had been in thinking he was a boy. "Look at me! I want you looking at me!"

He opened his eyes and blinked twice. "Bitch."

She inhaled. Counted to three. Exhaled. Squeezed the trigger. The *crack* shook the kitchen. His body jerked is if jolted by an electrical shock. For an instant, he remained standing. Then he melted into the floor. A puppet with its strings cut. A faint noise from the heap on the floor. A moan or a last breath. After that, silence.

Ransom lowered her arms. Heard scraping and screeching. Wood against wood. Someone was pushing against the door hard enough to move the bench away. She shoved the gun in her pocket, scooped up her purse, bolted for the service door. Tugged on the knob with both hands. Couldn't open it. Saw it was locked from the inside. She unlocked it and pulled it open. Froze in front of the crisscross of boards. "Shit." She fell on her belly and shimmied through the triangle opening with her purse. The back hem of her jacket snagged on a splinter of wood. She reached behind with one hand and yanked it free. Finished crawling through. Jumped to her feet. Ran toward the garage.

THIRTY-FOUR

WITH BOTH HANDS, Murphy gave one last push to the door. The space was enough for her to slip through. She went in sideways, lifted her leg and stepped over the back of the bench. She brought her other leg over. Her boots landed on the seat. She jumped down to the floor. Pulled her Glock out of her pocket. Ran for the room with the dim light. She flattened her body against the wall on one side of the open door. Listened. Nothing. She slid down into a crouch. Pivoted around and looked through the doorway with her gun pointed out in front of her. She saw the open door first and the heap on the floor second. She stood up, lowered her gun and ran to the door. Peered through the top gap in the boards. Heard the truck barreling through the alley. She slipped her gun in her pocket and pulled out her cell phone. Hit redial.

Duncan: "We're on the way."

"She took off. In her truck. Went down the alley."

"Got it."

Murphy: "Paramedics."

"On the way."

She heard him moan. She dropped her phone in her coat pocket. Turned around. Went over to the man. Dying boy.

He was on his back with his head propped against the cabinet and his legs splayed in front of him. She kneeled at his side. Took his right hand in both of hers. The shine from the flashlight on the counter combined with the neighbor's yard light to illuminate the room. Beyond Clancy's feet fell a dark cross—a shadow cast by the crisscross of boards over the door. She could see his clothes were covered with blood. The cabinet and counter behind him were red and wet. The floor in front of him. The dark spot in the middle of his chest was the most telling. Worse than a wound. A hole. She'd seen those holes in close-range shooting victims before. He was a breath away from death. She was angry. She'd gone through the work of saving him and the heartache of questioning that deed. Now this. A waste.

He opened his eyes a crack. "You."

"I'm a cop." He looked like a kid to her. One of her brothers, or her father as a young man. She had a vision of her father slouched on the floor, instead of recuperating in his hospital bed. She shook off the picture. "Who did this?"

"Serene," he whispered.

"Did she kill the guy up north? Professor Henry?"

He shut his eyes. His head fell to one side. She squeezed his hand. Bent her head close to his ear. "Catch?" She sat back on her heels. Kept his hand between hers. Thought about what Duncan had said. *Lives aren't interchangeable like that. You can't shuffle souls around.*

She heard her backup pushing the bench away. Multiple feet tromping through the door. Coughing and sniffling. Castro. She yelled over her shoulder: "In here."

Castro stepped into the doorway. Took in the scene. Holstered his gun. Pulled out his flashlight and punched it on. "Paramedics are right behind us."

Murphy: "They won't have shit to do."

"Dead?"

"Yeah." Murphy released his hand. Set it on the floor. Looked toward the open door. "The witch got away." She eyed the floor around her. No gun. "She's armed."

Castro: "We'll get her."

"He named her before he went."

"Did he finger her for the others?"

Murphy looked at Clancy's face. Noticed the dirt on his cheeks was streaked with tears. "He didn't have a chance."

Bergen poked his head into the room. Saw the body. "One down and one to go." He waited for someone to answer or laugh or tell him to fuck off. When they didn't: "Hey, get a gander at what else she left behind. Snagged it off a bench."

Murphy and Castro turned their heads and looked. Bergen had his right arm up. From his gloved fingers dangled a strip of material. A pink scarf. "That's hers," said Murphy.

"Cool," said Bergen.

Castro shined his light on the body. "Bergen. Clue in the paramedics when they get here."

"Right." Bergen draped the scarf over his arm and disappeared back inside the church.

Murphy stood up. "Let's get a better look at what we got here." She took her flashlight out of her pocket and punched it on. Both detectives ran their beams around the kitchen. In addition to the blood splattered everywhere, they saw fingerprints and smears in the dust on the counter. A flashlight and an opener and a can on the counter. Another can of food on the floor near Clancy's feet. A bullet hole in one of the cupboards. Casings on the floor. Murphy stopped moving her light around when it landed on the picture drawn on the dusty countertop. Clancy's artwork.

Castro: "Nothing but yum-yums. I'll see what else we can find in the church. Can't let Bergen have all the glory."

"Send someone topside," she said.

Castro coughed twice. Cleared his throat by making a grunting noise in the back of his throat. "Yes, Mom." He turned around and left.

Duncan stepped into the doorway with a flashlight in his hand. Took Castro's spot. "Garage out back has some treats. Fresh candy-bar wrappers. Cigarette butts. Fresh tire tracks."

"So they were hunkered down in the garage during the day and busted down the back door when it got dark. Smart."

Duncan turned his flashlight on the body. "Not that smart."

"Clancy wasn't in charge of this operation," said Murphy. "Ransom was using him. Playing him."

"Leading him around by his dick head?"

"Nice way to put it." Murphy trained her light on the dead man's face. "I think she's somehow responsible for the guy up north. Clancy didn't do it alone. She sure as hell planned Henry's murder."

"Think she's done?"

"Done with the killings maybe. Not with the boys."

Duncan: "On to the next cradle."

"Not if we can help it." Murphy clicked off her flashlight. She couldn't look at Clancy anymore. "Let's take this discussion out of here."

She walked out of the kitchen. Duncan followed her. Now that they were alone, she wanted to blast him for taking his time sending backup. Traffic or not, they should have nailed Ransom before she cleared the alley. Murphy held her tongue, however. She guessed Duncan was beating himself up about it. The two of them stood under a mounted ram to talk, against the wall with the kitchen doorway. Across the room, they saw Bergen. He was standing under a shoulder mount of a whitetail deer. He was pointing to the kitchen while yapping with two paramedics. A man and a woman. The man kept looking up at the buck and back at Bergen. Murphy couldn't tell if the guy was freaked out by the room filled with trophies, or envious of it. Probably a little of both.

Murphy: "She's a smart woman."

"Book smart is the opposite of street smart," said Duncan.

"Not in this case. She's both. Makes her more danger-ous. I think we've lost her. For now." Duncan opened his mouth to respond. Murphy held up her palm. "Forget it. It's over. On to Plan B."

Castro stepped next to Duncan. Folded his arms over his chest. Glanced up at the trophy before focusing his atten-tion on Murphy. "What is Plan B?"

"If she's in town, she might try to get back into her house," said Murphy. "Feed and water those cats of hers."

Castro: "We were gonna tape it off."

"Don't," said Murphy. "Make her think it's safe. We'll is-sue a press release tonight. Get it on the ten-o'clock news. Say we got Henry's murderer. A neighbor gave us a descrip-tion. Saw the killer fleeing St. Anthony Park on foot. We got his prints off the knife. Matched them to an earlier case."

Duncan: "We knew who we were looking for all along because we're such geniuses."

Castro coughed again. Cleared his throat. "What's our story on why the kid killed Henry?"

Duncan: "Random crime committed by a loser who wandered into the neighborhood. He was trying to steal the old guy's car. Couldn't break in and got frustrated. Stabbed the tires. Prof caught him at it. Got nailed. Shit. Half that's true anyway."

"Then we find our killer dead." Murphy paused. She didn't want to make things harder on Clancy's family. Dirty his name any more. "We don't even have to name him or give his age or hometown or anything. We'll say we're try-ing to notify relatives. Ransom will know who we've got chilling in the morgue."

Duncan pointed his index finger at her. "Wait. Why did we find him here? Who do we say croaked him? Do we say we're looking for a killer? Make up a bullshit description of a suspect?"

"That we're looking for someone could make her ner-vous. Make her stay away." Murphy thought back to Clancy's attempt to drown himself. "How about this? Neighbor heard some racket and banged on the door. Tried to get in. For all Ransom knows, that's who was trying to get in. A neighbor. She didn't see me. Neighbor called us or flagged down a squad or something. We got here. Pieced stuff to-gether. Examined the angle of the shot. The close range. Determined Clancy must have freaked. Killed himself."

"With Clancy's suicidal tendencies, she'll see how we could buy into that scenario," said Duncan.

Castro raised his eyebrows. "Suicidal tendencies? I never heard that about the kid."

Murphy and Duncan exchanged glances. "I'm making shit up as we go along here," said Duncan.

Murphy jumped in. "The point is, we don't even men-tion Ransom. Make like she was never a suspect. Never in the picture."

Castro frowned. Uncrossed his arms and adjusted his glasses. Coughed. "What about the shit she left behind at the scene here?"

Murphy: "She'll forget about the scarf. Figure she left it somewhere else. People lose scarves all the time. Otherwise there's nothing here we can't pin on Clancy."

"You sure she'll believe that we believe we got the right guy?" Castro scratched his forehead under his stocking cap. "For one thing, there's this suicide thing. Where's the gun?"

Duncan: "We'll say we're looking for it. Think some kids made off with it. Something like that."

Castro: "Who shoots himself in the chest? She'd know it wouldn't look right to us."

Murphy thought back to her brief visit with Ransom. The airs the professor put on. The show she put on. "Her weakness is she thinks most people are far less intelligent than she is. I would say she underestimates pretty much everyone. That would extend to the police. She probably underestimated Clancy at first. When she finally figured out she couldn't housebreak him, she killed him."

"How do you know all that?" asked Castro. "Shit. How did you know about the damn cats?"

"Jack's dad," Murphy said without hesitation.

"Oh yeah." Castro coughed hard. Wiped his nose with the back of his jacket sleeve. "Okay. Okay. I'm warming up to this plan. We make the lady prof feel safe. Like she can go home. Then what? We hide in her bushes? Jump out and yell 'Surprise'?"

Murphy paused. Castro wasn't going to like this. "There's no *we* in this plan. She'll hear you hacking from across the lake."

He sniffled. Looked hurt. "I could settle it down. Take some shit for it. That green syrup crap."

"You've been taking shit for it," said Murphy. "It ain't working. Sorry. This is a solo deal, at least for the stakeout at the house. You do the surveillance from the car. That's your gig anyway." She saw both men frown. Decided to downplay the likelihood she'd see any action. "Keep in mind, too, the house thing could go nowhere. She could be halfway to Canada, and we gotta rely on the troopers to nab her."

Duncan saw through it. "Don't try to minimize the danger of this house deal, Murphy. I'm not saying you gotta take Castro with you, but you gotta take somebody. Alone in that house with that head case? Don't like that idea. Not one damn bit." He nodded to the kitchen. "She's packing a handgun in addition to the sawed-off. Who knows what else she's got?"

Castro coughed again. "Duncan's right."

Murphy opened her mouth to argue with them. Closed it. She was outnumbered, and they weren't going to let go of this. It was like having two Jacks hovering over her. "Fine. Who then? Keep in mind my motto is A.B.B."

Castro: "Anybody But Bergen?"

She nodded. "This is a weenie-free zone."

Duncan: "How about another spin around the dance floor with your boss?"

She hesitated. Slapped her flashlight into the palm of her glove a half dozen times. Tried to think of a good reason to say no and couldn't come up with one. "Sure."

"So the decks are cleared on the home front?" asked Duncan. "This is okay?"

Castro: "Yeah. What's the word on your dad? The in-laws?"

"Jack's back at the boat feeding his folks pizza." She lifted her wrist. Clicked on her flashlight and shined it on her watch. "Actually they had pizza hours ago. I called the hospital earlier. Dad's doing good." She clicked off her flashlight. "So the decks are cleared. Let's get the show rolling."

"You go on ahead to the shop," Castro told her. "Whip out that press release and then head on over to Ransom's. I'll help the boss wrap this up so he can meet you there. Still gotta deal with the ME and his crew. Crime-scene guys."

Murphy gave the two of them the thumbs-up. Turned and cut through a row of pews. She punched on her flashlight as she went. Duncan went after her. "Paris. Wait." She turned. The two of them stood together in the pew.

She buttoned her coat up closer to her neck. "What?"

He shoved his hands in his jacket pocket and looked off to the side. "I'm sorry I didn't believe you at first."

Her eyes narrowed. "Having a hard time trusting me? Does it have something to do with that case we worked?"

"Hell no. You were great. Couldn't ask for a better partner—or a better nurse."

"Thanks."

"After all those years working the street solo." He paused. Pulled his hands out of his pockets. "I'm having a hard time believing anyone else's gut."

She took her keys out of her coat pocket. Jiggled them in her hand. Decided to use his first name since he'd pulled hers out. "Better get over it, Axel. If we're gonna work together. Otherwise one of us could end up like that kid on the kitchen floor."

He looked her in the eyes. "I know." She turned to step out of the pew, and he grabbed her elbow. "Paris?"

She spun back around and looked at him. "Now what?"

"Nothing." He let go of her elbow and watched her go. He left through the other side of the pew. Went back to the kitchen.

Murphy moved through the dark church, shining her flashlight ahead of her. She saw a dozen uniforms doing the same. They looked like ushers in a movie theater. She weaved around three officers standing in the middle of the aisle. One of them was shining his flashlight up at a moose head. The other two were reliving a moose hunt they'd been on together. She wondered if someone had called Xcel Energy to get the lights back up. Wondered what else Duncan wanted to say to her. Tried not to think about how pissed Jack was going to be when she finally got home.

THIRTY-FIVE

RANSOM TURNED ONTO West Seventh Street and headed east for no particular reason. She wanted to get as far away from the body as quickly as possible. She recognized her mistake as she neared downtown and spotted the tangle of cars up ahead. The Wild game. On the upside, she could blend in with the traffic. On the downside, there'd be plenty of cops directing the mess. She braked at a red light at St. Clair Avenue. Drummed her fingers on the steering wheel. Looked to her right. Thought about taking the High Bridge and crossing the river to the West Side. Too much driving, she told herself. Get the truck off the road. She crossed St. Clair when the light changed. Drove two more blocks. Turned left into the parking lot for Mancini's Char House. She'd been there before. Big eaters liked big wheels. She knew the lot behind the restaurant would be packed with pickups, sports utility vehicles and other trucks. Hers would blend in.

She pulled in between two other Fords—another Explorer

and an Expedition—and put the truck in park. She reached over to punch off the radio news. Paused with her hand on the knob. Listened hard. Heard a report about an armed bank robbery in Apple Valley. An accident on Interstate 94 in Minneapolis with multiple fatalities. Another snowstorm blowing into the Twin Cities. Nothing yet about a murder in St. Paul. Could be her caution was unnecessary. Perhaps whoever had barged into the church hadn't ventured far enough into the building to find the body. Hadn't called the police. She'd heard sirens as she fled the neighborhood, but maybe they were coming for something else. She turned off the radio. Turned off the truck and dropped the keys in her purse. Put her hand on the door and popped it open. Remembered her jacket and what was inside of it. She shut the door. Pulled the gun out of her pocket and dropped it in her purse. She'd get rid of the Ladysmith later. Toss it in the river. Even if someone found it and turned it over to the police, they couldn't connect her to it. It had been a gift from one of her boys. Her pot-supplying boy. He'd bragged about how it was stolen—and untraceable.

She set her purse on the passenger's seat. Turned on the dome light. Looked down. While her truck would blend in, her jacket wouldn't. Smeared with blood. She pulled it off, turned it inside out and folded it over her arm to see how it would look. No visible blood. She set the jacket on top of her purse. What about the rest of her clothes? She saw a couple of spots on the thighs of her pants. If she held her jacket a little low when she walked into the restaurant, it would cover it. Her sweater was another story. She held the wool by the hem and pulled it away from her body. Studied it. "Damn," she muttered. She'd had her jacket unzipped when she shot him; a band of red splatters decorated the swath that had been exposed. If she wore her scarf draped down her front, it would cover it. She lifted up her jacket and dug in the pockets. Felt her gloves. No scarf. She dropped the jacket on her lap. Looked over at the front passenger's seat. Turned around and scanned the backseat. Turned back around. Stared through the windshield. Chewed her bottom lip. She remembered. She'd taken it off and used it to wipe the gun. Was it still on the bench? Dropped in the snow between the house and the garage? In the garage? Sitting on the floor of the kitchen, soaking up his blood? None of the possibilities was good. Her hands tightened into balls. "Shit," she said, banging her thighs with her fists. "Shit, shit, shit!" If the police got their hands on it, could they trace it to her? How could they? They couldn't, she told herself. She put the scarf out of her mind. Returned to the sweater. Turned off the interior light. Glanced around the parking lot. She wished it wasn't so well lit. Wished the moon wasn't so bright. Still, no one pulling in or leaving at that moment. She yanked her sweater over her head, turned it inside out and slipped it back on. Turned the dome light back on. Looked down. A couple of spots had bled all the way through. Not too bad.

She pulled down her visor and checked her face in the mirror. Blood had clotted over the cut, but there was a red stain running from her forehead all the way down to her chin. As if someone had taken a red marker and drawn a line down the middle of her face. She snatched her purse off the seat, rummaged around, found some individually packaged wet wipes. Ripped open six of the squares. Unfolded the wipes and dragged them over her face two at a time. Dropped the soiled napkins on the passenger seat. She checked the mirror again. She'd rubbed too hard; the gash was bleeding again. She retrieved one of the bloodied wipes. Held it over the spot with one hand. With her other, she reached over and popped open the glove compartment. Fished around. Pulled out a handful of Band-Aids. Found the right shape and size—a rectangle as big as her thumb. She pulled the bandage out and dropped it in her lap. Shut the glove compartment. Took the wipe off her forehead and looked in the mirror. Dabbed at the bleeding cut. She dropped the wipe on the floor. Clawed open the Band-Aid. Slapped it over the wound. Smoothed it over her forehead. Patted it. Looked in the mirror. Wished she had bangs for more coverage. She flipped the visor back up. Turned off the interior light. She pulled on her jacket. Looped her purse strap over her shoulder. Looked over at the soiled napkins on the passenger seat. Brushed them onto the floor with the side of her hand. She popped open the door and hopped out. Shut the door and locked it. Turned around. Scanned the parking lot. Still no one coming or going. Good. She reached into her jacket pockets, took out her gloves and pulled them on. Noticed blood on them. She'd stash them before stepping inside. She went to the back of the Explorer, crouched down and scooped up a handful of snow. Packed it around the license plate. She saw the snow was cleaning the blood off the gloves. Good. She rubbed the gloves together to finish the job. Brushed snow over the bit of blood she'd left on the ground. She finished packing the snow over the license. Didn't see any blood there. She eyed the plates of the vehicles on either side of her. Theirs were covered with slush or snow as well. She went around to the front of the Explorer. Crouched down and piled snow over the front plate. Stood up. Stepped back. Scrutinized her work. Approved. She brushed her gloves on her pants legs. Took off her jacket. It looked odd inside out, and she didn't want to attract attention. Besides, it had warmed up. Was almost balmy out. She yanked off her gloves and shoved them in the sleeves of the jacket. She noticed two vehicles were pulling in. A minivan filled with gray-haired men and women. A pickup truck with a young couple in the cab. No

more fooling around by the Explorer, she told herself. Go
inside and act calm. Be calm. She tried to flip through her
mental literature collection but was too jittery to concen-
trate. The best she could do was to dredge up the first line
of Blake's tiger poem. The first poem she'd memorized in
college. It kept scrolling through her mind as she walked
through the lot to the back entrance. *Tyger! Tyger! burning
bright. Tyger! Tyger! burning bright. Tyger! Tyger! burning
bright.* The exposure to the night air invigorated her. Cleared
her head. She inhaled the aroma of charred beef. She
wouldn't mind getting something to eat. She put her hand
on the door handle and paused. Another bad thing about
Catch, she reflected. He'd been lousy in the kitchen. He'd
liked getting waited on, not waiting on her. That wasn't how
she wanted it. Her next one would have to pass a basic cooking test. She pulled open the door and went inside. *Tyger!
Tyger! burning bright.*

SHE slid into a booth in the lounge. Kept her purse and
jacket in her lap. A big-screen television and a couple of
smaller televisions carried the hockey game. The television
sound was off while a six-piece band dressed in black
played light jazz. No one was dancing. No surprise. It was
still early, and it took Minnesotans a few drinks to brave the
dance floor.

The waitress came by. A plump, busty woman with
Shirley Temple curls and a dimpled chin. "What can I
get you?"

"May I order food in the lounge?"

"Only shrimp cocktail and garlic toast."

Ransom didn't want to sit in the restaurant by herself;
she'd look out of place. "I'll have an order of each."

The woman scratched on her pad. "A cocktail?"

She was dying for a drink. Told herself to stick to one or two. She needed to stay sharp. "Glass of white wine."

"House chardonnay?"

"Fine."

The waitress finished scratching. Looked up. Her eyes went to Ransom's forehead. "You're bleeding."

Ransom raised her hand to the Band-Aid. Touched it and looked at her fingers. Red. "Fell on the ice," she muttered.

"Here." The waitress shoved a bar napkin under her nose. "You've got a good goose egg going under that bandage."

Ransom snatched the napkin out of the woman's hand. Held it to her forehead while she slid out of the booth with her purse and her coat. Ran to the ladies' rest room and pushed open the door. She bent down and checked the bottom of the stalls. Saw no feet. She stood up and went to the mirror. Pressed hard against the gash. Lifted the napkin away from her forehead. The waitress was right. A big bump surrounding the cut. She rinsed the napkin under cold water and pressed it against the wound. The bathroom door opened a crack. She stepped away from the mirror and went into a stall. Shut the door and locked it. Didn't want anyone asking her what had happened. She sat down on the toilet with her purse and jacket in her lap and the damp napkin pressed to her head. She heard two women talking. They were primping in front of the mirror. She heard them spray something. Smelled their colognes. Roses and something spicy.

"I wish Clyde would get off his ass and dance," said one woman.

"I'll dance with you," said the other.

The first one laughed. "I haven't done *that* since high school."

"I'm a good kisser, too," said the second. "Give great tongue." They both laughed.

Ransom hugged her purse and jacket close to her body.
Felt a headache coming on. She figured it was from the cut
on her head, and from her nerves. The giggling women and
their flowery cologne weren't helping. She bent over. Felt like
vomiting, except there was nothing in her stomach. They
left. She heard the door close. She took the napkin off her
head. Looked at it. A strip of red in the middle of the white
square. She opened her legs and dropped the napkin in the
toilet. Reached over and unrolled some toilet paper. Held a
wad to her head. Shut her eyes. Rested the side of her head
against the wall of the stall. Listened to the background
drone. The music. She sat for what seemed like an hour. Two
more sets of women came and went. She opened her eyes
again. Took the tissue down and looked at it. Another line
of red, but smaller this time. The bleeding was slowing. She
dropped the paper between her legs. Stood up. Flushed the
toilet. Unlocked the stall and stepped out. Went over to the
mirror. Leaned forward. The cut was oozing. She set her
purse and jacket on the counter. Opened her purse. Dug
around. Found another bandage. She ripped the paper package open. Pulled out the Band-Aid and peeled it open.
Brought it to her forehead. Positioned the gauze over the cut.
Smoothed the tape over the skin. Stood and stared at her reflection. Waited. Tossed the paper into the wastebasket.
Looked in the mirror again. She was relieved to see no more
dripping, but didn't like the rest of her face. The bump poked
out from the bandage. Her skin was pale and dry and tight.
She imagined it could somehow give her away. Tell strangers
she was guilty. She reached inside her purse and pushed the
gun to one side. Started pulling out cosmetics and dropping
them on the counter. She stopped and froze with her hands in
her purse. Frowned to herself as she remembered his words.
*What's wrong, Pink Lady? Forget to trowel your makeup
on this morning?* "Drop dead, my love," she said under her
breath. "That's right. You already did." She finished pulling

out cosmetics. She yanked the cap off a lipstick tube.
Smoothed a layer of pink over her lips. Pressed her lips together. Closed the tube and dropped it into her purse. Picked
a blush compact out of the pile of plastic circles and squares
and cylinders on the counter. Popped it open and brushed
some pink on her cheeks. Dropped the brush back in the
case and snapped it shut. Tossed the blush back in her
purse. She picked a cylinder out from the pile. Pulled off
the cap. Ran a line of cover-up over the bump. Blended it
with her fingertips. She pressed the cap back on the tube
and dropped it in her purse. She scrutinized her job so far in
the mirror. Decided it was enough. She plucked the rest
of the makeup compacts off the counter and tossed them in
her purse. Took out her brush. Gave her hair a dozen
strokes. Dropped the brush back in her purse. Gathered her
purse and jacket in her arms. Glanced in the mirror one last
time and forced a smile as she walked out.

She was happy to see her drink and food waiting for her
at her table. She slid into the booth, dropped her purse and
jacket on the seat next to her. Picked up her glass and
sipped. Dry and cold and wonderful. She set the glass
down. Picked up a piece of toast. Took a bite.

The waitress walked up to her table. "You okay? You
were gone quite a while."

Ransom nodded as she chewed. Swallowed. "I'm okay."

The waitress set a second glass of wine in front of Ransom. "This is from someone who thinks you're more than
okay."

Ransom dropped the toast on her plate. "Who would that
someone be?"

The waitress looked across the room. "A fella over there."

Ransom picked up her napkin and dabbed at the corners
of her mouth. Was glad she'd done something to spruce up
her face. "What does he look like, this fella?"

"Blond. Handsome. A little skinny for my tastes, and not much of a butt. But what the hell."

"What the hell," repeated Ransom. She picked up the toast. Took another bite. Chewed and swallowed. "How old does he look to be?"

"Looks like he's twelve." The waitress glanced across the room again. "But he's twenty-one. And eight months."

"How do you know?"

"I carded him." She turned on her heel and went to another table.

Ransom picked up a lemon wedge and squeezed it over her shrimp cocktail. Picked up a piece by the tail, dipped it in the sauce. Snapped the flesh off and dropped the tail on her plate. Told herself twenty-one was too old. She'd had enough of men for a while. She'd stick to boys. Bona-fide boys. Maybe she'd start carding. Anyone old enough to drink was off her menu. She picked up another piece of shrimp. Dipped it and ate it. Dropped the tail. Licked her fingers.

The band wound down another jazz instrumental and cranked up for some light rock. The male vocalist stepped up to the microphone and started singing some Eric Clapton. "Wonderful Tonight." Under the table, Ransom crossed her right leg over her left knee. Swung her right foot to the beat. A few couples drifted onto the dance floor. She was envious. She loved the song. She put her right elbow on the table and rested her chin in her palm. A flannel shirt materialized at her elbow. She took her chin out of her hand and uncrossed her legs. Looked up. The blond man. Ransom studied his face. Fresh and bright. He could pass for a teenager. She liked that. Still, she'd be violating the new rule she made for herself.

He stuck out his right hand, palm up. "Wanna dance?"

Big hands, she thought. Reminded her too much of

Catch. "No thanks," she said. "Came to be by myself for a while."

"Come on. One dance." He kept his hand out, but looked across the room.

She followed his gaze. Saw a table with three other young men, all of them in flannel shirts and khaki slacks. They were talking and nodding and bobbing their heads to the music. Monitoring their friend's progress. "I don't know."

He reached across the table and wrapped his hand around hers. Pulled her arm toward him. "Come on. You know you want to."

She hesitated. Considered the stains on her clothes. The lounge was dark. She could get away with it. "Why not?" she said. She hiked her purse strap over her shoulder and slid out of the booth. Stood up and followed behind him as he led her by the hand.

He let go of her hand and turned around when they reached the edge of the dance floor. It had become crowded; it was a popular slow dance song. He put both his hands on her waist and she followed his lead. Put her hands on his shoulders. They didn't talk or look at each other. Danced and glanced over each other's shoulders at the other dancers. The song ended, and the band eased into more Clapton. "Tears in Heaven."

"Like Clapton?" she asked as they swayed back and forth.

He was looking across the room at his buddies. Pulled his eyes off of them and looked at her. "Huh?"

"Clapton," she repeated.

"Yeah. He's okay." His hands slipped lower on her waist. He pushed away the purse banging against his hand. "Can't you lose the baggage?"

"No," she said.

"Whatever." He paused. Looked at her forehead. "So

what's the deal? Have a fight with your old man? He bang you up or something?"

She took her right hand off his shoulder. Touched her bandage. "What?"

"Why are you alone in a bar, on a Friday night?"

She returned her hand to his shoulder. "Can't a woman go out solo once in a while?"

He shrugged. "Ain't usual. Noticed the Band-Aid and the bruise. Thought something happened and stuff."

Ain't. Stuff. Catch all over again. She'd return to her table after this dance. "I slipped on the ice."

"Gotta watch that when you get older."

Her body tensed. "What's that suppose to mean?"

"My grandma slipped and fell. Broke her hip."

She stopped dancing. "I am not old enough to be your . . ." She felt his hands slip behind her. Wrap over her buttocks. "Hey."

"Sorry." His hands darted back up to her waist. "Lost my head."

She heard laughter over the music. Saw him looking past her and grinning. She felt his hands slide from her waist to her hips. She turned her head and looked over her shoulder. Two of his buddies were giving him the thumbs-up. She snapped her head back around. "What kind of crap are you trying to pull? Make some bet you could score with an old broad?" She dropped her hands from his shoulders and shoved his hands off her. Turned to leave.

He reached over and locked his fist around her wrist. "They're assholes. Come on. Finish the dance, ma'am."

"Ma'am?" She yanked her hand away and faced him. She took a step back and instinctively reached inside her purse. Wrapped her hand around the hard metal.

His eyes went to her hand going inside her purse, then back to her face. "What's wrong?"

"Nothing." She told herself to calm down. Withdrew her hand from her purse. Took another step back. Bumped into a dancer. Turned around to apologize. Faced a gray-haired man. "Sorry."

"No problem, ma'am."

"Ma'am?" she sputtered. Did she look that bad? The man's eyes went to her forehead. She reached up and touched the Band-Aid again. Still dry. She took her hand down. Clutched her purse to her midriff. Felt her face growing hot. This had been a mistake. She wanted to get off the dance floor.

She ducked between a knot of couples and went back to her table. Exhaled with relief as she slid back in the booth and dropped her purse on the seat next to her. She looked down at the food. Wasn't hungry anymore. Picked up the second glass of wine. She took a long drink. Almost spilled on herself. She set the glass down. She tucked a strand of hair behind her right ear. Brushed her fingers against the side of her neck. Felt lines she'd never noticed before. Dropped her hand into her lap. Longed to be back in her own house, where she always looked good. Where her babies and her books could always make her feel better. Younger.

The song ended. The dancers filed back to their tables while the band stepped off the stage for a break. Her cheeks still burned. She took the wine list off the table and fanned her face. She looked across the room as she waved the folder. The table filled with flanneled men had emptied. Good. The sound came up on the televisions. Ransom dropped the list back on the table. Expected to see the game on the big screen. Instead, she saw a male news anchor and below him, words crawling across the bottom of the screen: BREAKING NEWS. The camera cut away to a male reporter standing outside. Ransom started coughing. Took a sip of

wine. Struggled to steady her hand while she set the glass
down. The reporter was in front of her parents' old place.
She strained to listen above the clink of glasses and drone
of bar conversations. Wished she could stand up and scream
Shut up!

"Authorities are not yet releasing his name as relatives
are still being notified," said the reporter. "Police are also
declining to release details regarding the method of suicide. However our sources within the department tell us he
died of a gunshot wound to the chest and that the pistol
used is missing. Two homeless men found sleeping in
apartments above the storefront are being questioned. Police fear a third person—another man seeking shelter—
took the gun and fled with it."

The camera cut back to the newsroom. The anchor:
"These men are not being charged in the shooting?"

The reporter standing outside again. The camera shot
widened. Showed police tape staked around the house. "No,
John. As I said earlier, authorities are certain he died at his
own hands. He apparently had a history of depression. At-
tempted suicides. Police believe he became despondent
after killing Professor Henry during a botched car theft.
Rather than face prison, the suspect turned the gun on
himself."

Back to the newsroom. The anchor shuffling papers on
the desk as he talked: "Stay tuned for a full report after the
game. We'll have sports and weather. More details on the
warm-up."

The game came back on. Ransom took another sip of
wine. She set the glass down on the table but kept the stem
in her right hand. She wasn't shaking anymore, and her
face felt cool. Relaxed. She ran her fingers up and down
the stem. Reflected on how Catch's fascination with suicide had finally backfired on him. It helped that the police

were morons. She'd gotten away with murder—three times if she counted not only Catch but also the bar robber and Henry. She took another drink of wine, set down the glass. Ran her right index finger around the rim. Luck was on her side as well. Those bums living upstairs. How perfect. Finally, she gave herself credit. She was smarter than the average criminal. Better educated. More well-read. All that had to count for something. That's why Catch had died and she had survived. Made perfect sense. Why was she ever worried?

The band members started stepping back onto the stage and picking up their instruments. The television sound went off. The band launched into another instrumental. She recognized this one. "Beauty and the Beast." She picked up her glass. Offered a silent toast to the beast she'd left dead on the floor of her childhood home. He'd taken the blame for not only Henry's death but his own. Plus, to his credit, he'd never called her *ma'am.* She brought the glass to her lips, tipped it up and drained it. Set it down. Felt her higher senses returning. Her intellect. She remembered more of Blake:

> *Tyger! Tyger! burning bright*
> *In the forests of the night,*
> *What immortal hand or eye*
> *Could frame thy fearful symmetry?*

She wanted to get back to her journal. Put down some words. She was curious as to whether her writing had changed since she'd killed one of her boys. She guessed it had hardened. Sharpened like a knife honed against a stone. A tougher style would suit her. She felt ready to write another book. Ready to fight the university for her job. She reached inside her purse. Pushed the cosmetics and hairbrush aside. Touched the gun. Ran her fingertips over the barrel. She could battle the monsters within her walls by herself—and win.

The waitress came by again. "Another wine?"

Ransom took her hand out of her purse. "A split of champagne."

THIRTY-SIX

RANSOM WAS TWO miles south of home when Castro
spotted the Explorer. The truck was on Lexington Parkway,
heading toward the lake. Castro was alone in an unmarked
Crown Victoria stopped at a light on Thomas Avenue, a residential street that crossed Lexington south of the lake.
Bergen was touring the area north of the lake. Squads were
cruising along the other major roads leading to the lake and
the park from the east and the west. Wheelock Parkway. Ar-
lington Avenue. Maryland Avenue. Como Avenue. Midway
Parkway. Traffic was heavy and slow-going. The Friday-
night warm-up was bringing people out of their houses and
into the bars and restaurants.

Castro let two sedans pass him after Ransom. He hung a
right onto Lexington and followed her with the sedans between them. He radioed Duncan: "Murphy read this one
right. She's already headed home. Going north on Lexington. Just crossed Thomas."

"Good deal," said Duncan. He was parked in the alley

three houses down from Ransom's place. "Have the squads tighten the noose, but keep lights and sirens off. You follow her all the way home. Hang back when you get to her block. Park a few houses away."

One of the cars between Castro and Ransom hung a right. Pulled off of Lexington. Now there was one car separating the Crown Victoria from the Explorer. Ransom braked at a red light on Minnehaha Avenue. The car behind her slowed and stopped, and the Crown Victoria did the same. Castro eyed the truck under the streetlamps. "I could get this over with real quick. Slap on the lights. Pull her over and grab her."

"Murphy's got a feeling about this lady." Murphy had argued Ransom was unstable enough to whip out her gun and start blasting away. She told Duncan she wanted to take the woman in a closed setting, not out on the street where civilians could get hit. Duncan wasn't sure the situation was that volatile, but he wanted to show Murphy he trusted her gut. "Stick with the plan."

The light turned green. The Explorer rumbled ahead, kicking up slush at the sloppy intersection. The sedan and the Crown Victoria followed. Castro coughed. "You sure about this?"

Duncan: "I'm sure."

Castro coughed again. Cleared his throat. "Your call, boss."

"You're right. It is." He hung up the handset. He knew Castro was frustrated with playing a supporting role, but Murphy was right. The big guy's hacking would warn away an army.

Duncan pulled the keys out of the ignition and dropped them in his pocket. Unzipped his jacket, reached inside and took his Glock out of his shoulder holster. Checked it. Slipped it back in. Popped open the car door and got out. Slammed the door shut and locked it. Ran down the alley. Cut through a neighbor's yard to get on the sidewalk.

Jogged up Ransom's front walk and steps. He pushed open the front door and gasped. Slapped his hand over his mouth and nose while shutting the door behind him. "Jesus H. Christ it stinks in here." He stepped to one side of the front door. Murphy was on the other side. The two of them had entered through the front because boot prints already peppered the snow on the walk and the steps. The back steps were buried in smooth white except for the top of the stoop, where they found a few footprints and a heap of cloth. They'd pulled the material back and found a dead cat. Weighed what to do with it. Debated whether it would have to be opened up, and if the ME would be the one to do it. Decided to leave it where it was for the night in case Ransom broke with habit and entered her house through the back.

Murphy motioned Duncan away from the windows. "You're smashing the drapes. She'll see." Murphy was already aggravated with him. She'd been hunkered in the dark house by herself for better than an hour. Duncan wouldn't stay with her. Told her he'd sit in the car until the last possible minute because he couldn't stand the odor. He'd also refused to pull together any backup for inside. Told her they wouldn't need any. Murphy figured he'd been giving the stakeout short shrift because he didn't think Ransom was going to show. At least not so soon. She was glad he was being proven wrong.

He stepped away from the curtains. Lifted up his foot and nudged away a cat that was padding over the top of his boot. "I'm betting she's got zip for firepower. Shotgun was his deal. Handgun was hers, and she's already dumped it. Chucked it down the sewer or something."

"Could be right." They'd searched the place. Came up with the sawed-off shotgun. Sent it to the station along with other finds. Clancy's belongings. Ransom's journal. "On the other hand, they didn't even need a gun to do Henry."

"True."

"And even without the pile of dead guys, I'd say there's plenty of evidence she's losing it. The way she's got the heat cranked up. All these cats." Murphy crouched down and stroked the back of a Siamese that pawed at her leg. Stood up again. "Diary with stuff about scratching noises. The way she comes on to young men. Boys."

He peeled off his jacket and tossed it on the floor. "Your point?"

Murphy peered through a crack between the drapes. "We don't know what she's packing because crazy people are unpredictable."

He pushed his sweatshirt sleeves up to his elbows. "If you're so worried, where's the shield?"

"Same place you left yours." He'd never bothered taking his own vest out of the trunk, but he'd met her at Ransom's place with a shield for her. She'd sent it back to his car. Said she could hardly breathe because it was so hot inside, especially where she was stationed. Radiators lined the windows facing the street. She'd peeled off her jacket and her sweater. Was down to a turtleneck.

"See anything?" he asked.

"Not yet." She took her eyes off the window. Tugged at the neck of her shirt. Looked down and saw wet spots under her armpits. She looked over at Duncan. "How can you stand that sweatshirt?"

He reached up and with the back of his hand, wiped off a bead of perspiration trickling down his forehead. "I keep telling myself to pretend like I'm sitting in an outhouse in August. As soon as I'm done with my business, I'm outta here."

She wiped the moisture off her upper lip. "Smells like an outhouse, too."

"What is it about lonely women and cats? You never read stories about how someone found a dead old guy with a bunch of cats crawling all over him. You read that about old ladies all the time."

"Women need companionship," said Murphy. "Men watch television."

"That isn't true."

"How many guys have you heard about who died sitting in a chair, in front of a television? Ever heard of a woman who croaked that way?"

He paused. "You might have something there."

They heard a vehicle pull up in front of the house. Exchanged glances. Listened while a door slammed shut. Duncan pulled his Glock out of his holster and hunkered down on one side of the door. Murphy pulled her pistol out of the waistband of her jeans. She tipped her head toward the split in the drapes and peeked outside. Could see Ransom coming up the sidewalk with her keys in her hand. She leaned away from the curtains and nodded at Duncan. Took her place next to him.

AS she walked up her front steps, she eyed the windows. Expected to see her usual welcoming committee. She got to the top of the stoop and stood in front of the door. Put her left hand on the knob, and with her right, extended her key toward the lock. Studied her windows again. Waited. Took her hands down. This didn't feel right. No babies sitting watch amid the drapes. Not a single one. Something was holding them back. Someone was distracting them. She took a step back from the door. Eyed the ground around her. By the glow of the streetlights and the moon, she thought she saw unfamiliar boot prints. She wasn't sure. They could be Catch's prints left over from the morning. Perhaps her mind and her nerves were conspiring. Playing tricks on her. Ransom looked up at the windows again. Still empty. Her eyes narrowed. Her babies would never play tricks on her. She took another step backward. Tried to visualize who was standing on the other side of the door. Inside her house. A burglar? A rapist? No. Someone worse. A cop. She dropped her keys inside her purse. Felt around inside. Took out the Ladysmith. Pivoted the safety off. *Red means fire.* Wrapped both hands around the gun and raised her arms. Braced herself and aimed at the center of the door. Put her finger on the trigger. Inhaled.

MURPHY looked through the drapes again. Snapped her head away. "Hit the deck!" She and Duncan fell to the floor and covered their heads. A bullet splintered a hole through the door.

"Fuck!" yelled Duncan. "You okay?"

"Yeah." Murphy took her hands down. Waited a minute. Got on her knees and crawled to the windows. Peeked through the drapes again. She saw Ransom dash into the street. Run in front of an oncoming car. The Crown Victoria. It swerved and skidded to a stop. Ransom froze in front of it. Dropped her purse. Turned to face the car. Was she surrendering? Ransom raised her arms. Not up. Straight out. The sound of another gunshot. Murphy jumped to her feet and yanked open the front door. Took the steps two at a time. Yelled to Duncan behind her. "Check on Castro. I'll take Ransom." Murphy cut across the sidewalk and boulevard. Ransom was on the other side of the street, running up a neighbor's front yard.

Duncan went around to the driver's side of the car. The door popped open and Castro put one foot on the street. He looked shaken. "You okay?" asked Duncan.

"Ducky." Castro set his other foot on the ground and stood up. Turned around and eyed the top of the Crown Victoria. "She grazed the hood."

Duncan shoved his gun in the waist of his jeans. Slapped

Castro on the arm. "Secure the house and the yard." He turned and sprinted after Murphy. He saw her pursue Ransom between two houses across the street. He followed. The three figures cut through the alley behind the houses. Dashed through a backyard and between another set of houses. Emerged one after the other on the sidewalk in front of the houses. Murphy and Duncan stopped next to each other on the boulevard. They surveyed what was across the road. No houses. Only bushes and trees dotting an embankment.

Duncan: "Where'd she go?"

"There!" Murphy pointed across the street to a dot of pink amid the brush. Ransom was going down the embankment. It led to the drive circling Como. After the drive came an expanse of shore and then the lake.

The two detectives ran across the street. Followed Ransom down the hill. They ran halfway. Slid the rest of the way on their boots and their butts. "Where's she going?" Duncan hollered.

"To cut across the lake!" Murphy got to the bottom of the hill first. Jumped to her feet. Heard sirens. "They weren't suppose to use sirens! She's gonna freak out even more!"

Duncan jumped to his feet next to her. "Doesn't matter! Squads are circling Como!"

They ran for the street. Murphy saw Ransom start across the lake. "She's getting away!"

The two detectives ran into the street. Crossed in front of a van. The driver lay on his horn, slammed on the brakes and fishtailed. Came to a stop turned sideways in the street. A Suburban coming up behind the van honked and swerved and clipped the corner of the van's back bumper. A sedan rammed into the back of the Suburban.

Murphy heard the horns and the crashes but kept running toward the pink. She hopped onto shore. Had to pump her legs high to get through the deep snow. Got to the edge of the lake. Felt a tug on the back of her shirt and twisted her torso to disengage him. "Let go!" She was a foot from the ice when Duncan tackled her from behind. She landed facedown in the snow with Duncan's body sprawled on top of hers. She lifted her face up. Spit out a mouthful of snow. "Get off of me!"

He rolled off of her. "Stay off the ice! Let the squads take her!"

The instant she felt his weight lifted from her body, she scrambled to her feet and dashed out onto the lake with Duncan right behind her. The ice under the snow felt like slush. She scanned the surface of the lake. Saw the pink figure yards ahead of her. "Stop! Police!"

RANSOM heard the sirens. Felt her legs tightening up. Keep going, she told herself. Run through the pain. Run from the sirens. Think about something else. *Tyger! Tyger! burning bright.* A voice behind her. A woman calling out. She looked over her right shoulder as she ran. By the shine of the moon and the streetlights dotting the lakeshore, she could see the long, black hair. The woman who'd pulled Catch from the lake. The bitch was a police officer. She'd been inside the house. *Her house.* Spying. Setting a trap. Ransom whipped her head back around. Looked straight ahead. Set her sights on the other side of the lake. Had no idea what she'd do when she reached it. A cramp stabbed the right side of her ribs. *Tyger! Tyger! burning bright.* She told herself she could loop around and go back home. Run inside. Lock the doors and close the drapes tight and turn up the heat. Hide from the police in her warm house, with her babies and her books. *Tyger! Tyger! burning bright.* She felt her legs slowing against her will. As if they were operating of their own accord. On their own batteries. She heard the voice again, telling her to stop. Ransom slowed and stopped and panted. Turned and raised her arms straight out. Took aim at the head of black hair.

"GET down!" Murphy screamed. She and Duncan fell next to each other on their bellies. A shot rang over their heads. Murphy stretched her arms out in front of her. Steadied her hands on a hump of snow. Took aim and fired. Ransom dropped the gun and stumbled backward, but stayed standing. She slapped a hand over the wound, turned and ran. Tripped and stumbled forward. Kept going with her body bent like a comma and her hand pressed over her shoulder. Murphy and Duncan scrambled to their feet and ran after her. She was headed to the middle of the lake. Straight for the aerator. Open water, fourteen feet deep.

Duncan fired a warning shot into the air. "Stop now! Police!"

SHE heard another gunshot. A man's voice behind her. Ignored it. Kept running. *Tyger! Tyger! burning bright.* She told herself to think about her boys. Her boys would come back to her. Knock on her door. Even the ones she'd had years ago. They'd look the same, and so would she. They'd tell her she was young and beautiful. They'd get drunk with her and take naps with her. Catch would come back. Beg for her forgiveness. Love her the way she deserved to be loved. Prove himself the poet warrior she'd imagined. He'd slay the monsters within her walls. Her brother, Ezekiel, would come back with his wits and his body in one piece. They'd all come back to her house. *Tyger! Tyger! burning bright.* She was running out of breath. Her throat hurt from gulping the winter air. Her shoulder throbbed. She saw something in front of her. A black circle in the middle of all the

white. The pain was making her hallucinate. Her mind was
playing tricks on her again. Ignore the black spot. An illusion. Keep running. Keep thinking about the boys and the
babies and the warm, dark house. *Tyger! Tyger! burning
bright.*

THE aerator was close. They could see the edge of the
hole in the distance. Duncan was on Murphy's heels. "Paris!
Stop! The ice!" Murphy was too fast for him. She was pulling
away. Duncan launched himself toward her and slammed
into her legs. Knocked her down. Twined his arms around
her thighs.

She rolled onto her back and kicked at him. "She's getting away!"

Duncan crawled on top of her. Planted his knees on either side of her waist. Clamped his hands over her shoulders and held her down. His breath hung in a cloud as he
hollered. "Ice is too dangerous! Squads will catch her on
the other side!"

Murphy tried to sit up. "No!"

Duncan pushed her back down. He looked up and across
the lake. Heard a scream. Saw the pink disappear. Some
splashing. An arm coming up. Then nothing. Swallowed by
the lake. He lifted his hands from Murphy's shoulders. "She
went through. She's gone."

Murphy closed her eyes. Caught her breath. Felt the
snow beneath her back biting through her shirt. She tried to
imagine being surrounded by the cold water. Having it rush
into your nostrils and your throat and your lungs and your
stomach. Did it seep into your brain? All those smarts Ransom possessed. Gone. She opened her eyes and looked past
Duncan. Stared up at the moon. He rolled off her and stood
up. Extended his hand down. She hesitated. Reached up and
took it. He pulled her to her feet. Murphy looked at the

hole. Wondered if the pink figure would pop out and come after them, like a phantom in a horror flick.

They both turned their backs on the open water. Took in the action on shore. Lights blinking and flashing. Squads and fire rescue units. "They'll never get to her in time," Murphy said. "She's toast."

"You're right." Duncan threw his right arm around her shoulder. He pulled her close while she shivered. "Want my sweats?"

"I'm good. Let's get her gun."

Duncan rubbed her shoulder as they turned back around and walked toward the Ladysmith. "Sure you're okay?"

Murphy nodded. "She deserved it."

"She did."

Murphy looked over at the hole again. "They say it's like going to sleep."

THIRTY-SEVEN

RANSOM'S CORPSE WAS fished out of Como Saturday morning. The divers found her in thirteen feet of water, not far from where she'd fallen through. Duncan phoned Murphy on her boat that afternoon and told her. Van Hogan was hauled out of Whitewater the following Wednesday morning by a spear fisherman who mistook the dead man's hand for a northern. Duncan called Murphy's boat again and got Jack. He was on his way out the door; his wife was at the hospital. Duncan drove to Regions Wednesday after work to give Murphy the news in person.

He knocked once on the door to Sean Murphy's room and pushed the door open. Stepped inside. Murphy was standing in front of the window, looking outside. The meltdown had given way to another dumping, and the white stuff was coming down thick. *Mad Max* was roaring on the television, but nobody was watching. The bed was empty. "Where's the patient?"

She turned around. "In rehab. Swearing at the therapists

and my mother." She eyed the tin and the card Duncan had under his arm. "Sweets?"

"Pistachios."

"He loves those, but I don't know if he can have them." She walked over to the bed and took the remote off the covers. Punched off Mel Gibson. Set the remote on the nightstand. "Nice of you to come by, especially in this crud." She walked around to the end of the bed. Picked up her purse and hiked the strap over her shoulder. "Take off your jacket. Let's go for a walk."

Duncan tossed the card and tin on the bed. Unzipped his jacket and pulled it off. Tossed it over the footboard. He followed her into the hall. They walked side by side, past rooms with bedridden patients tethered to monitors. "They pulled the snowmobile guy out of Whitewater this morning," said Duncan. "He had a bunch of bills in his pocket."

Murphy stopped at a vending machine. Dug around in her purse. "So maybe Clancy popped him during a robbery. Freaked out about it and dumped the body."

Duncan pulled some change out of his jacket pocket. Fed the coins to the machine. "What's your pleasure?"

"Diet anything." Duncan hit the Diet Coke button, and a bottle dropped down. He picked it up and handed it to her. She unscrewed the cap and took a long drink. "Thanks."

They kept walking down the corridor. "Problem with that is, it looks like our bad guy was nailed by the shotgun *and* the Ladysmith."

Murphy took another sip of pop. Screwed the top back on the bottle. "Ransom was being helpful?"

Duncan laughed dryly. "I don't think so. More weirdness. Sheriff said all the shots were in the back. But who knows what went down that night?"

They got to the end of the hall and stepped into a lounge the size of a closet. A couch was wedged against the wall opposite the door. An end table with a lamp was stuffed into one corner. Murphy walked into the room, put the bottle and her purse on the table. Sat down. "Three people know."

"And they're dead." Duncan dropped on the couch next to her.

Murphy picked up the bottle and twisted off the cap. Took a bump. "The journal offered a little insight."

"I forgot you took it home." Duncan pulled the bottle out of her hand. Took a sip. Stifled a burp and handed it back to her. "Make any headway in wading through that bizarre thing? Read anything useful?"

"She admits to firing a shot at Hogan, but more or less blames Clancy for the mess. She hangs around because she's attracted to him. Wants to help him. She has a use for him. Sex. Muscle. Whatever. She talks about having him take care of her enemies at the university. Then it falls apart between the happy couple." Murphy took another sip of Coke. Held the container in one hand and fingered the cap in the other. "Other than that, I don't know what's to be believed in those pages and what's fantasy."

Duncan leaned back against the couch. Threw an arm over the top of the cushion behind Murphy. "That talk about monsters hiding in her house and all that. A sign of insanity?"

Murphy screwed the top back on the bottle. Propped the container between her knees. "The thing is, at least some of those noises were genuine."

Animal-control officers had discovered dead kittens rotting behind Ransom's bedroom walls. The animals had crawled into the spaces through holes in the plaster. The cavities were well hidden. In the closet. Under the bed. Behind the dresser. The warm, dark areas that had served as their birthing rooms had also helped kill them.

Duncan: "If she knew those sounds were caused by something real, would she have still imagined monsters?"

Murphy dislodged the bottle from between her knees. Twisted off the cap. Put the bottle to her lips and tipped it back. Finished off the Coke. Put the cap back on. "I think Ransom was waiting to go nuts. You know what I mean? It's like people who are hypochondriacs. They keep imagining they're sick. Pop pills like crazy. They finally land themselves in the hospital with an ulcer or something."

"You might be right."

Murphy tossed the bottle into a wastebasket tucked under the end table. "Or maybe I'm full of shit."

"No. I think you're right."

She shrugged her shoulders. Kicked off her boots. "God, my feet are killing me."

Duncan patted his thighs. "Give 'em here."

"What?"

"I owe you a foot rub."

She stretched her legs out in front of her. "How do you figure?"

"You were my nurse, and I haven't thanked you properly for that."

She jumped in. "You got hurt working on my case."

"You played Ransom right, and I haven't given you credit for that either."

Murphy shook her head. "If I'd played her right, she'd be alive now. Clancy would be, too."

"There you go again. Somebody's telling you that you did good and you can't accept it. That fucking Catholic guilt is the problem. Can't you give it a rest?"

She curled up her legs, pivoted her butt around on the couch and dropped her stocking feet in Duncan's lap. "Shut up and rub."

Duncan started kneading the ball of her right foot with his right thumb. Noticed skin poking through a worn spot in the heel. "I don't suppose I could convince you to take off these holey socks, Sister Murphy."

"Not a chance. Feet are cold." She paused. "Speaking of colds, what's the body count back at the shop?"

"Castro's better but Bergen's worse. Dubrowski's getting better, but he's not ready to drag his sorry ass into work yet. My guys who were out on that Chicago case are back in town, but Sandeen's still on vacation. Nash's job is still sitting there, waiting for me to fill it."

"Put down the violin, Axel. I'm off until next week. I want to get my dad settled in."

"That's fine. Family comes first." He patted her foot. "What's up with Jack?"

His switch to the subject of her husband made Murphy yank her foot out of his grasp. "What do you mean?"

He pulled her foot back to him and resumed kneading. "Why's he in Rochester?"

"Mayo wants him. I talked him out of relocating to Arizona. Wasn't easy, but he knows I want to be close to my folks after my dad's heart surgery. He got his second choice. Mayo down in Rochester."

Duncan stopped rubbing. "Are you trying to tell me something?"

She smiled. "Don't worry. You're stuck with me still. Jack's getting an apartment down there. He's going to be on four and off three."

Duncan resumed the rubbing. "Is that gonna work?"

She didn't like the question but decided to answer it anyway. "It has to."

Duncan massaged the toes of her right foot, rolling them one at a time between his thumb and his forefinger. "Am I too rough?"

"Feels great."

He moved his hands to her left foot. Started rubbing it through her socks. "Paris."

"What, Axel?"

He hesitated. Held her foot between his hands. "Never mind."

"You're always on the verge of asking me something. Can't you spit it out?"

He started kneading the ball of her left foot with his thumb. "Reading that woman's journal with all that personal shit in it. Didn't it teach you?"

She frowned. "Teach me what?"

He stopped massaging her foot. Didn't want to meet her eyes. He glanced through the doorway and across the hall. Into another room. One with a window. The snow was so dense there was nothing visible. Only white. A sheet of paper void of words. "Some stuff's better left unsaid."